INDIGO ROSE

INDIGO ROSE

Susan Beth Miller

BANTAM BOOKS

INDIGO ROSE
A Bantam Book / January 2005

Published by
Bantam Dell
A Division of Random House, Inc.
New York, New York

Cover art by Gary Kelley
Cover design by Belina Huey

Book design by Lynn Newmark

Library of Congress Cataloging-in-Publication Data
Miller, Susan B. (Susan Beth)
Indigo Rose / Susan Beth Miller.
p. cm.
ISBN 0-553-80396-4
1. Jamaican Americans—Fiction. 2. Separation (Psychology)—
Fiction. 3. Loss (Psychology)—Fiction. 4. Women immigrants—
Fiction. 5. Chicago (Ill.)—Fiction. 6. Women gamblers—Fiction.
7. Housekeepers—Fiction. I. Title.

PS3613.I5545I53 2005
813'.6—dc22
2004058364

Printed in the United States of America
Published simultaneously in Canada

www.bantamdell.com

BVG 10 9 8 7 6 5 4 3 2 1

For Lisa, Laura, I.C., and Dad

INDIGO ROSE

Prologue

September 8, 1988, Kingston, Jamaica

Louisa always trail behind me coming down the lane, on account of every lacy bug, bright butterfly, or brown toad catch her eye. She keep up a steady stream of "look Mama"s and make me stop my feet and bring the basket down from my head to turn back and see what she come upon. She have a blue powdery butterfly pinch between her fingers, and I marvel at a child of four years catch up to a flying ting and get ahold of it widoht do it injury. Or a slick red frog cup in her hand while she stroke him belly to quiet him.

"How you know that frog skin not burn yu hand, child?" I one time ask.

"Not this one, Mama," she say, and shake her frolicky head, and I see how she already know one small creature from di nex and know which one to look at from afar and which she can take eena di hand and pet.

When we come down to the stream, we bot pull off wi shoe and toss dem in the basket and walk the rest of the way home tru the water. That water is shallow, and clear as good well water, and it move so fast it sing. You can see the gravelly bottom and whatever likkle ting lie among di colored stone. We stop to pick up this or that, sometime just a bit of green frosty glass or a bottle cap or blue button. "Where this water go to, Mama?" Louisa ask.

"Go on oht to the sea."

"Where go the sea den?"

"Don' go nowhere, child, just eena di shore and oht again, as Water Mama tell it. But you can cross that sea and find a world neither of us see before. Someday, you and me we go there. Go on a sailing ship." John Crow buzzard float black overhead, high in the airstream, him eye fix on whatever him see below.

"When Granmada let us do that?" Lou ask me.

"There go some silly words. You don't know yu mama a full-grown woman who do what ting her mind tell her?"

"You too old for a papa, den?"

"What you ask now, honeygirl?"

"Where go Grandada? Granmada's husband."

"Just like yu own papa," I say. "Him go away. Like so many time. Only this time go for good, because Death him come and take di man."

Mi stand beside Papa and watch him wid di bright playing card-dem. Mi say in mi heart, Go, Dada, go *but mi put no words out into di air, which fill wid smoke and the orange and peanut snack the men eat that tease mi appetite. Mi a-feel shylike, but wide awake in mi head, though the hour be so-so late and Mama don' know that this time mi go wid Papa, when most time him go widoht us.*

Next day, mi and Doreen squat beside di river, each one of us wid a pile of colored stone, a-bet tree stone or six on which one of us turtle-dem cross over di wide path and win di race. Papa come by, a-tow likkle Vincent behind. Vincie smell like di hog pen near where him play.

"Mi put twenty on the red-face turtle," Papa call out, gleeful.

"Oh, Dada," mi say, "bet on mine—that one go for Doreen."

"Hah, hah," he laugh, a-vex me. "Maybe this race belong to yu likkle sister."

Lou and me keep on walking, the cool water drawing alla the heat ohta wi bare feet and alla the thoughts oht from mi head. Louisa frock sash slip its bow and follow behind her in the water, but bot of us too restful to badda wid it.

She start to sing a foolish song. *"Little Bunny Foo Foo, walking in the forest, scooping up all the field mice, bopping 'em on the head."* With her hands she makes the movements to tell her song.

I give her a "mother of God" kind of stare, then ask, "Where you learn that nasty-nasty song, child?"

She laugh, take up a nex verse. "*'Little Bunny Foo Foo, I don't want to see you gathering up all the field mice and bopping 'em on the head.'* That's what the Fairy of the Forest say. I learned it at school, Mom. All the kids sing it." She pull her tie oht the water and swing it in a circle like dem rodeo rider we see on the television.

"Since when?" I ask her, and take hold of her free hand, a-fear otherwise she slip on the bigger stone that now come underfoot.

She bring her likkle shoulder-dem up to her head in a shrug.

"That is nothing Jamaican," I tell her. "That an American song." I don't tell her I know that foolish song word for word, know a few verse she don't even hear. I remember Louisa father sing that same ditty and teach it to the local children in the dirt yard around the school. That was when Lou still in my belly. I look hard at her, try to see tru her skin to where that song come from inside. "You need a Anansi tale," I tell her, "to fill yu mind wid someting deestant."

"Tell me one," she say, a-jump up and down and a-splash my skirt till I shiver from the cold-cold water.

I tell her boht Anansi spider, who want to be a big-big man so bad him brag dat him no eat fi eight full day after him mother-in-law funeral, to honor she who die. Mister Anansi Spider soon find himself in deep-deep trouble for him big idea-dem. She listen to this tale from she own Ja home, a story that—far back in time—come from somewhere off in Africa, and her eye-dem grow round as the moon that turn the tide, so round that I see myself in them like in a mirror and feel a fright.

Louisa start to turn off down a likkle side stream she like, but I no wish to follow it, because the water there get muddy and red as spilt blood from someting nasty come down from the hills. I shut my eyes and wade blind eyed through the familiar stream, one hand held behind mi back, finger-dem a-wag at Louisa, my lip-dem a-say in a tease, "Me leave you now, honeygirl. Bye now, child." John Crow wheel overhead, easylike on the wind. After a few second I feel Lou join her hand to mine and follow along.

"I like that other stream, Mama," she say, sweet and wishful.

"Never mind that," I say. "Yu granmada she expect us home."

"Spin me, Mama," she say.

"All right, then, but after that we go on home." She offer herself to me to pick up and whirl around like she whirl her lasso.

Two days past that kindly day me and Lou spend together, the sun set wid a special beauty on a day that is hot-hot, the sun wid no mercy. Next day, Mister Gilbert come a-stride over the sea like a giant. Him kick up so much water you never see nor hear such a demonstration. The air grow black like all of us wear darkers over di eye. House door bang and rattle like nothing going to silence it ever. Hour pon hour, the wind keep on a-whoop. Wind send breadfruit, coconut, zinc offa di roof, the neighbor veranda, all of it scream tru the sky. No amount of time a-go to wear Mister Gilbert out. Only when him calm eye pass do him ease up, give wi a rest. The day is all a sudden lovely, air grow bright and friendly. But Mister Gilbert him just a-tease. Him return even more devilish, mek di wind raise higher, the air whistle and roar; it cork up wid flying tings. All of us huddle like a litter in the front room and pray the bang-arang soon come to an end. The grown one-dem tell tales and try to hold the jittering pickney close, but after some hour Doreen and Mama and me weary so from the fear the house will fly eena di sky that we all must have doze and take the wailing wind eena our dream-dem. I wake a-hear my Lou voice a-call from the other room, she a-cheep, "Mama, come here, Mama." I fly to my girl, my stomach 'im flip inside like a race swimmer at the end of the lane. I find Lou, find her face blanch wid fear, her hair caught tight neet a wooden case that the wind rattle to the ground, her blue frock jook tru by a rod that formerly hold the drapery, which now spread across the floor. Oh, Lord, my heart stall wid the sight of my baby trap so. Had that case weigh the same as alla the house, I would lift it off that likkle one.

Next day the Kingston TV news come to town to photograph wi trouble-dem, and flash wi picture across di nation, probably across di ocean to America and England. Then the camera-dem roll out as if all is finish and fine wid us, but we are poorer than we been before, and those first weeks our soup stretch so far, soup's just another name for tea, and we go to bed wid little of substance lying on wi stomach-dem.

Many folk go on so, half-starved to the bone because their crop spoil by the wind and, if not the wind, the waters that follow which take food crop and seed crop bot. Many body grow thin; even blood grows poor and maga. And the hunger take a toll on the people disposition, so dem brindle over every likkle ting.

At the hotel where I wait table, tings naa take as much time a-get back to normal. I am lucky that inside a month come a trickle of businessmen and officials and I can get some food there and take some home in my pocket. But even wid wi belly-dem full, someting change in my people that tourist neva see. Hunger a little closer to the door, giving us a quiet fear. Him hum like cicada in di air.

One

February 1991, Chicago

There comes a time you've walked so long on a twisted path you forget what you set out looking for and are content just to find your way home.

I walk the city's streets after winter's dark has fallen—that dark that comes at half past four and is strange to me even now, though it suits my heart. Most nights I wander in the chill air and have no direction, but this night I have a small mission, which pertains to Bertha in the flat across the hall from me, a kindly enough Mississippi woman ten years older than me who is big as a bus and so much blacker than me, we might as well be from two different races God set on the earth. Bertha's been complaining tru the evening that her belly's knotted with pain and cramps.

"You want a doctor, then," I tell her, standing beside her bed, my back to the door that opens to the dim hallway and onto my own front door. "You don' fool with pain in the belly. Might be your appendix want to burst."

"No, girl," she tells me. "Don't need no doctor. Don't be

bothering no doctor in the night. I'm certain it's fixing to pass. Might just be the change coming hard now I'm past forty, like it did for Mama."

"You and your mama not the same person, in the same body."

"Those things pass on down," she says.

I think she's just acting brave, because her face is drawn with pain. "You needing to be ox stubborn now?" I ask her. "Maybe we go to the Emergency and that way no bother the doctor at home. That satisfy?" I am ready to pack her up and take her to the clinic in a cab. Truth be told, I'm ready to get out of the house and don't mind the thought of babysitting Bertha at the clinic.

I've known Bertha since first I arrive in this city, settle in this apartment house June of '89. That's close to two years now of being neighbors, so I'm at ease with her company. It's peculiar to me how I feel like Queen for a Day when first I come upon my place, across the hall from hers, clean and spacious and three floors high so I have a view. Now it looks dull as old wax, and the stairs tire my back when I'm a-tote groceries. When I first come, my mood-dem change fast as the sunshine here, in and out of the clouds. I try to stanch the loneliness by thoughts of all the fine stories I have to tell Lou, Mama, my brother Vincent, sister Doreen, and the rest of them back home. The very first day I come, drag in all of my boxes, Bertha come across to say hello and offer me help. Time pass and Bertha come to be level ground to me. She tell me she been in her flat since her two girls go out on their own, first one, then the other follow, eight, maybe ten years past.

"Maybe it's gas," she tells me now. "That can hurt something awful and ain't worth no trip to the hospital."

"I'm a-go out, then, and get you some medicine. You need that. Seen?"

She lays her plump hand on my arm. "I don't need to

worry boht you wandering in the night, Indi girl. You just stay put, hear?"

It's a short walk I could make in my sleep to the Redding Road Pharmacy on account of all the times I've walked there for this ting or that. Bertha wants to keep on worrying aloud over my going out and about in the dark, but I tell her I'm comfortable as a cat when I'm abroad in the night and if she wants to worry she can go ahead and do it while I'm a-care for this little business. A scared look overtakes her eyes, and I see her pain is steepening. She clutches her belly and nods her head, finished with words, as if the pain jook her like an arrow.

The night air comforts me, releasing me from myself, but my mind soon fills up with the fear in Bertha's eyes as I hurry south down the road, with its a-sprinkle of storefronts here and there. I'm tinking that big woman needs a doctor, not a bottle of Alka-Seltzer tablets good for a running belly, but I go along to do what I set out to. I make it fine to Redding's, but the place is closed as tight as Heaven shut against a sinner, and a quick stop in each of the stores still open near to there turns up no medicines. The clock in my head ticks away the time and I wish I were back by Bertha to look at her with my own eyes and see is she holding up. Still, I want to keep up my search so I follow a picture I have in my mind of another little orange-fronted place I can check that can't be more than a few blocks down from here and over a little, to the east, I think. Used to be I could find my way over hills and through brush with just a snatch of moonlight, but in the city all the streetlights make my eyes see halos and I can hardly figure my way without stopping to read every street sign.

Before five minutes pass, I'm turned around, lost where the air is scented with motor oil and fried potato so that I've got to set my mind to my directions and forget awhile about Bertha. I feel in my bones I know the right way to walk, but what I feel don't add up to what I see around me, so I got to try to go by my eyes and ears, not my belief. I direct myself by the sights I think I know, like the beacon from the Stone Brewery and the white steam a-rise in two plumes from the Elvis Elevator Plant. The only person I see is a big bald woman slumped against a building who looks to be sleeping off her liquor. Then I'm caught by sounds that say I ought to be walking another way—fire engines screaming out of the north-central station, the laughter of seabirds—so I follow those awhile while I take up cursing Bertha for what her belly's done to my night. Pretty soon I know I'm just wandering, maybe even walking in circles.

Time past, I could bear some bit of danger without my heart a-jump like a spooked pony. But since Lou's death—can it be six months now?—fear's moved in like it's planning to keep me company all my days. When the feathers of steam on the horizon that might be my Elevator Plant landmark start seeming like they could mark some other place, I feel as lost as if I been stolen off the street, blindfolded, and moved through the city in the trunk of a car. And it's odd to me how the fear pounding behind my eyes says I'm afraid for my life, because haven't I wished away my hours these last days, and my days these last months, thinking how I would reach out my hand to Death, dance his dance, if it weren't for Mama, Dorrie, Vincent, and the others. Still the body knows danger like a field mouse knows a hawk, so now I've forgotten my search for the drugstore and I'm looking for my way back home, hoping to find Bertha more restful and preparing in my head to tell her, "Sorry, but Redding's was shut up tight—we got to wait till morning."

I've got no cause for worry after all, because ahead of me just beyond a peeling yellow hydrant and a wood slat bench with pigeon droppings all down its back, there's a strip of bright stores, their "open" signs still lit, and among them is the little hole-in-the-wall drugstore, Shepherd's, with the parrot-orange paint I'd been seeing in my mind. I go in and pull off the wool hat I crocheted to get myself ready for that first northern winter. I shake out my stiff hair and enjoy the warm air that's clouded a minute by my breath. The fluorescent light mimics a high sun that chases every shadow. I take my time in the aisles of boxed, cellophane-wrapped remedies, some past my reach, before I spot the Alka-Seltzer but pass it up for some strong-looking, wine-red syrup that says it's good for stomach upset. Then I pick up a bottle of Midol, too, because Bertha wasn't sure if maybe it's just her time of month coming hard. She told me she's coming up on the change, so her monthly isn't monthly, it's irregular as a lapsed Christian. Her phrase leaves me to wonder is she thinking of me with her word picture, since I haven't been near a church for Lord knows how long.

I give a ten-dollar bill to a girl behind the counter who has a head of black hair the color of shoe polish. She must have colored it from one of the boxes of dye they sell here. She's on the telephone making faces to a friend who can't see them. I've got to look hard at her to get her to notice she's holding my bill in her hands. The girl's got a silver pin stuck through her lip that ought to be outlawed. I squint my eyes at that painful-looking thing, thinking, *Lord, no child of mine would ever*... She puts down the phone and smiles at me.

"You old enough for working here in the night?" I ask her. "You're not much more than a baby."

"Oh, I'm old," she says, and squeals a little. "My parents wouldn't let me pierce before sixteen."

"Umm... is that so?" I say, and take my brown bag and pluck the few coins I'm due from off her cool hand. "Your parents, they let you do that damage to your body?"

"Well," she says. "I guess I didn't exactly ask."

"Jah, me no do that for a million dollars."

"Have a nice night," she calls after me still full of cheer. I glance back and see her wave a hand heavy with silver rings.

On the street again, I still don't exactly know which way is home. I ought to be smart enough to go back in and ask for directions, but how I a-go to put my faith in any directions come from that lost pickney, so I stand awhile on the street, just looking and thinking, trying to figure my way by someting my eyes or ears might pick out from the air. I don't see a soul outside, and my fear starts to flow again. This fear annoys me. I beat it back and bend my head down, clutch the package to my breast, and just start walking against the cold night air, knowing I'll recognize a street name soon enough and right away know the spot. Worst ting there is is to stand on a street corner looking lost—that much I know. I walk past the first cross street and it is Traylor and I say it aloud but don't know the sound of that name, so I mutter to myself *Just give it one more block before you turn back and search the other direction.* Maybe I've got to go back eena that store after all, ask that pierce-lip pickney to sell me a street map. I go on two more blocks past Cadwell and Smolen and South Apple, and though I pass some of those streets on the bus, they sound wrong for my path home, so I'm forced to turn back around and head the other way. Overhead, the moon is three-quarters full, its edge thin as torn paper, but its place in the sky doesn't help me like the sun would. When I turn back, the drugstore's still close enough to where I can see the faint lights in its window, which gives me some relief, but I can also see when those lights blink off. I hear a car start its engine and lay track on the road, leaving behind a burnt-oil smell. Oh, Lord, is it just me out here now with the temperature falling and the dark thickening and no living ting in sight but two winjy trees no higher than a man's head?

I'm back beside the store, looking at the hand-lettered sign set crooked in the window, telling its lie—"Open 24 Hours"—when a man steps out from between two buildings. I take his measure with my eyes, gauging his strength against my own. He's not a fit man. He's youthful, fair like the English, and large all over, but so big and soft in the belly he looks more woman than man. His hair is black, but it's short and curled up tight. I nod and head off the other direction from the one I just took, thinking I'll just go two or three blocks each direction till I find something I know. I see Bertha back home, her belly knotted, and now she's aching with worry, too, unless she's drifted to sleep. A sharp whistle cuts the air behind me, loud as a Betsy kick-up bird, and I don't like the picture I get of that big bafan man calling to some friend he's got hidden somewhere, tucked into one of these alleyways, to let him know they've got a rabbit wandered near to the net. I hear the heavy man's rubber-soled footsteps a-come up behind me. He hums, and the sound of a human voice against the silence is shocking. I get ready to hear him shout, "What's your rush, girlfriend?" How many times I hear that sort of ting. I prepare to tell him, "Don' you be fas' with me."

I think I got to make a turn now, can't keep heading in a straight line, waiting for whoever's going to jump out from back of the next building, making it two against one. Even one so flabby as this one, paired with another, would be trouble for me. Maybe I should turn my face to this slabba-slabba white man and give him the evil eye, pretend I'm old enough to be his mama and stern enough to be his granmada. But I can't bear to stan' steady and give up the little bit of sidewalk between us, so I take the next turn left, figuring that if I can lose him somehow, I may just hole up somewhere and wait till daylight—though I may freeze to death, because my finger-dem already wooden and the back of my neck and tips of my ears are ice. I try to keep my steps just a half pace faster than the steps I hear behind me. If I break into a run, I'll excite him like a squirrel stirs a dog to the chase.

I know he's coming up to the corner now, so what's he going to do—turn left and follow? I pass neet a streetlight that shines blue against a wall that's messed with dripping paint like someting hideous happen here. He whistles twice into the night and mutters. "Following me" is what I hear. "Why are you following me?" *Me follow him?—Jah! Crazy!* But he's not talking to me, I guess, he's talking to somebody else, to whoever he's whistling to, that's the one. I feel the neck of the medicine bottle tru the paper and press it tight to my chestbone. A black pickup truck drives by, polished so it shines back the street lamps, then a dirty blue city bus approaches. If the bus stops, I'll get on it—no matter where 'im a-go. I ask it with my eyes to stop, stop before I become the subject for a police investigation, probably be an unsolved mystery like on the TV, like Louisa's accident. The bus whooshes past, followed by a yellow cab, but I have no money for any taxi. *Don't worry,* I tell myself. *If this man was chasing after you, he'd have caught up to you by now.* His pace hurries, then I can hear he's running. I whirl around, got to stare him in the eyes, got to tell him, *Look, I see you, I know who you are now, so don't you hurt me unless you want to go on and kill me.* He slows, flushes, smiles a shut-mouthed grin at me, mouths someting that could be "You're in trouble," or maybe—crazy—it's "Don't you follow." Backward, fast as I can, I scurry, my eyes trying to make a dam to stop him while my feet hurry. His eyes ride out to the left of me. *Uch!* I hit my back up to someting, *someone,* it feels like—*oh, Jesus!* my heart is in my throat—I let the bag fall to the pavement, see the man begin to jog into an empty lamp-lit lot to the left where he's met by a person—maybe man, maybe woman—who trots off alongside him. I am faint. I want to shout for the police, but my voice lift out of me. Stooped next to my bag on the cement is an old black man, sturdy built with a milk-white crust of hair rubbed over his lip. "So sorry, young lady," he says, and his voice immediately relieves me. "I didn't see you come back-stepping out of the shadow. You oughtn't to be out in the street this hour. You're like to get into trouble out here." I stoop down to fish the Midol out of the brown skin of paper stained with the red syrup. "Careful, now," he says. My breath slows, relaxes. I feel like jackrabbit escaped from fox's jaw. "There's broken glass all over here. You're fixing to cut yourself." He hands me a soft, folded white hankie to wipe off the package, and I hand him back the red-stained, ruined cloth and tuck the box into my pocket.

"You know that man?" I ask.

"What man is that?"

"The fat man following after me."

He frowns. "Didn't see no man following, but I'm aiming to put you in a cab before some man that's trouble *do* come along. Out here at night, you're taking a gamble with your life. Courting trouble with a capital T."

"Got no money for a cab. I spend too much on that spilled medicine."

"Well, that's a shame." He digs in his pocket and hands me a ten-dollar bill worn thin as tissue. "Now you got money for a taxi."

"Oh, I can't."

"Hush, now. Do as I say."

Two cabs pass us by with their lamps darkened before he can hail me one that's working. He opens the rusted blue door for me. "Don't let me catch you out here in the dark again lessen you want a whoopin'." He gives me a wink and shuts the door, and the firm sound of it settles me.

"Thanks, Tata," I say through the glass.

Sitting behind a silent cab driver—an Indian, maybe a Paki—I have time to tamp down my shame and tell myself at least I'm coming home with the bottle of pills. When I see my building, I feel like I arrive back from the moon. I climb the stairs, my tired eyes too lazy to raise off the worn pink carpet that runs up the center. I go past the two doors on the first floor, another pair on the second, to our third-floor landing. When I push the door to Bertha's room, what I see there steals my breath, because Bertha's on her back on the floor, eyes shut, body heavy as a walrus. I'm not sure is she even alive. "Bertha!" I clap my hands like a fool as if that might cause her to rise from the dead.

She opens her eyes and pulls up into a heap. "Oh, Indigo," she says, sleepy and far-off. "Just trying to ease the pain."

"It still going badly with you?" I ask, and purse my mouth. "I brought you this." I hand her the Midol and feel ashamed it's all I have.

"Must be my time is all," she says. "Must just be that." I give her two dollars back from the cab fare and leave out telling her the tale of the other medicine I bought and spilled out on the street. "Thank you, girl," she says, her voice deep tired, her hand rubbing low on her belly. "Get me a cup of water, if you don't mind. This medicine is bound to do me good. Weren't you gone a long while? I took to worrying."

"Um-hm," I say from the kitchen. I bring back a teacup filled with water, take the pill bottle from her hand, and get her out two Midol. "But I'm back now and needing some rest, because tomorrow I'm off to the Silvers' to earn my wage." *And I got through this night's danger,* I say to myself, and glad of it, because someting on that city block wena pull me toward trouble.

Bertha gets herself back to the bed. "I'm grateful you found you some nice people, child. That lady employed you when you was just new in town was un-Christian." She shakes her head. "Taking advantage of you like that! It ain't right. I'm so glad you found you a decent family like you deserve."

"Um-hm," I mutter.

"Those girls don't have no mama, Indigo? They on their own till you come to care for them?"

"Oh, they got a mama. Got them a mama and a half some days, she so up in their face. But she and Professor divorce, and now she move out on her own to a flat."

"I ain't knowed of many flats out in the suburbs."

"All she needs is one, don't it?"

"She moved out before you lost Lou, honey?"

"A few months before that, close to Professor birthday last year."

"Lord, Lord, sadness all around," Bertha says, her heart big as always, too big for her own good.

I know Bertha has her own two girls she frets over. Neither of them married and only one have a good job. Fretting after Professor's girls must come easy to her.

"Go on, then," she says. "I'll be all right knowing you're across the way."

"You ought to call your girls tomorrow," I say, "let them know you don't feel right."

I go back to my own three rooms, the big one a living room that's got a few chairs for sitting and a dining table, too, that I put by the broad windows that give me my picture of the street. The kitchen's no more than a few steps one end to the other, and my bedroom has space for the big bed and a bureau and has a good window back of the bed that lets the air move tru, summer nights. There's one space in the house I keep my eyes from a-visit. That's where all my little Lou tings are kept, on the bookshelves cut into the wall. One day I feel brave, I en mek a shrine for my baby. Put her few photos there, the pictures she draw me of a girl and a orange sun, of Granmada, of Anansi spider how she see him when I tell her a tale. I find a few strand of her hair I untangle from my own comb. Oh, Lord. I set everyting back to the wall so mi eye no catch dem if me no have strength.

I go to the bedroom to ready myself for sleep. The light in here is low. The overhead's got two bulbs, but one's been burned out I don't know how long. The ceiling's so high I can't get to it myself and I haven't bothered to call the super. Used to be I never allow such a ting to ride, never look up at a fixture with one dead bulb and a pile of dead bugs a-show tru the glass widoht right away fix it. Now I can't imagine how I could trouble myself with dis ting.

I lie down, exhausted but feeling that sleep not planning to visit me soon. When sleep do come, trouble haunts my dreams like a hush-winged owl and I ride a current of fear to where even the morning would be welcome. When finally it comes with its white glow, I drop back to sleep until I wake again with a start to a picture image of Bertha flat as a cartoon and coming at me sliding out of a copy machine, once and then a second time so I have one picture of Bertha to hold in each hand. It's a strange thing to have all that bulk reduced to someting with no thickness at all. It's early morning still when I put my ear to Bertha's door, hear her slow-rattling breath, and go off to catch the bus, leaving her alone tru the day to battle whatever punish her from the inside out.

Two

Clair holds my hand like a child of three, though she is eight going on nine any day now. She and I are in the Surprise Shop in the little shopping strip the girls call "uptown." We're here because the feeling's come washing over Clair that she's got to buy herself a "surprise ball" this afternoon or she might die of longing. I tell her those balls are just a bunch of junk for throwing out Professor's money, because whoever makes them just winds some colored paper into a ball and every few meters they slip in some trinket you could get from a gumball machine, someting that don't be worth a dime. But Clair's got to have it this day or her heart's going to break. So we make a trip into town and take our time strolling because the midday weather's even and fair for February. It's only three or four blocks to this town. Though I been here one and a half years, it's still hard for me to accustom to how neat and tidy this little town is, with all the stores set in the few square blocks, all the merchandise inside the closed shops, everyting for sale brand-new and cellophane packaged, nothing spilling out and spreading eena the street like back home. Not even music carries out to the street.

Everything's in its place except Clair's mother, who sure don' belong in this store hand in hand with somebody else's child, some girl Clair's size we never before set eyes on but holding Clair's mama's hand just like she belong to her, the child a-pick up one ting after another from the row of bright buckets—tiny baby dolls with eyes that open and shut and windup dogs and stickers and tiny checker sets. Clair's eyes open so big you could fall into them and drown yourself, and I feel the sweat slick her palm and know her heart is fluttering. Mrs. Silver comes direct to us, this stranger-girl in tow, and gives us a ugly kind of smile I've got no words for. Someting's playing behind her eyes, someting telling her she's scored some class of victory in the battle she's waging with Professor, and she wants to introduce this stray child she's got to Clair and tell Clair how this girl is her new neighbor child at her town house where she's living and don' they spend a lot of nice time together going to the ballet and movies and shopping.

Clair is yanking on my arm like it's a bus cord, wanting to get us out of there, but I turn away from Mrs. Silver, feeling a mind to throw up, and grab Clair a super-size purple surprise ball and quick throw some money at the woman behind the counter so Clair will at least have something nice for later.

We're halfway back home before Clair's got a word out of her mouth. "Why does she *do* that?" she says, her eyes wet. "Who is that girl? Why was she with my mother?"

"Your mother's her own kind of person," I say. "She's cut from a different bolt of cloth."

"She had blonde hair," Clair sniffles.

"And yours is brown," I say. "But that don't mean a ting."

"I want to see my friends," she says. "I want Franny. Her hair's prettier than that girl's."

"Tomorrow," I say. "You'll have her over to the house tomorrow."

The kitten climbs my breast slowly, like it's making the climb up Everest. I feel the pressure of each paw. I am sore and tender and know I am coming up on my time of the month. Here comes Bertha with her belly pain, and I can see right into her belly through a little window and so I see there's a snake curled up in there, sleeping. The kitten starts up purring and kneading my flesh. Now I am a ball of dough. The cat's claws prick me. *Jah!* I push it off me, and my eyes come open and I start rising up through the layers of sleep. My thumb presses a nipple, expecting the dream's soreness, but there is nothing. Half-asleep, the light still low, I see Clair's surprise ball on my table, beside the clock, because she said "no" to it ten times or more. I get up and dress a little, wake a little, sit on the hard edge of the bed and rest my head in my hands, stand and dress a little more, till I am finally in this early-morning room that's pink with the three girls' flotsam and jetsam. Professor's voice calls me from down the long hall, and I go his way—ten steps, twenty steps in all—and slip myself inside his little room, next to his desk, where I wait quietly, everyting still hushed with morning.

The air in here is dry. It parches my throat and eyes. I close my eyes to comfort them while I wait on Professor and think of how back home in Jamaica I never knew air could sting the eyes from dryness, though it stings when the cane burns in the fields or Mama goes on a-fry her fish and bammy all the day. Professor sits at his desk in the short-ceilinged study he's crowded with books and little photos and art statues, everything neat as a museum, and there I stand beside him, flat-footed and straight as one of his statues, while he opens one last bill with a silvery blade and chooses the right stack to set it on.

"Indigo," he says, his eyes still considering his papers, his mind only half turned to me, "do you know where North Apple Street is, in the city?"

"Yes, Professor," I drone. "Apple Street is near to where I live. I pass it on the bus most every day and walked past there just the other night, so it must be in the stars for me to hear the name of that street every place I go." *I passed by the low-class end of it,* I think, *wandering like a lost child.*

He glances up at me, his eyes bright with revelation, as if he is just now realizing that I have a place to live that is not his house in the suburbs and a community with streets whose names I know. By some twist of mind, he's forgetting the day he came to my house and stepped inside not long after he changed my world forever with his phone message about my Lou. I rub my breast for a second where the nipple feels sore.

"I bought a puppy for Clair's birthday. I want you and Jilly to go pick it up on Tuesday or Wednesday. It's paid for. You'll pick it up at a Mrs. Perkins's house on Apple Street and drop it off at the Tabors' on Arbor Street for a day or two so we can have it for Clair's birthday Thursday."

"Yes, Professor," I say, curling my toes against the floorboards, thinking, *Why am I so lucky to be running all these family errands?*

"You've heard me talk of Dr. Tabor. She's one of my colleagues at the university."

"Um-hm."

Professor turns away from his work and laughs about something he must be seeing inside his head. "Clair should be old enough now to take care of an animal. By the time I was her age, I'd had two dogs come and go."

"Your girls had Lopey to care for, before she run off." I don't tell him all the hard planting and picking work, all the hauling loads up into the hills and tending babies many a child in Jamaica do by that age, and do in the heat of the sun. Professor thinks he lives in the big, hard-knocks world, so I don't need to tell him different.

"One of those dogs was mean. Buster, we called him. I was glad to see that dog go." He laughs so hearty, remembering, it's hard to resist his good spirits. "I think Grandma Silver took him to the pond. She told me he ran away, that same dog that followed her home in the first place, hoping for a bone, probably getting a bowl of borscht instead."

Professor's little fat-cheeked mother died soon after I arrived, from all her years of rheumatism. I see Grandma Silver on swollen knees, drowning the dog at the pond, and wonder what Professor finds to laugh at in that picture.

"Clair's new dog is a purebred Shetland sheepdog, not a pond dog," he says.

Now I hear Professor's meaning, how he says "pond" when he means "pound." So that's where Grandma took Buster. Took him to the pound when he got to be too much trouble. Told Professor and Aunt Esther that Buster run off.

"So you'll go? With Jilly."

"What else I have to do with my time?" I say, knowing that Professor stomachs my meanness these days. Could be this family needs some kind of sheepdog to herd them, with Mrs. Silver off in her own apartment since some months before Louisa's gone, and the girls and Professor flying off in all directions. Sometime seem alla them may go the way of Lopey.

"Jilly can drive. I gave her the house number for Mrs. Perkins and also Dr. Tabor."

"Jill drives very nicely, for just turning sixteen," I say, telling him a lie because I feel in a deceiving mood.

"Do you think Clair will like the puppy?" he asks me, though that is as silly a question as ever been asked.

"Oh, Clair, she'll be so happy with that puppy, she'll be squealing. She miss that old dog."

Professor smiles his lovely smile, now that he's heard what he needed to hear. "I hope so. Too much worry for these girls lately, and now their mother's talking custody suits, which is bound to be a nightmare."

"She would take those girls?" I ask, and shake my head. "Lord, I don't know what kind of mother she sees herself. Flaunting other folks' pickney in front of Clair."

"She'll do what's good for herself and not worry over anyone else's *tsuris*." He looks at me, knowing I won't know his strange word. "*Troubles.* A Jewish word for troubles. But you know about that, Indigo."

"Yes, Professor." I cross my hands over the darts that run like two scars up the middle of my white uniform. Professor gives me a look as if 'im no begin to understand me, because I put no grief into my words. I'm not in the habit of telling him all of my truth. When I talk to him about Louisa, my words are dull as ash.

I see in my head a photo picture of a white car, a plain, innocent thing shining in the sun, sleek and trimmed in silver like what you might see in an advertisement. Might as well be a teif's shotgun for how it steal the life from my child, just run her down in the road and drive on past like she count for less than a field mouse. Sweat starts to run neet my arms and on my forehead, and I want to go off to where I can take some breaths stretched long as taffy. I feel like maybe I'm going to pass out. Could be I *want* to pass out, to keep my heart from sinking one more time into a place so cold and evil no decent soul ought to know of it.

"Indi, Indi," I hear, the words dragging me. "Indigo," Professor says, his voice pulling at me determined as a tugboat, "I know what you're going through, and the girls understand, too, and we'll help any way we can." Now he lets time flow by. "But I have to say something." He pauses again, and I see that Professor, normally so quick with his words, has to work at this one, whatever it is. "It won't help anything to take it out on them. Your anger, I mean, the way you've been so sharp with all of us lately. And they could use a little more affection from you, like you used to show them. They've got their troubles, too. You know that."

Oh, Lord, Professor's going to poke at me till I want to creep into a cave and hide. I keep my silence awhile, until my fear hardens into stone. "How can I show what I don't have?" I prick him. "Tell me that."

Now Professor's got his hurt-face look. He lets the room fill up with time. I feel him wanting to push back his chair, scraping it rough against the floor, and walk off from me, but he keeps to his seat. "Fake it, then," he says, his voice suddenly stern, not wrestling any over these words.

What am I going to say to that? I've got no words to answer with. I turn my head to the wall.

"Let me put it this way. Those girls need someone who can care about them, at least a little. It's my job to provide that, so don't gamble with *your* job, if you value it. There's no malice in what I'm saying. I'm just telling you what needs to happen here." Now he stands up from his chair, and his face makes a home for a scowl that looks like it has settled in permanent.

"I don't have a gambler's luck, Professor."

"All right, Indigo, but you know what I mean. It's just you and me that those three girls have got for guidance. No one else—no mother and no magic business from up above. At least that's my philosophy. So you think it over."

"Why do you send the girls to religious school, then?" I ask, forgetting any idea I might have of my "place."

Professor shrugs. "It's their people, the Jewish people—they have a right to know where they came from, and a right to choose their own path ahead. But for me, it's about who we are and where we've been, not about God on high with the long white beard."

"Some would call that sinful thinking."

"Yes. Some would. And they're free to call it what they will, just like the girls and I are free to find our own way."

I turn to go. *Free.* Professor sure makes a parade out of that word and dresses it in fine feathers.

"Indigo," he says, calling me back one more time. "Today in my office, I interviewed a man for my study, for my project, the refugees project—you've heard me talk about that. This man's family were French Acadians who fled Europe to Canada, then fled Canada to Louisiana, to bayou country. There was too much interbreeding among them, and they developed a genetic disorder that caused this man and others in the group to be born deaf. Now he's gradually losing his vision, which is another part of the disorder. Soon he'll be altogether deaf and blind."

"Troubles all over, Professor."

"That's just my point, Indi. It's a hard road for many people. Everyone's cast out from some place, going from here to there, with struggles along the way. Do you understand?"

"Who that's suffering in this world's going to understand that, Professor?"

He drops his head. "Sorry," he says. "I guess I don't know what I'm talking about. Sorry." He starts mumbling a song in his broken singing voice as if he already let me go and he's sitting by himself. "How the winds are laughing . . ." is what I hear. I wonder who are they laughing at today.

I go on out from his study and wander toward the library, my mind a blur. There in the library is Jill, squatting beside the bookshelves, her back to the door, so most of what I see is her head of hair so bushy she might have sprung from a black mama, though the color's about like wheat. She jumps up when she hears me, scared as a wild creature and pressing a small book against her chest like I'm not supposed to see it.

"Hi, Indi."

"You got something you need to hide from the light there, Jill?"

She shakes her head.

"Well, you can keep what secrets you like," I say. "I'm not here to put my nose in your business. Just come in here to sit awhile." It comes to me how I've not seen Clair for hours, not since her friend Franny came over to visit. "Where's your sister?" I ask. "Those girls go out running around in the cold, Clair risking her asthma again?"

"I don't know."

"Child needs to take it easy outside, she need to carry that inhaler like Professor tell her alla the time."

I change my mind about sitting and wander out and head to my room. Then my mind changes back, so I go on down to the kitchen, straying like a spirit. Some mousy squeals come from back of the basement door. I go ahead and wander down there next. Clair and Franny are off in the far corner, past the furnace, with only the one bare ceiling bulb shining on them—could be some kind of prisoner-of-war scene from the movies. The two of them sit giggling like a chorus, half-naked and cross-legged on a piece of rug, plastic playing cards fanned open in their hands.

Clair looks at me and claps her hand over her mouth, discovered. She pipes out some shrieking sounds that could come from a baby animal.

"You girls into that strip poker again?" I ask. "You're not out of that childishness yet?"

"We just started it this year!" she answers back, and gulps air.

I look at Franny, and that plump child's face closes like a flower in the moonlight. "Should have finished it soon after," I say, and think, *This is what happens when a child's mama don't care a wink what she do.*

"Don't tell—*please,*" Clair appeals to me.

"I got more to do with my time than bother Professor with how his young daughter go on like she big."

Clair grabs Franny's hand, then releases it and pats Fran's shiny hair, still jumping with excitement.

When I've made the evening's meal and left it labeled in

the fridge for the girls to set out on the table, I say good-bye to Clair and Jill and Professor and tell Julie, the oldest at seventeen, she can drive me the long block to the bus, since it's dark out tonight. Julie groans a little, always glad to be grudgeful, but then she brightens and her hand reaches up to fluff her hair like her mind's conjured a picture of somebody looking her up and down with eyes full of interest. Must be she sees she's got an excuse to get her car keys and go prowling about in the dark world.

As we walk to the car, Jules shoots her eyes up toward the pearly bit of moon laid out on its back like a foolish woman. "Better go on home after you drop me off," I warn her. "Right on home."

"There's one bright star just above the lower tip of the moon," she says. "It's like a big diamond. See?" She points. "Do you think it's a wishing star or something?"

"You can wish on any star you like," I say. "Don't make it necessarily come true."

"If I could get my wish, I would change everything," she says, and sighs, "change everything there is, change it all around so you wouldn't recognize my life."

"That's you, Jules," I say, "always the restless one, wanting what's not to be." The wind stirs the air, then stops like it's holding its breath a second before it looses its grip on what bits of things it's picked up from the earth. I hear in my head Professor's song about the wind that's laughing and think, *Maybe this gentle wind's playing a big joke on all of us.* Can't no wind come, though, no matter how whispery and sweet, that I don't think some of Mister Gilbert, the hurricane wind that raked the islands and grabbed all of what lay in his way, dropped it down to smash into bits.

I am relieved to get home, into my own space, where I have nothing to do for any person but Indigo Rosemartin. I don't even take off my coat, just sit down in my brown-checked armchair that used to be in the Silvers' library and smells a little of the cigarettes Professor smoked until the girls formed a unity and got after him so much he went ahead and quit. Now it's got the center space in my living room, between the dining table on the left side of the room—beside the big front windows—and the little kitchen across the way, opposite side to the big windows. I have an old leather footrest I got from the resale down the road that I keep in front of the chair.

Before I can put my feet up and rest them, my friend Jewel from the flats just across the road is at the door, her long body fidgety as Big Bwoy when he's made to stand in front of teacher and do his sums. Jewel is from here, not Jamaica. I know her from when I used to go to the Baptist church, in what the churchwomen call the "old days," which means the days before the pastor they got now, a Mr. Davis. Now I just watch out the window Sunday morning when Jewel hails her cab or, on a nice day, sets out to walk the eight or nine blocks that take her past the shopping section and a little ways toward the lake.

"You come with me tonight, Indi girl," says Jewel. "We'll go on down to the new Grill and Games Pub over on Webster Street." She lifts her hand to slick back her cap of straightened, oiled hair, always styled in the latest fashion. Looks like shellac to me; could be the head of hair on one of Clair's Barbies.

"When you ever see me drinking, Jewel?"

"Play some cards, then, or dice."

"When you see me gamble? Don't even play no Drop Pan back home, 'cept on occasion."

"Oh, hush, girl," says Jewel. "You just come on out to a restaurant with me, then, eat you some dinner. Or ain't you the eating type, neither? You done give that up, too? You so proud."

Lord knows I need someting, but it don't be that. What

I need don' even have a name to it, that I can give. Just someting to fill a dead space that's swollen up in me. I wonder how can a place be empty and full, dead and aching, all at once. I hear a story one time of a man who lose a limb, but what's gone still hurt him and there's no relief he can find. Can't very well salve what don't be present. No easing massage or balm of sinkl-bible plant a-go to help that hurting. I remember Bertha across in the silence, not even stirring up a sound with a chair that scrape or a pot lid fall down. *Lord! I got to check on her.*

"Go ahead and poke fun at me," I tell Jewel. "I am what I am." I keep my words shrill, but she urges half a laugh out of me with her talk. "Come across the way with me and see to Bertha. Then we'll go."

Bertha gives no answer to my first knock, then answers the second one in a groggy voice to where I know we en wake her. "Never mind," I shout in through the door. "Go on back to sleep. I'll check you later." The door stays closed, so I never set eyes on her to see her condition.

"Did you know her when her mother was sick and dying?" Jewel asks.

"No, ma'am. Un-um."

"Lord, that was something painful to see. Cancer."

We walk down the street, keeping clear of the buses that spin up slushy snow, and enter the Basin Blues Bar at the far end of a three-block stretch of businesses, half of them owned by people from countries I never even heard of. I order a cheddar cheese burger and fried potatoes. Jewel stays with some kind of tomato and cuke salad, which is why she keeps her stringbean shape. Me, I just as soon have me some fat to get through the winter, just like an old black bear. While we wait on our food—Jewel's eyes roaming the place one end to the other, her foot a-jiggle—some big, muscle-bound man come over to the table, show off a grin broad as a rainbow, his skin the color of eggplant. He gives us a look ought to shame him and says, "Well, how about that. Two beautiful gals. Fine, fine evening, ain't it?"

"Ain't it the truth," says Jewel, and right off gives up her own broad and coaxing smile to this stranger.

"It'll do," I say when he turns his eyes my way.

He grabs hold of a wooden chair from the next table, sits backward around it so it looks like a baby's chair under his big frame. "I'm Francis—most call me Frank," he says, "and that I am. Never a word of deceit ever cross my lips. You ladies have some names you want to share with me?" No fool, he looks to Jewel for his answer, but he glance my way to study my face and figure, like men always happy to do if you got any kind of curve to you.

"Mary Lou," Jewel says with a giggle, and gives me a kick under the table, silly as a schoolgirl.

"You all got any plans for after your meal?" he asks.

"Not likely," says Jewel, Miss Sassy-pants.

"You like to play a little dice? A little cards? Easy stakes, of course."

"Um, not likely. My friend Cindy here ain't likely to be in the mood." She pushes her elbow at my arm on top of the table.

"Pity," say Sir Galahad, and pull a plain white card from his wallet, scratch down someting for Jewel in a blue pencil. "She sure would pretty up the place, with them big red lips."

Lips for spitting, I wouldn't mind say to his licky-licky self, but know enough to keep my mouth shut awhile. "That your business card?" I ask, aiming to bring him down a rung.

Jewel reads the card. "Brother Man?"

"Some kind of fool Jamaican?" I ask.

"You ain't a Jamaican?" he says, as if he's going to surprise me with that fact.

"Cindy," Jewel repeats with conviction. "That's her pretty name."

He dismounts his chair with a high swing of the leg, like he ride some fine stallion. "Maybe you come your own self, Mary Lou. Or maybe Cindy here change her mind when her mood done pass." He squeezes the top of the chairback with both hands. "Though some men crazy about a hard-hearted woman." He turns around, points to the bar, to a little gnome of a white man, pointy headed and old as the earth. "Brother Man's place is ecumenical, taking all color and kind of folk. Mr. Borotsky there comes all the time. Yo, Mr. Borotsky," he calls softly, and the old man lifts his face to us, his eyes buzzard sharp. "Come meet some folks."

The old man jump down from his stool like his body full of spring despite the silvery hair and skin that fold down over his eyes, all the fat behind it leached away like it do with old folk. I see him slip a hand behind his ear to fiddle with a hearing aid, then he walks to our table, as fast-foot as any youth.

"Good evenink," he says, his head curtsying, his English stiff and funny like Grandma Silver's, even though she been in the country from Julie's age, leaving Europe before the Second World War, so Professor tells me in his long stories. This Borotsky reaches his liver-spotted hand to me, giving a hard squeeze, pressing his second hand over mine as well, then on to Jewel he goes. "Friends of yours, Francis?" he asks, his breath powerful with garlic and lemon.

"Hoping to make them friends. I'm inviting them over to Brother Man's. I told them you go there all the time, Mr. Borotsky. That way they can know it's a decent place."

"Decent?" the old man questions, pushing out his bottom lip. Even the skin of his lip is brown-spotted. "But Francis is a good man and tells the truth," he says. He makes a fist and taps his chest and says, his voice slow and knowing its own mind, "Myself, I am a regular customer. Whenever I have money to burn, as they say, or throw away, that's where I am to be found, but I have a strict policy, ladies, never to risk what I dare not lose, understand? You don't want to throw away your life there, like the sad young people with their drugs. You just want to engage in a little sport, and know the difference."

Francis laughs. "You don't want Brother Man dogging your steps. He dog you clear into the next world."

I see this old man has a blue tattooed number marching up his forearm. Even in the winter he wears a short-sleeved shirt that opens it to the eye. My eyes settle on the inked numbers, and he watches me see what I see.

"What is that, do you know?" he asks me like a schoolmaster, and touches it with his finger.

"Yeah, mon, me know that, surely me know," I say. "Professor him tell me all aboht them camp-dem when him a-want to lecture me on the suffering of alla the human race."

His voice comes slow, each word by his choice. "You think maybe I should wear a long shirt, cover it up? Is that it?"

Jewel looks at her feet, aiming to hide her face, moon behind clouds, disappear herself.

I shake my head and shrug. "Not for me to say."

He opens his eyes full wide to me. "Good," he says. "Good. So I am glad to meet an intelligent woman."

"You live here in this neighborhood, Mr. Borotsky?" I ask. "A Jewish man, here in this neighborhood?"

"You believe that all Jews are rich and live on the Gold Coast?"

"Maybe."

"Actually, Miss—"

"Cindy." Jewel lifts her head and declares my name once again, then hiccups.

"—Cindy, I could afford a more, as they say, upscale neighborhood, but here in this neighborhood I am more at home. *Versteh?*"

"You're most welcome, then," Jewel says, as if she's social chairwoman of the neighborhood.

"So. Who is your Professor who enjoys lecturing you?" Borotsky asks.

"Professor Silver," I say. "My employer."

"Silver. The Jew who studies generations of refugees. I know of him. I know his work. Some interesting ideas, he has. And a decent man, a mensch, I've heard, though I haven't had the pleasure of meetink him."

"He's good enough to pay my wage and put food on his children's table, so I guess that makes him a decent man, compared to many." I think of Professor's words the other night and wonder will he find me decent enough to stay long in his household, or will I find myself out in the street.

Borotsky's left hand takes hold of the bottom button of his brown wool sweater and pushes it through the buttonhole.

"It's a mite chilly in here tonight, ain't it?" Frank asks. "Mr. Borotsky, how 'bout you and me go on down to Joselyn Street?"

"Yes," says the old man. "We'll go and take our chances against the House." He winks at me. "A little contest I have. Me against the House. An amusement for an old man."

"Ladies?" Frank asks.

Jewel shakes her head. "We still be waiting on dinner," she says, some kind of fear livening her voice. "But thank you kindly. Maybe another time."

When they go, she says to me, "I like that Frank, honey. Ain't he a doll?"

"Umm. Nice enough. Don't be nothin' special."

"He thinks you're pretty. You see how he reads you with his eyes?"

"He can think what he wants. Wish I never born a woman."

"Hush, girl. That's evil."

"At least that old man's got some sense." I think of the old black man who picked me up off the street the other night after he knocked me down.

"I don't like seeing those slave numbers on that old man's arm," Jewel says, and shudders. "He ought to cover them up. It like to give me the creeps."

"We ought to stroll by that place after we finish up eating, just stroll by and poke our face in the window and get a look at what alla them so het up about."

"You think we should go there, Indigo? Ain't that wicked?"

Poor Jewel can no make up her mind which kind of person she be. First, she the one want to go a-gamble. Now she the preacher. "How it cyan be evil to go peer tru di window? You tink one of dem men go on reach a hand out and pull us in, force us wager wi money?"

"Oh, girl, ain't you something!" Jewel starts laughing so hard she got to lay her head on the table.

I start up laughing, too, like I haven't done for Lord knows how long.

"What would our mamas say, girl, see us crazy like this and fixin' to go out gambling?"

"You right on that," I say. "Mama was no big fan of gambling when my papa do it." I remember the time Papa sneak me off to the bar. It don' surprise me he do such a ting to Mama, but surprise me some dat I go along with his plan. Mama my hero when I'm small, she my fairy godmother, my angel, the way I love her. She loves me in return. I feel I warm her heart, brighten her eye, quicken her laugh. But by the time Papa take me off with him, alla that start to change. Somehow the heart goes out of her love when I am four years old, maybe five, still a baby. There is someting that happens to Mama's love that cannot happen, because a love like that cannot change, never can wither. A love like that makes the mada feed the baby before she feed herself. I think how they explain on the airplane for the mada to take the oxygen for herself before she do for the child. Mada no can do so, she prefer the baby life above that of sheself. But someting do what can *no* be done to Mama's love. Too many babies, perhaps, too likkle baby fada, spoil Mama heart. Seem like someone jook her heart with a thorn, drain oht alla the love. "And Mama get mad as a bull," I tell Jewel. "She throw dishes and tear up papers, shout till she's hoarse when Daddy go to the bar and waste her money. Finally, he just give it up, no can take her hollering more." *Of course, later,* I think, *he just give all of us up. Maybe go back to his pleasure-dem.*

I ask Jewel, "What we got to hurry home to but Bertha sick in the bed and not much better off for our company?"

"Don't think like that, girl," Jewel says, sitting up straight now, a proper Christian. "We can't go prowling in the dark. You right—we got to get home and look in on Bertha."

"All right, then," I say. "We stay back this time—don' even go squint an eye in the window. I guess you be the good one, Jewel, even when I be wicked."

Three

Next evening, I open up my door and there's a white paper that's slipped under there while I'm at work. *Indigo,* it says. *I'm back to the Coopers house all the way through till next weekend. That handsome Cliff came by three times looking for you. I saw him out the window. He's sweet on you, girl, and ain't he something fine to look at. Jewel.*

Cliff is a fellow thinks he's a fox, God's gift and alla that nonsense. I en meet him one year ago now, the first time I feel winter, when life skip along fine for me. Back then, I save up money from my work at Professor's, send dollars and nice tings for dem back home, feel my pride in all that sustenance that make a likkle river flow from me in America to all my people back home. I miss my girl someting awful alla the time, but I hold steady against that hurting, knowing I offer them some hope and joy. I en meet Cliff during those days at a party spindly Mary give one day for us from Jamaica and for a few folks she know from here and there. Mary is a girl from down the street. She want to be a fashion model so don' eat nothing but carrot sticks. The black girls from here tease her she fixing to look like a carrot stick herself the way she eat, tease her how she got no booty. Old Cliff him show up in leather and tight pants, skinny little beard hanging off his chin. *Billy goat,* I think, but I like his bright smile and stories of working on the railroad, so I take him into my heart. Back then, my heart's a warmer place. I like Cliff's come-and-go spirit. All the ones I love got that spirit about them, even my own self.

Today that note Jewel writes gives me no pleasure; men no longer season up my life. I rip the note top to bottom in four strips and rise to my feet, drop it in the waste can, then settle back into my chair.

Some skinny streaks of sunshine slip sideways through the curtains and lay across the floor. I stare at the light as if it might start up dancing, but the sun gives me no joy either. My heart has no more use for sunshine.

It's funny how sunshine means different to folks here than to them back home. There the sun is too much and wears you down. You get to wishing you could go off and find some nice shade. Here, for all the winter months the sun is just a faint, flickering thing, like a pretty moth everyone want to catch hold of and save in a jar. I remember laughing with a happy feeling when the sun en come a-dance out my first northern February. This February it mek me no difference what the sun do wid himself. Him no friend of mine.

Restless, like more and more these days, I go on and knock once at Bertha's door across the way and hear her call me in. Bertha sits on her bed, watching the TV, eating some ice cream. "Is that how you spend the Lord's day?" I ask her, my praise of God a leftover thing.

She laughs, full of her good nature. "Indi girl, what a pleasure," she says. "Come and sit by me. I'm having me some mint chocolate chip. You want some?"

"Thanks, no. Glad to see you're feeling yourself again."

"But look at you—you're wasting away to skin and bones, girl. How you keep strong enough to do your housework?"

I pinch my waist and show her my three inches of fat under my purple sweater.

"Oh, okay, child," Bertha says. "You're ample. Suit yourself, then. I won't fuss after you like I do my girls." She pushes away her half-eaten bowl of ice cream. "It ain't setting right with me today," she says, and for a bit her face gives up its glow.

"I thought you were fit again."

"Not entirely," she says. "Come sit beside me here, watch this little movie with Meg Ryan. She's such a sweet-faced gal and it cost you a five-dollar bill or more to see her at the theater."

I shake my head. "Just a heap of nonsense."

Bertha gives me a steady look. "Your heart's still broke, child. That's why you talk so harsh."

"Got to go," I say, sorry I came across. "Got to get some housework done."

Back in my room, I take out some of the leftover five- and ten-dollar bills from my purse and lay them in the drawer of the Singer cabinet I use for a phone table. That drawer is full with paper money. I got more money than what I need, now that I spend so little on them back home. Money piles up in that drawer like the burdens heaped in my heart. I think crazy thoughts about papering the walls with it, just to show how little it means to me, this fruit of my labors, but I hear the American government might lock a body up for that kind of foolishness. Not in Jamaica, where if you can find the government at all and it's not drinking rum neet a mahoe tree, it's got more to worry over than what cover your wall. My door swings open, and it's Bertha come chasing after me. I turn tail and walk toward my kitchen, let her trail behind.

"Indigo," she says. "I done made you mad."

I turn and look her in the eye. She comes toward me, her big brown body moving like a pudding, same as Mama's always did. *Oh Lord, Lord.* She puts a hand atop the chair back to help support her weight.

"Some things you don't want to be talking about just yet," she says. "I understand that, child. Don't you worry—I'll leave you be, till your time comes to share your heart."

"All right, then," I say.

Her eyes travel past me to the open drawer full of bills. "You ain't got a bank to put that in, gal?" she asks. "You never know when someone can break into these rooms and fill his bag with all of that money you work so hard for."

"Me got an account at the Chicago Avenue."

"Clifford's cousin Zach works there as a teller," says Bertha. "He's a fine young man, smart as a schoolteacher. I like to see a young man raised up fine as that. His mama certain must be proud."

"Zach must not have much in common with that idle Clifford, then."

"Clifford, yes, he's cut from a different cloth."

Bertha leaves and I beat my fist into the wall, taking care to blunt the sound. I try to draw some calm into my spirit, but no way can I find peace now in these rooms full of Louisa's pictures and the old black radiator that's taken up groaning. I go and stand at the small mirror, run my hand over my cheeks, over the skin of my neck. *Old,* I think. *You're getting old and worn and losing spark, not no young girl anymore like Bertha's two.* Better to go on out into the night and let the lights and traffic noises fill up my head rather than fill it myself with hurting words. I grab a light coat and rush out the door, don't even lock it behind, don't care a thing about the money that lies in the drawer, useless as leaves that drop from the trees here. For all I care, someone can walk in and take it for his own. Maybe I put a little gift tag in there that say, "Help yourself, mon."

The air is full of mist, like something's crawling up out of the earth into the space above, making a life for itself above ground. The heavy air seems to settle on my skin and give it cover from the cold. No need to put the coat around me. The street is light enough for clear seeing just with street lamps and the little house lamps people turn on to flood their front steps at night so they know what danger's coming their way. I see two orange tiger cats casting about in the bushes in front of the low building next to mine. They don't see each other, but each one sniffs the air. Then they come face-to-face and explode into hissing and spitting till one screeches so horrible it seems he must be clawed to death, then he runs off.

I go on past two, three tall houses, my eyes browsing the bushes and sitting porches. When the street is empty of cars, I hear a few night creatures I can't name. See a fat raccoon struggle out of the sewer grate, hiss at a cat, and waddle back to the silver trash cans set between two buildings.

From up on one of the high cement porches comes a man's voice. "Hey now, woman." I can't see a face but know the voice as a Jamaican named Henry P, a man bald-headed as Anansi spider. Two times or three, him and me have pass the time of day. Him the one work as a fireman for the city. Jus' sit all day outside the fire station till a call come in, then at night like to sit out on his high porch with a tan hound dog the man say he get at the pound. Always he got the long rifle set across his knees like he have some hunting to do right here in the city, and his radio plays soft, spreading music out eena di street, like him back home in Jamaica.

"What you say, Henry?" I call back, and move to the middle of the quiet street so I can peer up to his porch, see him sitting in a wood chair, his heavy boots resting on the cement wall of the porch. Can't see his dog till the animal ambles over to the top of the stairs above me and stretches his neck skyward, blaring once so loud he might be sounding out Judgment Day.

"Just out walking?" Henry asks me.

I nod.

"You feel safe to do that, sister? Late as this?"

"What? Now you my mada?"

"Why you no come up here on the porch and let me give you a drink of rum, keep you from a-walk in the streets all alone. This city 'im a tiger in the night. You mus' be a tiger yourself. Mus' be wary."

"Me no need a drink right this minute, Henry P."

"All right, then," he says. Hound dog start to creep down the stairs to take a better look. "Come on now, Tosh," he calls. "Indigo, you come on, then, and have a cigarette with me."

"What kind of fireman need to start his own likkle fire-dem, give himself cancer in the lung?"

"Oh, Lord. You sure want to give me a hard time, gal. You got no vices of your own?"

I shrug.

"Jus' come sit by me here, right on the bench. I got it covered with a little linsey-woolsey shawl to keep it warm." He pats the cloth beside him. "Once I take my feet off the ground, we're swinging."

I feel a tide a-push me on past. "Keep your feet on the ground," I say. "Me, I got to go on a-walk," I say. "Someting pull at me."

"Sound like a fish on a line," he says, and chuckles. "Go on, then, Indigo gal. Get you some air. I'll keep a watch on you if you stay close. Anyone bother you, Toshie and me we come straight to the rescue."

I walk on down the street, thinking I am getting too rude even for me. I know my meanness aims partly toward Bertha for spoiling my peace every which way, remarking on my

Louisa, bringing back the picture of Mama's full bosom. Better show a little friendliness to this Henry P next time I come by, or pretty soon I'll start sprouting fur and claws like a jungle beast. I get a sudden sad feeling that takes hold of me so strong it seems it can make the blood flee my veins in fright. All of it circles on Louisa, that much I know. When I think of the days stretching on without her, I get a fear so deep I don' cyan put words to it. Life spreads ahead of me, an ocean of empty hurting I no cyan bear, its waters flowing forever. Best those waters trade direction and wash back over me.

I pull on my coat and step faster and try to nail a lid over all this thinking. It must be near eleven when I get into the business area, so the only thing I come to that's open is a 7-Eleven store with a pack of teenage boys hanging about the door, their pants sagging down over their batties just pitiful, though Julie, who always knows the fashions, tells me that's the look. Can't see how flashing your underclothes can be a "look," but Julie says I must be getting old before my time if that's how I think. A liquor store no bigger than a phone booth has its door flung open to the street, calling out to sinners. Likely, that Basin Blues is open if I want to walk two blocks more, but here comes an arcade of some kind, the door swung wide as the liquor store's, the noise of talk and laughter and peculiar whistles and bells tumbling out like its own kind of music. I think of that Brother Man place that Francis hyped and of all them foolish Jamaicans thinking they know how to throw their money away so it don't hurt. But don't my own money sit back in the drawer, ready to buy birthday presents for my child that's buried? A young man and a woman some bit older stand together on the steps, smoking something they rolled themselves that's got a sweet smell. I know the smell of ganja well enough to know this is a good class, maybe what we know as sinsemilla back home.

It's cold now and the dampness that slithered out of the earth has climbed over my feet and into my pores like they are doors I forgot to shut. I go on past the couple and up the cement stairs, which are splattered, by accident or art, with all color of paint in a psychedelic pattern. When I walk in the door, there's nothing to see but men—half of them bent over the old-style pinball games, half setting on stools along the front wall, staring into video screens. Whenever one looks up at me, he soon glances around to the others, tries to catch somebody's eye, maybe give him a wink. Mek me wish one more time I born an old woman or one that shape like a post. I walk past one or two pinball machines that are not in use but I don't know how to manage them. A monitor's free, so I go over there feeling like half of them men's eyes are warming my back while I take a look at the screen, see what game it's got. I can only half decipher the theme of it.

The air around me darkens, and I look to my side to see a skinny white fellow in high boots and a leather jacket, 'im long, uncombed beard looks pasted on, who leans against my monitor without asking, just like he's got a right to be here. This boy appears young enough to be in high school and thin as a sugar cane.

His slick smile lifts jus' one side of his mouth. "Bet you five bucks your dude there won't score a hundred." He points to the cartoon figure on my screen.

"Not here to bet my money," I say. "Just playing a game."

"Best little game room in town," he says.

"Yeah, mon," I say, "and me have a keen preference fi enjoy it by mi own self."

"Just jiving, you know, like 'best little whorehouse' in town. Hah. Hah."

"You see some fine humor in that?"

"Hey, easy does it, miss. Or Ms.—whatever. You're not from here, right? You got an accent."

He wanders off, and I go on and sit down on top of the stool, slip in my quarters, and start jerking that joystick like this is my idea of fun. Pretty soon the men had enough of watching my back—I feel the heat go off it—and return to their playing. I notice how I feel almost jealous of them playing their foolish games, because I catch someting in their eye, some kind of light I see, that tells me how their play fires them up, makes their heart-dem pound. I hear how they holler out like it's jubilee day when they hit a prey. "Holy Chicago!" one man whoops each time he gets the high score.

No one's worrying about me anymore, so I can stand up and walk out of there without all those eyes swarming me. I walk around the town a little more till it's past midnight and I can go on back home knowing I've made my way through the rest of another evening doing who knows what, all of it meaning nothing. I am pushing time past me like I'm rowing in a boat, hauling back the water.

Sleep comes to me slow, but when I sleep, I have an odd dream that is in my head as I wake the next morning. In my dream I am not Indigo, I am Jill, away from home on her long summer trip, only I am my own years and not a foolish teenage girl like Jill. In the dream, I am stretched on my belly on the ground inside a canvas tent, trying to find some coolness in the earth that's beneath while the heat of a July night keeps me restless. The air is so wet it hangs about me like a cloud, so thick I tink I might slice it like a melon. I open up my eyes to the light of the full moon, and the counselor I like, dressed only in his short pants, squats just outside the door to my tent, his bare, broad feet the closest thing to my face. I see him like it is not the first time he greets me this way. Already he has pulled loose the white bow of ribbon that closes the outer flap of canvas. I lie there watching while he slides the zipper of the mosquito netting and pokes his head inside, his black hair shiny with sweat. Then he slides one dusty foot forward onto the canvas, which is littered with sand as if we are camped beside the sea.

I moan and the scene blinks out and then I am Jill in her room at Professor's house and I am making my bed, folding the ironed white sheets into the square hospital corners I learned in the Girl Scouts. There is no end of corners to fold. One follows after another and another.

I get up from the mattress and know I have another day to face. So I wash and pull on my uniform, comb out my stiff hair, wondering who put this strange dream in my head that must've been meant for Jill's young head. Must have come my way because I'm back to the Silvers' this morning. Tomorrow morning I go with Jill to pick up that animal at the high-class end of Apple Street. Here or the Silvers'—Lord, I don't know which place I would least rather be. There is no home for me in this world anymore, not in one place or the other, so I just row back and forth between them, finding no peace.

Four

"You can put those back," I say as Jill draws her car keys up out of her bag, along with a green hair band that's caught a ride like seaweed come up with a fish. "We can take the express bus into Chicago." The day is warm enough—past thirty, which is just about a heat wave—and the sun is high.

"We're bringing home a puppy, Indi," she protests. "How can we take a bus?" Jill looks at me like she's thinking she doesn't know me anymore, the sharp way I act.

"I've been on buses carrying two live chickens, one under each arm, and a pig on a rope following behind."

I see Jill stop herself from speaking. She wants to try and be good, because that is her nature, and she remembers when we were friends. I only remember the idea of that, and it is weak as a breath of smoke left over from a doused fire.

Jill picks the hair band off her keys. She reaches up to make a ponytail out of the hair she's always brushing to tame its wildness. "Daddy gave me directions to the house. He said to take the Escort."

"I'm not driving in the car with you, Jill. You'll get us in an accident and your father will have some more doctor bills to pay."

Jill's eyes slip sideways trying to get past that subject. She knows what doctor bills I'm talking about—all her mother's bills from the psychiatrist because of the crazy tings she do all the time, like driving her car right into people's gardens. "They won't let a dog on the bus. It's against the rules."

"There's not one single driver I trust, Jill, young or old. If you don't get us killed in that car, some old drunk willing to do it."

"The bus has a driver," Jill says in her soft but firm voice.

All through the bus ride, Jill's been clutching the paper Professor gave her that is printed "Educational Institute" in blue letters at the top and has directions written with Professor's black-ink fountain pen below. Now we walk two blocks through cold slush that seeps right into my shoe leather. We get to Mrs. Perkins's house, and I see the north end of Apple's not much like the south. Must've left all the worms for the south end. At the door, after we tap with a brass bull, barking dogs greet us, and then a skinny, fine-boned white lady with a narrow nose that juts out like a breakwater.

"Oh, Miss Silver," she says to Jill. "You've come for the pup. And who is this?" She looks down at my wet shoes, though I'm standing square on the mat and I swear red letters say "welcome" clear as morning light.

"Indigo Rosemartin," I say, and look around and find myself admiring whoever keeps this little parlor dusted and polished, because there is no dog hair in the corners and no odor of dogs here, just a scent of lemon oil.

"Indigo," she repeats, turning my name in the air like an odd thing but saying no more. Her hair is black as paint, and her blouse and skirt just the green to wrap a Christmas gift. I wonder who is older, her or me? She is as light-boned as the four midget collie dogs that circle around her feet, each dog with clean white fur climbing up its legs, which puts me in mind of the white-gloved ladies at the hotel in Montego Bay. Mrs. Perkins and her dogs make me feel like I am made out of clay, but I would rather be my way—with some meat on my bones—than sickly like them. Even Jill looks built like a field hand compared with them, though she's lighter than me by forty pounds. Mrs. Perkins clucks and calls out names like she is gathering Santa's reindeer, then leads her four pretty dogs out of the room. She comes back, carrying in her arms Professor's little dog, and sets it on the floor. I take a peek and see that this one is a boy dog, though it is shy and delicate as all the others.

The dog doesn't want to make his showing. He hides himself behind Mrs. Perkins's feet. "Come now, Tennyson," she says to him, using his high-flown name. "This breed is shy of strangers," she explains, talking mostly to Jill because I am dark-skinned and wearing a servant's white uniform.

Jill squats down and baby-talks to the dog and tries to get him to come to her. I don't have that much feeling for pet dogs and cats. They're like goats that can't give milk. Don't worth a dime; just eat from your cupboard. But Jill is more softhearted than me.

"Your father's already given me a check," Mrs. Perkins says. "Your father's a professor, isn't he? Of American history? I like to know where my dogs are going."

"Not American," I put in. "Just history . . . of displaced peoples of the world." I wonder what does this woman's maid use to give this floor so high a shine.

"Oh," she says, and hands Jill a large envelope with the dog's papers. "He's a champion, you know. You can show him."

I see how one ear of the dog is bent down limp and think, *What makes this skinny scrap of dog anybody's champion?*

The lady walks us to the door and pats the dog a few times on top of his head. "Where is your car?" she asks Jill.

I tell her, "Thanks. We're just around the corner, Mrs. Perkins. No distance at all for us."

* * *

We are out walking to the bus, keeping up as fast a pace as the clouds that hurry overhead. "Jill, you let that dog breathe. You'll smother him to death." She kisses him on top of the head with her little lips, both of hers together thinner than one of mine and pale as a cut pear.

Looking down the road, we see a silver bus whoosh past the stop. Jill starts kicking at the cindery snow, which has melted down to something dry as Styrofoam. I look her square in the face and say, "Now, stop your worrying. The driver's not going to lay an eye on that dog. Just you watch."

Soon the next bus swings round the corner. I unbutton my big coat as the bus bunks the curb. The brakes hiss like a jungle cat, and the dog presses to Jill's chest. "All right, Jill. Now, you give up that dog a little while." She is slow as treacle about it, but she hands him to me piece by piece. I tuck the creature under one flap of coat and keep my right hand snug under his skinny bottom. Then I let the coat lie over him and fold my left hand across him to keep him still. "You climb up first, Jill, and pay the driver for two. Watch how he don't even see this animal."

Jill does what I say and finds us two seats near the back, where there are no more than three or four other people. I let that puppy slip down onto my lap, still hidden under the coat. Jill is silently giggling with nerves because we have a dog on the bus against the rules. A little China girl sitting across the way with her white mother stops bouncing her glittery yo-yo and gets up and comes over to snoop. I give her a devilish look, and back she scurries to her seat. "See that, Jill," I say, and laugh. The laughing in my stomach must rile the puppy, because he starts to kick. Maybe too hot in there, under my coat and his own. That little dog nips me on the wrist and I yell out, "Jeesam," and lift my hands and the dog hops onto the floor and right away shakes himself out and looks more sprightly.

Jill is useless now, she is too much in shock, eyes round as headlamps. I got to crouch on that gummy yellow linoleum to try and coax that dog. At the same time I give the China girl and her rougy-cheeked mada and the two or three other folks a look with my eyes to say, *This is no business of yours.* They keep quiet until Tennis-something squats down and—oh, Lordy—begins to piddle on the speckly floor. Then everyone starts up laughing and pointing and saying "Uh-oh" and "Oh, God" and "They should never have brought a dog on the bus" and the bangarang stirs the driver to turn his head around. When he spots the dog, that young man kiss teet and his pale hair stand up like cut grain. He right away swerve the bus to the side of the road, then jam the brake so hard the dog skitters into an old lady's ankles and starts yipping and I come off my toes and fall back onto my batty, though I'm lucky nuff not to fall where the puddle is. "Raatid!" I mutter, and Jill, hearing me, starts to giggle. Jill has got the dog in her arms now, and she is staring at the puddle and stroking the animal rapid enough to rub fur coat right off skin. The driver strides back to us. Him look ten foot tall.

"Out, you with the dog—both of you, out," he says, and takes Jill's arm in his hand, not hesitating to squeeze it hard, and marches us like pickney right down the aisle to the front stairs.

I wooda like to get eena cuss-cuss wid dat man, but I just say, "Well, thanks a lot" to his gruff, long-cheeked face as I climb down the metal steps. "Just a little dog and a little piddle and we got to get off the bus."

Jill is laughing too hard to talk, and stomping her feet. "You better give me that dog," I say. "Till you control yourself, Jill." I think Jill just now broke a rule for the first time in her entire life. "You can't all the time be licky-licky, Jill, just because the man wear a uniform.

"Now, how we to get to that lady professor?" I ask her. "Too far still to walk. We're only to Evanston."

"Get another bus?" Jill asks, still laughing too much to say more than a few words.

"No thank you. One bus enough for today. We can go to a phone, Jill, and call Julie at the house."

We find a tilted phone booth sitting alone on a patch of gray stones next to the Shell station. I send Jill to call the house while I stand holding the dog and breathing in the gas fumes. Jill steps out into the air and leans on the door frame while she holds the phone to her ear, hoping for her sister to pick up.

"Don't lean on that rickety thing," I warn her.

After a while we get lucky, because for once in her life Julie is home and not out chasing around with her friends, and she says she will come for us, though I know already how grumbly she's going to be.

When Julie gets to us in the blue Escort Professor bought for her and for Jill, Jill and me and the little creature pile in the back and I say, "Now, don't you tell Professor, Jules."

"Let me see the puppy." She turns around in her seat and stretches her neck over the seat back.

"Ooh! He's so cute. Scott will love him," she squeals in the way these teenage girls have that drives me crazy. "I like the white racing stripe down his nose—that's so cool. All my friends are gonna love it." She turns back to her steering wheel and eases the car out of the Shell lot. Already the sun is close to down. "You guys are nuts. I can't believe you took the bus with a dog. Whose brilliant idea was that?"

"Never mind about whose idea," I say. "We paid our money to that driver, should have got our ride. That bus business one big bandulu. So you just take us home, Julie. We've heard enough about what we're not supposed to do to last us. We're not needing more, thank you."

"What if Mom gets custody of us?" Jill says as if she's been thinking all along about this. "What are we supposed to do with the dog then?"

"No way she's taking me," Julie says. "I'll run away. I could never have a friend over if we went there, never. I'd be too embarrassed."

I remember another day like this one, Julie and me side by side in the supermarket line, her mother just weeks before moved out from the house because Professor could no more abide her nonsense.

"You better phone your mother once in a while," I say to her. "Otherwise, could be some trouble coming."

"Trouble with who?" she says, always a sharp-mouth child.

"With your mama," I say.

"So?" she challenges me, watching herself in a mirror she's spotted across the store, brushing smooth her nice brown hair.

"Well, with up above, then," I say, and lift my eyes up toward the ceiling. "Don't forget, she's still your mother, Jules."

"I wish I had someone else's mother."

"You too red eye, wanting what others got. Mrs. Silver, she your mother now and all the time."

"Who would ever know," she says, cold as someting I set in the freezer for next week supper.

"You'll feel remorseful if someting bad happen to her and you no call her in three weeks' time."

"What bad is there that hasn't happened already?" she asks me, keeping up her argument.

I am sorry I put my nose in where it don' belong. That night I write a little letter to my own mada and leave Julie be, though I put that letter I write in my nightstand and never post it.

The girls and I drive along, Jules's car riding nicer than any bus, and I remind them, "Professor instruct me to drop this likkle dog at another professor house for a few days. Professor Tabor, friend he have from the university."

Both of them whine with sadness. Can't bear to let this little pup go.

"Well, it's not me doing it," I say. "You voice your complaint to Professor. But now we got to do as he say."

Professor Tabor lives right beside the bus stop that's closest to the Silvers', which is how I planned on the bus in the first place since I no deh fool. Now Jules slides us up to the curb, over the crunchy ice, and we all of us troop out, me, Jules, and Jill, who's got the dog in her arms. Jules kicks her way down the sidewalk—a mosaic of ice and salt stain—and up several stairs to the door. So here we go again. She pulls the brass knocker and lets it snap against the door. Along comes a blonde-haired lady to the door. "We here for the professor," I say.

"I'm Professor Tabor," she says, surprising me. I look her over, see is she attractive. I'm thinking, *Lord, is Professor out looking at the ladies?* Well, I wouldn't hold it against him, I don't suppose.

She takes that little dog in hand like she has made a second career of receiving babies passed along in the night, quick and quiet. I see it's going to drive Jill crazy, leaving the nervous dog a couple of days, but we've got to follow Professor's say-so, so off we go, Jules leading the parade, back to the car and on home, empty-handed.

Five

I wrestle off my snow boots and rub life into feet that's frozen, lean my chilled backside to the black metal radiator that sound like hungry belly. I'm glad to be home, where I can set my feet up and rest, but it's only a minute or two before three knocks shake my door. Might be it's Bertha, which wouldn't be all bad. I could fix her a cup of tea and let her laba-laba keep my mind from lighting on Louisa.

I go to the door, and Lord if it isn't that Jamaican, Cliff, Jewel warned me about, his hook-shaped pipe dangling from his lips like he's aiming to be Mister Sherlock Holmes. Same scrawny beard he take pride in. Alcohol on his breath. "Oh, Jesus, Cliff," I say. "What you do here, mon? Me no looking for company, especially when you don' trouble yourself to call me on the telephone, let me know you come to mi door."

"Indi girl," he says, "ease up, now." He tries to take hold of my hand with his own hand, which is hot as bread just out from the oven.

Now me brindle. "Don't be grabbing at me, Cliff," I say.

"You go on along. What make you think I'm a-want your company?"

"My heart tells me so," he says.

"Best nah trust your heart when you full up wid rum."

"Stop, girl, everything cook and curry."

He comes in and sits in my brown chair, stretches out his long legs so I see the bulk in his calves and thighs, then flips the skirt of his long wool coat over them. With a little stone-handled ratchet, he digs around in his pipe, then sets the pipe on the wood table beside the chair, wipes the knife, and slides it into his coat pocket. I latch my eyes onto the pipe to make sure it spills no ash on my table.

"What's the matter with you, Indigo? I just come to visit with you, sister. Why you act so dogheart?"

"I en tell you," I say, my arms folded across my bosom. "Men no good for a ting nowadays. What you think of but rum and pum-pum?"

Cliff stands up, still wrapped in his long coat. He steps my way and tries to circle me in his arms. "I don't believe your words, Indigo," he says. "How you get so coldhearted and rough? Never used to be."

"Me got nothing against you personally. Got no feelings for you one way or the other, mon."

Cliff shakes his head. "You jook me heart with your words. What your mada think if she can hear you talk this way to a gentleman en pay you a call?"

"Don't be considering what's in me mada head when you never meet her once in your life."

"Lord, Indi, you treat me worse than if Mister Gilbert come to call, knock your house down with him big winds."

"Men do as much disruption," I say.

Now Cliff has had enough of me. "Okay, Indigo, I'll be going, then. Me no bother you again, gal."

"Everyting about that fine with me," I say, and nod.

"First let me use your chimmy, if you can be so generous."

I gesture him to the back of the flat while I stay on my feet, waiting. Me, I'm laughing in my heart. *Men hurt so easy,* I think, *same as little pickney.* But men don't know a ting about the kind of hurting women feel. My own father was a spoiled small boy, greedy for his comfort till the day he die, four years before I come here, long past when he break Mama's heart—*Lord, I don't send Mama that letter.* Papa a good one for laughing and playing games with the pickney, but that is where the fun stop. Professor him someting better than that, the way 'im take proper care of his girls. Professor is more grown than most, though I believe sometime he think he some big general, not a man with two feet set on the ground.

Cliff must write a book in that bat'room. I wonder should I send that letter, though it don't say a ting, just labrish and other nonsense. I make a frame and leave out the picture. To pass the time, I wash down my stove with Ajax and hear in my head Professor singing "Ajax, the foaming cleanser" in his cheerful voice. *Mama no write to me. Why I think to write to her?*

Cliff struts out of the bat'room, his feathers still mussed. He looks me over and changes his face. "What is it, girl?" he asks, worry smoothing his voice. "What happen? Someone come to the door?"

"Yah, mon," I say. "Jamaica come to di door."

"How you mean dat, Indigo?"

I shrug. "Just thinking, mon, thinking of home, while you spend the afternoon in the loo."

"What you thinking boht, then?"

I shake my head. No words come for this. My hand opens to the air like I let fly a bird, but nothing there to fly.

"Got to get your pain oht your mind now and then, girl." He touch his hand to my cheek, then run a bit of that woolly beard across it. "Come now, Indi. Let me give you a lilly bit comfort. Not going to hurt a ting." He slides his hand back of my head while I'm shaking it and, Lord, he press his mouth direct to mine. I can't believe he takes hold of me so, when my heart so vexed, at him, at Mama, at alla the world. How he don't see that I'm fuming? I struggle and get so mad I bite his ear so 'im yelp like a hurt-foot dog and draw back to give me a look with eyes round as supper plates. "Lord, Indigo, you are out of your right mind," he says, so now I know he's seen what's in me.

"That's right," I say, screw face. "Now, you get oht my house."

"All right, gal, ease up, now, ease up," he says. "I see you mean business. You don't have to holler and bring forth the neighbors."

"Go on, then."

"You never miss your water till the well runs dry. Remember that, sister woman."

He's gone and won't come back, but my peace is spoiled six ways. I lean against the wall beside the front door and move my head over it like a rolling pin on dough, angrier than I can say at that man. Jah! Why he no leave me be? Why alla the world don' let me be?

Though I try not to see it, I can't help but know that one part of my suffering this moment comes from the feeling between my legs when Cliff put his lips to mine. Cliff don't know, but I do, that if he had stayed a heartbeat longer, I would have given my angry self to him, liquory breath, ugly face and all, let him spin me like Mister Gilbert, maybe whirl me away from where I'm at, make me forget about Jamaica.

Truth is, I've always been a weak woman. That weakness is what got me Louisa without a proper father to support her. Louisa's father not a bad man, but I might as well have got her a rum-drinking, card-playing rude boy as get her a sailor father who right away take his sweet self back to America when Captain said, "Board on up, boys."

When Steve left us, I told myself it was all right with me that he go off. So long as Louisa and me remain together, why do I need the moon and the stars? But later I saw that had I a good working man around me, I wouldn't have need to work so hard to keep my Lou fed and clothed deestant and pay for her school fees and have something left for a plaything. And later still, when everything gone so bad and I am looking back from this shore to that, I see clear as light that had that pretty man stayed with Lou and me, stayed by our side, I wouldn't have need in the end to leave her with Mama and come to America to make a little money to have some nice tings and let some brightness into their lives. I would have been there, would have been there to keep my child safe from that murdering car.

But then I never was one to be lucky. Except for my Louisa, not a thing ever was lucky about me, a child of a wandering, soon-forget-you father, a first child from a mother who run out a string of three pickney in the space of time most women spend to nurse the first, a child born to a suffering land where folks say they rich if they got two billy goat or a pig. What could I find in all that to make me feel blessed? But when Louisa came, that was blessing enough for a lifetime. When my life seemed bare as an unplanted field, I would look at that child and feel, *The Lord loves me, look at this child Him give to me.* She was perfect as any child could be, black or white, rich or poor, born in the country or in a fine hospital on a hill, wrapped in satin. Louisa was how I made my way, she was my boat over rough water, my shield from anything come to harm me. Earlier times, some foolish man come and take his pleasure with me, lead me to think he planning to give me his love. Then, come first light, he go off, crooning, "Guess I goin' now, honeygirl. See you sometime. Hope you enjoy them purty flowers I brought you." Once I had my Louisa, I could say "Never mind seeing me sometime" to any such ram goat.

Day after he took in the telegram telling that Louisa is

killed, Professor came to my apartment. Though somehow now he en forget that visit. "I'll pay for your ticket home on the airplane," he said. I just turn my face to the wall—this wall here in this same tainted room—and roll my eyes up in my head and act like I'm stone deaf. "Indi," Professor said, "don't you want to go? I think you should. It would be best to go."

I turn my head to the side like I'm turning it away from someone smack my cheek till it's afire.

"I am sorry," say Professor. "Oh, Indigo. There are no words for it. I am sorry."

Inside I moan and want to pound my head against the wall, but outside I keep quiet for Professor's sake. My *child*, Professor, my baby, my treasure, my Lou. You have three that's living, and I lose all I ever have. That's what I'm thinking, and my heart wail and bleat, this past any pain I ever imagine.

Now I don't see how I'll ever go home. All my aunties and cousins and sister Doreen and young Vincent, the sweet one, and of course Mama, worst of all Mama, always Mama, all of them looking at me, blaming me, saying with their worrying eyes, "If Indi not gone a foreign, this never occur. Poor child. Only just past her six-year birthday, and her mada not even home to rejoice in that."

So I blame it on dem like Cliff, how they get you weak and get you with child, then out the door they go, laughing and dancing and thinking they so fine because they give you some posy. And what choice do they leave you but get a job and try to support the family? What choice? And where are the good jobs but in America—that's what everyone always say, all of my life, when they send their eldest one a foreign. *America. America. America.* Like singing a song. I hear it ringing in my ear like parade music you got no choice but follow till it take you far from home.

I tell Jill about it, about the brightness I used to feel when I think of America. It must be what she felt when she brought home that flute she'd been waiting and waiting for and flipped open the metal locks on the slim case and saw inside such a silvery sweet thing. I tell Jill about how it was for me and just the word, *America*, brings it all back and hurries my breath. "But still—you listen up, Jill," I say, "—I wouldn't never have come here if I don't need to provide for Louisa and Mama. You can believe that, true as you believe Professor loves you girls." That's what I told her. "I wouldn't have come, not ever, not Indigo, not leave my baby without a mada."

A police siren screams down the dark street, shoots me out of my memories. I go to the drafty window and search, but see only a far-off smudge of red light against the night. "Oh, Lord, Jill," I say aloud, "the Devil must have made Indigo. Not Him who makes a natural mother."

How can I soothe my heart? I think about Bertha, how I can't ever do a thing wrong in that foolish woman's eyes. Maybe I got to knock on her door, maybe her kindly face going to ease my sorrow. I take some time to clear the red from my eyes before I go across to see about Bertha.

Her voice so small saying "Come in" that when I twist the knob and push the door and see her tucked up in the bed, I think of poor Granny in the Red Riding Hood, a story my own granmada tell me.

"Indi girl," she says. "You caught me lying in the bed." She wears a spotless white flannel gown that shows off her deep skin. The gown is tied below her throat in a bow tiny enough for a baby doll dress.

"What's the matter with you, Bertha? You don't look right." She brings one hand out and stretches it toward me, then sets it on the white coverlet. Her hand is puffy and the palm pink as a kitten's nose.

"Oh, Indigo," she says, her voice a murmur of leaves. "I been fearing something awhile. I been feeling too much pressure in my belly." She lays a hand on her stomach and pushes against it, then says in a voice she hushes so I have to labor to hear her words, "The doctor says it's cancer of the female organs." Her broad bottom lip starts to quiver until her mouth opens like she is taking a great gulp of air that finally stops her trembling. "Can you believe that, girl? Just like Mama had, only hers in her breast." She cups her left breast with her hand to show me which one and keeps her hold on it a long while. "Took her away from us that loved her, took her bit by bit and cost her terrible pain, and me and Daddy and the girls just forced to watch her suffer. Watch her lose her hair, lose all of her meat and her spirit, and can't do nothing to help."

Lord, I'm sorry I come. I can't face this right now. I see my own mother's breasts, large and long. They fall near to her waist when she takes off her brassiere. When I buried my head there as a child, that was the time I felt safe from all harm. Don't no Obeah woman or no terrible duppy come and harm me.

"Cancer." She puts the word forward another time almost with curiosity, as if she is holding up to the lamp some strange object she found in the street. "Now I got that same disease ready to eat me up, just like Mama. Can't believe it, girl. Can't believe Jesus gonna let me go that same way, go down that same hard road Mama traveled. Cancer." She shakes her head.

I don't like to hear that word. It gives me a sick chill feeling. Even though Bertha's hand bids me set on the bed, I keep my feet. "You feel poorly alla the time?" I ask her.

"Very run-down, girl. And achy. Gas pains and such." She puts her hand back to her belly and gives her face a sick-stomach look.

"I must fix you a nice meal and get your strength up," I say. "Something mild that won't sit on your stomach."

"Thanks, Indigo," she says, "but I'm too wore-out now to eat."

"You must keep your strength up and don't get weak." I wish I had a nice young coconut in my fridge, to give her its jelly and milk.

"Girl, something of your own troubling you?"

"No," I say. "You don't need talk. You need some rest."

"You don't look yourself, Indi. Turn your face back where I can see it better."

"I'm fine, just bothered by that old tomcat Cliff."

"Cliff don't redden your eyes like that most days."

Bertha picks up two photos, takes one of the pictures in each hand. She looks so weak and pitiful, she makes me think of the people Professor likes to instruct me about, though I always try to close my mind to his talk of all that pain and suffering. She studies the photographs of her two grown daughters. Tears flow down her cheeks steady as two streams. "Heart and soul," she says to me, and rocks herself a little. "I say to my girls, 'I love you heart and soul.' Who will love them that way when I'm gone, Indigo? Won't nobody." She shakes her head slowly, then says to me, "Sit yourself down, child. Tell me how your people doing back home."

I carry a chair to beside the bed. "You've got time. Don't be leaving them girls yet. Cancer can be a slow, slow thing. Sometime it stop and don't start up again, like a turtle stop in the road. Sometime the doctors cure it. Don't be hurrying it so. You got to keep some hope." To take her mind off her misery, I get up and pull the deck of red-flowered cards out from the sewing drawer where I know she keeps it and deal gin rummy on the bed, then crazy eights, which Julie showed me one day while we waited for the ambulance and hoped Clair wouldn't get home from school before it came and took their mother off yelling and screaming to the hospital one more time for some kind of treatment that quiet her down awhile but never so far do her lasting good.

I play my card and wait for Bertha to figure her move. She is slow, like her mind is moving at half natural speed.

Bertha lays down her seven of clubs.

"You don't mean to make that move," I say. "You could use that card. You're giving up the game."

"Just tired, girl," she says with all the world's weariness, so I sweep up the cards and stand to go so she can get her rest. "Leave open the door, child," she tells me. "Don't turn the lock. Be sure and come tell me another time about your people, your mama and all and what you hear from back home."

Even big as she is, Bertha looks small lying in that bed in the darkening room. Out in the hall, I whisper, "Jesus, protect her," out of my old habit of prayer.

I go in my room and sit awhile, feel an aching in my legs and shoulders. What would I tell her about Mama? No one in the world now I love more than she, now that Louisa is gone. And no one ever cause me more pain, how she give her heart so freely, then take it back like the giving never meant to be. When I am small and her love is steady, never could I picture such love a-run dry. Love like that never can fail, no more than a river stop its own flow.

My eyes fall on the bookcase, where I keep some of Louisa's little things. I have a box that's got her first tooth that fell out not long before I left. I think how I never saw her big tooth come in, just left her with that gap in the mouth. I always told myself, *Don't worry so over that. Got all the years ahead to see her grown teeth. The big ones don't go nowhere.* Lord, why did I leave? And why not go back and see her, instead of spend my money on gifts to send? Now I never will see her new teeth. And so much that child never see herself. Some things just too sad for telling. Too sad even for feeling. I wonder will these moments come over me for all my days. Every time I got to comb Clair's hair, pick out a tangle, or fasten a bow, will Lou be there breaking my heart again? And which way is the worst, if she's there or if she's faded, when, either way, all I got is heartbreak?

Sharp fear runs a course through me, through my flesh and all through my bones and down into my fingers and feet. I get up and pace and think to myself, *I'm better off at the Silvers' nights, not in this lonely place just across the way from dying.* I grab hold of my coat, and my hat and gloves, and hurry into the dark. This time I just walk up and down the block, try to walk off the shivers in my heart. I've got a searching feeling like there must be something out here I could find that could settle this fear, but Lord only knows what that might be, so I'm left to walk the street like I'm still pacing my room, only now I got a big big room with walls no one can see, but Jah, I feel their strength, how they trap me. Got to be someting out here in the world going to sparkle like quicksilver, like *America*, to ease my pain. Some kind of medicine out here I can find. But this night I find no medicine for my body, and none either for my soul. All I do is wear myself out walking and shaking and bearing the coldness in my bones, until I crawl back up to my flat, look one more time at Bertha's door, and fall to sleep, not a-bother even to fill my belly.

Six

All through dinner I don't know who of this group is the most restless. Jill is a worrywart, thinking will the dog she's got tucked away in her room bark so that Clair hears him even with the radio Jill left playing. Julie is in a big old rush. A rush to get done with dinner, to get out of the house. She always hurry like wind over water. Professor, he is just tired, I think, always tired these days, working from early to late and responsible for these three girls.

Clair keeps asking, "What about my cake? Don't I at least get a cake?" Now that her mother is gone, she don't know who to ask, so she ask her questions over and over. Ask me. Ask Professor. Ask Jill. Ask Julie. Pretty soon she a-go ask that dog. Though she is too old for it, Clair still keeps a picture book, *Are You My Mother?*, about a likkle lost chick a-go from dog to cat to pig to cow, asking, "Are you my mother?" That story is this child's life. Lately, with Mrs. Silver dropping all her nasty hints about taking the children away from dey father, Clair all the time asks me would it nuh be better for her to be wid her mada. "What makes you think that going to be better," I ask, "peculiar as your mother acting, and Professor loving all three of you girls?" Clair gets a look like her thoughts can't find a straight path to follow and says, "She's our mother, Indi."

"No cake for you, Clair," I tell her, even though I know Jill's got a chocolate cake hiding in the pantry that she baked late last night. "I couldn't find nine candles in the drawer. You just too big now. Sorry boht dat."

"Oh, Indi," she whines, and hits her forehead on her fist. "You're just joking. You could go to the store and get more. You could send Jilly."

"Too much trouble, Clair," I tease her. "What have you done so good this week that I should go to alla that trouble? Anyway, you have you a nice cake last year. You mus' get a cake every single year?"

Clair knows I'm playing with her, but her face falls. Professor gives me a sharp look aiming to cut out my play, and I remember his warning words from the other day and put a rein to my evil talk.

"Do you think Mommy will call?" Clair says in Jill's ear. Jill nods, rolls her eyes a little at Julie, who tightens the corner of her mouth. Even though I haven't yet cleared the plates, Jill trades looks with Julie and her father, then goes out through the swinging door into the kitchen and soon comes back with the cake flaming with ten candles, one for good luck.

Professor starts singing "Happy Birthday" in a voice that makes fun of itself because he can't keep a tune, and I recall all the times Mrs. Silver said her cutting words, like she so stoosh, about Professor's singing voice. She fancied herself ready for the opera stage.

Jill gives her dada another look and slips out like a spirit, and I hear her on the stairs, then hear the long groan of her bedroom door. Professor and Julie search the ceiling to keep their give-away eyes from Clair.

The phone rings once, and I think, *Oh, Lord, Mrs. Silver*

calling already. "I'll get that," I say, and hurry on out to the living room, to the phone at Professor's desk.

A man comes on, saying, "Hi, sweetheart," as if he knows the sound of my voice from my hello.

"Who is this?" I say, and hold the receiver out so I can fix on it a moment with my eyes.

"You don't recognize my voice, girl? Don't you remember meeting me—it was just a few days past—you and Jewel? Call herself Mary Lou that night. Frank's my name, Miss Indigo."

"How you come by this number? Jewel do this? Don't be a-call this number, mon."

"Just want to give another invitation to you ladies to come on down to Brother Man's place, have a right bit of fun with some of the sisters and brothers there. That's all."

"You don't hear Jewel tell you I don't party and don't gamble? Don't know a roulette wheel if it come rolling down the street."

"I want to make sure you know the invitation's still good, that's all, girl."

"You nuh call me again at my workplace, mon. Got enough trouble from Professor right now over my job."

"Sorry then, Indigo. I'm not aiming to make trouble for you. Actually, just needing to check this number for someone, see if it's really the right one for your Professor Silver."

"What? Someone planning someting against Professor? What kind of nonsense?"

"No, no, girl, nothing like that, and I can't say exactly, as it's private business. But nothing for you or your professor to fret over. I best let you go, then, girl."

I grumble my way back to the dining room, wondering what on earth made off with Jewel's senses. Can't think what somebody want with Professor, either. Lord, that man sure talk sugary.

"Wrong number," I say, back at the table.

Jill must been waiting for me to return, because she just now walks into the dining room, cradling the puppy. I hear a tiny pained cry, "Lopey," from Clair and then she fly out of her seat squealing just like I said she would.

"Daddy, you got me a puppy," she cries, jumping into the air. "You got me a puppy. I love you. You got me a puppy." She run between Professor and the puppy, hug them each. She comes by me, too, and gives me a squeeze, and back she goes to the dog, then lays down on the carpet on her back and rolls over and over in her excitement like she's got a fire to quench.

"Don't treat him like a doll, now," Professor says, warning against all this excitement. "Don't fuss over him. He's a dog, not a baby."

"Oh, Dad, we just got him," Julie says. "Leave us alone. Don't be a party pooper."

After dinner Clair sets out trying to tame the dog they call "Tenny" now, to shorten that hitey-titey name Mrs. Perkins give him, and Jill follows Clair around the house, coaxing her to be gentle with the creature.

Julie comes in and perches next to me on the arm of the sofa, which is flattened from so many years of girls setting on it. She is waiting for Professor to come out from the bathroom so she can say her good-bye and go off in the girls' little blue car to meet Scott, her boyfriend. Professor take his time in there, maybe just sit and think his thoughts. The long while he spend in there puts me in mind of that Cliff. Jumpy as a cat in a cage, Julie is up and down and leafing through the stack of papers on the coffee table. She picks up Jill's pile of pictures from her camping trip last summer and looks at the counselor named Ben Sands we all say Jill is madly in love with but won't admit it. Jill tracks her sister with a nervous eye.

"Are you going to the dance Saturday night?" Julie asks Jill.

"I sold my ticket," Jill says. "I've got a huge paper due Monday. I won't have time to go out."

Julie drops the pictures onto the table so that the pile topples and deepens Jill's frown. "You sold your ticket so you can write a paper?" Julie is in shock. "You must be mentally ill."

Jill twists up her face.

"I bet you won't even ask anyone to the Sadie Hawkins dance next month," Julie says.

"She's too in love with Ben Sands to dance with another boy," Clair says. Proud of her smart words, she jumps up from her chair with a laugh, facing Jill.

"Shut up," Jill yells, and lifts her fist over her head, because Clair has got her goat now and Jill's got a temper that fires up like Professor's.

"All right, Clair," I say. "You let Jill be. You, too, Jules. I don't need a ruckus." Clair flops onto the floor and hugs the dog. Jill's got every muscle in her forehead clenched.

Professor comes out. "What's all the yelling about?" he says, stiff faced, just wanting to stop the noise, not to hear any answer out of these girls. "I just got you girls a new dog and already there's arguing."

"There you are, finally," Julie says. "I'm going out, Dad. I'm meeting Scott and I'm late."

"Just stay off that motorcycle of his or I'll kill you," Professor says with a gruff voice.

"I know, I know," Julie complains. "And you don't have to tell me every gross injury you've ever seen on the TV news."

"Hey, I'll tell you if I want to," Professor says. "You're still young enough to learn a thing or two from your father."

Professor goes into the hall and then through the swinging door into the kitchen to scrounge for a sweet. Julie pets Tennyson on the head, tells him she might bring Scott by to see how cute he is, then goes out the front door, not bothering to close it all the way behind her, so I have to follow after and do her job. Jill and Clair trail their dad like ducklings, the dog trotting along, too. I see Lou coming next in the line. She's like the last little duckling coming across the pond, the one that all of a sudden disappear from sight when the snapping turtle open 'im jaw and pull it under.

It's just me alone in the living room, and the girls' phone line rings. *Oh, Jesus,* I think. *Here we go now. Here comes trouble.* I cross over to Professor's desk to answer it, and this time I'm right. "How are you, Mrs. Silver?" I say, lifting my eyes to the up-above. "The girls are fine. They off busy in the other room, maybe best to call later." That was worth a try but not going to work with this woman who is fierce like a she-tiger. "Yes, Mrs. Silver," I say. "Just a minute, then. I'll go." I lay down the phone and go back to the dining room, where the three of them have settled with their vanilla wafers and milk. I could be an English butler, the way I stand beside the table and make my announcement. "Clair," I say, shoobing my voice through their chatter, "your mada on the telephone. She say she want to wish you a happy birthday." Clair's face flushes, and she jumps up and hops off like a bird. Professor and Jill tail after her with cookies, milk, and Tennyson and sit back down in the living room, Jill on the sofa and Professor at his desk chair because Clair just stand beside the desk, shifting from one foot to the other, and does not use the chair. I can just boht see Mrs. Silver on her end of the line, face pale and puffy and so full of angry suffering I want to wipe it like a greasy mirror, her mouth spitting her words tru the mud alla those drugs make of her talk.

Clair is wanting to say something but having to bite her tongue to keep from interrupting her mother's long speech. "A *puppy,*" she says after a while, her eyes on the animal that's standing beside her. "He's little. He's so cute." Then she listens a long while more and shakes her head and makes the screw face that's going to give her a line between her eyebrows before she's thirty. "I couldn't. No. I *couldn't,* Mom." Professor starts making his own rough and tough faces. "We were having a birthday dinner at home," Clair says. Her mother talks on and on at her, and it's no trouble to guess the poison in her words. Clair twists up the phone cord with her free hand so I'll never get it straight; I snap my fingers at her, but she don't look my way. "Indi made dinner. I couldn't go out with you. Yes I do go, sometimes. I had dinner with you last week."

Jill goes and hovers beside Clair like one of the rescue helicopters they send from the hospital.

"Could a puppy be at your house?" Clair asks, worry digging deeper into her voice, her eyes seeking Jill. "Do they allow dogs in an apartment?"

Now I know just what track Mrs. Silver's heading down. She has to bring up custody if nothing else is going to cut a big enough wound into the child. Jill sets down near to Clair, on the cushioned bench beneath the front window, then all of a sudden jumps up and stretches her hand for the black receiver. "Let me. Let me talk to her."

"Jilly wants to talk," Clair says, and hands off the phone to Jill, then runs to find her puppy, who has wandered into the front hall. I see her drop to her knees and follow the puppy on all fours like they are two of a kind.

"Hi, Mom," Jill says, her voice dull but tense as a drawn bow. Now Jill listens a long, long time while her foot and free hand tap the air. I know she is holding her anger. "All right, Mom," she says, stiff as a zombie. "*We* told her we're having dinner here, at home. She's nine. It's not up to her." She listens again, her eyes roving the wall beside her. Professor's face is stern, but he looks like he's gone to some other house. "I know custody may not be up to her either, but it's not up to you. Just leave it to Judge Jaworski, or whatever his name is." One time Jill left her diary open, and I saw how she wrote, "I hate that Judge and I don't even know him. How could he choose who's better for us to live with?"

Mrs. Silver must be starting up again, because Jill closes her eyes and holds her silence. Finally she says, "You didn't even invite her. Maybe that's why she didn't have dinner at your place. Anyway, I have to go now. I have to go. I'll talk to you tomorrow. No, I'm not putting Clair back on, and Julie's out. I've got to go. Right now. I'm going now. Good-bye." Jill hangs up, and I wonder is her mother still holding the phone, talking into the air. I see her sitting on her unmade bed, her lips—bare of that red lipstick—gummy and pale next to the receiver, her breath stale enough to turn your face away.

"Same old stuff?" Professor asks, his eyes fixed on his paper.

Jill nods. "She's upset because Clair didn't have dinner with her and she was home all alone and doesn't feel well."

"When does she ever feel well? She's just manipulating you kids, like she always does. You've got to stop falling for it."

Jill's face looks angry and ill. I look hard at her, at her pasty skin with the pimples white girls are quick to get. Maybe she sees my eyes on her, because she reaches up and gives one of those red spots a hard squeeze, jus' make it redder. "She's bringing up all that custody stuff, talking about her friend who's a judge and saying she's sending her lawyer, Mr. Goldfarb, who used to be my Sunday school teacher, to talk to us. Is he going to preach to us about God or something?"

"You don't have to listen to anyone's preaching. You can make up your own mind on that. That's what I expect of you," he says. "I think I'll get myself a Bloody Mary," he announces like he's just had some bright idea. "Do you girls want some tomato juice? Indigo?" I don't know if he's offering me liquor or tomato juice. No one answers him, and he goes off toward the dining room to the wood cabinet with its two bottles of drink he opens maybe one time a month, stopping on the way to put some sorrowful songs on the record player. "Mahler," he says to no one. *"Songs of a Wayfarer."* I recognize the German sounds from when I worked in the hotel in Montego Bay. Plenty of German guests there, and English, and Dutch, all of them just "foreigners" to me, except for the Americans, who I took some care studying.

I go back in the kitchen and begin with the dishes, washing off every scrap and aiming to make the china shine like Mrs.

Perkins's floor. Jill comes in and hangs around me, dries some dishes for me, and puts them up in the cupboards. "Thank you," I tell her.

"Do you think Clair likes the puppy?" she asks. Her voice has all the life of a plant that's sat a week in the sun without water.

"What kind of question is that? Of course she likes that puppy. Likely gone off to spoil it right now." I stop and wipe my hands on the front of my apron.

Jill nods soberly. "So I guess we did okay with her birthday. Except for Mom calling. We couldn't help that. That wasn't our fault."

Those pleading words are just the kind that get me angry when they come from Jill. "That's just like you, Jill," I say, "trying to control what you can't and feeling burdened about the whole world's business."

Jill frowns. "I better do some homework."

"You always have some more homework to do. That's one thing surer than the sun rise in the morning."

Jill goes off. She knows she will get no comfort from me tonight. I can't help it. Her licky-licky face angers me. And she feeds me those foolish lines to coax some words that aim to lift her mood. Some children sparkle like the sun, others are like Jill. She gets all A's or A pluses in school. Julie says it's just from always doing the homework, never skipping one thing, but Jill's teachers say, No, it's not just that, Jill's mind is on fire with ideas. I don't see that these days. I only see a child slow moving as a milk cow. I can't help what I feel.

Tonight I guess I'm part of this family and got to spend the night here, because it's too late to get on the bus at this hour, just to turn right around again in the morning. I hang up my towels and go to my room. Though it's only nine o'clock, I've had enough of this evening, so I stretch out on my bed on the pink ribbed coverlet Julie gave me that used to be on her own bed. The three girls' rooms huddle around mine. Julie's not even home yet and the others are all awake, but I am ready for sleep. The trouble is, sleep may not be ready for me. I put some cream on the dry patches that mark my cheeks by this time of winter, try not to bother that fassy skin, make it worse, and lay on my back with a framed picture of Louisa in my hand. My finger goes to the tight braids at the side of her head, their tails tied off with blue ribbon. I remember the day Louisa born. The midwife tie off her cut cord like that, before she lay that warm, squirming, precious child 'pon my breast. And I remember the day I snapped that picture, Louisa's fourth birthday. I took her for a picnic by the water, bought her everyting she love—ice cream and balloons and candy—and a book, too, because that child always want stories. We read the story of the cat who walk tru di red paint and eena di house, and Louisa said Granmada wouldn't like that. But the pictures brought her a smile, and she put her arms around my neck and pressed her face up to mine and held it there till my cheek was damp from her warmth. Then I made her sit still while I walked off from her and snapped her birthday picture, just like I did every year. I remember leaving her hugging arms and stepping back just four or five steps to snap that picture, and my heart cries not to let go, not even to step those few paces from her side. I loved that picture best of any of them, because it caught my Louisa's sparkle. That day she came back to my arms, gave me a hug, said, "Spin me, Mama."

Later that day there was something else happen. I think Louisa track Mama's house wid red dirt. She pretend to be the cat in the paint, making a big joke, seeing how bad would her granmada take it.

I look into her face a minute more, then lay her picture on my breast and feel the emptiness I feel every night when I finally put away thinking about the family that crowds around me in this house. There's a poem Jill likes to recite to Julie, when Julie's mad. It's about fire and ice and which is the one best suited to end the world. The poet thinks it's fire. My heart is both ways; it's like a fire that burns cold. Lord, how do such tender loving of a child turn to such hate?

Okay, Louisa, I say, not wanting her scorched by my fire. *Okay, girl. You are with the angels now. Don't worry about Mama.*

I think awhile about Clair with her new little doggie, her new joy, her someting to love, someting to look forward to when the school day's done. Nothing for Indigo, though. Since Louisa's gone, none of what used to gladden me moves me at all. There's no joy in these girls, no joy in Professor or Jewel or none of them. How many nights can a person go to bed empty, wake up empty, drag on up out of the bed with nothing that fills the heart?

First thing next morning Jewel calls me, and I know it's trouble, because she never before call me at Professor's. "Indigo, some bad news." I hear her suck in her breath, then she tells it fast. "It's Bertha. Bertha's passed."

"Dead? No. How can she be dead?" I dispute her. Julie walks into the living room and stands a few feet from me, impatient for the phone. "Cancer don't hurry like that," I say to Jewel. "She only just got it." Julie is paging through a *Seventeen* magazine while she waits. When I say "cancer," she lifts her blue eyes to me and looks close at my face. The younger girls always worry over what will be the blow that topples me and sends me out of their house, but this oldest child never studies me so. I sometimes wonder would this one care at all if Professor trade me in for the next maid in the line. Yet there are her sober eyes set on me, taking me in.

"She had a heart attack," Jewel tells me. "Stout as she was and the cancer on top of that and all the worry, it like to be too much strain on her heart. The funeral's at the church, Sunday morning."

"Is someone sick?" Julie offers a meek question when I put down the phone.

"Not anymore," I say, shaking my head. "Friend of mine dead from cancer. Seem like jus' overnight it mow her down. Seem like it can't be so. She lives direct across the hall from me, too."

"Huh?"

"She lives direct across the hall."

"Sorry, Indi," Julie says to me in a whine, like a youngster. "I'm sorry. I hate all the stuff that happens to people's friends." Julie looks like she wants to cry.

"To their friends, to their enemies, to any person on this earth."

"It's not fair." Julie kicks at the wall. "It's not fair."

Seven

On Sunday, I go to the Baptist church to attend the funeral. The bench is hard and I feel fidgety as a child as the preacher raise his voice and call on the Lord. Used to be I went to church every week. That was the way all through my childhood and beyond. It's been a long, long time now since I sat in a church pew; it feels like a foreign country I don't care to visit. The ladies in the choir sing from their hearts and wail their grief, their white robes swinging in one wave with their dance, taking my mind back to Bertha's white nightgown that made her look like she was readying herself to be an angel. I listen to them shouting their jubilation songs and moaning their sufferation songs, but my heart won't stir. This is supposed to be Jah's house, but I find no God here, no more than anywhere. What I do feel is so hateful I am glad no one can see through to my black heart. I am thinking how it looks like they had to give Bertha a casket extra wide. I consider that if she'd died from the cancer, she would have pared down to a regular size and saved some expense with that casket and saved the pallbearers some strain on their backs.

I don't think about my Louisa's burying. I don't think about what that day must have been like, with the sun pouring down warm and even, the way it does most all the time at home. I see the hill where my people lay their dead, the hillside decorated in almond trees and blue-flowered tree of life, the women dressed in colored skirts lifted by the sweet breeze off the water, mango hummingbirds sucking nectar from the crimson flowers. I hear my people singing hymns and the old African slave songs that ask the Lord to deliver us. The breeze passes through the leafy trees like spirits whispering. There is my baby in a small, small box, her face closed off from mine this day and every other by the lid shut between us. And the most cruel part, she is not the child I left, because a year has passed day by day by day. I always told myself that when I returned to her and looked direct into her eyes, I would see there every little ting I missed. I would see the tings so sharp and clear, it would be as if we'd been side by side through each of those days and not missed a moment together. What a lie to tell myself, to keep my heart calm in this faraway place.

Now I can't keep my mind going from Bertha lying dead in the coffin to Louisa lying on the street—as helpless as a bouquet of lilies that toss down on the ground—and it comes to me in this moment how I don't even know who lift that child's dear body off the road. I feel the weight of her in my arms as I did a million times, and the feel of her a-go to drive me mad with losing her. Did an ambulance driver, a man, perhaps a woman, a mother, in a white smock, stoop down and lift her onto a stretcher and put her inside a van? And where was Mama? *Jah.* I see her sucking the insides from a cigarette to draw some sort of strength, walking in circles to lose the frantic feeling that flood tru every limb. Where is she standing? In the house? In the road? And where is my Louisa? In the ambulance? Is Mama in the ambulance beside her, running her hand over Louisa's forehead and up through her hair, sticky blood now on Mama's palm as she stroke her hair and rock and pray, feeling desperate to get the child to the hospital before it's too late? Maybe turn her mind for half an insane second to me over here, ignorant but soon to know what's gone so dreadful bad.

I picture Louisa struck down in the sweet blue dress with reindeer around the middle that I bought her at Marshall Field's the first week I had money enough after I come to America. But I don't know. I don't know what my girl was wearing. I don't know did she ride in the ambulance. I don't know who in the world was the last person to hold my own child's body, and was Lou awake or sleeping, was she calling for me. . . . Oh, Jesus. Don't know where Mama was, or Vincent, or Doreen and who dress her little body for the burying, and did they dress her first in tears before they put a pinafore—which pinafore?—over her head and small arms. Don't know who took in the telegram at Professor's house that night. Suddenly all these blank places flood my mind, and I fear each thing that's missing will be one more thing to haunt me. My heart pinches with pain and—devil that I've become—I curse Bertha for dying and bringing all the empty spaces to my eye, because here I am at Bertha's burying, and where was I for Lou's?

I think I may have to get up and run, but I focus my attention on the front row, where I see two stout, smooth-skinned girls that must be Bertha's daughters. They turn around to glance nervously over the crowd and see who come to pray for their mada, and I see them both with faces awash in tears and see how they cling to each other. And I remember their names are Rosie and June and see how they both have kindly light-colored eyes like Bertha's.

When I step out from the church, the dry cold air flows into my nostrils and makes them tingle. Just past the doors, the young black preacher, Pastor Davis, stands greeting the mourners. He shakes my gloved hand, then I quick move on past. I've got no use for the Lord's servant this morning. Jewel runs after me and hugs me from the side as I climb down the wide steps to the sidewalk. The tears lie so thick in her eyes she doesn't see that my face is smooth as a cold gray stone. She holds me tight, and I want to shake her off, want to say, Jesus, give me space to breathe before I fall down dead myself.

Back in the hall outside my apartment door, I recall how just one week past, I pushed open Bertha's unlocked door to check on her and bring her some supper. Now I grab hold of her doorknob and turn it, and the door surprises me by yielding. Bertha's kin already have come and carried everyting away, even the dishes from my plantain and chicken, not even a rug remains on the floor. My heart is just as bare as that. Not much in me left that's human, and it may be that nothing can pull me back, so close am I to the edge. A chill comes through me. Must be the body fearing for itself because the soul's already lost.

In the afternoon, I go out to walk in the bit of sunshine and see if I can draw any of it into my bones. I get one block from the church, and here comes that Pastor Davis sailing down the sidewalk in a fine navy-blue wool coat. His face opens up like a break in a bank of clouds, and he hails me with his laughing eyes and a lift of his bare black hand.

"You were a friend of Bertha's," he says, warm and gracious like a preacher's meant to be.

"Indigo," I say, and look him in the eye and lift my chin. "That's my name."

"Why don't you come round to the church another Sunday and worship with us," he says, looking at my face, calling me by my name. "You carry God's blue sky inside, in your given name."

"What makes you think I'm a Baptist like them in your church?"

He shakes his head as if I am an ignorant pickney who brings pity and amusement to his heart. "There's only one Lord Jesus, dawta." He calls me that as if he knows my people. "Whatever you are—Baptist, Methodist, Adventist, nonbeliever—Jesus is your savior if you take Him into your loving heart."

I am thinking what a fine coat he has, soft like lamb's wool, and wondering did he get the money from his parishioners' pockets. It pleases me to suspect him as a hypocrite. "I'll be sure to come, then," I say from out of my loving heart, "now that I know I'm welcome." I know he knows I am flat-out lying. I like the feeling I get lying to a man of God and not fearing damnation. I like that he won't have courage enough or rudeness enough to tell me what he knows of what I am. He has invited my loving heart into his church—I want to laugh like a hyena.

That evening I am soaking in the old claw-foot tub when the phone starts to fuss. I climb out of the water and drip bare skinned across the living room. It's Jewel saying, "Indigo, come out with me. Let's go dancing, girl, or some such thing. I'm low as a beetle in the grass. I know you're not keen on partying now, but come with me this one time. Do me a kindness, honeygirl. My heart needs cheering."

"All right," I say, thinking it don't much matter where I keep my body, in the house or out. Same me, either way. I might as well humor Jewel, who has been good to me except for her foolishness of late in giving out my number at Professor's. "Come across to my flat in 'bout an hour," I say, "and I'll go where you want." I set down the phone and stand and feel the heat from the radiator lift the water from off the skin of my thighs. Then I go back into my tub and lay awhile, look at my breasts rising out of the water like hills out of the sea, look at my belly underneath the water, smooth and large as a whale.

I remember Dada tell us how Jonah him swallow by the great fish and find himself in the fish belly like a likkle beenie baby. Him so unhappy to be caught in there, him railing to set free. Wonder what did Jonah see in this world to make it more to his liking than that whale belly. When my nipples come to attention from the cool air, pucker all around, I press them with my fingers—Lord, here come Lou again at the breast, and here come she fada, too, how him stand at attention in the house, click him heel-dem, show me what he mus' do as a sailor when Captain say jump. Then him come to my breast no different than pickney, suckle, and lay down di head. Time now to get out of the tub, flee to some other space inside my mind.

Jewel comes at quarter past eight, her body tall as a cornstalk and dressed in a tight blue dress the color of the flowers Jill calls bachelor's buttons, the dress hugging her little bosom and her batty and stopping a hand's length above her knees. She jingles with silver bracelets, sounds like Christmas when she moves. "Whoo-ee," I say when I look at her.

She looks at me screw face, because I have on my white uniform dress I bought my first week in this country. "You ain't fixing to wear that sorry thing, are you?" she asks. "You aiming to change?"

I shrug. "Me put it on a-come oht di bath."

A frown settles between her eyes.

"Then what you have me wear, mada?" I ask, giving up my stubbornness, ready to do what she wishes. She takes my hand and pulls me to my clothes closet in the bedroom, draws out a red rayon dress not fit for winter, and hands it to me. I roll my eyes but take the shiny ting and zip it up the back with Jewel's help because it's tight against my ample flesh.

"There, now," she says as she spins me around. "Don't you look nice."

"Look like a redbird is what."

"Hush your mouth," she says, and tells me to take along a little extra money if I've got it. I go back into the living room with Jewel trailing me and look in the small drawer of the Singer cabinet. There I see plenty of green bills, so I take out twenty-five dollars for my purse. My mind goes back to Bertha and the red-flowered cards I pulled from her drawer that day, me foolish enough to think a game of cards going to take her mind off her trouble-dem.

Jewel no tell me where she a-take me and I no ask, but I don't think it's a dance hall we're aiming for. We walk the half block down our own street until we get to the bus shelter, then wait five minutes until the local southbound bus arrives and she nudges me to climb aboard, where we settle into a seat beside the rear door. The vibration in that transport could shake a person to bits. Must be a wheel's spinning off-kilter. "You fixing to kill me tonight?" I ask Jewel, imitating the black folk here.

"Hush up," she says, but laughs a little. She pulls a paper out of her pocket and studies some notes she's got. Ten minutes pass as we rattle through one city neighborhood after another. Jewel hears the street name she's after and tugs the yellow cord beside the window. We get off into the cold, misty night and walk a block down a street named Joselyn into a neighborhood that seems as full of Jamaicans as my own. Guess we don't visit Mrs. Perkins tonight. Not one high-tone little dog prance along this street, splash mud on 'im white gloves.

Three blocks down the road, some island music spills from the windows of a house that stands out too much for its own good, with its peeling red paint and wide front porch sagging like a smile. I think perhaps we go in and find nothing but Rastafarians all in natty dread. "This a Rasta house?" I ask Jewel.

She shrugs, not knowing and not wanting me to worry her about it.

"Them an odd bunch worship the Emperor Haile Selassie like him a god."

Jewel's eyes stay quiet. "They say he's a righteous man."

We climb up onto the broad porch of the wood-frame

house. Its planks complain of our weight. "This just a place to play a little cards, girl. Maybe some roulette."

I stop a minute. "Gambling?" My mind jumps with surprise. I never know which way Jewel going to turn next. Half the time she hold to her church's sayings, half the time she go wild.

"It ain't nothing. Just a few games is all. Just for tonight." She gives me a look like she beg me for someting, when she's got no need to ask my permission to seek her comfort.

I go on up to the front door. There is a carved wood knocker shaped like a pouncing tiger, but the door is cracked open. "You sure this place deestant?" I pester her.

"Hush, girl, and take your money out your purse—set it in your pocket before you go in."

"What? Bumbo! You take me to pass time with criminals?"

I turn away from the door, but she takes my arm and steers me back around, then looks me right in the eyes to settle me. "No, I ain't, girl," she says. "This here's Brother Man's place, the place all of them's talking about."

"Wah!" I say, and let my mouth and eyes fly open.

Jewel shakes her head at me. "We're just here this one time, to have some fun and put poor Bertha out of our minds."

"I already did that," I say.

Jewel frowns at me but holds her tongue, though I see she wants to say, *Shame on you*. All of them still make their allowances for what the Devil plant in me.

Music I recognize from Henry P's front porch as a new reggae group call itself Burning Spear meets us as I shoob the door. The room we step into is smoky enough to burn my eyes but broad enough to give me room to breathe. Color posters for Jamaica, "the island paradise," are taped to the paneled side walls with tape that's turned nasty from the smoke. Beside a yellow door on the back wall is a white-painted board with a faded photo of Kingston harbor on top neet the words "Burma Shave" and a clock undaneath the photo with round beads of red glass to mark the hours. The gold hands tells us it's five past nine. Beside the yellow door is a great slabba-slabba white man, his brown eyes following the spin of the old vinyl record someone just now put on. Maybe he's the one who change the music and give us rock steady. I hear the voice of Bob Marley, know him as a child of St. Ann who come to Trenchtown, live there like my own family, his father no more regular than my own, from what they say. Same ting everywhere.

Heads turn our way as me and Jewel bring our bright colors into the smoky room. I see about ten men, a couple of them light skinned, but most black, most sitting or standing around two green-draped tables, one long and one square, the two set apart from each other. The long table has a cloth printed with numbers in red and black and a spinning wheel at the end. That one is cork up with players. A fit-looking man in a tight T-shirt and snug black leathery pants spots me in my poppy red and jumps up so fast from his chair he throws it over. He flushes for half a second with shame, then shakes himself till he's right and comes direct to me and Jewel. "Come on in, ladies, come right on in," he says, his voice in a deep curtsy of welcome. His hand runs down his beard—so stiff it looks sharp—then shakes my hand as if I'm not to mind whatever oil comes off from his ugly hair. Next, one arm goes around my shoulder, the other one around Jewel. "I'm Brother Man," he says, his eyes switching this way and that between the two of us. "And this is my place." Now his chest is big with pride and his arm sweeps the air.

So this is the one, I think. *Odd how him take that name like a title.* I wonder what is his real name, name he raise up with. I think to ask him, take him down a notch from his boasie high horse, but don't want to hear Jewel hush me just yet.

Jewel is in a hurry to open her mouth before I open mine. "This here is Mary Lou," she says to Brother Man, and gives me a nudge with her elbow. "I'm Cindy."

Oh, Lord. Here she go again with this deception. And why she have to give me *that* name, wid my baby's name tuck inside, I don't know.

"So pleased to meet you," the man says, and he raise his finger, like "wait," runs off to behind a desk for a minute, and hurries back and hands me and "Cindy" each a small stack of chips—mine blue, hers red, opposite of our dresses—"on the house." So eager he seems to welcome us that I think women must be the big-time spenders here. Most likely the big-time losers, too, like everywhere else. There is only one woman here besides me and Jewel. The men are calling her Lucille or Lucy B, and one man calls her "Lucille Ball," I'm guessing because her hair has a bright orangy cast that don't fit her skin tone—must be by Clairol. When I get close to the woman, who's tall as a tower, I smell lilies enough for a whole garden, so maybe, I humor myself, it's Lucy Bee or some other such nonsense.

Though I see no bar, everyone here got someting to drink. After a while, I see how the drinks sail in with Brother Man from behind that yellow door. I give Jewel the evil eye, my look saying, What kind of place you take me to?

Jewel lifts her chin and points me deeper into the place with a stern, "never you mind" kind of face. The fat man shuffles to the long table, where most of the others sit around the numbered cloth and the pretty silver, black, and red roulette wheel like those in the big hotels in Jamaica, this one every bit as high-tone, and circled in light wood polished lustrous as a mirror. Must have cost Brother Man plenty dunsa. No wonder his chest swelling big as Anansi, since when he still back home, likely all the gambling that man do is Drop Pan, like all the men in-country. The roulette and such are lef' to the rich foreigners, many of them American, or the stoosh uptown Jamaicans with foreign money in they pocket.

Jewel and I still stand, milling, not knowing what to do with ourselves. Brother Man wander off a bit, bend over this one or that at the tables, say a word into their ear. My eyes go to that one woman mongst them. I study Lucille for a minute and see what I can read in her face. If I pretend away that orange hair, she is a handsome, big-boned black woman. Layers of colored cloths flow around her body—one dress atop another like an African princess, all of them rich with her lily scent. She sees me looking at her and smiles as big as a jack-o'-lantern and says in a lilly-bit shy voice, "Welcome to some fun." Her body so big and her colors so bright, her winjy voice surprises me.

"We'll see about that," I say, and tap-tap my foot on the floor. Jewel gives me a dirty look like "How rude you got to be to these strangers now?"

Scattered glass ashtrays show drawings of Jamaican beach resorts spread out under the sun. Coasters lie on all the tables, though no one's using them to set down their drinks. Even the coasters have color pictures from home that look like magazine photographs under a varnish. On the littered desk to the left side of the room is an old electric typewriter makes me wonder is Brother Man a writer by day. Maybe he write his coming-to-America story, hope to make himself a million dollars.

The desk looks to be the center of Brother Man's operation. It's where he went to draw out the chips and where he keep a-visit to check his books and notes. I wonder what could I do with a typewriter and think of Professor, who spends so much time tapping at his keyboard that I feel those quick keys are part of his fingers. Sometimes I covet the quiet I see on his face when he sits at that machine, setting down his thoughts. I think of Papa laying fresh paint on a wall, white or yellow, thick as butter, getting his good feelings that way.

An ambulance coming down Joselyn Street whines and then screams until it drowns out Bob Marley, who sings now with Tosh and another of the bredren. Jewel's body tenses. "Oh, Lord," she says. "Now somebody else took sick."

Brother Man takes up pacing. "Wa mek? That sound is

spoiling our peace," he mutters, and pulls a cigarette from a drawer neet the typewriter, lights it, and sucks hard at it. "Can't even hear my dealer." That means the fat man; I got that part now. Mama used to drag hard on a cigarette when she was troubled, like when Daddy come and brighten our house awhile with his cheer, then 'im gone like the cooling rain that the sun dries up. The ambulance reaches this house and passes it and its siren softens. I see Louisa lying in the street, so I know it's time to shut my mind, try to fill my eyes and my ears with this odd room and nothing else. When I look around me, there is that silver wheel pretty as Jilly's flute and decorated black and red. When it spins and sends the marble bouncing along its track, it gives off a sparkle of excitement and looks like it wants to whirl up into the air.

I walk right up to Brother Man and ask him just what am I to do with the blue chips he put in my hand, since I never before been gambling. Can I use them to bet that wheel? I wonder. "Never mind not knowing," he says, his voice taking a gentle, tata tone, and shows me and Jewel to the long table, to what he calls "Joshie's wheel," because it is tended by the mountain of a man, Joshua. Brother Man moves two of the seated men oht their chairs, though they grumble a minute, and sits us down like we're royalty—though we still mus' set our batties on a cold metal chair. "Look at the table, ladies. See how the numbers are one to thirty-five and they're set up in columns—three of them. You choose your bet. You can bet a full column, or one of the four corners, or a straight-up bet, which means you pick your one lucky number." He goes through a few others, but it's too many to track. I look at Jewel, and her eyes shine like Jupiter. I bet she's thinking of Pastor Davis all of a sudden and wondering what on earth she doing here. I laugh inside. She a puzzle to me. "You need to place your chip—one or two, however many you want—on your number to show what you're betting. You're free to place bets until Joshie here says, 'No more bets.' Even when the wheel spin, you can put your chips down. But when he says so, then you got to hold your bet. Then you keep your eye on where the ball lands. When the wheel stops, the dealer's going to put his marker on the table and show you who are the winners, who are the losers. Some of your bets pay two-to-one odds. Some have long odds, as long as thirty-five to one. That means the odds are against you, so if you win, you win big. You bet one dollar, you win thirty-five."

"No!" says Jewel.

"Open your ears, Jewel," I say, forgetting her "Cindy." "Heed the odds. Most likely you lose that dollar in a hurry."

The men laugh and I see Lucille is there, laughing, too, down at the far end opposite the dealer. "Mary Lou's caught on," she teases in her soft-spoken way.

"You better have a strong hunch before you bet thirty-five-to-one odds," says a small man direct across from me. Behind him, his back to the table, is a dark man with arms thick as tree trunks. He turns to face the table and gives me a smile. I see it's that Frank, who bothered us that night at the Basin Blues Bar and again on the telephone Clair's birthday night. Jewel gives him a big smile, and he comes around to our table and pours a few more chips into our hands from out of a cloth bag, like he is passing out popcorn.

"I'm going to sit right behind you here, make sure you don't make no beginner's mistakes," he says. "I know my way around this table—that's for sure. I'm a regular here. You'll find me most any time you come."

"You so proud of that?" I say. Jewel right away lifts her eyebrows, shoots her eyes my way, giving me her warning.

"I'm an honorary member of Brother Man's staff, and I'm honored to welcome you," Frank says, too busy pounding his chest, I guess, to catch my tone.

"Francis will bust your ear talking," a man across from Jewel says in a high, Southern style of voice, his skin rosy brown like he's part Indian, his build short limbed, but square and solid as brick. "My name's Curtis," he says, making his introduction. "And you all are . . . ?"

"Indigo, and this here's Jewel," I say emphatically, to Jewel's scowl, because I see no point to her charade—Frank already knows what our right names are, and I can't tolerate "Mary Lou" too long.

Joshie tells us, "Place your bets," but Frank reaches out from back of me and places a hand on mine and says, "Watch awhile, get the hang," so I sit and watch the men and Miss Lucy hurry to get their chips set up, and then Joshie starts the wheel in motion and I watch it spinning and hear the ball bouncing. I like the way the wheel spins recklessly like nothing's going to slow it or stop it. It's like a top go free and easy, spin long as it please; it catch the light from the green glass globe overhead. For a second my mind brings back the light flashing over that ambulance that riled Brother Man, but then a cup of rum comes into my hand and sparkles under the green light and I am drinking it, though I swore off drink a time ago, because I couldn't help thinking that someone with too much liquor in him struck down my girl, and that thought fix drink in my mind as an evil fit for an Obeah witch.

I'm ready to get in on the fun, so I put a chip on the middle column, but that one wins me nothing. Jewel is still sitting. "Come," I say. "Why you come here if not to bet?"

"What should I bet?" she asks me.

"Bet what you please."

Jewel follows me, betting a column, and wins herself two dollars. "OO-ee!" she whistles.

Joshie's voice is as whispery as his body is large. Seems to have a permanent laryngitis. When he shoobs the wheel, he bites one corner of his mouth and twists that same side of his face like a lover who is coming in a clench of pain. I wonder does he see in his own mind what look his face has.

Lucille gets up from the far end of the table, and her long skirts wind around the leg of a chair and catch, so she has to pull free. "Lord," she giggles. "Now the chair is aiming to undress me." She is such a big, tall woman, her frame seems more a man's than a female's, but her laugh is soft and girlish and sounds foolish to my ear, coming from so big a package.

"Oh, woman, you bust me up," Curtis says, and jumps up, goes over, and gives her a happy nuzzle on the back of her neck to where I wonder are they lovers, or soon to be. Lucille gets busy saying her good-byes, getting fixed to leave this warm room for the cold just beyond the door. Brother Man sashays over and wraps his arm tight around her shoulder and draws her to his desk with the typewriter and half a dozen small locked drawers, all the while su-su in her ear. He writes something in a ledger book and shows Lucille with his pointing finger what he's set down. She nods with a sudden serious look and a troubled glance to Curtis and gets herself to the door with no more small talk. She is out so fast she don't let in a single breath of cold.

There is no game to play at the square table, which sits between Brother Man's office area and Joshie at his roulette table, but a few men sit there laughing and smoking. Soon the front door opens, and in comes Henry P, and it shocks me a little that in this strange room I already know three people—Jewel and Henry P and Frank. I wonder is the old Jew, Borotsky, going to show up and make it four. "First time I ever see you without your hound dog," I say, and call Henry P's attention my way from where I sit.

He comes over to me at the table and smiles and says, "Oh, sister woman. She who don't drink or smoke or dance."

He holds out a cigarette to Jewel, who shakes her head. He offers one to me and I take it. "Yah, mon," I say. "Me wid none of dem vice." I don't care that he teases me. I don't care what he or any of them tink of me. I'm not here making friends, just here a-please Jewel and please myself.

Francis moves to the second table and Henry P claims his seat, slides it into line with Jewel and me, crowding Joshie some.

He puffs out rings of smoke so he can watch them float up and away. "Fireman mus' love di fire," I say to him. He gives me a laugh that's happy despite my evil tones.

"You too-too faastie, dawta," he say.

I turn my thoughts to what numbers to choose. I learn that some of them just lie flat and lifeless as dry leaves when you call them up in your mind, so I go ahead and blow those aside. But others carry a strong, sweet feeling and got some heft. I spin each number around like Clair's gig she call dreidel and see what emotion comes to me and imagine the thrill I might feel if I pick right. I make my way just like that, as if I am feeling along a hand rope in the dark but that rope is as jump full of life as a viper. I win two column bets, then take a chance on a corner and win that, too, eight-to-one odds that get the whole table oohing. Soon I'm thinking about nothing but the spinning of the wheel, with all its sweet good luck numbers.

After a while, old Mr. Borotsky does come in the door just like I predicted, so I figure this place must give me a gift of knowing what's to come—no wonder they talk about it alla the time. Still, must be careful, trouble no set like rain. The old man nods his greeting to all he knows, which includes me. Brother Man looks at the Burma Shave clock and gets up from his chair by the typewriter, goes over to the smaller, square table, and starts up a game Henry P say is "blackjack" with Borotsky and the men who been waiting, but Jewel and me stay with the roulette, where we learn our way.

I can't say why it is I feel so easy in this place, since I never gamble in all my life, except for the Drop Pan lottery back home, which don't count for much. I saw some gambling at the hotels in Montego Bay, and there was that one time, when I was a girl, that Dada angered Mama by taking me into a bar where he drank and played cards tru the night. I stood at his elbow and kept quiet, but I knew well enough, and proudly enough, who chose to have me there beside him. When Mama raised hell with Dada, I knew that was the last time I would go there, but for a long while I held on to the noise and perfume of that place in my mind, even after Dada packed his things into his brown canvas sack and went off one more time.

Tonight as my mind tests out the different numbers, sees them take a form in front of my eyes so real that I could reach up a finger and tap the one that's best and pluck it like a fruit, I can tell I have a gift for this game. It's just a matter of fact, not a brag. I look over at Jewel, and she concentrates on the other players and on the wheel and the betting, and it's clear to me she don' have the knowledge of how to instruct her mind to sort tru the various numbers. But I know how to do that like it's a born gift, like some folk have the gift to heal or to know they future. For me it's natural as knowing the sweet melon from the green. I just never happened across it before.

The last old vinyl in the pile starts up, plays through, and stops. Joshie tells us in his sore-throated whisper, "Break time." He retires to the back of the room, puts some Cuban rhythms on the CD to play, and picks up a set of bongo drums to beat along to the music, his lip captured in his teeth, his face twisted in that look that draws me because it is such a peculiar face for a man to wear in public.

When Jewel says we ought to be going, it's only the sting in my eyes tells me I'm ready. I stall a bit till Joshie comes back from his break and sets up his next turn of the wheel. I lose my first bet because I don't think about what I do, then I concentrate and win an even-odd, and then, Lord, I win a trio, my longest odds, eleven to one, and get all of them talking, and when I cash out for the night with Brother Man in his little office space in his corner of the room, I have thirteen more dollars in my pocket than when we come in the door, all from betting what chips I was given. Jewel, she lost all of Brother Man's chips and those that Francis give her, too.

Brother Man keeps on working at his records after Jewel and I stray from his office. Time's come to go out into the night, so we move toward the door. I see Brother Man look up and notice we are ready to leave. He surprises me by speeding across the floor to catch us. Suddenly he reaches his arm around my shoulder just as he did Lucille. He grips me tight as a bull dog. I notice he don't give Jewel the same show of his strength. He walks us the rest of the way to the door, with me still inside his arm, and bids me and Jewel good-bye with a smile that could melt a body.

My back shoobs the door as I slide the last button of my jacket through its hole. The door opens fast from outside and almost brings me to the ground. As I catch my balance, a sickly-thin old white man dressed in white from his shoes to the bow tie at his throat walks past and crosses over to Joshie at his roulette table. Joshie says, "All the time, sir. We're open all the time," to the man, who must be a newcomer like me and Jewel. The old man is so pale in his skin and his dress, he could be what we call *doondoos,* a man who lacks color in the skin, even the hair and eyes, or could be an actual duppy man. That and the little white bow at the throat take me back to Bertha and where she's gone. If I believed in such things, I'd say this old man might be an angel sent down to put some thought of Bertha in my mind.

We walk down the steps, and my eyes are happy for the cold night air.

"I guess you got all the luck there was to go around tonight, Indigo," Jewel says, laughing, as we stand on the sidewalk, still in the shine of Brother Man's lights, pulling on gloves.

I like the winning but don't care a dime about the dunsa, and I try to stuff some of my bills in Jewel's handbag. She won't have any part of that and squirms and says, "Stop that, girl," acting as if I'm some sassy man want to get into her business.

As we stroll to the bus, I think how I been like someone hypnotized by mampi man's spinning wheel and Lord, I have forgot myself and forgot the passing of time, and I swear it may be the first time for that since Louisa's been gone. I marvel at my free spirit and tell Jewel, "Some good time. Nuh?"

She looks at me like she is well surprised, but nods and says, "Yeah. Some good time."

"You go there to Brother Man's regular?" I ask her.

She laughs and says, "Hush now, girl. You know I ain't never been there before. And I ain't got the money to go there regular." She looks at the ground and says, quiet, "Only tonight. Because of Bertha. That's not a place it's decent to go, not most days." Then she sighs, and I know she is back with Bertha and holding faith with the Baptists again, which brings me down some.

That night I sleep a peaceful sleep. Me and Louisa play in the river, then lie side by side on the green hillside. Mister Sun shine down on us like in the camp song the Silver girls always sing. No evil things have happen. No evil things going to happen, not to me, not to my baby. Both of us safe for all time.

Eight

Winter's rolling on, so at least the sun come up before I board my bus. I sit and watch the people, some still lazy with sleep, though others must have waked themselves by now with the bright red sweaters and hats they wear, one lady with some sort of dangly earrings fashioned into red hearts. Across from me, two men black as Africa are talking and jiving like they're putting on a show, the older one full bearded—an uncle, I think—and the young one so full of bounce and flourish he can't keep his bumbo set in the seat. Must have swallowed some of them Mexican jumping beans Clair likes to play with, or someting worse he buy on the street corner. He's got his hair in shaggy twist braids that look to make a righteous home for some wild creature. If you ratchet off that rag mop on the head, this boy remind me of Vincent when sun en come up.

"Danny, I'm getting me a tattoo," the pickney say, and catch the eye of his uncle, him a good-looking, talawa man himself.

"I'm fixin' to get me a tattoo of my face, put it on my arm right here."

"Say again!" say the uncle, tall-eyed. "Tattoo your own likeness? So people can see your butt-ugly face, then see it all over again on your arm? The brothers say, 'Hey, man, there go Ethan Jones two times in one.' Maybe you best get you a tattoo of your booty and put it on your backside."

"Hey! What you talkin' about?" asks the boy. He jumps to his feet, feelings hurt, make me wonder why Uncle don't use his big head a lilly bit more.

"You young fellows," Uncle says. "What you want to get you a tattoo for in the first place? Let some witch doctor stick a dirty old needle in your arm like that, cause you an infection."

"Tattoo's *bad*, man, don't you know that? Don't you know nothing?" The boy twists at his hair a minute, sits back down, muttering, "*Bad*, man. You too old to know a damn thing."

"Oh, easy now, I'm just foolin' with y'all," the older man says, trying to mellow tings now. "But you got to think about HIV. That ain't no joke."

Though the young man's face puts Vincent in my mind, Vincent have a steadier nature. Besides, never would Mama let him in the house with hair so leggo beas'. The youth grabs the metal post and stands, lets his weight swing around it like a small one on a carousel.

It's eight in the morning when I make it to the Silvers'. Before I get my key to the lock, that dog yappy-yaps on the other side of the door. Then I'm inside, where the girls scurry like they do mornings, noisy as birds in the bush, as they get themselves set for school. Professor, he is long gone, sailed off in his navy-blue Honda to the city to work, Professor so full of life and ambition he's oht the house even before the sun awake. Before he goes, he takes a peek at his girls sleeping, probably hears Jill snoring to beat the band, sees Julie cuddling the pillow, her mind on her Scott, and Clair twisted in her sheets like a toffee in its wrap.

The girls are no longer asleep when I get in the house. Clair sets right in on me in the front hall. She's got a red sweater she's holding in my face to show me the button that spins from 'im thread like a child's tooth set to drop.

"Can you fix this, Indi? I need to wear it today."

"Sky gonna fall, Clair, if you wear some other sweater this morning?"

"Do you know where Mommy's thread box is? Did she take it with her?" She's got to know.

"All right, Clair. Why you need to have this one sweater here? You have a closet full of sweaters with their buttons lined up straight as soldiers."

Clair looks at me like she is too disappointed in me for speech. "It's *Valentine's Day,* Indi."

Oh, Lord, I forgot—Valentine's Day—so that is why this child is more nervous even than her usual runaround morning self.

"Do you think I'll get a lot?" she asks me in her wheedling way.

"Now, how am I to know that, Clair? Move that dog off from me." I lay down my coat over the banister, then go on to the closet at back of the hall and pull down Mrs. Silver's orange shoe box with the black line drawing of a high-heeled dress pump on the top. Inside are a hundred spools, each with thread spilling out into the box, tangling with the others, making a terrible knot. With Clair at my elbow, I stand and search until I find a spool of red thread and a Chinaman, made of colored silk, who is stuck tru with fine needles. This pincushion must be one of those little presents the girls bought their mother for this or that occasion, most of them left here in the house when she a-go. Clair has a way of picking out those leftover things with her eyes when I am opening a cupboard or a drawer. She's always ready to say how she bought this little glass vase or that pot holder for Mommy, but here it is still in the drawer. Biggest ting her mama lef' behind was her tree daughters.

The child follows me upstairs so she can keep attending me till I'm done with my sewing, steady as a bee at a flower.

Finished, I say, "Here," and hand her her sweater. "Now you're all ready to be some boy's valentine."

Clair doesn't know what I mean by my words. "Child must creep before him walk," I say. Her face can't settle on a grimace or a smile, but she's glad for the sweater and I'm glad she can let me go on down to the kitchen now.

Julie and Jill sit down to their bit of breakfast in the eating nook that makes a corner to the house and joins up the kitchen and the dining room. Julie is already teasing Jill about asking someone named Nathan to the dance that's soon to come.

"Ask him right after English," Julie says, half standing and leaning Jill's way across the table. "Just trap him. Don't let him get out of the room without asking him." She lifts her head to me and says, "Tell her she should do it, Indi. Tell her 'just do it today'. Otherwise, she'll never do it."

I lift up my eyebrows and cast my eyes to the side.

"You would have told her *before,*" Julie says, the tone of her voice saying that just the look of me this minute disgusts her.

"Then I would have been a busybody before."

Jill comes into the kitchen with her dishes. "Will you keep an eye on Tenny while we're at school?" she asks. "Try and take him out if he looks like he has to go, okay?"

"What you *think* I do, Jill?" I say. "Just stan' and watch him piddle on the floor so I have the pleasure of a-clean it up?"

"Dad says we've got to get him well housebroken if we want to take him in the car with us when we go to Indiana this summer."

"You speak for yourself about that trip, Jill. I nah go to any Indiana. Got a lake right here and don't ever pay it mind."

"It's the same lake," Jill says.

"Then one more reason not to drive tree hour to visit it."

Julie chimes in from the breakfast room, saying, "We're going to drop Jilly off at the old people's home." This is a joke they have. They always like to tease Jill about leaving her at an old folks' home they pass when they go to Indiana, due to some of Jill's cautious ways. I think this year they can drop me off there, too, if I get as far as that.

Before she goes off to catch her bus, Jill sings out, "I already made my bed, Indi. You don't need to do it."

"Well, kiss me neck," I call out.

After the girls leave, I go make up Julie's room, then go on to Jill's. Though she's steady as a field hand when it comes to her schoolwork, Jill's ting-dem look like an angry wind scattered them. I don't clean up Jill's personal things—she's too old for that. I usually just make the bed and dust a little and gather up the laundry.

I get curious why Jill suddenly straightened the bed linens when nothing else in the room is set straight. Could that bed hold a secret? I turn back the coverlet and lift the pillow to see, and sure enough, Jill has got a letter under there. I know the name on the back, Ben Sands, penned in blue marker in a script as pretty as a schoolgirl's. This man's been writing Jill once a week ever since summer. He's the same one crept out of Jill's dream the other night and into my own.

I am dumbfounded to see how this letter nah even open. Jill must hide it here to give her someting sweet to think of while she's at school. Julie tells me Jill used to save her Halloween candy so long in a paper bag on the floor of the butler's pantry—doling it out to herself in dribs and drabs—that it got to where Professor made her throw it out as rotten. She's like the hamster those girls had when first I come here.

You could offer that likkle creature a piece of lettuce big enough to make himself a bedsheet, and it would draw it up into its cheek bit by bit till it looked ready to bust. That's how Jill hides away her pleasures, tucking them deep inside. Maybe it makes them sweeter, or maybe just keeps them safe from Mrs. Silver, who's sure to spoil any child's joys. Seeing that note from Jill's friend, I know it's more than a homework paper that put Jill in a upful mood this morning.

Here is a note from Mrs. Silver, too. This one's laying out on the desk, in plain enough sight to where I can stand over it and take a look to see does Mrs. Silver say someting about the lawyer Julie says her mother wants to send to bully these girls. But no, she is harping on someting just past. "I was very upset about Clair's birthday," she says. "You're old enough to take some responsibility in these things, Jilly, especially when you know your father won't. It's heartbreaking for me being separated from my youngest child on her birthday."

Rass! Why she pyu such stuff? You think she could stop with alla that, figuring she stung the girl nuff by now, but not Mrs. Silver; she don't know what stopping means. If there is any dogheart ting she can think to say, she going to say it. Here she go some more. "Valerie, the neighbor girl next door who's in your history class, had to comfort me by spending some time with me. How do you think I felt, relying on a stranger when my own children are only five minutes away? I would have expected more from you, Jill. Maybe not from the others, but from you."

I remember a time when Mrs. Silver all the time begging this girl to "help me, help me" as if the child were the Lord Jesus you could pray to in your hour of need. Sometimes Mrs. Silver seemed feeble as a whimpering baby, sometimes howling like a hurricane, but always picking out this one child, maybe think she have a gentler nature than the rest of us, though I doubt that. Back then, Jill still do what she can to help her mother. She bring Campbell's chicken noodle soup to her or a clean, pressed blouse and skirt, thinking those lilly bits of comfort can help her mother get up oht the bed. She look at tings like any child would, asking, What would make me feel better if I was sick with a cold or flu? then try to do those tings for her mother. But her mother just push her off, whatever little helping ting she do, saying, "Oh, no, don't bring me that. That's not going to help me." She would wail it out, "Don't bring me that, don't bring me that," as if the child was set to harm her, bring her a snake in a basket or a match to set her afire or someting. Then, after she sparked up in anger at Jill, she would go right back to moaning how great her misery was and why won't Jill help her none.

When first I come here, Julie already was independent as a working girl, though barely sixteen, but Jill still tried to get some mothering oht Mrs. Silver, instead of the other way around. When Clair pester Jill all tru di morning, Jill say to her mama, "Clair won't leave me alone," and her half expect some help.

Her mother say back, "Look at you. Seven years older than she and carrying on about a little child."

Then I see Jill's color rising. My own color rising, too, as I fume on Jill's behalf.

"She won't leave me alone," Jill would try again. "I have work I have to do, and she keeps bugging me."

"She's no more than a baby. You ought to be ashamed."

"Why isn't it important for me to get my homework done?" Jill would ask, trying one last time but now looking mad as a bull.

I remember one night her mother stand in the hall in front of the girls' bathroom, she say to Jill, "Look at you. Just look at you. You're a wild animal, a beast. You're not to be trusted around that child."

Jill stepped away then. I saw her go glance at her face in the mirror, her skin red and dark like an Indian. She studied her face and dropped her eyes, ashamed. Ask me what does she see in the mirror and I'll say, "a wild animal," that's what she sees, viewing herself through the mother's eyes. All that afternoon Jill so sweet and careful, do this and that for Clair, walk on tippy toes. All that afternoon, watching, I want to spit. In the evening I find her cross-legged on the kitchen floor, a flat smile like a scar on her face, their wild spaniel dog, Lopey—she run away later that same month—asleep on her lap. "See, Indi," she says, "as long as I don't breathe, she'll quiet down and stay by me."

"What do you care that she sleeps on your lap all night," I say, "when you have your homework to do and other tings more important than this?"

Jill looks up at me with that unnatural smile and says, "Look, Indi, how sweet she is, so sweet when she's sleeping."

These memories give me no pleasure. I put them away and go on to Claire's room, where the child has pulled out last year's Valentine's cards and got them sorted and stacked according to who she likes how much; then finally I make it to Professor's. Though it's easy cleaning, this room is the one I put off till the end. Always it was Mrs. Silver's room to me, because she was the one home during the day, often just lying in this bed, suffering and whining, until she decide to go out and pounce on somebody. This room has no air to breathe. I wouldn't set a plant in here and bet any money on it living. I pull open all the curtains, but still the room has no light.

The upstairs library I save for last. This room is the one I like the most. No one's private life is lived in here, and the high ceiling with its wood beams puts me in mind of a church, and even though I am done with churches, the room still gives me a quiet feeling. The little dog follows me like a shadow and tucks his bottom under him and watches me do my dusting and straightening as if this is the most fascinating activity he has seen in his eleven weeks in the world. I keep my eye on him to make sure he's not set to piddle on the floor, and think of that floor Mrs. Perkins had, shiny as a bald head in the sun.

When I go to dust the shelves of books that run all up and down one wall, Tennyson comes and stands beside me and barks at me, ceaseless, in complaint. "Hush, Tennyson," I say. "Leave me be. Indi no do a ting to trouble you."

Here is a book, *Facts of Love for Teenagers,* pushed back and squeezed in by the others. I don't like to see Professor's books set like crooked teeth, so I try to pull this one forward so it's even with the others, but they are all of them pressed in so tight that a dozen or more spill out onto the floor and I have to place them back one by one. I take up the sex book, such an old thing that its pages are yellowed like ugly tobacco stain—they make me think of that filthy tape all over Brother Man's walls. The book must have been Professor's once or Mrs. Silver's. I see how the book wants to open to one page, so I take a look at what is there. The dog still yappy-yaps at me, but I try to shut him out my mind.

These pages I see make me rumble with laughter. What they write here looks like some wives' tale they en write up and set in a real book. I look to see who put his name to it and it's a man, which is no surprise to me. Men always filling your head with lies. Whoever wrote this strange nonsense is talking about how a man's wood can get caught in the woman if her muscle-dem clamp down during the act of sex. "Caught penis" is what he calls it, like the name of someting real and commonplace as fever or influenza. He tells a story of a man and his wife who have to make a trip to the hospital in that condition, the man clamped inside the woman. If Jill reads this, that be the end of any thoughts that timid girl ever have about men. Jules might as well drop her sister off at the old folks' home this very minute.

The ringing phone stops my fun and forces me back into Professor's bedroom, where he keeps a phone beside the bed. A voice I seem to know puzzles me, saying, middle of the workday, "Excuse me, is the professor in?"

"Who is this calling?"

"This is Indigo, is it?"

"Um-hm. Who dat a-ask?"

"You'll remember me, then. It's Mr. Borotsky. We met at the restaurant. A man named Francis introduced us. Then we met briefly again at Brother Man's."

Now the voice come clear. "Oh, yes, the old man."

"The old man, that's right." He laughs, his voice bright like bells.

"You're wanting someting with Professor?"

"Yes, if you please. Just to say a few words to him is all."

"Well, you not likely to find him home in the middle of the afternoon. Him a hardworking man."

"Of course, yes, of course. I wasn't thinking of his age. He's not an old man like me. I'll call again."

"You nah wish to cause him trouble, seen? He got trouble enough."

"Oh, no, no, of course not. Just to speak to him, you see. About his work, about something I've had on my mind."

"You want to give Professor more stories of wickedness to carry in his heart, is that it?"

"But that's his work, isn't it? To know these things that happened, especially to his own people, the Jewish people? For history's sake."

"Well, it's not for me to say. Professor cyan decide."

I hang up the phone, sit down on Professor's bed, start to think of those places, those "camps," Mr. Borotsky mus' been to get the blue numbers printed on his forearm. Professor tries to tell me sometimes about those people's suffering. All the husbands and wives dead, babies, old people dead, and on and on and on. Would have been Grandpa and Grandma Silver mongst them if they not leave just beforehand, come here to this country. I feel another river of fear run my way. Feel I have to brace for it like a wave heavy nuff to knock you down to di dutty. I bend and grab my ankles like they tell you to do when you ride the airplane, if the air get rough. Oh, Lord, here come Louisa into my head. Here come her laughing, and her smiling, and the feel of her hair and her little head in my hands as I make her pigtails. *This going to pass,* I tell myself. *Pray God, this going to pass.*

I go downstairs and distract myself getting a pork roast into the oven for supper. Then I go back to the library and see that silly book again, but now I take no interest in what I read.

Tennyson still gives me that hard little bark. Jill says it means "Won't you play with me," but that's not what I hear. Sounds more like he's angry over someting I do to upset him—he make his complaint.

"Hush." He won't quiet, and my nerves are jangly. "Just hush. Me nah wish to hear it," I tell him. "What me do to you? Just ignore you best I can." He won't let up, so I say, "All right, then," and let him lead me down the stairs and out the front door.

The day is so warm I need only my sweater. It is a day more April than February, though there's none of April's perfume in the air. The little ice left in the ground crackles like it's feeling pain melting. What can Mr. Borotsky want with Professor? Too many neighborhoods crossing here that ought to keep to their own side of the road; don't need Trenchtown run to St. Ann.

Mr. Borotsky's been in those evil places, and Professor studies those who come through evil times, the people that must flee from here to there to survive. I can't see why Borotsky need to speak with Professor and tie up the one life with the other.

The dog sniffs the sallow grass alongside the driveway, and I lean my back against Julie's and Jill's light-blue car that Professor bought them from a friend. The retired man next door lifts his hand to wave to me, and a breath of wind whips his light hair into a peak like an ice cream. He has a head of hair so silvery you could cash it in for someting of worth. It puts me in mind of Clair's storybook *Rumpelstiltskin,* about the man who promise to spin straw into gold. I nod my head.

"Beautiful little dog," he says. "Nice for the children, replacing the old dog."

I turn my ear to him like I can't hear him unless he shouts it louder. This old man is in his driveway every day of the year that the temperature rises past freezing. He polishes his red car till it looks like the waxed apples they sell at the Dominick's. I wonder what he sees in that car that makes it so precious to him. What fine ting do his fingers feel neet the sliding cloth? He runs that cloth over the car's fender as loving as if it were a baby's bottom.

Now I see the strangeness it holds for me when a man loves a machine like the one run down my child. I straighten myself, not wanting to lean my body on an evil ting. I cross my arms in front of me and clamp my palms to my elbows, think of Jill and Julie driving this car, young as they are, and driving it with Professor's blessing the same as if they were to use a typewriter or a telephone. All of that raises a fury in me. For a second, I put their faces behind the wheel of the car that killed Louisa, but that is too much for me. I don't know what face belongs behind that wheel—old or young, white or black, man or woman, I don't know. Hit and run, it was. Some inhuman soul just run down my child and drive on. The police say there is an investigation, but I nah hear a single word about who murdered my baby. Not one blessed word.

For a while, I lose track of where I am. Maybe I lean back against that hateful car, pulled off by my thoughts, my remembering.

Nine

Professor always tells the girls the way to pull off a Band-Aid is to do it quick. Going slow won't stop the pain, it just draws out the misery. But telling me about my Lou, Professor nah keep his own counsel. I remember the burden in his voice as he come up to it, as I stood holding the black earpiece tight to my ear, the cord snaking toward the base on the low table. Hearing that darkness in Professor's voice, my heart knew it could only be one thing. Only one thing in the world was that precious for me to catch such an ill wind flowing from Professor. I feel I may pass out even before the word-dem come. Pass out to try to stop my world from forever a-change. I hear the roar of the waterfall and know, once over that fall, current don't never take you back.

When I dropped the phone that fearful day, I was like someone whose head shot through with a spray of bullets. My mind was filled with broken pieces of itself. I was dazed and my legs weak and the only words I had were NO and NO and NO Lord NO. My mind would not let this ting be so, yet my spirit began right away to ache and shiver from a terrible fever.

I remember a blur of time—hours perhaps—that is nothing but this fever of pain; then came a moment when the phone cawed at me like a black crow, because I had set it down without getting it back on the carriage. I think of that day now and remember that small thing—setting back the phone after Professor delivered the news he took from the telegram—and I see how I could not allow myself to set it back straight. Doing that would mean the world was in its normal working order and I was in mine, and the nightmare ting I had heard was real and somehow had to be fitted in with other real tings. I needed to believe that every single ting in the world, from the phone to my baby being dead, was cockeyed and all of it would be set straight only when the world got back to itself.

I sat in the chair and rocked like a daft child, in a state that was all at once numb and on fire. Finally, after many hours, I felt sleep coming to me in the chair where I sat, but I fought it off out of a terror of waking in the morning to the life I now had. How could I rise up that next morning, rise up any morning beyond that, with the sun gone out of the sky? The days ahead stretched on with an emptiness the fear of which stole away my heartbeat.

I think now of how a world can change just like that, just a few words coming across a telephone wire and all that you know is gone, like a shadow picture on the wall flees when the lights come on. It is gone as if it never were. When you think like that, it seems a miracle, or maybe an idiot's act, that any of us ever pick up a ringing phone or go to greet a knock at the door. How we know what awfulness can meet us there?

I lay down and slept for a minute or two, then started awake, slept again and started awake, time and time again, until finally sleep was stronger than me and took me down.

When I awoke in the early morning, I had not even a part

second of peaceful forgetting. I had not rescued myself from misery with any easy dreams, so there was no shock of remembering, just the ache of knowing, which was going to be mine forever.

Later on in that most dreadful day, Professor came to my apartment and tried to talk to me about going home to the burying, but I could not speak to him. I drove him off with my silence. Days passed me by, me just sitting rocking in the chair, clutching all my baby's little tings that I had dug out from my closet in some dumb state and dragged back to that chair. Bertha and Jewel and some others forced their way in from time to time, made me tolerate their hugging and holding, their soups spooned to my lips, but none of it mattered. And the phone would ring and ring, but I did not really hear it, because I am sunk in the deepest winter a body can know. At times I rock, hard and fast, and then I am limp, too far lost even to blink an eye. Finally my mind begins a blind searching for someting to take hold of out in the world, someting that remains to grab on to to pull me back from death. I think of all the small tings I used to love—a red dress Mama made me with cotton lace around the neck, ripe mango spilling its juice down my chin, curry goat for the Sunday meal, Clair's laugh when Professor tickle her middle. But nothing warms me, and suddenly I am scared, I am terrified, and that is when I know I am alive still, in some far-off corner of myself.

In four days' time I go back to Professor's, because what else should I do with my wretched self? I pack a few things in a paper bag and go on over there without even picking up that black phone to call, and they are shocked to see me standing in the doorway. I am there like a ghost, and I want no one seeing me or speaking a word to me. I feel too fragile to be spoken to, and feel I will break up into tiny glass threads if someone tries to get me to speak. But they don't respect the thinness of my spirit. Julie finds me dusting in the living room and stands still for once in her life and says a few words to me.

"I'm sorry about Louisa, Indi. That's horrible. . . . What happened is horrible." She tries to put all of her feeling into that one weak word. "How could someone have done that?" she says, puzzled at the universe. She has slowed down and looks sad and timid, but when she's said her piece, then she's done with it, and soon she is back to normal, making such noise around me I could scream in pain.

Clair is too young to feel she has got to make a speech about what has happened to Lou. She just sneaks a look at me every time she thinks I'm not looking. She tries to see am I the same Indigo I used to be, and tries to distract me from my own insides with her chatter, which grates on me now. My mind pictures how that child saw her own mada go from bad to worse, and now she's got me before her eyes, sunk into quicksand, but even that is not enough to move me, though I have loved these girls most next to Louisa.

Jill, she can't say a word, but I see her dancing around me, careful and concerned, thinking she should speak but not finding the words. She's the one who gets me angry, the way she's thinking her words could hurt me if they're not perfect as her schoolwork. What could she say or not say that would hurt me now?

Sometimes Jill looks at me so earnest, wanting to speak something but not daring. She is hoping I'll guess at what she yearns to say. In my mind I tell her, *I can't help you, Jill. If you can't say what you want, go away from me. I'm not a dentist. I can't pull your words out from your mouth. You come back when you're ready, or don't come back. It makes no difference to me.* Then if she stays hanging around me in spite of my ugly thoughts, I think, *Why do you follow me around, child? Have you no place of your own to be going? I don't need an extra load to pull behind me,* and somehow I hear my own mama's voice in my voice.

Some more dark days pass and Jill gets braver, and now

from time to time she comes up beside me and says, "Indi, how are you?" She slips in her words so careful, as if she is setting a fine sliver under my skin. I turn my head Jill's way and say, "How are *you*, Jill?" in that singing voice we Jamaicans have that Americans all think is sweet like a melody, but to me it is just my own voice. "How are you, Jill?" I say the words, though I'm not caring how she is. Sometimes I want to say to her, *What is worrying you so, Jill? Why do you look like a nervous lamb?* I would be saying this all in meanness. I am trying to say, *What problem can you have, child? Has your life gone flying apart like a haystack set on by a hurricane? No? So then why are you such a cloudy day?*

Yes, Jill is the one who brings life to my anger, when she looks at me like my pain is hers. Maybe I should thank her for that anger, because I swear it is the only thing stirring in me some days. I think of the child I lost, my fat sweet pretty baby. And then there is Jill, already with the pimples and skin dull as dough. How could God make the two of them? And seeing the two of them that He made, how could He take my pretty, dark-skinned girl and leave this one that looks to me like a mud puddle? So there it is, as evil a thought as one of His creatures could ever have, and it is mine.

I come back to myself again, out beside the driveway, my back to the blue car, my eyes on the silver-haired neighbor who has nothing better to do than polish his own cursed car, the dog gone off a ways so that I get a heart jump of worry until I see him and call him and, smart thing, he comes already to his name.

Jill is the first of the girls to come in. She looks like the air is out of her balloon now, not like this morning, when she went off all happy-go-lucky. She piles her heavy load of library books onto the coffee table and sets down on the couch. Next comes Julie with her boyfriend, Scott, trailing her. He enters like a man, big and noisy and filling up the house with nothing but himself.

"Hi, Indigo," Scott says, and gives me a big, slow smile. He's a polite boy, but I know he is doing more with Julie than Professor would like, so I make it my habit to frown at him.

"Hey, Jill-O," he says, his little joke. Jill doesn't even know how to talk to him, grown and manly as he is. Soon she will get uneasy and excuse herself to do her homework. But Julie gives her no chance to run.

"Well, *did you?*" Jules needs to know, going right at Jill with her questions.

"What?"

"You know."

Jill glances at Scott but finds no way not to answer. She nods.

"Can he?" Julie turns her head and says to Scott, "Jill asked somebody to the dance." Clair comes in and plops down close by Jill on the sofa and bends her head to rest on Jill's shoulder.

"Can he?" Julie repeats. She walks this way and that across the carpet, leaving a tangle of trails behind.

"His family is going skiing in Sun Valley. They have a condo there."

"I can't believe you actually asked him," Julie says. She looks down at her little fashion wristwatch.

"Who did Jill ask?" Clair asks Julie, her eyes full of her curious nature.

"Nathan Bigelow," Julie says. "He's nerdy, but he's cute."

I can see Jill has had enough of this. She gets up and escapes to her room.

When Professor comes home, looking weary, he gives Jules and Clair a little peck and goes right up to his study. When I mount the stairs to call him for dinner, he looks up at my face. "Do you know a Mr. Borotsky, Indigo?"

"Um-hm. Not by my choice."

"Why?" Professor looks up. "He seems like a nice man. He called me at the office this afternoon, about an appointment. You have something against him?"

I shake my head. So some way he got Professor's work number.

"Would it be best if I go out to his home? Maybe he'd talk more freely there? What do you think, Indigo?"

"Don't think much about it one way or the other, Professor. You hear that buzzer calling in the kitchen? My mind's all took up with the pork roast I got to go pull out the oven."

Ten

I'm back at home, trying to clear my mind of those girls and their problems, knowing I got to go right on back there come first light. The evening's got me walking the street again like a yellow-eyed potoo bird aiming to hunt someting down in the night, but can't say what I might be hunting for. I go on down the street and into the town, but all I do is just look in windows. I look in shop windows and study what's inside, even peer in the people's houses, look at the families in there and the lights and furnishings. I see a handsome man playing cat's cradle with his likkle girl, and my foolish heart stops, me thinking him Steve Jones till I look closer and see the set-back chin this man has that don't look a ting like Steve.

Henry P must spend his night looking out at the street as I look in at the rooms. As I pass his ground heading home, he calls to me from off di porch.

"What you want, Henry?" I call to him.

"You always prowl so in the night?"

"If di mood take me."

He walks to the edge of his porch and bends his bald head over. "I heard something. Come closer, gal. I no wish to yell my business to di whole street."

I move in a little.

"They say your employer him a big professor," he says, "a big expert."

"You might say. Who tell you that, mon? You talk wid Jewel? She's one bigmouth woman."

He shakes his head. "Over at Brother Man's they go on a-talk. Because the old tata, Borotsky—him the blackjack king—him have an appointment set with the professor, and the professor offer to visit Borotsky home to put the man at ease a-tell him story. You know dat old man past, Indigo? How him en send to one of dem concentration camp where dem burn people alive in di gas oven?"

"Someting like that," I say, thinking how the people were killed by gas, so Professor say, then burnt in the ovens. Henry makes it sound like the people roast in the Tappan range. "People suffer over di whole world," I say, copying Professor.

"Truly."

Enough of this talk, I feel. "The city pay you sufficient to spend your night-dem at dat bredda gambling joint?"

"City pay me fine, to where I can throw away a dollar or two. Nothing more than that, though. I nah plan to be one of dem who get themself in deep trouble. Some of dem do, you know. Too gravalicious, dem." He touch his stomach. "Hungry belly, dem, for the big win. I, I jus' take it for entertainment, like when we all go to the dance hall back home, listen to DJ music. Play the Drop Pan. You come again, Indigo, to Brother Man place?"

I shake my head. "Me no see the thrill."

Now Henry P's the one who have enough. "Hey, girl, perhaps if you listen to you professor whenever the chance come, you get to be some kind of expert, too."

"So far, I come to be expert on bedsheet and fried potato, mostly."

"Then mus' be you nah wish to know more than that, sister," he tells me, gentling the words with his calm voice.

Next day takes me back to Professor's, where I guess I'm meant to get an education, according to Henry P. I don't learn much that day, but next morning we all learn one ting or two about Jill, because Jill finally lets go of her secret and lets us know she has done more than what Julie thought she would, she has asked another boy, Keith, to the dance, and this one say he wi go wid her.

"Well, at least you're going," Julie says, "even though the guy's not too cool." Julie wants to give her some skimpy bit of credit for her nerve.

"Is he cute?" Clair asks her.

Jill shrugs.

"Come, Clair, and eat your breakfast," I say. "Jill is stingy. She no a-go tell us a ting, and that is her privilege."

I see Jill trying to find her way with these boys and I think, like a sinner, *Maybe Louisa is the lucky one,* because what a trial it is to be a woman. Though in all of my own troubles with boys as a young girl, I never was quite as clumsy as Jill. That child don't even know which way to point herself—might as well have a blindfold and play pin the tail on the donkey. She is that lost, even though she has a fine figure plenty of boys would admire.

When Friday night comes, I walk by Jill's room and see she is standing looking at what she's laid out on her pretty blue bedspread, that bedspread the last ting Mrs. Silver bought her before she left this house. Jill's laid out a brown wool dress she sewed for herself over the summer, nylon stockings, and a pin that is nothing but a gold-colored X. "Jill," I ask her, "why do you not wear a dress with some color? Someting red or pink that's nice for a party and brings out your color?"

"This one will be okay."

"Okay is not what a girl wants for a party."

The phone rattles and I go into the library to get it, and it is trouble coming right this minute, because here is Mrs. Silver again. I want to lie and tell her Jill's not at home, but I say, "Just a minute"; then I return to Jill.

"For you, Jill," I tell her, standing stiff and stupid as a wooden post. "Your mother is on the telephone."

I follow her back to the library and pick the receiver up off the cabinet and put my hand over the speaking end. "You better be careful, now, and not spoil your evening," I say, then put the receiver in her hand. I go and stand in the hall and squint my eyes at the picture of her holding the telephone, as if I can see more of what's happening between them that way—see it and scorn it. I wonder will Jill stand up to her mother this time, but I know, watching Jill's face, that Mrs. Silver is taking that girl apart like a puzzle box. Jill tells her mother, "No, we don't have any trips planned for spring break" and "No, I never heard of that woman" and "No, Daddy isn't having an affair." She tells her, "I'm sorry," and again, later, "I'm sorry." I expect her mother must be telling her how she isn't sleeping and isn't eating and has a deadly ting of some kind growing in her breast or her belly. I think of Bertha, who had a real sickness to kill her, and then of Mrs. Silver always casting about for a disease like it is some kind of jackpot. Jill looks out at me in the hallway, and I roll my eyes to Heaven. Then I have too much of watching this, and I go down to the kitchen and wash my hands, soaping between the fingers like a surgeon.

After a while Jill comes down. She's put on her slippers and her bathrobe and is cradling that little dog in her arms as if he's a baby. She might as well have a nightcap on her head like a picture from an old-time storybook, because she looks like she is ready for bed. I pretend I don't think anyting about what I see. I just say, "You better get your shower and get yourself ready for that party."

"I don't think I'm gonna go, Indi," she says to me in a winjy little voice that makes me ashamed of who she is.

I turn away from the burner plates I am scrubbing and wipe my hands on my apron. "What do you mean, you don't think you're going?"

"I have so much homework. When will I ever get it all done if I don't do some tonight?"

I put my hands to my hips and look at her. "That is just nonsense," I say.

"Really, Indi," she says, her whine deepening. "I do."

"Jill, are you staying home from that dance because your mother calls and makes you feel you are responsible for alla her misery?"

"I don't know," she mumbles. "I have a lot of work. I'll tell Keith I'm sick."

"Too much schoolwork, then, to have a life? Is that how it is for you? Maybe you *are* sick." I twist her heart just like Jules do.

She winces. "Too much work right *now.* Not always."

Now I am angry. "Jill, you are a fool. You let her play her little game with you as many times as she wants to, like she is a cat and you no more than a ball of yarn. Now, I suppose, you a-go take yourself upstairs and lock yourself in your room and dream about that secret boyfriend who is how many miles away and ten years too old for you. Meanwhile, you turn your back on a boy who goes to your own school and is looking forward to taking you to a dance like it is the high point of his life. You are a fool, Jill. That is for sure."

Now Jill does what she has never done with me, which takes me by surprise. She starts to cry. Jill always been strong as a board, but here she is, spilling tears and turning her head in shame.

Oh, Lord, what have I done now, and how many people's troubles do I have to bear? I say that to myself, and to her I say, "Stop that now, Jill. I don't mean anything by what I say. I'm a fool myself, just as much as you, and I am double your age."

Jill is going to surprise me all day. She is too upset to watch her words, and she says, "You hate me since my mother left and I went on that summer trip. I know it." The little dog stands by Jill's side and yips at me.

"That is not true, Jill," I say, shocked by her. "You are off your head, talking like that." I look at her pitiful, crying face and suck in my breath. My words are soft but steady. "I hate everyone this last year. That is what's true, and nothing else but that."

"Me," she says. "You hate me more. Because I'm selfish."

I shake my head no, but feel confused. "You are more selfish than Jules?" I ask, unbelieving. I give her a tissue to wipe her face. "Now, you go up and take your shower and go to that dance. You wear that plain dress if you want but you go." Jill sniffles, done from spilling what's in her heart and walks off, and I am left to work my mind over this. Because in truth it *is* Jill who angers me more than the others, but not because she is selfish. Maybe it's that she tries too hard and cares too much about every small thing, where I care about nothing. And in her mousy way, she wants to crawl inside my heart, which is a fool thing to do, black as that heart is.

Later, we all have our dinner, including Julie's Scott, who eats as much as the three girls together and twice what Professor do, which gives me more occasion to frown at him. Jill finally goes off to her dance, looking sweet in the blue dress she put on, and Julie goes downstairs with Clair to listen to Scott strum his guitar.

I hide in my room awhile, just lay down on my bed, on my back, and spread over me the pink woolen blanket Clair gave me, its satin edge against my cheek, and remember her offering it to me, folded perfect as a flag, making a ceremony over giving me her treasure, her baby blanket from when she was little. Here comes Jill into my mind, asking me why I drive her so to go to the dance. I don't understand it myself, except that I want her to move on from this place, to push on to some sort of freedom. Julie's freedom light is Scott, though I can't say if he leads her right.

My own freedom light was never a man; it was America. I would see the moving pictures that showed America and see it had big, big fields of corn and wheat so no one go hungry, and house-dem huge as hotels, with clean linoleum floors, each house with a telephone, and streets lined with stores selling how many thousand fine tings. Some people over here, they think, Oh, Indigo, you are from Jamaica. You are from an island paradise. Why do you come over here, where there is ice and snow and hard living? They don't know that living in a place is not the same as going there on holiday. They don't know that the sun can wear on you same as the cold, and hunger close by the door tires you worst of all. Still, when Louisa come into my life, I think my heart is done with America. The big, empty place I carry all my life is filled. Louisa would come over to me while I rest from the heat, and she would push the hair off my damp forehead to look in my eyes. "Mama, you're so pretty," she would say. She thought my hair was beautiful because it was all in one piece, not parceled out like hers in little braids.

I met Mrs. Williams when I was waiting on customers out beside the swimming pool at the hotel in Montego Bay. All I remember from that beginning is her blonde curls and tall, well-fed figure. One day she complimented me on my serving and asked me did I want to come to America to work in her house. I was shocked and I was flattered, and so I was speechless a minute, but I finally told her, "Oh, no, Mrs. Williams, no, I couldn't do that, because of my little girl." She said, "You think about it, Indigo, and let me know if you change your mind." She walked away, then walked back to me and said,

"You could make some money and give your girl advantages the other Jamaican girls will never have."

That day, my work is hard and the sun is hot and tires me out. In the evening I go with my friend Yoli to the American movie show and watch an old picture of Burt Reynolds romancing Sally Field. The only time I ever thought about Steve was when I went to the movies, and there he'd be, sitting beside me, rubbing my hand with his warm fingers, making me quiver. I remembered how he said, before he got on the American navy boat, "My Indigo Rose, love of my life. . . ." Then he got on the boat, and I watched it rocking so hard in the water it gave me the feel of Steve rocking me in the bed when he was all inside of me, which was just the feeling I nah want to call back. Now he don't even know what our life's become since Mister Gilbert pass through and leave us laboring just to get food enough for the table.

When I get home from the movies, Louisa is still up and playing with her baby dolls. I go on and tell Mama a little bit about the picture, then sit awhile on the floor with Lou. I offer to comb her dolly's hair and put it up in a knot like she always wants. Louisa says, "No, Mama, I'll do it myself," and grabs that dolly back with both hands. I can't recall she ever told me no before when I offered her someting nice. My heart lets out a whistle of pain, like a pricked balloon. I think how she is growing fast and she will need different tings from me as time goes on. I wish she had a fada to get her what she need, like I wished I had one myself how many times? Hers is even more lost to her than mine was to me, though Lord knows I never intended that deprivation for my child.

In the morning I see Mrs. Williams again when I am out by the pool gathering up glasses. She is sunning herself, her hair pulled up above her head so she can brown herself on every centimeter of her face. I don't say a word to her—just nod—but all the day after I've seen her, I am thinking about America.

Mama, she was the one most to confuse me, because all the

time I was growing up, Mama was nah one to want me close. When I was little and I went up to her on a hot day, tired from the sun leaning down on me, she always said, "Indigo, you go off. Don't hang round my neck in this heat, child." How many times she said that. "Indi, you go off. I've got babies enough hanging on me."

Then when I'm grown and I say a word or two about going to America to work for Mrs. Williams, about maybe leaving Louisa with her awhile, she is cork up with disapproval and I swear she wish me to feel I am a-break her heart in leaving her. But soon enough I go off anyway like Marcella Howard from the next town up the mountain, and I send Mama all the fine tings she always talk about, and hope those will lighten her heart.

I think of Mama's heavy heart and wonder is that why God sent me such misery when first I come here. And is that why God . . . but I leave off with that thought, which is more than I can bear.

My first airplane ride takes me through the sky toward Chicago, and I am so full of excitement I think my pounding heart will break free of my chest and fly to Chicago on its own. Naturally, I am missing my Lou, but in my head I am telling her everyting I see and feel as if she is right beside me in the next seat, instead of the purple-dressed woman from Negril that clutch her Bible to her breast. *"We're in the airplane now, Lou, and the stewardess is bringing me a little cup of coffee and a nice meal on a tray. Everyting's beenie, like it's made for your dollies. The stewardess gives us pillows, but who could sleep when we're flying over clouds puffed like giant cotton balls."* I can't get the grin off my face, especially when the plane hits some hard air and bounces up and down a little. Ooh! Scary! But I like the feeling. *"It's like when we go to the amusement park, honeygirl, and go on the rides. Mama got to see if she can stand up and wobble down the aisle to the little bathroom in back; 'im no bigger than a broom closet."*

And later: *"The airplane just touched down on the ground and I'm in America. Your mama's in America, sweetie girl! And you're right beside me, pressed to my heart."*

I get here full of joy and hopes, and when the sleepy, sweet young black man Mrs. Williams sent to the airport drops me off in front of the fine house and I see her walk to greet me, I give her a big, big smile and want to give her a hug, but her flat face stops me. I don't see her eyes sparkle like they did in Montego Bay. I start to fear all that shine come from di bottle. When she settles me into that dank-smelling basement room where I'll have to sleep each night after I'm done attend the family, worry stirs in me, but I don't want to give it run. Next day, the sun restores my spirits and I go through that first day of cleaning and ironing happy as a canary let out of its cage. But when she locks up that big, untrained dog in there, too, come evening, not asking me how do I feel about dogs, not telling me that big shepherd dog doesn't trouble himself to do his business out in the yard more than half the time, a film starts to spread itself over my happiness like a cataract. I get brave and complain to her about the dog, but she just raises her plucked eyebrows at me like, Who do you think you are, some kind of royalty?

Well, poor and scared though I am, I have more pride than that, and after two months go by and I come to realize from the other maids in the neighborhood that many a family in the suburb search for a full-time housekeeper and many of them happy to have a Jamaican, I do a little scouting, and soon I'm ready to tell Mrs. Williams, Thanks very much for a-sponsor me to come here, but I no come to America to clean up after a dog and live beside him in a dark basement—I could have nicer than that back home in the ghetto, and I have found someone else—a professor in Wilmette City—to sponsor me now.

When I get to Professor's and meet the three girls, life brightens up again for me. I start to get my excitement back, and so I write Louisa and Mama and the others about all the fine tings in America. Some of my work is hard, but there are easy days like when I take Clair to the library and let her sit and read her books for hours and I thumb through the telephone books from all over the country, just get a feel for the thousands of towns, with their strange names, and looking at the different names of the people, some of them very odd sounding to my ears. There are simple names, too, like Silver, or White or Jones, that hundreds and hundreds of families have, so if you want to find one Silver or Smith or Taylor, you'll never succeed unless you know which one of the thousands of towns they're in.

I am tired of remembering. I wander in and out of each girl's room, looking for I don't know what. In Jill's room, tossed on the bed, are some old, scratched records must have belonged to her mada or fada as a child, maybe even to the granmada. Jill don' even have a record player now, just the CD and tape deck, but I guess she still look at these old records. I see Mamas and Papas, Cher, and the Beatles. Here are some older ones still. Elvis and Harry Belafonte, a name I know well enough. I study the list of his songs and see that many are known to me, like "Jamaica Farewell" and "Brown Skin Girl," that speaks with its words to my own story, since it tells of a sailor who visits the island, makes a baby, and leaves the Jamaican girl and the family to care for the child while the fada sail off over the blue sea. That sailor's a white man, not like Louisa's sailor fada.

Steve came to us on his leave, a young black man so fine, so talawa, with polished skin and a voice rich as honey, and he was full to overflow with him sweet music. I first meet him at the corner store where we go sometime to take a rest after work, never expect to find so fine a package there. First time meeting, he gets me talking, gets me to answer a thousand questions, then tells me this and that riddle and rhyme until I can't stop myself laughing. After that day, sometime we go to the dance hall, hear the DJ play his riddims, but other times Steve just sing me his own music from America—sing me old-style songs like Otis Redding, then some Sam Cooke, "She's Only Sixteen" for the young girls and "You Send Me," and the best one, Percy Sledge, singing "When a Man Loves a Woman," Steve sliding his voice all up and down Percy's song. A person has to dance to that music, got to embrace and dance cheek to cheek; the music give you no choice. *That man* gave me no choice. Lord, I didn't want one. I think back on that sweet boy, and then my mind skip over to Louisa, the precious child he gave me, and I feel what it was to tickle her into rolling like a log while she lay on the ground, to lift her heavy, sleepy body off the dutty and up into my arms, to pet her damp hair as she sleep, and suddenly I am caught again in the fresh pain as bad as a fox that just caught a trap across the leg and is a-go to gnaw the leg off sooner than stan' in that pain, and I am wondering one more time, how will I rise the next day. I can't go to bed now, because I'm a-fear for the morning.

Finally, around midnight, Jill comes home from her dance and turns on a light and is spooked to find me sitting there. "Oh. Indi," she mumbles, and blushes. I ask about her date, and she is very cool in saying, "Oh, yes, it was nice. It was fine." But I swear I see a glow come from deep inside that girl, like a hot charcoal's hid in there. It's a wonder how she is so set on a-keep her pleasure tucked away, but set or not, there it is, shining out from her. I suspect she may fuss a little less over that far-off Ben Sands now she has somebody closer to home and closer to her own age.

Next afternoon around five, I walk by Jill's room and see her there at her desk in a dreamy pose, a white notepaper held out in her hand like she is waiting for a wind to pick it up. I figure it to be another letter from Ben Sands, who may be nothing more than a make-believe Prince Charming out of a fairy tale. I guess she's going to hold on to such pretend pleasures even when someting real come her way. In my heart, I lacquer my contempt over Jill. "Better get on with your schoolwork," I say to her, and she looks at me, puzzled. Later, I go in to bring a stack of clean laundry. She's back to her books, and I see the note set on the corner of the desk, so I start to find some more words to sting her. Then I catch enough of a look to see the paper is signed "love Keith" in a big, looping script. So it's not a letter from far away—it's a little love note from the boy who took Jill to the dance last night, which startles me.

Through the rest of the day my mood sours. I am so hungry for some sort of pleasure, I go hunting tru my mind for a shred of it, like an old woman rifling tru a chest full of keepsakes. Used to be the men that excite me so, they turn me inside out. And Steve, the most fine, most high-tone, of any of them, how he held my heart in his hand-dem, stop mi breath, fill mi belly with life. Lord, bless him, punish him. Jah have mercy on me, a confused, lost woman. I got to run some other direction, I so certain that sinting's going to bury me under. Finally I vision myself back at Brother Man's with Jewel, because wasn't there some sort of life in me that one night, first time in forever. I think of the green cloths over Brother Man's tables as if they are lawns of green grass where I can lay my head and dream, or race across them on a fast horse.

Eleven

I am off for three full days while the girls go to visit their auntie for their late-winter break. Friday morning, I step out onto the black plastic runner in the hall and am surprised to see a man turning the lock of Bertha's rooms. I'm accustom now to the rooms being vacant and forgot someone would take them some day. He turns around and it's Zach, a man I recognize as Cliff's first cousin. I only met him one time, at Bertha's niece's christening, but I hear he's a man with no wife, a serious sort who works at the bank.

"Indigo," he says in a even tone.

"You take that flat?" I ask.

"Yes. I signed for it yesterday." He gives me a smile. He is some bit bigger and handsomer than his cousin, except for his ears that poke out from his head like they are set to hear sounds from halfway around the world. I want to ask him how does it feel a-take those rooms where somebody just die, but I know that's unwelcoming, so I keep my mouth shut for once.

"Maybe you'll come in and have a cup of coffee sometime," Zach says, and tips his head of short, wiry hair to me so that I see he already has got one or two pieces of gray twisted in there.

"Maybe," I say, and get on with locking up my door so I can head out and get some tings I need at the March Madness sale. His place is Bertha's place to me. I won't be quick to visit him there. Can't tell anyway if he wants me or just being Mister Polite.

Before I climb down the stairs, I glance back and see that Zach follows me with his eyes. Maybe he is not as much a scared rabbit as he appears. Irritation jumps in me when I think that now I will have this one knocking on my door come evening, spoiling my peace just like Cliff. It turns out I am wrong about that part, because the day comes and goes and then evening comes and I hear him return to his rooms and I think, *Now him bex me,* but the evening stretches on and nobody come to disturb me, which is good by me.

Saturday, Cliff catches me in the hall midmorning as I carry in my mail that's cold and damp with the weather. He gives me a stony face and presses his open hand up to his green leather jacket like he is saying his pledge of allegiance, and pats his heart with his hand. "Good morning, Miss Indigo," he says, as if we are meeting up at church, though he is unshaven and not fit for any church I know—more fit for the dance hall. I think he may take that hand and offer me a shake, but Zach comes out into the hall and shines his peaceful smile.

"Zachie!" Cliff says, happy as a pickney come upon his best friend. "Me pleased to see you, braa."

"Star! Bredda!" Zach puts his arm around Cliff's shoulder and opens his door to him. I see Zach look my way and start a greeting, but Cliff rush him into the apartment and leave me to stand scuffing my feet on the floor, no one left to speak to.

I go into my rooms and I'm standing by the open door, thinking that—though Cliff is someting pitiful—with his deestant manners Zach is a man a woman might have as a neighbor and not have any nonsense between them. Cliff comes back into the hallway, still wearing the jacket he must have paid dear for. I face him and set my feet apart, put my hands to my hips like I am a cowgirl. "What you wanting now, Cliff?" I ask. "I thought you come to visit your cousin, not me."

"Let me come down and sit, Indigo," he says.

"Do as you please," I say, and move aside to let him enter my place.

Cliff perches on the wooden chair next to the small round dining table I've covered with a lace cloth that some great-auntie brought my granmada from England. I stand across the room, my back to the wall, my head disturbing a small photo of Mama and Dada set in a wooden frame.

"Pretty color in you dress today, girl. Me like the salmon pink. 'Im become your skin. Cyan you sit, too?" He smooths the leather over his breast with the flat of his hand.

I go and sit across the room from him like I am interviewing him for a position.

"I'm just here to say *sorry,* Indigo. I shouldn't have come here uninvited, when I'd been drinking. That wasn't right."

"Well, then," I say. "Now you talk some sense."

"You've had a bad, bad year, I know. Worst ever. I wish I could be a friend to you."

"What makes you think I need a friend?" I ask. "That meddling Jewel tell you that? She put her nose where it no belong just like another time recent?" The slant of Cliff's eyebrows trouble me. I see Steve Jones in that portion of his face. In the smooth skin, too, though that's the end of the likeness. Not one ting more they hold in common.

"I've got a child of my own, a son who lives in New York with his mother. I can imagine what you've been through is all."

"No need to waste your imagining on me," I say. Jah, I need this man out of my space. Someting in me wants to smack him, but my mind startles with the sense of his skin's smoothness. Too much of Steve come into my fingertips if I smack that cheek.

He shakes his head back and forth. "Why do you have to be so hard?"

I stand up and turn my back to him. Next thing I know, I feel Cliff's hands around my middle and his lips roaming my neck, his cheek rubbing over the spots he has kissed. He turns me around in his arms and then his lips are soft to mine and at the same time his hands are running down the dress over my back until both are behind me on my hips, pressing me onto him, no air between us, making me feel his excitement. Now I know he has brought me right to this place where two roads cross, where I have been before. And each time I've come here, I let the feelings in my body carry me off like a river at high water and any objection in my mind I let wash away like a leaf in the flood. But since Louisa was lost to me, I tell myself, *Never again*, tell myself, *Next time this moment come, if ever it do, my mind going to stay sharp and stay strong, and that man will hear my words* No *and* No *and* No.

But Cliff is cunning as a fox and him give me no time to steady up my stubbornness, only a quick look into my eyes to see what they might be telling. So here I am, and the weakness in my legs is like always and the lightness in my head is, too, because all my feelings have gone to make a commotion in my female center till I am nothing but a purring cat. And so I say nothing to this man, not one ting, not a whisper. Then I am in the bedroom, my own bedroom, where he has carried me or led me—I do not remember which—and I am without my clothes and sweat is over my skin and I have given in to my body like always before and Cliff is half sleeping beside me, twining my hair around his finger and looking with kindness at the broad face my Louisa always said was "so pretty, Mama," and I can only shut my eyes to his because of my shame and listen to the deep sigh the radiator makes as it brings up the heat.

When Cliff leaves, he thanks me and kneels over me on the mattress, which is spongy from the weight of two, and gives me kisses all over my face and neck, even on the spots of fassy skin that the winter air has left, and both of us got to ignore how he's getting excited again. "I'm going to New York awhile, Indi girl, to see my cousin Lily Ann. One love, dawta. I'll call you when I get back."

"Don't worry about that. Ma Bell's got enough customers without you," I say from flat on my back, and shut tight my eyes.

He runs his thumbs over my closed eyelids so lightly I can just feel his touch. "I'm not listening to your words," he says. "You enjoy yourself while I'm gone. Remember, I'm not owning you, sister, just try to give you a little pleasure, and have some for myself."

Who would want to be owning me? I think. Like owning a pot of poison. "You go on, now," I say, my eyes open but sharp against him, my mind thinking, *I won't be seeing him again now that he get what he come for.* I tell myself, *Good riddance.*

"Poor Indigo," he says as he stands, "always angry with her men." But I don't want to hear any of that nonsense, so I turn onto my belly and let him leave.

I try to tell myself he is just one more bag-o-wire not worth my worrying, but I know I am in trouble now. Lord, such deep water rise up over my head.

Sunday starts off with a dream of Louisa froze in the wintery ground of the North, when she ought to have a bed in Jamaica's warm soil. It's so bad I got to hurry and forget it, and since I got to forget what I did the last day, too, I turn to cleaning my rooms like a gale wind. When I finish cleaning, I feel the space in the day when I would visit Bertha, but now there is nothing across the hall but an empty room filled with Zach. The day stretches before me, and my mind finds only the thoughts that unravel it. I try to shoob off thoughts of Cliff and what could come of my weakness, but finally I sit down to do what I should have done yesterday, figure where I am in my cycle. I see that I am right in the heart of it, and that makes me feel pressured as a kettle on the flame. I am sorry one more time to be born a woman.

I've got to search out some peace. I remember how my mind rested and my heart sparked a little at that Brother Man's place and wonder could it be open even on the Lord's day. In my head I hear the fat man Joshie mumbling, "All the time, sir, all the time," and it comes back to me how that pale white man tall as a telephone pole, with the small bow at his neck, asked the big man when can he come there and find a game.

This time I don't need any red dress to please Jewel, or any white uniform to annoy her. I put on the one pair of long pants I have, which are plain dark-blue trousers with a good crease, and I put on a white shirt and tuck it in and make my hair into a twist so it fits easy neet a wool cap, and that way I look more man than woman. Most of my money I pull out of my purse, and slide the bills in my front pants pocket along with someting extra from the drawer. Nobody get into that snug pocket without me know it, so I feel safe a-carry however much dunsa I want.

The ground is bare of snow, with only a few flakes dusting the dead grass so slow that nothing will build up. The wind tugs hard at my coat and at my near-empty bag—maybe that wind's drawing in some colder weather—and I curse it and tell it, "Leave me be," and threaten it, "Just watch yourself." I wait just half a minute for the express bus, and when I climb on, I see the bus driver and notice he and I are dressed about alike. Sometimes I watch Ralph the Honeymooner on Nickelodeon with the girls, all of us lying on Jules's bed, since she's the one with the upstairs TV and the double-size bed. Even Professor likes to come in and watch awhile. He won't sit down, because he is too busy for such nonsense—that's what he states—but he laughs till tears line his face at Ralph and especially at the blundering one, Norton, who lives upstairs, him so dege-dege him fit eena di sewer pipe. Then when he's laughing his hardest, Professor walks out like he can't admit to a-want to see the rest, but the girls and I nah proud and watch to the end. I think I may get myself a bus driver's cap and wear that instead of this wool one. Then if I run into Cliff on the street, he won't know me from a stranger.

I get off the bus and walk down the street and am surprised how well I remember my way. As I near the house, my heart pumps fierce and I wonder what am I fearing. Getting closer still, I hear the African drums, and this time the green light overhead have turned into a pinkish color shining in the window, and my heart finally settles down till its beat matches with the drums. I wonder is Joshie in there tapping on his bongos in his deep peace, his teeth raking over the softness of his bottom lip like he is drawing out a burr.

When I shoob the door, it opens directly and I walk in out of the cold and feel a flow of energy that's part of this place. It is only the smoke in the air that I don't like, knowing it soon will burn my eyes till they run with tears. Brother Man comes directly over and greets me, "Hello, Mary Lou."

"Indigo," I say, annoyed by his forgetfulness.

"Indigo," he repeats, but then he hums the words of that old song "Hello, Mary Lou, Goodbye Heart" and chuckles.

"Yeah, yeah," I say, wondering why is it men always got to sweet-talk a woman.

"You friend no wid you tonight?" Brother Man asks, but when I shake my head, he says, "No surprise in that, sister woman. Don' everyone belong here. You one of them that do."

I wonder what is that supposed to mean, but don't have the right style of words to ask him.

He carries my coat to the old brass coat tree for me—attentive as when I fix up like di redbird—and layers it over the others. Frank is here again, just like he said he'd be most of the time. The man must not have a job, or maybe him a professional gambler who's figured a way to make some big money off Brother Man. I wonder is that possible or does Brother Man have everyting figured for his own gain. Frank hands me a cigarette with an arm that bulges with a muscle the size of a mango.

"Henry P's been by looking for you now and again, angel face."

"He lives just around the corner from me. Don't have too far to look."

I have no matches, so he flicks a flame out of a purple plastic lighter and reaches for my cigarette, but I take the lighter and light the smoke myself, then hand his lighter back. Before I know it, I am sitting at the long roulette table, watching the play, and have forgotten the day and the time and everything outside these walls.

I buy twenty dollars of Brother Man's blue chips and shake them in my hand with a sudden rush of nerves and just watch the wheel spin till my heart settles; then I place my first bet. *Tapatapatap* is running behind my thoughts all the while, but I'm not noticing, it's just a background riddim like at the dance hall. When I finally hear it, I realize Brother Man is at his typewriter. After a while he strips the sheet out of the carriage and holds up what he's written, to study it by the pink ceiling light. Then he laughs loud as thunder and blood fills the vein at the side of his neck that's ropey and thick as an umbilicus. I think of Zach, who's got heavy veins on his hand, but know these two men no can be brothers.

"Oh, someone is in trouble," Frank says. "That's what it means when Brother Man types a letter on his machine and gives out his hoot. You don't want such a letter from Brother

Man, Indi girl—one of his 'declarations of dependence,' I call them."

"As long as you pay what you owe, you have no trouble from him." Joshie's words come quiet from his big face, which is always attending the wheel, its flash so opposite to his soft, mumbled self.

Each time Joshie calls for bets and I put my money down on an odd or even or on a square of four numbers, I get a fine delight and don't worry at all if I lose on the spin, just go on and try another time and get that pop of excitement again.

"Look at that devil woman take away my money," Brother Man says as he strolls over to stand behind me and watch me shimmy my chips twice for luck while I think about whether to wager just one or maybe two blue chips and where to place them. He pats me on my shoulder as if we're old friends, him happy with my success. This time I win two chips playing reds at two to one, and I see this sport is easy, there is nothing to it once you get the feel.

"Man smart, but woman smarter," says Frank, taking his line from out of a song I know well nuff, but then he gives Brother Man a wink and I make myself a note to watch my step here. Woman don't seem so smart to me either, not after last night.

"She don't look near as womanly as last time she was here," says the mottle-faced man named Wiley, who I scarce recall. "Why is that, Lady Luck?"

"Better hush your mouth with that kind of coarse talk," says Frank, spouting some steam. "Ain't you heard a thing boht what go on in society today? She sue your ass, talk like that."

"I'm not coming here entertaining anyone but me," I say. I keep on playing, but my luck fades some.

Redheaded Lucille comes in out of the cold. She shakes some snow out of her hair and nods and smiles to everyone from across the room. Here she is, trying to please the lot of them with nods and curtsies, though no one spoken to her yet. She crosses over and sits down next to Frank.

"Hi, doll," he says to her, and puts a hand on hers. "Oooh, Lordy, you're cold as ice."

"Ice cream be nicer," quashie man Wiley says.

"Mmm, ain't it the truth," Lucille says. She takes off her outer wrap and shows I don't know how many flimsy layers undaneath, as if she put on all the summer dresses she's got, to add up to something with enough weight for winter. Makes me want to laugh out loud, the way she dress herself.

I see Lucille's hand searching mongst her flowered fabrics. She is smacking her lips, so I expect she will draw out a lipstick when she finds her pocket, but her hand comes out with a small square snapshot instead. She lays the picture on the green tablecloth beside Frank as if she play a card.

"This here's my grandbaby," she says to Frank, keeping Wiley out of it. "I just got the picture in the mail from my daughter Zelda in Tennessee. It's a little raggedy, coming through the mail." Frank slides a pair of glasses from his breast pocket.

"Well, ain't she a precious doll," he says. Then he lifts his hip up off his seat and pulls out his worn wallet and flips it open to show her a picture that shines through a dull plastic window. "Here's my son and my little daughter. Harry's grown, but my baby's only eight."

"What beautiful children," Lucille says, looking close. "What treasures."

I see a tear run from the corner of her right eye like a leak out of a water pipe. *Jah*, I think, *where we going here?*

Brother Man has his watchful eye on my frowning face. He gets up and goes to the back room and comes out carrying two half-filled cocktail glasses. "Here, friends," he says, handing them to Lucille and Frank. "Now, put them private tings away." With his beard, he points to the photographs. "I'm sure they're fine children all, but not for here. You see"—he motions his chin to each corner of the room—"this place, Brother Man's place, is its own separate country, not part of whatever you have or don't have out there. We want to keep the shade-dem drawn between here and there. We don't need all of that from outside a-come in. Don't need to see a tear in Lucille's eye. If this a place where Lucille going to shed a tear, this place don't be worth a dime." Brother Man milks his stiff beard like a teat. He looks frustrated, as if nobody going to grasp what he mean, but I know and am grateful to him and say in my heart, *Yes, Brother Man, you got that right.*

Lucille and Frank put away their photographs, out of respect for Brother Man, and take his drinks. Then he relaxes and says, "Yeah, mon, see how it go better now with everyone." He takes a close look at me, then walks over to his typewriter and flips on the electricity and listens to the machine's rough purr, but he puts in no paper, just sits and leans his chair back on two legs and rolls himself some ganja smells sweet as sinsemilla and blends that nicer smoke with the tobacco smoke that already is burning my eyes. I go to his desk, give him my coil, and get another pile of chips from him.

I have a strong sense that Brother Man went to that trouble just for me, because of some special kindness he feels. But he's just a fine businessman is all, one who knows how to make his business run cool as that wheel. He gets up and goes over behind Lucille, his back pressing right up against her chair. He takes to doodling his finger across her back like he write a little note there with his fingernail, then lift her hair with his finger-dem and whispers a ting or two close in her ear. She places one last bet, then says some quick good-byes and heads out into the weather.

When I am thirty dollars poorer than first I come in, I know it is time to leave, but I don't regret spending my money this way. Truth is, I am glad to be free of it, as if it had some kind of weight about it that would carry me down, like stones in a drowning man's pocket. I know, too, it is an odd twist what happened with my money tonight. Because I was not concentrating, not giving my full attention to the numbers, which means they don't come up round and full in my mind. So there's a lesson for me in that, for next time.

Old Borotsky steps inside as I am buttoning up to go out.

"Oh, Indigo," he says. "Good evenink. You're not leaving us, are you?" He shivers as if the cold outside still chills him, but begins to unbutton his wine-colored coat.

I nod.

"What a shame, because I've had a talk with your professor. So, sometime I want to tell you about that. A good man, your professor, a mensch, *versteh*? Listening to an old man's story about such a troubled time. But that is his field of study, is it not? Still, a decent man, and one day I am going to tell you a little. Just a little, my friend. That is all one can ever tell of such things. Maybe more than one can tell."

"Another time, then, Mr. Borotsky." *Why does he want to tell me at all?* I wonder. *Why does he want to tell anyone?*

"Abraham," he says. "My given name. Do you know, Indigo, that already I can tell you that Lucille with all the dresses is not in this room, which leaves us, when you go, with an absence of ladies, with no lovely ladies at all. The atmosphere will be incomplete, but so it is with life. We must not seek perfection. Do you know how it is I can say there is no Lucille, without even looking?" He throws both his arms high into the air to show me his vision of Lucille, the big one, tall as a tower.

I shake my head, though I think maybe I can guess.

"The nose," he says, pressing a bent, spotted finger to the tip of it. "Because of the lily of the valley perfume. That fragrance I love. It makes my heart dance. Why? That is my secret, but maybe sometime I am going to tell you, sometime when you would like to know. Maybe I will. Good evenink."

Walking to the bus, I think how Brother Man knew to tell Frank and Lucille to keep their family show 'n' tell outside the door. There's a man who knows his business, which is something I admire. He lets a body know there's a place to go where you can shut the door, keep what's outside the door out and enjoy a bit of what excitement they're selling inside. Mr. Borotsky is just the opposite. He wants to cross over to my world by talking with Professor. Can't believe he went ahead and did that, and now he wants to carry his news to me like he's offering a basket of ripe papaya.

After I get off my bus—me and the bus driver looking like kinfolk dressed up about the same—the sidewalk takes me right into the path of that preacher, Mr. Davis, in his fine navy wool coat. He knows me even in my busman's clothes. "Where are you off to on this good evening, sister?" he asks me, all pretty in his speech like him a character out of a tale.

"Doing the Lord's work," I say, slick as the wolf cajoling Little Red Riding Hood from undaneath Grandma's bedsheets, and I hurry on, don't give him the time of day. I wonder am I looking to be struck by lightning. I turn back toward him and shout out, "My cross-the-hall neighbor a-come for supper, Father." Lord, I make that one up in a flash. "Got to hurry home and make him a fine cake."

"First better give him a plate of beans," he launches back, and I take that to be his lesson about what's best for nourishing a man, body and soul. Beans before cake. Work before play. I think of Bro Anansi and the story they always tell about him and his hunger and say it come straight from Africa, but who knows truly about dem tings. Bredda Anansi is the spider who also is like a man and sometimes showing all the foolish traits a man can have. Anansi wants to look like the big man at him mada-in-law's funeral, so him say he'll not eat but keep a fast till the eighth day after the burying. Then, on the fourth day, when Anansi's stomach is clean as a brass bowl, him find some beans a-heat over a fire and try to gobble them down on the sly, but the other animal-dem come tru the clearing and Anansi must quick-quick hide di beans or be shamed. So that likkle spider pour alla them beans into his hat hot-hot and steaming and set his hat on his head with the burning beans inside. Him hop and holler from the beans in the hat, and them beans scorch the hair right off the head. And that is why Anansi spider him bald till this day.

I wonder where did I pick up that old tale of a man's foolish pride. I think maybe it come from Papa, who of anyone I know as a child could best tell a story. I see him hopping and hooting like Anansi, making all us children roll with laughter, before he set his own hat on his bald-as-a-bissy-nut head and dance out the door for who knows where. Or maybe it was just Miss Lu or Mas Ron tell us the story on the Saturday-afternoon TV. *Ring Ding,* they en call it, and all of us children come in regular as the tide to watch.

When I get back to my room, I open my dunsa drawer and take from the scattered bills twenty dollars more to put into my handbag, thinking later I may go back out to the grocery for some tings. I take off my wool cap and begin to pull off my trousers that smell of ganja and tobacco, but the thought of Cliff and what chance I took last night stops me all of a sudden, and I pull back on the pants and lay down on my bed without zipping the zipper, and lay there just running my hand over my belly. A weight passes into my eyelids and is too great to fight, so I let myself slide into a strong sleep.

When I sleep, a crazy thing happens. I dream my own memory of the day Papa showed up full of talk and joy and told us he had rented a better house for Mama and us three children in a finer part of the town, away from Trenchtown with all its dangers. All of us were jumping with merriment. I wondered would this nice house be enough to keep Papa home with us, or would he keep up his wandering ways. Later that afternoon, he en go out in the djew rain to the house he got for us and took only me, the oldest, to help him ready it, because I was a good worker even then and not afraid of the weather. I remember that day, remember how I felt so blessed to be with him, how I loved his laughing and the jokes he made, caring more for that than for the house itself.

Me and Papa we sweep and scrub all tru di morning, till we get hungry as Anansi on the fourth day. In the cabin, there is nothing to eat but a single can of beans, and I wonder will Papa share it with me—since I am mighty hungry. He wants to build a fire, but little is dry enough to burn. We find a few half-dry sticks sheltered under larger branches and make a smoky fire outside the house. Papa removes the paper label and sets the can directly on the fire for a while. The fire is tiny and soon burns out, but we are too hungry to make a search for something more to burn. Papa offers the can of beans to me. "You first, daughter," he says, and my heart grows full with his tenderness in letting me have the first meal. Because we have no utensil to lift out the beans, I have to use a blade I make holding together three peeled green sticks, but I don't mind, because the sipple wood seems clean. I eat some beans, but they are cold and the sauce watery. I eat nearly half the can anyway, because Papa is sharing them with me and I am hungry as John Crow. But hungry as I am, they are not good to eat, and I make faces while Papa watches me. When I hand back the can, I say, "They're cold, Dada." He takes the sticks and stirs what is left in the can and puts a little pile of beans into his mouth. "Not mine," he says, and laughs with all his body, and I see how he has offered me the cold beans from on top of the can and thinks it funny that he saved the warm ones for himself. I laugh at his joke, but my heart shrivels and the rest of my day's got more chill than an English winter.

I wake later in the evening and am glad to be out of that dream. I lie in bed and see Papa's one silver can of beans, the label torn off, the raised rings circling it. Brother Man's spinning wheel appears, and his hands reach out drinks to Lucille and Frank, stopping their talk of babies and grandbabies, easing my misery. That morning dream of Louisa in the hard ground comes back to me. Jah! What a painful thing. Alla that hurt wants to overtake me, bring me the old thoughts of my baby's cheeks and hair, most of all her smile and bright, bright voice. I hear her voice in my head, saying, "Listen, Mama," and the ache wants to kill me. Then I can't hear her voice, can't find it when I search, and that wants to kill me worse. I shake off the pain, play stubborn with it. I have nothing in me of Mr. Borotsky—*Abraham*—who wants to recall and recite his fearful tales.

Out my bedroom window, past the neighboring buildings, just a thin crust of blood red sunlight lies across the broken bits of horizon I can see between the buildings. Too late now to go out on the street alone to do my shopping—I'd just tempt whoever's out there hungry to steal my groceries out of my arms on my way home.

I am reading my *Reader's Digest* at the dining table when a knock comes, and I open the door to find Zach. Standing in the door frame, he seems taller than when I last saw him. I'm not in an arguing mood for once, so I invite him in for a cup of coffee. A thought scoots past me fast as a hare that says, *Now I'll be pushing this one away, too, just like the cousin,* but I let him come in anyway. I wonder does he know what Cliff got just for knocking on this door, and I recall Cliff's words about taking my pleasure where I can while he's away and wonder did he intend to pass me on to this shy cousin with the motherly eyes.

Zach sits down, but he is stiff and uneasy with himself. He lays his hands on the table, one atop the other. "I went to the church down the road last Sunday," he says, and his words fit with his pious look. "That preacher is as good as any I've heard. Do you know him?"

Pastor Davis. Seems he don't stay out of my life for long. I nod. "All I ever hear from the ladies of that Baptist church is how their preacher is so fine and comely a man, pity he don't find a wife." The radiator is making noises like a sick stomach.

They fight with Zach's words as it pumps out heat. I'd rather my eyes burn from Brother Man's smoke than from this parchy air.

"I don't know about that part," he says. "He was preaching about God's light come into your life, which we feel as joy and reverence." He turns his eyes to me. They are big and white, with a center so rich a brown it looks like a dark cherry.

"Not much light shine here in winter."

He hums me a little tune, self-consciously. *This little light of mine . . . I'm gonna let it shine. . . .* "You know that song, Indigo? That's the light they're talking about, sister. Inner light."

"God's not been around here much lately, old man."

He frowns. "Why you call me that?"

"Your mind's so full of deep thoughts, not like young men I know."

He nods, thoughtful now.

"I had a dream right from the Devil this morning," I tell him. "Sent right from him to me, Express Mail to Indigo Rosemartin."

Interest crosses with worry in Zach's face. "What made your dream the Devil's doing?"

"It came just to cause me pain, to give hurt, like a child that pinch you just to hear you scream."

"What dream give you such pain, woman?" He reaches up and lays his warm hand across mine on the table. I see how this man relaxes when he can give counsel, but I don't mind. Don't mind nothing about him this moment.

I turn my chair so I am sideways to him and move my hand to my lap. "You know about my Louisa?" I ask him, figuring whatever Cliff knows of me, this cousin of his likely to know, too.

I glance his way and see him nod. Seems he's trying to hold all of me with his eyes.

"I dreamt my Louisa was buried alive in the cold ground. She was under the ground alive, struggling with no air and no light and no loving." I glance over to Zach and see him shake his head at me. His face takes so stern a look I have the thought he's angry.

"Louisa's with Jesus," he says. "She's not in darkness." He gets up, and I think he may come around behind me and kiss my neck and give me some loving to tease away the pain, in his cousin's way. But he walks across to the window and parts the white curtains and looks down at the lamp-lit street.

I bring my coffee cup to my lips, but a shiver goes through my hand and I slosh the coffee down the front of my shirt. Its heat makes me jump to my feet, and another wave of coffee leaves the cup and catches my blouse. "Aiiii! Look how I'm clumsy. Spill on a white blouse, too."

He turns and sees what I have done and smiles his pity. I go into the bathroom and wet a cloth with cold water and walk back in, soaking the spots of coffee until the lace of my white brassiere shows through and I am looking down at one nipple stand up from the cold.

"You better put on a dry one and soak that in the sink," Zach says, "before you catch cold."

"Yes, Mama," I say, and go off to my room. Still I can't keep it out of my mind that Zach will follow me in and put his hands on my shoulders just as my blouse is coming off, so I am careful to push shut the door till I hear the metal piece click into place. When I go back out into the living room, Zach hasn't moved from the window. I can barely see his face in the low light. What a gloomy thing winter is.

"This chair here's got a little wobble, Indigo," he says to me. "I'm going to fix it for you when I get the tools."

Suddenly I can bear his visit no more, so I make an excuse of needing to fix supper so I can send him off. When he goes, I sit awhile in the stiff chair across from the wobbly one he's vacated and feel the last light ease out of the room. My mind goes again to what I chanced with Cliff, and I lay my hands on my belly. I can have no baby now. If I am pregnant, I believe I might take my own life. Zach and Preacher Davis would find plenty of sorrow and affliction in that act, but not me. I would set like the winter sun and become like dark night. I find no sadness in that. The thought of flowers in the spring gives me more grief. They jump up eager from the earth and flash their colors and lift your spirits till you think to dance. You spin around one time and they are gone. Life is special made for breaking the heart. The child would be born in November. In America, that is Thanksgiving month, which sends you down the dark chute into winter. Louisa's birthday was in May, the first month of real springtime in this new world.

I vow I'd take my life if a child's coming, but fear jumps in me and makes the sweat wet my brow.

Twelve

Overnight, we go back into the freeze. Snow streaks through the light of the moon, and the weather seems more like it's meant to this time of year. By morning, every tree branch and twig carries a coat of snow, and I have to admit the world looks like a fairyland. Winter's beauty and its roughness no longer surprise me, and knowing that makes me count the months and add up that in the spring it will be two years I have been in this odd part of the world where half the year you stay so bundled up you forget the look of your own flesh under all that layering.

I wrap myself against the cold to wait for my bus back to the Silvers'. The bus comes late, leaving me to worry about Clair getting off to school. I got to count on the big girls, I guess. Finally, the bus rolls through the slush into its spot alongside the curb. My breath clouds the air as I step inside. When I get to the Silvers', the girls are dashing out in a group, and I see it's hurting Clair to have her sisters hurry her along and not allow her time to stop and be with me a little. Inside, alone but for Tennyson, I've got to stomp each foot a dozen times before that soft snow gives up its grip on my boots.

By afternoon, snow is falling again as if it wants to make up for the two unnatural weeks of warmth we had and hide the house up to the roof. The girls tumble in, and Clair talks with a dance in her voice about sledding in the park with her friend Franny, each on a spinning saucer that puts the smooth glide of Brother Man's roulette wheel in front of my eyes. I put my face to the strip of glass beside the front door and watch the snow come down and cover everything, and I am glad to see the whole world buried before my eyes.

The big snowfall shuts the schools and keeps the girls home the next day. The older two are jittery, and I have to summon Professor's warning in order to muster patience with them. Only after some time pass do I understand there's something particular that's itching at them.

"The lawyer's really coming today, on our snow day?" Julie questions Jill. "That's not fair. It's our day off."

"Not till this afternoon, till after school hours," says Jill.

"So what," Julie says. "He's still coming, isn't he?"

"What's a lawyer?" Clair wants to know.

"A giant asshole that swallows you up in his big butt," says Julie.

Louisa's voice comes into my head, saying, *That's nasty*. "Jules, watch your mouth," I snap and I am shaken to feel these girls and my own together in this room.

"What is it?" Clair presses. "You tell me, Indi. They won't."

"Someone your mother's sending over to talk to you girls."

"He taught my Sunday school class in fifth grade. I hate this," Jill says, her voice filling with the embarrassment she anticipates.

"Why is it bad?" Clair whines. "I don't get it."

"When does she send us anything good?" Jules complains.

It's a long day being around these children. By midafternoon, my eyes look out at the red sun and see it already starting to tuck in for the night. All three of them mark time in the front hall.

"When he comes, tell him I'm sleeping," Julie wheedles me. "Tell him I have pneumonia from going out in the cold. I think I really might. I don't feel well."

"Clair," Jill says. "Your show is on. *Party of Five.* It's already started."

"Oh," Clair frets, torn because she loves that show and can't ever miss it. "Do you think he'll really come? Call me if he gets here, okay, Jill?" Clair races up the stairs and we hear her show booming up above. The furnace fan springs on and blows hot air into the living room. Within minutes, the doorbell rings.

Julie starts with her nervous faces, and Jill says, "I'll get it," her voice tough as shoe leather like it gets every once in a while. Maybe because Julie's feeling babyish, Jill's got to be the big sister. Still, she surprises me.

I follow along like duppy man to keep my eye on tings. Julie disappears into the dining room.

"Mr. Goldfarb." Jill greets the man at the door, her voice cool as the outside air. The blue scarf he unwinds from around his neck must measure a city block. I wonder, when he finish unwinding will his head fall off. He kicks the packed snow off his shoes and runs a hand up over his head, which has a path of baldness down the center. "Come in," says Jill. "You can sit in the living room. I'll get my sister."

"Won't you get both the girls?" he asks, hurriedly wiping his boots on the brown mat inside the door. "Your mother said there are three of you lovely girls." Mr. Goldfarb's glasses fog from the warm air. He wipes them on a hankie and sets them back on his nose so crooked I want to laugh.

"You want Clair to come down?" Jill asks, disbelieving. "Clair is nine. You want her here?"

"Well, whatever you think, Jill. I'll defer to you. I know you're a girl of uncommon good sense."

I guess he's remembering how smart Jill was in that Sunday school class, since Jill's going to shine in any class once she gets up nerve enough to speak. Still, the mood she's in, Jill's going to hate this lawyer's licky-licky way of talking.

He turns to me and says, "Nice and warm in here, compared to outside, Miss . . . ?"

"Rosemartin. Indigo Rosemartin."

Jill's gone off to coax Julie, who's still hiding in the dining room, maybe behind the curtains like the likkle ones do.

"Sit down, Mr. Goldfarb," I say. "Dem girls be back shortly."

They come in and perch on the two chairs, leave Mr. Goldfarb setting alone on the long couch and me standing back of the pickney, beside Professor's desk. The lawyer gives me an uneasy look that says he's waiting for me to leave, but I just smile back.

He sighs. "Now, girls," he says, "your mother wanted me to come talk with you because I'm her lawyer, and her friend, and she's very concerned you're not getting her side of the story, since you're living under your father's roof and you're"—there that grown man stops and giggles—"under his influence, so to speak. Even though you're extremely bright girls, you're likely to see things from his point of view. It's only natural, right?"

I would have thought Mrs. Silver would hire a more clever variety of lawyer than this Goldfarb.

He squints and giggles again and mutters, "Oh, gee, maybe we should have had this meeting somewhere else. But here we are, right here, so at any rate, it's something like propaganda—even if it's accidental—that's what your mother's worried about. She doesn't want you girls brainwashed. Do you see what I mean? Of course, it's so, well, I—" He stops as if his supply of words cut off like air from a slashed hose.

I want to laugh, but my eyes go to Jill and I see that girl's color rising and know this idiot lawyer has got her anger boiling. Still, her eyes are cold as ice.

"No, I don't see," she says.

"Well, your mother loves you—of course—and she's worried about you. Do you see how that—?" He shakes his head. I don't think Mr. Goldfarb ever tried talking to a teenager before.

Jules works her lips and wriggles like a toddler. Her pale face says she might be set to vomit.

Jill opens her mouth, but it takes a minute before the ice inside her thaws enough and the boiling simmers down sufficient to let her words come. "That's why you're here?" she jooks him. "Not about the divorce? Not about custody or anything with the law? You're here to tell us who we're supposed to listen to? Who we're supposed to love?"

Mr. GeeWhiz lifts his pinky finger to the middle of his bald strip and digs away at one spot in a way to make you think he's got a tick he's got to dislodge with his nail. "No," he says, and shakes his head. "I would never . . . not who you're supposed to love, Jill. I know you're an altogether loving and conscientious girl—I know that, from being your instructor—remember what a fine student you were?—but just hoping you'll give your mother your ear, your attention, don't write her off and listen only to your dad. Oh, I know he's Daddy, okay, and he's taking care of you, and of course you love him, of course you do. But your mother's been sick, girls, so have some compassion for her like the Torah teaches, and give her a chance. That's all—just give her a little of your devotion and attention."

Jill stands up and takes so deep and slow a breath I think her heart must be firing like a machine gun. "What do you know about us?" she says, getting ready to shout now. "What do you know about our family?"

Mr. G picks up his hat, and you can see he's sorry he said he'd do this job and he feels twitchy as can be in Professor's house. I'm happy for that, thinking, *Don't it serve you right, foolish man, coming here thinking you're some angel of mercy, spouting the Bible. Lord, these girls don't need you setting them straight—you can't even set straight your own eyeglasses.*

"Of course," he says. "You just think about it, girls, if you care to." He turns to Julie, who's squirming, where Jill's looking like I might have to hold her back from strangling that man. "Can you just think about it a little, Julie, for your mother's sake?"

"Okay. I guess," Julie whines. "Just don't tell people our business, okay? Especially at the temple. Don't tell everybody about all this stuff."

Mr. Goldfarb nods and smiles faintly. "I'm sorry I didn't meet the youngest child," he says. "She must be out playing."

"You think so?" I ask. "Out after dark in alla that snow? You think that's how we take care of a child here—me and Professor?"

The man giggles and says, "Oh, surely not."

"What time is it?" Julie asks. "Daddy's coming home at eight."

Jill whispers in my ear, "I lied to Clair."

Mr. Goldfarb looks at his watch. "I should be going, girls, and Miss Rose . . ."—he nods to me like I'm someone important here—"a pleasure to meet you all—and to see you again, Jill."

I show him to the door while the girls stay in the living room. "How can you look at your face in the mirror?" I say, calm and whispered, not wanting the girls to hear. "You've got some little bit of nerve. You and Mrs. Silver." He reaches up and fixes his glasses all of a sudden and grimaces.

"Good-bye," I say, and practically shoob him out into a blast of wind.

Suddenly Julie is on her feet, peering out the hall window, watching Mr. Goldfarb whip his coat around him and sidle into his car. Jules is sticking her tongue out like a six-year-old, and Jill is stretched full out on the couch in the living room like she's gone into a faint. "What a turd, what an asshole," Julie shouts. "I can't believe he came here. If he talks to people about our family, I'm gonna sue him in court." She turns and looks at Jill. "You really gave it to him."

Jill shakes her head. "Jerk," she says.

"Putz," says Julie as Clair hurries down the stairs with the puppy in her arms. "Gold fart."

"*Party of Five* is over." Clair looks around, then sits down on the floor and squeezes the dog to her chest.

"He's gone," Julie says. "Jill told him off."

"Gone already?" Clair asks. "Did you call him a putz, Jill? Out loud?" Her eyes fly open. "Wasn't he nice? Why did Mommy send him?" The dog squirms out of her lap and goes to lie down alongside the front door, where the cool air seeps through.

Clair jumps up and turns to me. "Did Jill call him a putz?"

"Shut up, Clair," Jill says.

"Stop with that word," I say. "I don't even know what it means."

"Like schmuck, or prick," Julie tells me.

Jill lies cradling her stomach like she's ill and exhausted. "What's the matter with you, Jill?" I ask. "You sick now you tru a-be faastie?"

"When's Daddy coming home?" Clair asks. She turns to Julie. "Did Jill call the lawyer a putz? Maybe he'll tell my friends at Sunday school that she said that."

Jill jumps to her feet, shouting. "Shut up, Clair. I didn't call him names. I'm not two years old."

"Yeah, well, sometimes you act like a baby," Clair taunts. "That's what Mommy always says. 'Jilly thinks she's so sophisticated, but she acts like a two-year-old baby.' "

Jill grabs Clair by the forearm and squeezes her arm and shakes it, then drops it like a hot poker. "God, I could kill you," she says.

Clair whirls toward me, her victory won, and shouts, "Did

you hear her, Indi? Did you hear what she said? I'm telling Daddy."

"I didn't mean it that way," Jill shouts. "I meant, you're so . . . breakable. Your bones are just like sticks. I could break your arm."

"Don't say that," Clair yells out, as if in pain.

"That's enough, you two girls," I quiet them. "Professor'll be home soon. Just settle down. Let him get some peace when he comes."

"He always gets peace," Julie grumbles. "We stay here with the asshole lawyer or have to go visit Mommy and see the gross place she's living, while he's out having a good time somewhere, probably with some lady we don't even know."

"Hush," I say, "Professor's just working, and driving home is slow and dangerous with all this snow and ice," but I don't blame this child for her complaining.

"Probably we'll have to go live with her, and he won't even stop it. He won't even care," Julie whines.

"Are we going to live with Mommy?" Clair asks. "Is that what the lawyer said?" She looks at me, looks at Jill, looks at Julie.

Jill shakes her head and takes her lip between her teeth. "No."

When Professor comes home, looking weary, he gives each of the girls a peck and goes right up to his study, flicks on the light. I see all the electricity sparking still in the girls, but they keep it from him.

I follow him upstairs and say, "Good evening, Professor. Do you want some hot tea?"

He shakes his head. "The day go okay, Indigo?"

"A visitor come."

"Oh," he says. "Right, I forgot. The lawyer."

"Lawyer and teacher."

"How was that? The girls handle it okay?"

"Well enough, considering."

"It's all for show. She doesn't want those kids. There's nothing to worry about."

"Nice if you tell that to those frightened girls, then."

I go to my room, thinking those girls don't get free of their mada, whichever way they turn. Jill can draw up fierce as a lion and pitch poor Mr. Goldfarb out the house, but she don't rid herself of Mrs. Silver and the ratchet that woman twist in the heart. Jules can whine and complain all the day, or throw a fit, don't nothing going to come of it.

Saturday belongs to me, and I'm grateful for some rest, but I wake in bed Sunday with a black feeling lying across me heavy as a horse. Back home, Sunday was church day, for me, for the family and most of the town. But I no wish to see Preacher Davis at his Baptist church or to find a Methodist church like that back home. So what me left with is another hole in my heart. So many holes there, feels like a moth make 'im lunch fran me. I have a list of house chores to do, and so I start in sweep the floor and then wash it and press a few clothes, but the passing of time and the steadiness of work do nothing to light up this dark. I ponder a-go to Brother Man place for a beenie bit but don't that be a foolish waste of a day—as bad as Bertha's soap operas—so I put the thought out of my mind. The gloom is stubborn, though, in how it clings to me. I can't rouse myself to any of what chores are left. I pace like something caged, then sit in the chair, fidgety and useless, until a knock rumbles the door.

"Cho!" *Who's that going to be?* I complain, but at least whoever it is a-go lift me to my feet.

I open the door and find a young ting who just move in—two, could be tree weeks past—into the flat below. She just a smiley face and a cloud of wiry hair to me plus some clanging pots and clomping feet I hear time to time neet my floor. She smiles so sweet you think she never en have one bad day in her young life. "I'm Terry," she says, and giggles a little like young people do and shakes that hair that need some braid.

"Indigo," I say.

"I know," she says, and giggles again like this supposed to be some kind of achievement that she know my name. "Oh. I think this is for you." She puts out her hand with an envelope. A bill, I guess, that went astray, something else I don't need. The girl gives a little wave and heads down the stairs. "Nice meeting you," she calls back, and I wonder at how the Lord make the young so fetching and foolish all at one time.

This here not a bill. The address is penned by hand. *Oh, Jesus. Oh, Jesus Lord.* I got to sit. This is from Vincent, my brother. I know his careful schoolboy writing and the pretty blue ink pen Papa give Mama. I set down that envelope like a hot stone, put it on the table beside my armchair, the one that holds the black phone, then I jump up to gain some distance from it.

I don't need this now. No, not in any way I can figure do I need this now.

Vincent's like a hot wire run to Mama. Me don' be afraid of him for him, just for how him carry me to Mama. She's the one. Jah, she is, truly. She's the one twist my heart. I circle round, circle round, circle round, then circle back the other way. Finally, I lift Vincent's letter from where I drop it on the table. Can't feel worse than now. Might as well open it. Get it over wid. Get it done fast, like Professor say you rip off di Band-Aid. Inside, the letter is typed, so I know Vincent go to the library in Kingston to do it. I see his slim, fidgety figure, a boy's shape still when last I beside him, and see the coffee-colored darkness of his skin, his always deeper and finer than my own. His letter tells me, "Hello Indigo" and "How are you sister?" and then tells me that he is coming to America for some kind of work, so he will visit me and see how I am, and maybe I can show him the sights of Chicago that he hear about since him a boy. He wonders can I show him the place where Al Capone conduct his business. He must think those mobsters still alive and still fussing and fighting boht the city. I think of Vincent as a boy hiding out behind the corner of the house, hanging on to the edge while peeking round it, playing cops and robbers with his friends. Maybe that small boy's heart still pump in this grown man who writes me a nice, polite letter on a typewriter. I read on to where Vincent tells me he's to arrive in April. Lord, he's put a date on it, like a real thing with a set plan in back of it. I wonder can I write him back and get him to change his mind. I a-go tell him Al Capone is long gone and Chicago is not the high-living place he thinks and April can be a cold, disheartening month in the North. But when I think about what he would feel to get a letter like that when he is hungering to come to America, I know I must let his plan stand. Don't no one get free of what they left behind, not those girls, not Indigo.

I think again about Brother Man's, because I have a pretty good idea I could slip free of all this pain and worry if I go there even an hour, maybe two. And don't it be more wasteful to spend the day in gloom than to do what might ease it, so I put on those same drab-as-winter man's clothes I wore last visit and walk out into the cold, and Lord, don't the slap of cold air across my face relieve me some.

When I get to Brother Man's and enter that room patchy with smoke, I don't waste much time with greetings, because I am here for a purpose and not to eat up my hours. Brother Man senses my mood, on account of that deep gift he has, and lets me move right to the roulette table without delaying me even by a word.

I am still in a bad place, and it's terrible enough it frightens me, because I can't see how it will take its drowning hold off me and let me float up to where there's some clear air. I start out making my bets. I play a few dollars' worth of chips at two for one and lose all of what I put down. Then I think maybe I take too little chance here, so I pile up a few more chips on my bets, keeping those same, easy odds, but still luck is against me. Soon I get an idea in my head that I've got to risk a little something more to win something—like there's some kind of Anansi lesson in this about putting forth your whole heart or your whole effort—so I go ahead and sample eight or nine numbers in my head, looking them over, touching them like gemstones I'm selecting for a fine brooch, then I pick the number eighteen and lay down four dollars on that one number with thirty-five-to-one odds against me. And Lord, if I don't hit it and get a whole pot of money and prove something to myself about what a person's got to give to get something back from this game. The miracle is that all of my mind is concentrated now on the next bet I'm going to place and my pain is wiped as clean as the board Joshie sweeps free of chips.

Brother Man comes over and lays his arm across my shoulders. "I'm so happy you find us to your liking, Indigo. I want to see more of you here, make you part of our family."

I give him a smile of thanks for his good medicine, though today, with Vincent's letter in my mind, I don't need to hear his talk about family.

When I am set to leave and feeling lifted high as the sky, Henry P senses my mood and steps over beside me. "Come, Indigo. Now you come out with me, have a little bite to eat at a restaurant."

"You don't worry for Toshie home alone without you?"

"Him a big bad hunting dog, sister. Plenty tough all on his own."

"All right, mon. Tonight you win me over."

Henry P gets my coat and helps me into it. My mood's so bright, I take down my hair and shake it out.

"Ooh-ee," says that half-Indian, half-hillbilly Curtis, a man built like a jailhouse wall. "Look how pretty, Miss Indigo, with your hair let down. Y'all ought to wear it that way all the time."

"Maybe I do, come future."

"Mind if I join y'all out to the restaurant?"

"Fine. No kya," Henry P says.

As we three are leaving, here come Mr. Borotsky up beside me. "Hello, Indigo."

"Mr. Borotsky, sir," I say, "I don't even know you here tonight. Where you hide yourself?"

He pushes his lips into a pout and shakes his head. "Who says I'm hiding? All evenink, I'm just where I always am, Indigo, but you have your head in the clouds tonight and can't see out. Still, I keep my eye on you, watch what happens to you, and see a great deal."

I shrug, not needing to hear an old man's riddle now, when my spirit's found a fine riddim.

"You won a lot of money tonight?" he asks.

"Very lucky this night."

"Better you should lose," he says. "Better you should lose the first three times you visit Brother Man. But you are off now to celebrate?"

"Yes, mon, Mr. Borotsky."

When we leave, I am glad for the clear air. Only thing in Brother Man's I can't stand is the burning smoke that clouds his air.

In the Red Dog restaurant, we arrange ourselves in a booth in the corner, order drinks from a fat young woman who floats over the linoleum in some kind of slippers, holds her order pad right to her nose.

"Child must be half-blind," Curtis says as she slides away.

"Hmm," mumbles Henry P. "Indi here had her eyes wide-open tonight at the Brother's. Got the best of the house, I'd say. Making you real happy, sister woman."

"Brother Man bless me tonight."

"Got to watch that man's blessing," says Henry P, holding up his pointing finger.

I feel curious about Brother Man. Truly, 'im the one wid di

sharp eye. Henry P's hand lays on the table beside his glass. I pat it a few times to catch his attention. "What you know of that bredda?" I ask.

"Him a hurt and lonesome man, and you mus' be careful you no tread on him toe."

"Son of a bitch, I say," adds Curtis.

"All of it coming from what galls him," Henry P says, sipping his ale, brow pulled tight.

"I reckon that, too," says Curtis, and chugs some liquor.

"His American wife, Teisha, up and left him for another bredda from the islands, not from Jam-dung, this one a Haitian businessman. All of that make for a powerful meanness in him."

"You know her?"

Curtis says, "That's just what Miss Lucy says about him. All of it is the Lord's truth. Bet your life on that."

"You know the man, then," I say, "so you no need fear him. You know Teisha?"

"Understanding don't dull an arrow," Henry P says, and shakes his head at me.

"You think about that, girl," says Curtis.

"All you big men so fearful," I say.

"Maybe," says Henry P, "but best don't be like the rat. . . . You fire him tail, him tink a cool breeze."

"Pff," I snort. No one need take me for a fool. "You know the woman you say break his heart?"

"Teisha?" Curtis asks.

"What kind of name?" I ask.

Both of them shrug.

"Teisha from here," says Henry P. "Used to come in long time ago. Very sexy woman, with the spike high heel-dem, plenty jewelry, plenty perfume."

"Broke that man's heart," Curtis says. "And whipped up a hell of a fury in him." He stands up. "Got to go home to my lady," he says. "It was a pleasure, y'all." He lays a couple dollars down on the table. "That should take care of mine."

"We all best go," Henry P says. "Me best feed Toshie."

"Teisha," I say, shake my head. "What kind of lagga head name that?"

Curtis can walk home from there. Me and Henry P catch the bus, get off at our stop, and he walks me near to my steps, says, "Good night, Indigo." The sirens that come so regular up and down this street drown out my good night to him.

Thirteen

Professor's fiftieth birthday will be coming up in May. Jill already got Professor a special briefcase she saved her money for. I'm in the laundry room off the kitchen, doing my ironing, when Clair comes in.

"Indi, how can I get some money?" she asks me as she makes herself comfortable on the sagging yellow-striped sofa, her eyes focused out the window, where the sun is lowering through a white sky. "I want to buy Daddy a fountain pen."

I keep my iron moving over the blue sheet, erasing the wrinkles. I know there's still a pile of green bills in my drawer at home, less than before but still plentiful. "Better get you a little job."

"What job can I get?"

"Didn't Mrs. Grinwald say she'd hire you to walk that big liver-spotted dog of hers? Her boys can't rely on to do a thing."

"If it was summer, I'd sell lemonade. That would be better." Clair looks directly at me as if she'll milk some bright idea out from my eyes.

"Seem like summer to you?" I ask, and pull a pillowcase onto the board. I like the way the wrinkles disappear beneath my heat.

"Oh! Maybe hot chocolate."

"How you plan to keep it hot all day while you wait for your customers to come by?"

"I don't know. Can't you think of an idea, Indi?" Clair flops onto the sofa on her belly and digs her toes into the pillows.

"Can't solve all your problems, Clair. I'm not a magician." I feel Brother Man's cool plastic chips in my hand and wonder am I telling this child the truth.

Clair goes out and Tennyson comes in and starts circling the way he does when he look for his spot to settle. As he walks, his chest begins heaving, and I see he is getting ready to vomit. I cluck at him and try to draw him out of the room and into the kitchen, where the floor is linoleum, but he stops and stands steady like a statue, then goes ahead and vomits on the wood floor beside my ironing board, right up against my green plastic basket full of clean linens. Nothing comes up from his stomach but some hugly yellow slime, so I think his small belly must be empty. Something just irritate it. He keeps his head down and trudges onto the brown and white checkerboard rug, trailing a slick string from the mouth. I try to shoo him off the rug just in case, but he won't budge and starts heaving again as he drifts, head down, from square to square. Finally he spills another puddle of the yellow slime. "Jeesam! Now I mus' clean the rug. As if I no have drudgery enough widoht you."

Cleaning the floor and then the rug busies me for a half hour. The puddle won't clean up, because it is nothing solid, but not a liquid, either, that I can sop with a sponge. I might as well be taking up a dozen rotten egg whites.

I get down on my knees, trying to coax the mess into a box, using a stiff piece of blue cardboard from a Tampax box one of the girls tro away. My knees remember the rough wood flooring of wi house in Ja. Louisa's been eating all tru the morning, stuffing herself on more food than what we can afford to spend on one small pickney and ignoring my words when I tell her to leave off devouring everything like a likkle pig. I threaten to put all the banana and bread on top of Mama's tin bread box, which is over the cupboard and out of reach of the pickney.

"Me eat all me want, Mama," she says to me. "Granmada say there's always nuff for me to fill me belly."

"That belly look like a balloon ripe to pop," I say. "You jus' tro away good food Jah make for wi nourishment."

"Granmada say I must never go wanting."

"How you wanting?" I ask. And I add, "Let Granmada wash dishes down di hotel till the skin of her finger-dem look like waves on the sea."

Sometime after that, Louisa starts vomiting, first giving back all the bread and banana, then cleaning her stomach of its fluid, emptying everyting onto the floor like an afterbirth or some other hugly ting. I give her a full plate of "see what I told you"s as I clean her mess. She runs off crying from my words, and maybe from the vomiting, too, which always scared her, as if her inside organs were coming out before her eyes.

Tennyson's mess takes me so long cleaning that I have no time to finish my ironing but must get on with thinking about dinner. I go on out to the kitchen and pull some green beans and pork chops and salad out of the refrigerator and rinse all of it in the strainer. Then I wander into the hall and take a stroll around the house, just needing to stall a half minute before I set in working on the next job.

Jill is tucked away in the corner of the den, perched at the end of the long window seat. She is using the last bit of light from the windows to work on some blue-flowered cloth.

"What you doing there, Jill?" I stand across the room from her, in the doorway.

"I have to fix this dress."

"That dress is for Mary Shetland's party tonight? You going with that boy Keith again?"

Jill nods and starts to tear out some stitching.

"Looks like you're tearing it, not fixing it."

Jill's lip quivers like she's set to cry. "It's not working."

I go over and take the cloth out of her hands and hold it up to look at what she's done. She is stitching a line of navy-blue braid along the neckline, but the braid makes a crooked and lumpy line. "Why are you ruining this dress? Where did you get this dress, Jill? I haven't seen this dress before."

"My mother bought it. She gave it to me a week ago last Saturday, when we went out for lunch."

"This is a nice dress. Why do you want to ruin it?"

"It's cut too low. I have to wear it because I promised her I would. But it's cut too low."

"Stand up a minute." I hold the dress to her shoulders, noticing that it smells from the same perfume as everything that comes from her mother's closet. "Now, why you say this dress is low cut? Julie would wear this dress in a heartbeat and be proud of it. Why can't you, Jill?" I hand her back her work. "Go try on this dress for me. You come find me in the kitchen when you got it on."

Jill comes into the sharp light of the kitchen and stands in front of me, her hands in back of her. The dress has a scoop neck and long sleeves, with a little balloon puffing the fabric at the top of each sleeve. It's nice fitted around the bust, then it swings out like a bell and falls to just above her knees.

I rinse my hands and dry them on a rag so I can fuss with the dress if I need to. "This dress is darling on you, Jill. Getting you that dress might be the ongle nice ting your mother do for you this entire year. Why you want to ruin it?"

Jill starts to worry her mouth a little. "It's not too low cut?"

"You got a bust, Jill, but not that big a deal. This dress is fine. Your mother know a ting or two about party dress-dem. When she's not so sick, she go to plenty of party."

"Now she doesn't go anywhere."

"So what? So you stay home, too? Is that how you fix everything? Stick yourself in the closet?" I want to tell Jill she's a lagga head fool, but I stop myself. "All right, Jill," I say. "Go get yourself ready now. By the time you're done fussing with your hair and makeup, Professor will be home and dinner on the table."

Jill nods.

"You look pretty as a picture. You gwan to jump and spin till di sun come up."

Jill goes off seeming a little steadier. She is in her room, dressing, and I am moving about the kitchen, wondering can she get those red webs out of her eyes before she has to go. I wish I bought some Visine at the drugstore last time Tennyson and I took a little walk into town. That was a more peaceful day. Suddenly, I ache to be sitting at Brother Man's table, all my thoughts gathered around the numbers, choosing one number or a group. Next I pray for the right one to come up on Joshie's wheel, jump with excitement when it does, my mind nowhere but there. I am surprised how that longing cuts so deep, how it sharpens from time to time no different than a birth pain.

I take a few potatoes out of my drawer to cut and fry up, and cut the tops off the beans. Out in the living room, the phone jingles. Usually I just let one of the girls get it if they're about, but only Jill is here and I want to let her get herself together.

Standing beside Professor's desk, I pick up the phone. "Indigo, is Jill there?" comes this spindly voice that is set on sounding weak and wavery as a candle flame in the wind. I don't know what to say. I know what comes next if I put Jill on the phone, but I never en make it my business to interfere with that. The air stays empty.

"Indigo, put Jill on the phone. I need to talk with her."

I hold my breath a second, then let it go. "Jill can't come to the phone right now, Mrs. Silver."

"She's not there?"

"Jill is getting ready for a party."

"Well, put her on the phone. She can take one minute away from what she's doing to talk to her mother on the phone."

I cross my fingers. "No, Mrs. Silver, Jill can't come to the phone. She's putting on the nice dress you gave her."

"Indigo!" Even my own name sounds bad to the ear, coming from her mouth.

"I have to go tend to the dinner, Mrs. Silver. Jill will call you tomorrow."

"Indigo, you get her right this minute. It's an emergency."

"If it's an emergency, best to call a doctor." Before she can say a ting more, I say, "Jill can't come to the phone. There go the timer on the oven. Sorry now, Mrs. Silver."

In my mind, I have her grumble, "Okay," and I quick hang up the phone. My legs are rubber. I sit right down on Professor's chair, wondering *what is it I have done,* hanging up on Mrs. Silver like that. She might jump in the car and drive here. Then *what kind of trouble am I in,* and not helping Jill any, either, to have her mother's hot breath in her face ten minutes from now.

I hear a key in the lock and feel a flow of cool air as Professor pushes open the door and finds me sitting still as a corpse in his chair. "Hello, Indi," he says as he comes in from the dark, and seems to carry in some darkness with him.

"Hello, Professor." I stand up and smooth the straight skirt of my uniform.

He looks at me. "Is something the matter?"

"Oh, no, Professor," I say, but I feel like biting at my lip the way Joshie does.

"Then let me put my things down." He comes over to his desk, and I move out of the way so he can set his briefcase down and pull out the pile of mail he brought home from the office.

"Everything okay?" he asks again. When I nod, he says, "I'm tired. I had a long day."

"You ought to take your weekends off."

"I could use some dinner." I glance at the phone and pray it won't ring; then I nod to Professor and excuse myself to the kitchen.

Jill gets herself to the party, looking adorable in her dress, and the evening goes past without any more word from Mrs. Silver. Maybe she just took a pill and went to sleep and left us in peace. Jill comes home acting like she had a good time again with Keith, but my mind is still on what I've started.

After a day or two, when nothing has come of my mischief, I let my breath flow again. Just my luck, then, that later that same afternoon, Jill gets another call from her mother and I'm the one to answer the phone. This time I behave myself and pass the phone directly to Jill.

When she hangs up the receiver, Jill picks up her winter jacket and finds her purse.

"Where are you going?" I ask her as she stands beside the front door and fishes for her keys. "You're going back out in that icy rain?"

"I've got to go to the drugstore."

"Why is that?"

"My mother needs something."

"What does she need in such a hurry?"

Jill shifts her mouth sideways, embarrassed. "Pads."

"Napkins?" I ask her, my voice loud enough to reach throughout the house.

"Yeah," she mutters.

"You don't even like to buy Tampax for your own self, Jill.

You have me buy them at the Dominick's and bring them home with the groceries."

Jill slides her eyes away.

"Why can't she go herself, or make do until tomorrow? The roads are icy, and darkness fall within the hour."

Jill shrugs. "She's sick. She's got a high fever."

I remember the time Jill and Jules and I went into Mrs. Silver's apartment house and found Mrs. Silver lying in bed, "sick," stains all over the sheets like someone bleeding to death. I think Jill must be seeing that scene, too, thinking that's what tomorrow will bring if she don't do this errand. Or maybe this time it can be something worse, maybe she truly bleed to death, and all of it on Jill's head.

"All right, Jill. You do what you need to, but please drive careful."

"I forgot to ask her what kind," she says, twisting her face in discomfort.

"Just get Kotex," I say. "That's what she likes. Get one box extra thick and one regular. She'll be fine with that. And try to get home before dark so Professor don't have to worry about you on those slippery roads."

Jill nods.

"You want me to drive along with you?"

She shakes her head.

"You sure, now? I don't mind. I'll drive along with you, help you watch the road."

"That's okay."

"You got money?"

She nods.

"You sure? You checked?"

"Twenty dollars," she says. "I've got twenty dollars."

The next night, Jill has gone to bed early so she can get a good night's sleep for a big United States history test she's got in the morning. The phone yammers, and I quick pick it up at Professor's downstairs desk to stop the sound. Mrs. Silver is asking for Jill, sounding plenty worked up. I tell her Jill has gone to bed and is sound asleep. I think maybe Professor will pick up the phone upstairs and take this call for me, but no luck there. Jill stumbles into the upstairs hallway in her nightie and calls down to me, "Is it for me, Indi?" I cover the phone and tell her, "It's your mother. I told her you're asleep now, so go on back to bed."

"I'll get it," she says, and gives me no time to warn her how her mada sound.

I hear Jill pick up the phone and say "Hello," and I say into the line, "I'm hanging up," but Lord help me I don't put down that phone.

Mrs. Silver's voice is clumsy, like she's been drinking, and she has so much trouble finding her words she might as well send out a search party. "I splashed ashid—ash—acid—in my eye," she says to Jill, with no hello. "I called the emergency room, and they said I'll go blind if I don't get some medicine. I need you to bring it to me, Jill, right away. There's an all-night pharmacy. You can go there and get it. It's an emergency. You understand? An emergency."

Jill is quiet for long enough to count one hundred. I am imagining acid in my eye and a trip, in pain and fear, to the hospital; the thought makes me shudder. I think of blindness, what that means, how you don't see a thing, not even your own child's face after that. Ooh, shake my head, shake my thoughts away.

"Will you get me the medicine?" her mother asks again, her voice sluggish and drunken, but still demanding as a general.

Jill says nothing for a while longer. I hold my breath to fix on the silence, and after a while I hear Jill very softly say, "No."

Now Mrs. Silver's voice sparks. "Didn't you hear me?" she demands. "I'm going to go blind. That's what they told me. It's acid. It's burning my eye right this minute. The pain is god-awful."

"I can't help with that." Jill's voice is soft and slow but steady, like a train that keeps on its track through a bad storm.

Mrs. Silver is furious. She is hollering. "You can't? You can't? What do you mean you can't? You can drive a car, can't you? You have a car, don't you? I believe your father bought you one. You can bring the medicine I need."

"I won't," Jill says, soft and low, but cold as steel. "Maybe they'll deliver it to you if you call them."

"You don't care if I go blind?"

Now Jill is trapped and has to take time to consider. "No," she finally says. "I don't care. I don't. I really don't."

Mrs. Silver starts in telling Jill how bad she is, how wicked, how selfish, how ungrateful—her words coming easy now—and on and on about the eye that is burning its way to blindness as they speak. But I question if her heart could burn so hot while her eye is burning. Then she's got to tell Jill how now she'll have to call on the neighbor girl, Valerie, who's more to be counted on than her own child.

Jill says nothing. Finally, Mrs. Silver slams down the phone. Then over the line I hear the click of the upstairs phone. I soft-step up the stairs, and Jill is in the library, sitting on the sofa, crying like her best friend's dead and gone. I sit down beside her. She tries to explain to me what happened on the telephone.

"I know," I say. "I did something shameful. I listened on the line." Jill looks shocked, but I think she is glad she doesn't have to tell the story.

"What if she does go blind?" she asks.

"Jill. Use your head. She going to holler like that if her eye on fire? She the one got better vision than the whole family. Only one that don't wear glasses. True today and still be true tomorrow."

"But what if she *does* . . . go blind?"

I shake my head. "On the phone, you en do the right ting. No doubt."

Julie wanders in, dressed for bed in her short flannel nightgown, her hair pulled on top of her head and rubber-banded.

Jill looks at her. "Why doesn't she ever ask Julie?"

"What are you upset about?" Julie asks, coming over beside us.

"Mom asked me to get her some medicine. She said she got acid in her eye and she's going to go blind."

"Are you doing it?" Julie asks.

Jill shakes her head. "I told her no. I told her I didn't even care if she went blind."

"Why do you pay any attention to her?" Julie asks. "You know she's making it up. She always does."

"That's why she doesn't ask Jules," I say when Julie walks out. "You're the fish that bites at the bait. Jules don't even sniff it. And Clair, she's too young to count for anything with Mrs. Silver. She'd take the bait, but Mrs. Silver no care to hook her—she's too much a baby still. Wait till later, till she's more grown. She'll be on the hook, too, if she's not careful."

Professor comes in in the gray cotton pajamas he always wear. "What's the trouble?" he asks, his face tired, his voice stern.

Jill shrugs. She isn't going to tell him.

"Trouble with her mother," I say.

"Oh," he says. "More of that." He bends and kisses Jill on the forehead and says, "Don't let her get to you so much." Then he tells us both good night and goes to his bed.

Jill stops her crying and turns inside herself, darkness pulled over her face.

I feel angry at Professor. Why can't he stay and talk with this child? How does he think she's to work out all of this worry without some help? He must think these girl-dem were grown and wise from the day they put aside their nappies.

I can't offer her anything if her own father can't, I say to myself, and besides, I am spun around by my anger. "Good night, Jill," I tell her, and get up to go to my room and put on my nightgown and make myself comfortable with a bit of crocheting while I sit in the bed.

We don't hear anything more from Mrs. Silver the next day. Jill is stomping around the house, making twice the noise of her usual, quiet self. I catch her in the kitchen, pulling a pot from an overhead cabinet so she can boil some eggs for her school lunches. She draws out that pot so careless she's going to pull down half a dozen others along with it, right on top of her head. I have to reach up both my hands to catch what's coming down so don't all of it land on Jill.

"Lord Jesus," I say. "What are you doing?"

"Getting a pot."

"Going to get ten pot smack you on you head if you don' careful." Then I tell her, "I guess no phone call come today from your mother."

She shrugs and runs a hard stream of water from the faucet into her pot so that half the water splashes back onto her hands.

"You don't think you'd be hearing from her if she half-blind in the hospital soon?"

Jill shrugs again, and her face takes on a bitter look. "Maybe she's dead and lying on the floor in her apartment."

"Don't you believe that. Next time she calls, she'll have forgot all about the acid she splash in her eye, and you'll be the fool for worrying."

"You like to call me that," Jill says, catching me calling her a fool one more time.

I shake my head no.

"Yes you do. You do."

"Oh, sorry, Jill," I say. "Don't take me so serious. Most of us can be fools one time or the other."

Jill pulls a white piece of stationery out of her pocket and holds it up to me.

"What is that?"

"You probably already know. It's a letter from Ben, my friend from last summer. I think that's why you hate me so much, because he likes me and writes to me. He doesn't forget me even though he's far away." Jill takes her letter and rips it down the middle, then rips across it a second time.

I am shocked. "You are off your mind, child," I say.

Jill kicks her foot into the cabinet below the sink hard enough that I worry she could break a toe. "I go away for the summer. She gets worse and worse. Everyone's angry. Nothing's right. I come back, and everyone wants to make fun of me and be mad at me for having a good time. Nobody can stand that I went away from this awful house and had fun."

"Jill, you are putting too many things in the same pot that don't go together. You get yourself all mixed-up."

She shakes her head. "No. I know it. I know how it is. You tell me to go out with Keith just so I'll forget about Ben. You don't want me to have a good time, because *you* never do."

"That's what you think? How do you figure all that?"

"Then if Keith touches me, what am I supposed to do? Tell me that. What am I supposed to do?"

"Is that what's troubling you so? Do what you want to do, Jilly, just like all of us do when it come to that." I hear in her words that Keith is not so shy a boy as he seems. I take a good look at Jill as if the touch of that boy's hand would leave a shine I could see. "Just don't get yourself in trouble."

"You don't have to worry about me," she says. "Mommy will talk the judge into letting her take us even though she's a lunatic, and you and Daddy won't have to worry about me, or about Clair or Julie either."

* * *

The next day, Jill seems more her regular self, though she is embarrassed by all she said and she's fearful to meet my eye. She busies herself with her schoolwork, then disappears into the dining room to practice her flute. At the upright black piano that supports her music, she goes over and over her notes.

Julie comes into the kitchen, where I'm slicing yellow onions. "How long is she going to play that thing?" she complains. I see that today is Julie's turn to be in a temper. Usually that girl just comes and goes, about like Professor, while Jill and Clair spend more time with me. But Julie is hanging around the house today, and something mean is working in her. She is looking to fight with all of us.

"How am I to know?" I say. "You ask Jill."

Jules goes into the dining room. "How long are you going to play that squeak box?" I hear her demand.

I am fighting off tears from my onions.

"I don't know," Jill says. "Till I'm done."

"I can't think while you're playing," Julie says.

"It doesn't squeak," Jill says. "Flutes don't squeak."

"Yours does."

"Clarinets squeak," says Jill. She must be thinking of Julie's old clarinet, that she played for six months, then quit. She's giving a little back to Jules.

"I'm going upstairs," Julie says, and leaves Jill to her music.

I leave the kitchen and follow Julie up the stairs, at half her speed, because I'm going to take a rest from the onions and clean the girls' bathrooms. I clean the toilet and the tub, then turn to the sinks. Jill's super Tampax box is out on the long sink counter, half-empty, but against the mirror sits the box of regular Julie had me buy her five days ago, and the cellophane covering is unbroken.

I remember last month how the girls were on the same exact schedule. I think, *This must be why Julie is mad at the world and calling Scott on the telephone every five minutes, whining like a wet cat, making empty talk.* I have a hunch and I go in the library and look for that little sex book, and sure enough it is missing. I know which room I would find it in if I cared to look, and what section it would open to. Here is one more trial this family doesn't need. If it has to be me, with my foolishness with Cliff, or Julie with hers, it might better be me, though the thought of that still gives me a shiver.

When I finish in there and come upon Julie in the hall, I say, "You're not using the Tampax I bought you. Are you using Jill's?"

"Uh, yeah," she says, but her face flushes. She rubs her foot on the wheat-colored carpet I have to work so hard to keep clean.

"I see what's going on here, Jules," I say. "Professor don't, but I do."

"Just shut up," Julie hisses, more faastie than her usual self as she sees Professor is coming down the hall. He wants to know from Julie if she's got any receipts to give him, because he keeps track of all the household expenses for when tax time comes.

"I don't know, Dad," she whines at him. "Why do we have to do that stupid stuff?"

"Just remember to give me those receipts," Professor says. "It's not that hard. You girls always forget." Then he goes back down to his study. Before he goes through the door, he turns back to Julie and says, down the hall, "You girls could think about me for a change. Especially you, the oldest. You could set an example and not act like a baby."

You wouldn't call her that if you knew what I know—I talk to Professor in my head—*but then maybe you don't want to.* When Professor is back in his study, I say to Julie, "Better do some thinking about whether holding on to somebody is worth all you're chancing."

"Can't you leave me alone," Julie says, and looks like she may burst into flames and into tears, all at once.

"I know you," I say. "You feel if you lose Scott, you are no different from Jill down there working away at her music. You are no girlfriend of the football captain, no class secretary. You are nobody special." I wipe my forehead with my wrist, because I am sweating. "You are who you are, Jules, whoever that is, good or bad. You're not who Scott is, and never will be."

"I can't talk to you now," Julie says, turning away. "I'm in a hurry."

"When aren't you in a hurry?" I say. "Always running off somewhere, you and Professor, like two rocket ships."

Then she turns and faces me like she is ready to fight and brings her eyes to mine, her hands to her waist, and shouts, *"You know what she did?"*

I shake my head to say I don't know what she's saying. Don't even know which "she" this child is talking about, though maybe I could guess.

Julie's eyes are shining with anger. "She showed up at the luncheon for Scott's mother's fortieth birthday. Don't ask me how she even knew about it. I didn't invite her, even though all the other mothers were invited. I was so embarrassed. She sounded drunk, and she asked Scott's mom if she'd put on weight, and she was wearing a see-through dress that looked like a nightgown. I was so embarrassed I wanted to die. Why does she have to be my mother, Indi? It's just not fair."

I shake my head.

"I ask Daddy why can't he stop her from doing these things, and he just shrugs and acts like it's no big deal and says, 'You can handle it.' But I *can't* handle it. And I don't want to. I hate it. I hate all of it."

"Okay, Jules," I say. "What is it you think Professor can do? What you think any of us can do? You just be you. Don't think about being your mother's daughter, or Scott's girlfriend either. You just be who you are, then you'll be okay. And don't think about giving away too much of what's yours either, because no one you tie your boat to is going to make you anyone but who you already are."

"You don't understand anything," she says to me. "Not any more than he does."

"Well, maybe not," I say, but she has put her hands over her ears to shut me out.

Professor walks back in. "What's going on?" he asks.

"Julie's a little upset is all," I say.

"What's the matter? You're still mad about those receipts? Or did you have a bad day in school?"

Jill comes in and stands quietly beside me, then Clair follows.

"No," Jules says. "No. No. No. It's *here,* not school. It's here."

"What's the matter here?"

"How can you ask me that, Dad? Do you live in a paper bag?"

"What's the matter with Julie?" Clair asks.

"Do you know what she's talking about, Jill?" Professor asks.

Jill shrugs. "I don't know. Probably Mom and all that stuff."

"All what stuff?" Professor asks.

"Well, you know," says Jill. "Mr. Goldfarb and all that sickening stuff."

"Why would you girls get so upset about that?" Professor asks. "Indigo said that lawyer was a flyweight, a nobody."

"It's not the lawyer," Julie complains. "It's Mom and what she's trying to do, and what she's already doing. Do you know what it's like to have her do the stuff she does?"

"I think you girls are exaggerating," Professor says. "After all, you're safe here with me and Indigo. You don't have to worry. You girls don't know what real danger is."

I shake my head. "Best to keep your studies in the office, Professor. These girls know a ting or two boht life."

"Do they, Indi? Am I being a blockhead?"

"You got me watching my manners, Professor, so I don't say a ting."

"You're not a blockhead with me, Dad," Clair puts in. "And Mommy's not so bad with me, either. Everything's okay, isn't it, Indi?"

"You're just looking through your rosy-colored glasses," I tell her, "but that's okay, for how old you are."

Before I go on back to my place Saturday morning, Clair is after me again about her pen money. I hold firm and tell her, "Better find yourself a little job, Clair."

Fourteen

Finally I'm home, but before my eye can find that typed letter lying on my table, in a film of dust, I am at Brother Man's, which feels more like home than my rooms. I put down the last five chips I have and let Joshie spin the wheel, two chips on the even numbers, three on the number twelve for Louisa's birthday. The wheel spins and stops and Joshie says, "Black fifteen."

"I'm finish," I say as if I am content to quit for the day, but I get a sharp, empty feeling, strong as a sickness, as I stand back from the table.

"Night's young, Miss Indigo Rose." Brother Man sends his words out playfully, like he is tossing me a rubber ball. He is across the room, savoring his ganja, offering none to no one, leaning back on his elbows, which are perched behind him on the wooden table that holds his typewriter.

"May be the night is young, but I'm cash poor," I tell him. I bend over and smooth the front of my trousers and retuck my shirt.

He spins around on his chair and starts up some typing, his back to the room. "I never hear you say you salt before." He talks over his typing. "You all the time flush."

"There's a first time for everything, don't it so?" I use the words Julie likes to say to Professor when she want him to change his ways.

Frank is across from me at the table, sitting in a white plastic chair. "Brother Man don't begrudge a little loan to you. Maybe get you on his list." He teases, his dark skin flushing one shade blacker.

"Dem tell me none but di fool enter him name on Brother Man's list," I say.

"That's right. I don't want a pretty lady on that ugly old debtors' list," says Brother Man, whirling back around toward us. "That spoil your beauty sleep."

"You just as soon get you a kiss from a barracuda," says Frank, and laughs, then flexes his right arm to show the muscle neet his yellow T-shirt. "Take it from one of Brother Man's best friends."

"Ongle friend," I mutter, faastie.

Joshie keeps his head bent to his wheel but curls his eyes up toward me, gives me a close look, then calls for bets before he spins the wheel again. "Brother Man won't put you on his list the first time," he mumbles.

"Sure enough," says Frank, his eyes straying to Brother Man. "He'll play the gentleman and give you an interest-free loan."

"Oh, don't tempt her," Brother Man says.

When the wheel stops, everyone but the house comes up empty. All of them are losers, don't know how to place their bets with some care, like I do. I wish I brought just a few more dollars to put down on number twelve for my Louisa's birthday.

"Yeah, don't tempt me," I say.

"It's the interest that kills you," says Frank. "Without the interest, you've got no problem. Brother Man charges what we call *usurious interest.* He like to make you a sharecropper got no more money than to buy next year's seed corn. Then you got to do his bidding."

"Where is Lucille, lately?" I ask. "I don't see her in a long, long while."

"Just my point, sure enough," Frank says. "You ain't seen her, but I bet Brother Man know just where she's at, and whether she had any hospital bills of late."

"Why you let them talk like that, mon?" I ask Brother Man.

He shrugs. "Dem got alla the smart-smart words—look who got the coil."

I guess words don't get in his way.

"We just his raggedy-ass brothers is all," says Frank.

"My mood's too high for any type of bredda to spoil it," Brother Man says. "Have a new gal in my life. Lovely, mampi gal." He chuckles, spreads his hands to a meter, then sends his glee into his rat-tat-tats.

Brother Man surprises me. Him usually keep him private life most private and expect the same from alla the rest. I get a whirl of irritation in my belly.

Joshie spins again and this time hits the twelve. "Oh, Lord," I say, and snap my fingers. "Look at that." There is Louisa's number, and I let my girl down just sitting by, not putting so much as a dollar on her birthday number. But I don't speak my private business out loud like these others.

Next ting I know, there is a neat stack of blue chips in front of me on the table even though, soon as I look, Brother Man is at his typewriter, tapping out words to look like he never get up from the chair. I pick up the top chip in the pile and inspect it, like I gwan to find some secret message stamp upon it. For a while, I only sit and watch the play. Then, with a quiet mind, I put down five chips on the "first twelve numbers" spot and five on the number twelve. The number comes up thirteen and I win two times nothing, but thirteen is close enough to twelve for me to know Louisa spirit cyan be near. I put down five chips more, four on even and one on six, the six for my baby's age when she die and for half her birthday number, and this time I hit, just like I knew I would, and get an instant flow of good feeling. I get up and stack the rest of Brother Man's chips on the table corner for Brother Man to come get and take to his bank behind the desk. After that, I cash out my winnings and pay back to Brother Man half of what I borrowed.

The wind grabs the door from me and slams it and I am out in the cold, my coat over my arm. Walking and dressing against that wind, I wonder did Brother Man see how I'm gifted with good luck, or did I leave him in there clucking, thinking he'll catch me in his web with his skank moves because I don't know this little interest-free loan from the one that gets you in trouble. Probably he's feeling like a happy man, his night gladdened by baiting his trap plus finding a new woman, a new gal, fat and nice. But he thinks too low of me. I took his lilly bit money this one time only to give him a tease, pick up his interest a little.

Wet snow catches on the wool of my coat and takes its time melting. Flakes fall on my eyelashes and icy melt dribbles into my eyes, feels cool and nice after the smoke of that room. I go ahead and catch some on my tongue, like a child. When I get home forty minutes later, my eyes fall on Vincent's letter and I quick stash it neet some papers in my desk; not the time for alla that now. I take off my shirt and pants and I see I am not a man after all, because though it's some days early, I am bleeding. There is the end of my worry. No child going to come and spoil my peace. I make a chocolate in celebration, stir out the long streaks of dark that marble the color, then hot it up to warm my insides, think a little of Clair and her money mission for Professor. Lord, that child! I settle onto my chair, sipping my good chocolate; I try to play up my easy spirit, tell myself *oo-ee* what a misery to carry a child by that renk Cliff, knowing how the Jamaican them all the time laba-laba one to the next. No child on this earth for Indigo but Lou, though a next child of my womb could have some lilly bit of Lou in the chin, the ear, the smile in her voice, the clever bright eye. Oh, Lord, Lord oh Lord help me here, because nothing make peace for Indigo. Whether I turn toward the sun or against it, always going to burn.

I'm in a dream where I am at Brother Man's and I hit my bets, time after time. My play is so far past what's ordinary that everybody stop what they do and stare my way. All I have to bother my pleasure is a cut on my finger that's bleeding. I dab at it, attempt to stem the blood, but it don't let up. But it no matter to me, such a scant bit of bleeding's not worth a care. No, mon, nothing can stop me when I'm at the wheel. I sail higher even than Brother Man with his new woman. But Jah, in the end don't all the blood drain right out mi body from that small slit on the finger, and I am pale as any pink-eye doondoos you ever see. When I catch sight of my bleached skin in the mirror, with Vincent, worried, a-stand behind me, I get a terrible fright and wake.

Half-roused, I see the time when Louisa's daddy and me dance the rumba Papa taught me and all the other dancer-dem stop to watch. Most times, I am not so fine a dancer, but that night I am high on Steve, his body a ting of beauty to my eye, my skin. I have to dance to keep from kissing and hugging him there in public.

I get up from the bed to put that crazy dream and my mind's walkabout out of my thoughts. I make my tea and toast and wonder should I venture over to Brother Man's to pay the rest of the little loan and clean the smile from his face.

Probably do no gambling at all this day, or no more than a spin or two of Joshie's wheel. Just get that loan paid with what I still hold in the drawer and get Brother Man's mind off contemplating how he add me to his list.

I put on my trousers and cap, but then comes a knock at the door, and I open it to find Zach. He looks surprised to see me in my own house. I see it must be the cap covering my hair that makes me look like a burglar opening the door to a house he just now break into.

When he recovers, he says, "I have a problem, Indigo." His voice sounds embarrassed, like a schoolboy.

"Seems like whoever lives in that room always do have a problem," I say. "Big one or little. Well, don't stand out in the hall."

I pull off the cap and let my hair free, and that seems to relax him. Though I want to get to Brother Man and pay off his loan, I try to chase that from my mind and act a proper neighbor.

"What's troubling you, then, Zach?" I say to him.

He smiles that shy smile again. "You know how to make saltfish and ackee, sister? I've got such a hunger."

"That's your problem? How can I be a Jamaican woman more than thirty year and not know how to prepare ackee and codfish for a wanga-gut? You have what tings you need in your kitchen?"

He nods, then stiffens his nostrils. "You been smoking, Indigo? You know that's bad for your health, nuh?"

"Skip that, now where you find ackee near here?"

"They have an islands grocery on Siena. The fruit don' the best, but it can make do."

I nod. "I hear of that place." I feel my own hunger want to cut a hole in me, try to put me on the bus that roll toward the sound of Africa drums and Bunny Wailer, Pan Head, the Lieutenant, all them rude-boy voices I heard alla my life. Most of all, the soft whirl of the wheel calls me. *Mek we go there to-*

gether, I want to say to Zach, but he no even know the place and never would approve it.

"Oh, listen to you, girl," Zach says, because I am humming something widoht my mind on it. " 'Miss Daisy, she make me crazy,' " he sings along with my tune. "You have that old album?"

I shake my head. "It just come up in the head."

"You miss the dance hall, sister? Alla them days? 'Johnny you too bad,' " he starts singing. The music must free him some. " 'Jus' a robbing and a stabbing and a looting and a tooting and a . . . too bad.' "

"Go on home and set your food on the counter. I come across soon and show you the way."

He beams like he just win the big jackpot. "Yes, sister," he says, a sweet lamb with a smile in his voice.

I set my hat on top the television set and go to the kitchen and yank at the swollen wood drawer.

"You tie on your apron," he says when I walk into his place with the red cloth wrapped around me.

"You telling me something I don't already know?" I say.

"Indigo, you a woman who truck no nonsense," he teases.

"You tink I can teach a man cook saltfish quicker than I cook it myself?" I ask. "Curry goat is what I miss."

"You tink of the fine feast days."

He turns and walks to his living room window, and I hear him humming the tune that's on Jill's mama's old calypso record. "Ackee, rice, saltfish is nice, and the rum is fine any time of year. . . ." Jill must hear those words and not have a hint what some of dem foods are. Those girls, they live in their own small world, thinking everyone eats what *they* eat, wears what they wear, lives how they live. Sometime Professor can seem in that world, too, though he study North to South, East to West.

After I fry up the fish and feed him the meal, Zach sits in his cushiony chair and puts his feet up on a raggedy-edge ottoman. He lights a pipe and seems too contented for me to bear his company. My thoughts again draw me to Brother Man's, so I get up and go toward the door.

"You don't want to relax a bit after you cook all that fine food?"

I look at him and see my brother, Vincent, in his thin figure and can't help but stand a second and watch the line of smoke rise between his eyes and disappear. "Later mon," I say, and go on out and across to my own place.

As soon as I am home, I am in my bedroom, digging in my desk drawer. First I see the Holy Bible that live in that drawer. 'Im a Gideon Bible like you find in the motels; this one come wid my rooms. I can't say why I need to read again my bredda letter which I no wish to set eyes on since I open it. Though it is Vincent's words I read, it is Mama who is most in my mind. What was Vincent but an overgrown vine when last I see him, halfway between boy and man? What words of his own cyan trouble me?

When I was a girl, I often strayed to the hills on a hot day when Mama had too much of me hanging around her skirt. I would wander this way and that, study the weeds and flowers, find on logs galliwasp lizards I make sure not to touch, or lie on the ground, looking up at the clouds that flow past. Sometimes I would set my feet to point up the hill so I feel the blood a-run to my head. Then I would turn onto my belly and rub my face into the grasses and see cyan I pick out the soft ones from the sharp with just the skin of my nose and my cheeks. And I would open my eyes and watch the ants crawl right under them, only a quips or two from the shine of my eyes. If I shut them again and twist to the right position, I could roll down the hill like a log. That was a good way to spend an afternoon, until Mama create Vincent and he have three or four years to grow. After that, each time I wander, when the sun come to hang low in the sky, I would see

Vincent lumber up into the hills and hear him call my name. It wasn't that Vincent was wanting something for himself. He wasn't coming for help or to join in my delightment. Mama en send him to fetch me back. "Indigo, you out too long," he would tell me. "Mama needs you to help with the cooking." Or "Mama needs you to help with the wash." Or the ironing or sorting need to done. It got to where Vincent no more bring his own voice than the postman bring his own letter. They oughta put a stamp pon his forehead and Mama address on his back, because he just bring messages from Mama, who send me out in the morning but now she need me back.

When I see Vincent trudging up the hills in the heat, doing his duty, I never think, *Here comes Vincent,* but *Oh . . . Mama's calling me home.* Doreen she stayed close by Mama all day and never trouble Mama's nerves. Must be I was more like Papa, who never pleased her being close or being far, so she send me out in the morning and call me back night, till I come to be like the tide.

When finally I arrive at Brother Man's, I find him back by the record player, where he is putting on his dance hall to replace Joshie's drumbeats. He carries on with loud talk like a dub poet. I pay him back his joke loan, and he makes a little speech to me: "I see, Indigo, that all those others had best model theyselves after you, the way you pay back your debt quick and no fall behind." His voice is kindly, but the vein on his neck bulges as if his blood is kicking as it pass. Him nah happy that I rein in my indulgence. The lamp light's a sickly blue tonight, not a color I like all around me.

Joshie looks our way and does that odd biting business with his mouth and drums a quick pattern on the green cloth with both hands. Only the man's hands are quick. He has gained some weight since the first time I saw him, and can scarcely make his way around the table. Poor mampi man's getting as round as his wheel. May soon be stuck in the corner with that playting and no get out.

On the way over on the bus, I told myself *I'll just pay Brother Man his money and walk out,* tell him, "Be seeing you another time, mon," and neva woulda go near the wheel. But I get a thought that as long as I come this long distance on the bus, I should make best use of this time to try someting different, maybe find a way to make a quips more out of my money. I hang around the roulette wheel awhile, not buying chips, just watch, then when Brother Man goes to the smaller table to deal blackjack, I go over and sit down between him and Frank and across from an Indian man with skin like sandalwood and speech as elegant as some of the English who come to Jamaica and spend their money in the shops and hotels. I never before sat down at this table, but I looked over enough shoulders to noh how it works, so I have no need to ask a lot of ignorant questions.

The only thing I nah get is where is Mr. Borotsky tonight, because usually he's the one who gets Brother Man to start up dealing blackjack. Brother Man slices and dices his cards like an expert. I buy a few chips and let him include me in his dealing and I start my play with as much confidence as when I bet on the wheel—knowing I got an instinct fi whether to stand or to keep pulling new cards. But I learn I don't noh my way in this game, because damn if I no lose what money I en bring before I even get warm in my chair. I take a shock seeing how fast my stack of money is eat up.

The Indian looks kindly at me and says, "Ah, I see you have not played blackjack before." I don't like him training his light on my ignorance, but I have to nod, my eye-dem shut, because his words are the simple truth as all can see. He reaches his hand across Brother Man's table offering a neat mound of chips and says, "I am lucky tonight."

Because of someting my eyes caught when he lift his midsection to stretch across the table, I am slow to speak. His left arm is cut off below the elbow, and the skin is closed as smooth and round over the end as skin over the tip of a man's wood. I shake my head to tell him to forget those chips, and he makes no fuss, but takes back his money just as gracious as he en give it.

"What happen to your arm?" I ask him, my eyes meeting his.

Frank looks up, surprised I'm so straight out, and says, "You ain't met Sanjay before? He's here most often as you, girlfriend."

I shake my head. "Why I can't noh him and not noh what become of his arm?"

"To answer your question, Miss Indigo," Sanjay says, "I was in an accident."

"Automobile?" I ask.

He nods. "Some young people's prank."

"That left you like that?"

"Yes. Two children removed the stop signs at an intersection, and I drove through in my Chrysler and collided with a large dairy truck."

"Jah!" I say. "What terrible mischief."

"It was a long time ago," he says. "I seldom think about it."

"Truly? I don't believe you," I say, and stand up, lean over his way, see again the wicked deed.

"Sit, please," he says. "They were young people, little more than children. I saw them in court. I don't think they had a real idea of people sustaining injury, real injury. Maybe they had watched too many videos."

"You forgive too easy," I say, shaking my head. I think for a minute about Julie or Jill, out doing their practice driving with Professor. Once or twice, I sat in the backseat, on the way to the Dominick's, while Professor gave Julie a test of how she drive. I remember how he'd shout out, "Jesus, Julie, you just about hit that boy on a bicycle." Julie would answer back, annoyed, "I was a mile away, Dad. Don't have a cow! I already got my license."

Cool, Jules was, like driving that car is no big deal. And boasie, feeling she know how to drive already and nah need Professor's lessons.

I tell the Indian, "Someone ran down my girl with a car and left her to die in the road. I nah go forgive that person so long as I live. Mek no difference whether he's eighty or eighteen." My heart is pounding, and I cannot believe I'm telling these people my story, but there it is, out on the table big as a beast.

"Your loss was greater than mine," says the Indian, his voice steady.

I no can argue with that, so I keep my silence.

"Too much talking," Brother Man says and shakes his head. "You make it hard for me to deal. Where's the old man? Anyone noh?"

"Too much of your income staked to him, eh?" says Frank. "You miss the old dude."

Frank always insults Brother Man with a laugh, and Brother Man takes it from him like Frank means nothing by his words.

"We two go way back," Frank says to me, gesturing at Brother Man.

Though my money dry up, I've been at the blackjack table such a lilly bit I've had no chance to slip eena that happy feeling that always come about with time. I've got to find that place before I go, especially now that Sanjay enlighten me with his philosophy of life, so I hang around awhile, talking with Frank and Sanjay and whoever else comes and goes, thinking I can get where I need to just by breathing the peculiar air of this room—mix in with sandalwood today—widoht put my money on anything, not on the wheel or the cards.

But I am wrong about finding my tranquillity just by rooting here awhile like a garden plant, because the longer I stay and do nothing but let Brother Man's tobacco and herb burn my eyes, the further I feel from that high-in-the-sky, easy feeling.

Still no Borotsky, I notice, and my wish to see the old Russian surprises me. Brother Man concludes dealing and I've moved no nearer to my breathing space, and I get to feeling a warning of that awful panic. I am still sitting at the blackjack table, all by myself now, when the door opens and Mr. Borotsky hobbles in. He looks up and sees me and frowns, then hops directly to me, his movement looking painful. "Good evenink, Indigo. What? You are playing blackjack tonight? Taking an old man's place at the table?"

"Why you so late tonight? Fi dat?" I nod to his leg.

"Oy! I twisted my ankle, so I had to stay home with the ice bag until the throbbing ceased. Such things happen all the time to the old." He smiles. "Why do you sit here all alone?"

"I make a fool of myself playing my first blackjack. Go ahead and lose all my money, so I don' cyan go to the wheel."

"Good!" says Mr. Borotsky. "Better you should lose all you brought with you tonight, better that than win on your first night, which will make you feel like Zeus on Mount Olympus, then you'll lose all you own in the next month."

I laugh. "Funny words for you, king of the blackjack table. That's what they call you."

"Yes. My title."

"Why do you like the blackjack, Mr. Borotsky, better than that nice roulette wheel?"

He sits down beside me. "I have given that one some thought, Indigo, so I will give to you a better answer than you expect. I find two reasons, thus far. One is Brother Man, the dealer. He and I have a small competition. He is 'the house,' tryink every minute to relieve me of my money. And I am determined to outsmart him, crafty beast though he is. Of course, in the end I always lose, because he tilts the odds in his favor, but I seldom lose by much."

"The other reason?"

"Twenty-one," he says, and smiles.

"Twenty-one? What's that supposed to mean?"

"It's the number itself. I love that number."

"Twelve is my lucky number," I say. "Has to do with my little girl who died." There I go again.

"Same number, then, for both of us," he says, considering my eyes, slowing his words so it's the space between them that matters. "Only turned around."

I'm going to stop this talk, go to Joshie's table and at least look on.

Borotsky puts his right arm out on the table, takes a look into my face, so deep it makes me want to leave my face behind. "It was my twenty-first birthday, Indigo, when the Russians liberated the camp I was in."

"Give you back your life?"

He shakes his head no. "Gave me a chance to piece my life back together, from a million broken bits."

I nod. "This the story you tell Professor, Mr. Abraham?"

"Part of it," he says. "I told him part of it. I'm telling you part of it. Do you think there is something wrong in telling that story?"

I shrug. "That one is for you to choose. But alla that misery. Lord. Why you want to talk boht it, bring it back into your heart?"

"It *is* my heart."

"You feel no pity for yourself? You don't feel a deep-deep hate and more hate after that and more the next minute?"

He shakes his head. "Not anymore, Indigo, though I used to overflow with it and fight against drowning in it. Now I'm close to the end of my journey, and I feel pity for humanity, for all of us, because we don't know how to be what God surely meant us to be."

God meant? And what that suppose to mean? I wonder.

"You're a nice man, Mr. Borotsky," I say, "but now I mus' go to the other table."

"Just stay away from the blackjack, my dear. Stay away from our 'brother.' You leave him to me."

I wander to the roulette table and stand beside Joshie, swallow his soft smell of perspiration, and watch the way his clumsy body moves with grace when he shoob his wheel, like he gets something magic from that shining, spinning ting. I am missing my roulette and feeling sorry I gave up my money so fast on the cards, which never meant to be my game. Seems I must get just a little taste of that top-of-the-world, easy feeling before I go. Brother Man come beside my elbow, so I whisper in his ear, "Let me have just twenty-five," and he acts like he cyan know what I need before I speak it, because the chip-dem come to be sitting on the table next to my hand and I swear he never move from his place.

Brother Man goes to his sideboard desk and busies himself with his ink pen, leaving me to my pleasure. Joshie bends over the table and sets his chips on the numbers I pick. When he straightens himself, he taps the edge of the overhead fixture with his head and sets it swinging, and the light—the blue bulb tonight—moves over the table in a wild dance, mek you tink how you head can feel if you take too much of di rum. I try scattering my chips over many number and think of stars dotting the sky. I'm not in need of a big hit, just the little thrill of making my picks and watching the wheel spin and spin and make its pick. The one-one extra cash from Brother Man is plenty to get me just what I seek, and I am glad I can tell myself I only borrowed this small amount that I can pay back easy as can be next time I come. In fact, I could have brought more cash from home and need no loan at all, so in a manner of speaking the loan's already paid off, since the money's set aside in the drawer. I just planned poorly about what to bring with me is all. Not much more to it than that.

Just as I prepare to get up from the table, along comes a brand new face, a young white man with a measly braid down his back and bad acne on his chin that look like he fassy with his nails and make it worse to where I want to tell him, like a mada, Leave that skin alone.

"You sure know your numbers," he says. He looks hard at me, and his face jumps to life and the dege braid flip like a fish on the dock. "Hey, you're a girl! I thought you were a man."

"Wa matter? Mek no difference here which one I be. That's part of Brother Man's good sense."

When I'm feeling restored and I en turn in my chips and have my coat on, set to go, Brother Man must sense my leaving even though he's at his desk with his back to me. He slides up alongside me, his face calm and relaxed once more, not agitated like when I first come in and give him back his dege money, breaking the string he'd tied to me. His eyes are on me different from any other time. They look at me without blinking, and his nostrils yawn. He takes one of my hands in his and looks me in the eye. "I'm seeing you like when you first come in with your friend—I forget her name—without those man clothes, sister. You and me ought to go out for a drink sometime."

"I thought you were permanent here," I say. "My mind naa see you oht in the neighborhood."

"Much about me you don't see," he says, and smiles as if he's got an idea of how to charm me. "Much about you I'd like to see. Where I cyan find you tomorrow, sister?"

"Nowhere," I say, and put on my gloves.

"What? You disappear into the air Mondays? Like a witchy spirit?"

"My job come and get me."

"Oh." He sharpens up. "Caring for white folk and their pickney-dem, like so many of our women."

"Making a dollar to buy the groceries," I say.

"Mek a dollar caring for white folk," he says, "tending their needs and plenty of their whims, putting your loving where it no belong. What your own family back home, your own people, tink?"

"Me nah consult their thoughts that regular." I think of Julie how she tells Professor, "I don't have the faintest idea."

Brother Man walks off, and I think how I praised him too high in my head. He likes to parade his idea of keeping the outside world far from di door, but his philosophy don't worth a dime if he break alla the rules whenever he care to.

The long-hair young man comes up beside me, puts his fassy-skin face to my ear, and whispers, "You hear about Brother Man's girl, his jelly roll?"

I frown and shake my head no. I don't know Brother Man's jelly roll. I barely know or care to know Brother Man.

"She dropped him like a stone."

"So fast?" I say.

"Yeah, man. He's settin' the record, poor sucker."

When I get home, my belly is cramping, so I go in the bathroom and sit down on the stool and stretch my legs out in front of me to relieve the pressure some and try to pass some gas. My belly aches, but I tell myself how I am lucky that foolishness with Cliff ended with this and not the other. God willing, Julie's foolishness can end the same way.

Fifteen

This week at the Silvers' I have a hard time keeping my patience. Though Brother Man caused me aggravation and my respect for him dwindle some, I never before have the heetch so bad to get away to his place and, truly, I'm glad I've got it, glad for wanting someting and believing someting going to get the blood moving tru my veins, glad to be dusting the Silvers' tings, or sweeping their floors, or cooking their dinner thinking of that wheel a-spin and the ball a-patter and the excitement raising the hair on my skin as I wait to see what sweet number the silver ball going to choose. I am scheduled to work all through the week and Saturday as well. But Thursday morning, the weather is bright and almost mild, and all the girls gone to school and Professor to work, and it comes into my head that there's nothing I've got to do in this house till it's time to make dinner, and Professor's always telling me I'm free to take some personal time during the week if I need it.

I throw a coat over my uniform dress and slip out of the

house as fast as an intruder that never did belong there in the first place. I hurry down the block to the bus stop to get the express bus and the transfer that will get me right to the bus I always take from my own yard to Brother Man's. I am nearly running when I get to where I see Brother Man's red-painted porch that smiles in the distance. I wonder at the picture I make racing down the road, coat flapping, but that nah stop me flying.

When I get to the house and find all the lights are out and the place is quiet as a tomb, I can't believe it, can't make sense of it, want to tell myself I've come to the wrong house or someting to make sense of it. Worst part of all is to accept it. I go up to the door and knock and knock with the wooden tiger and peer in the windows, though it's clear as light the place is shut down. The only sign anyone's been there in a year is the smoke that lingers.

I can't go directly back to the Silvers', because I'm too sheg-up. I hear Julie in my mind, saying she hate everyting, that life—all of it—*sucks.* I don't care what a dirty, low-class word that is. I go back to my own place—just for a minute, I tell myself, because I've got the family dinner to prepare and Clair will be getting home and she need to find someone there. I knock on Zach's door, but the one time I want to see the man, he don't answer. May be I'm crazy, but I feel like the floor's gone out from under my feet. At home, I take a little glass of rum, even though I bought that liquor for Vincent, in case he needs a taste of it to warm his blood against the shock of winter.

That rum does nothing for me. I wait half an hour, try to steady my breath, then Lord, don't I leave off thinking sense altogether and run out to the bus stop and get right back on the bus and on back to Brother Man's, knowing no way should I be doing this. I am off my mind, going back to see what I just saw—a door shut against me. I get there after the same ride and same walk, and Jesus Lord, I can't believe this sight any more than the last one. Must be the last visit was a bad dream or somebody slip drugs in my breakfast, because there is Joshie's music and the lights and talk and alla that. I walk in just like always and get the usual greetings from Henry P and Frank and Brother Man himself, but I am not my usual self, because I'm still sheg-up through and through. The only ting I see different from most days is the group appear somewhat sparse.

"Wh'appen here?" I ask the few that's there.

"Um. How you inten' dat?" asks Henry P.

"I was here one hour ago, and none of this go on. Everyting shut. Now all is back like usual, like some kind of stage play that start up."

"Every business mus' close up shop on occasion," Brother Man snarls. "I do some accounting is all."

"Weather got a mite hot, girl," says Frank, "if you know what I'm aiming to say. We got to make ourselves scarce awhile."

"Police?" I ask. "You speak of the police?" Strange that never cross my mind when I find the place empty and shut.

Henry P laughs. "She the one to say it out straight. We got to hot step awhile."

"How you come to know when the weather get hot?" I want to find out.

"Little birdie told us so," says Frank.

"Jah put no delicacy in some womenfolk," says Brother Man. "What you wear on your feet today, sister woman? Got you some army boots?"

"Hush, now," says Frank. "She's a fine gal and a guest."

The room hushes, and I look toward the door and there's Lucille just come in, her head bowed as she busies herself with a long line of small buttons that run from her neck down past her knees.

"Lucille," I call out. "Mi tink you go away from town or someting."

I watch her timid eyes search Brother Man, see a stiffness

in her smile, but her voice says, "No, girl, why you think that? Just had me a little chest cold is all." She puts her hand up over her heart and moves toward us and right over to Brother Man's side like the two of them are joined. I swear that woman gives him a nervous blink of di eyes. He must have seen it, too, because he lays his arm across her shoulder like he's owning her or someting.

I play my roulette same as usual—except for watching the clock on the wall—and come out a quips better than even. Most times that would suit me fine. Woulda been more than fine today if not for the dead house that greet me my first visit. I wish they coulda send around some letter or someting, give me a warning, though I know it's pure foolishness to wish fi dat from a gambling house. Brother Man typewriter no mek kindly letter-dem like dat fran Vincent. Oh, Vincent, Vincent, soon him come. That visit a spin of di wheel itself.

When I get back to the Silvers' and start up my cooking, I feel dangerous restless like some hot-stepper ready to do a nex' job.

Clair comes in and starts spinning in stocking feet on the kitchen linoleum. "I heard a dirty joke."

"Um-hm."

"What's the difference between a nut case and a whore?"

"Where you come by such speech?"

"A nut case has a screw loose and a whore is a loose screw."

"Lordy, Clair, you way too young for that sort of ting!" Clair's joking and hopping about is hard for me to take today. At least I have most of the dinner done, so I can sit my batty down awhile, try to stop my head spinning. Clair runs up to the attic, shouting that she's going to pull out a box of dress-up clothes used to belong to her mother. The phone rings, so I'm back on my feet to answer it.

Professor is on the line. "Indi, have you heard from Julie?"

"No, Professor."

"Damn it. I was supposed to pick her up at school at five

o'clock and take her to the dentist. I waited there half an hour, and she never showed up. I phoned Scott on the cell phone and got him to call her girlfriends, but no one has seen her since school let out."

"That's peculiar," I say.

"I'm worried. Do you have any ideas? Where could she be? Scott said something might have happened with her mother."

"That coulda done it for sure."

"She's got my credit card, too. She was supposed to give it back after she got gas yesterday. I asked her three times, and she just got mad about my not trusting her. She's an hour and a half late, now."

"That's not usual for Julie."

"There's no point in my waiting here. I'm coming home."

I sit back down and think about where would Jules go if someting upset her. Got to be Scott; he's the first place. Where else Julie going to go? I picture her at the mall and know she can get there on the bus. But I don't know. Maybe just a foolish idea, me tinking I can see what don't be there. Still, I'm almost grateful to Julie for planting some thoughts to take my mind off my self.

Jill comes in, late because of after-school band practice. Looks like she went to the library after that, from the way her arms piled sky-high with di book-dem. "You see your sister, Jilly?"

"Clair?"

"Jules."

"No."

"She's gone missing. Professor en wait for her at the school an hour and a half. Where would she go if she upset? She's not at Scott's."

"I don't know. The mall, maybe."

So could be it's not so foolish to picture Jules there. "Jill, when Professor comes home, you tell him I took the bus down to the mall to look for Jules. You put the dinner on the table for me. Everything's ready and on the stove. Just hot up the tomato soup before you serve it. The rest of the tings should hold their heat."

I get off the bus and trot across the parking lot, closing my coat over my middle against a damp wind. I go in tru the Crate and Barrel store. I no waste time there but go out eena the big center space, where the teenagers like to hang out, annoying the older folk. Then I just got to wander and keep my eyes open. I nip in and out of some of the stores Julie might like but don't see her, then I take up a post in the middle, but start to wonder was it some sort of false pride a-tink I know where that girl's gonna go if she upset. Cyaan help but tink of me and my numbers, how I get that feeling cyaan nothing go wrong because I know, I just know, what number's coming up. But look how I lose money of late. So maybe I not so smart as I wish, just foolish like Big Bwoy and boasie like Anansi.

But whether luck or wisdom sit at my side today, here come Jules, walking out of Nordstrom and heading across to Lord and Taylor with one full shopping bag in each hand, looking like a big-time spender, either that or a bag lady more choosy than most. I head right to her, calling out, "Julie, Miss Julie Silver." She gives me a hard scowl that looks like it could turn right to tears.

"Wh'appen, Jules? What is it? How you cyan run around here when Professor wait on you, worrying."

"Just leave me alone," she says. "Why are you here?"

"Someting's the matter, Julie. Must be." I whisper, "Are you pregnant, Jules? Is that it? If so, we manage it."

"*No.* Why would you think that?" She says in a hush, "I got my period two days ago."

Jules seems like thirteen all of a sudden, not seventeen. "Well, that's good, so nothing to worry about there. So what's the matter?"

"Nothing. I need some clothes."

"Need them so bad you got to steal your fada charge card?"

"He won't mind. He doesn't care. He doesn't care about anything."

"What you need so vastly?"

"Some clothes. Some nice clothes—something with class, not junky stuff."

"Oh. All of what you have now is junky? Is that what you're saying?"

"Our whole family is junky. And I hate it."

"What's going on here, Jules? Why you suddenly got to be some sort of fashion model out of *Vogue*? Why it's not good enough to be your own self?"

"What's so good about being me? What's so good about being Julie Silver?"

"Your mother up to someting again, Jules?"

"Do you know what she did? She called up Scott's mother on the telephone and started complaining about Scott and how he's not polite enough and not serious enough. To his own mother, she said that stuff. She just wants to make a fool of me so everyone will look at me and say what a weird family I come from."

"So you going to fix that with new clothes?"

She shrugs.

I put my arm close around Julie's shoulder. "You're gonna have to take the bus with me now, the city bus, like ordinary folk. It will get us home just fine, for a good supper."

Julie tears up.

"You're not all grown-up, Jules, not so much as you tink. Some tings going to get clearer in your eyes in time—that is, if you give it some time and don't always be in such a fool's rush."

"What about all this stuff?" she says, lifting one shopping bag in each hand. "I spent a lot of money."

"Oh, Jesus, Professor's going to have a cow!" I laugh. "Maybe tomorrow you mus' return some of them tings. But for now, you got a bunch of new clothes."

We get home, and Lord, if Jill hasn't done a fine job setting the table and laying out the food. Jules sees her father and breaks into tears, till he have no choice but sit her down and put his arm around her.

The Silvers tire me so with all their troubles that Monday, when I'm off work during the day, I feel I deserve a little fun. It wi be hard to go back there next workday widoht some enjoyment first. I bundle myself against the cold and walk down to the Chicago Avenue Bank and take out half of what's there, get myself ready for Brother Man. When I go back home and put it in my drawer, suddenly that drawer is layered thick with cash, just like when Jewel first drag me over to that gambling house. I right away begin to get that old misery about that money and what it used to be good for.

I head out to the bus but Jamaica is too much wid me. I wonder how will Vincent bear up if the weather is wintry in April, him with no meat on 'im bones. Will he have any proper clothes to wear? Will he feel like he's gone to the moon and want to hurry and get home to where the wind carries some breath of life?

Brother Man's not at the red house today, which seems stranger than I can say, since he's sewed into that place tighter than a pocket. The folks left under Joshie's watch are a serious bunch. Their eyes take in nothing but chips and numbers. Some of dem new to me, so everyting boht this place seem new, which troubles me. A tiny black woman smokes a long cigarette and studies her numbers. Her face is full of lines sharp as knife cuts, her hair is pulled into a bun look like a rubber ball, no strand loose from the bundle. She must be sixty, maybe coming to this house for years, learning what she knows now but somehow I miss her. I go over and stand beside her, watch her study the wheel like her mind is full of careful thoughts. But this is my night. Don't belong to her, nor anyone else but me, that much I know. I see myself clear as a photograph walking out two hours from now, my leather purse cork up with Brother Man's money, though he's not here and don't know who or what walks oht his door. Money in the drawer troubles my mood but walking out with money lifts me high, though I can make no sense of that.

Brother Man must hear me thinking. He comes in the front door and walks over and stands before me, his eyes as angry as the day the police interrupt his business.

"I'm still looking forward to that drink, Indigo," he tells me, no laughter to his voice, just scolding.

"One of these days, mon. Soon as I make dege-dege money so I can pay for my liquor."

"Drink's on me, woman. Don't need no private funding."

"Okay, then, but today is for the numbers, not for socializing. What happen with your fat little gal, then?"

"That don' be your business," he says. "Just do what you come for." He strides off, his hands deep in his front pockets like he's ashamed for the world to see them, greedy as they are. I go to the wheel, and soon I am up by two hundred, so I know it's not just me dreaming, today truly is my day. For a time, I go with one of my systems, playing the last digit of the number that en come up time before last, joined with the last digit of the last number to win, which means I got to concentrate and hold the winning numbers sharp in mind. I get to where I'm ahead by four hundred and the people interrupt their own play to look at me. Should stop at four hundred, but this day I no plan to satisfy easy.

When I am up by six hundred, my system starts to corrupt, and I find I am losing equal to what I win. I just stall, hold steady at six hundred, so I tell myself, *Okay, okay, here is the moment. Now you choose, sister. Do you cash out with the man or go on to a next system, maybe one you never before try?* I am glad for the six hundred, but it's not the large number that would swell my heart tonight, so I say, *Okay, Indigo girl, today's your day to go ahead reach for the moon.* I think hard and deep and discover a new system, one that challenge me more even than the last. This one ask more from my brain, because I got to call on the last three spins, not just two like before. I can't talk to a soul or even move my eyes around the room, chancing distraction, jus' get hold of my numbers and play them.

The people get quiet and fix on me, them keep still as ice. Must be my concentration spreads a tension through them, too. The first time I try the new system, I hit it at twenty-four-to-one odds and feel myself weak from what I en do, weak like a woman can feel when a man who's been filling her head walks in the room unexpected. I get myself together so I can remain attentive to the numbers and figure what to play this next round. When I come up empty, I wonder did I call my numbers wrong because the weakness cost me my focus. So I play again, using my three-spin system, but again I miss on the winning number, though not by much. Now I am down to five hundred, and I stop again to parse my course. I step back from the table and let Joshie go ahead and make his next spin for the miniature woman—Amaria, she calls herself—and for the Indian man, Sanjay, who's come in along with two others.

Joshie takes bets and spins a second time, and I watch a big Cuban man who Brother Man calls Ernesto. He wins a small bit of money, which gets him excited, then he takes off his shirt to show the people how he's got tattooed roses draped across the back of his shoulders like a shawl—don't know why winning a quips of money mek him want to strip off his clothes. Could be he's got the same chemicals running tru his brain as Clair, who don't take much of an excuse to pull off her garments. Lucille comes in and sidles up to Brother Man till she's close as a shadow. After a while, she goes and loses some more money like she always do.

Ernesto hits some long odds on twelve, my number for Louisa's birthday, and I watch him jump a mile into the air and give a yell and give a hug to Sanjay, who most don't touch because of his stumpy arm. And then I'm back in the game, not liking to see what should be mine today going somebody else's way. I realize, too, that the slide down to five hundred is only testing my courage, because if I stop here and take that sum home, what do I have but a half-filled drawer that gives me no good feeling, it's just a wan thing, but if I keep on and take some risk, then maybe I get what I come looking for, that feeling I look to and long for that makes my heart full like a pool fill up from neet the ground.

That's how I decide to stick wid my new system even while my dunsa sink from five hundred to four hundred to three. I hold to my idea of keeping my courage and taking risk, but today is not my day after all, and pretty soon all the eyes are on me—who knows, maybe they take me for a fool—because I have nothing more to spend. In the end Brother Man is by my side, and I am too maga in my spirit and confused in my mind to resist what help he offers me, so yes I do, I take some money from him, more than any time before, two hundred dollars in all or maybe a little more, but in the end somehow I go home without those dollars, too, and without my good feeling, and have a sorrowful evening and a black and wakeful night.

Next morning, I have no choice but go back there and try to win someting so I can pay him back. Though I never do such a ting before, I call Professor and tell him I have personal business and mus' come in late. Then I climb back on that bus one time more—the step-dem seem more steep than usual—and me go again to Brother Man's, feeling like a duppy man abroad in the night. I set everyting straight, but I worry all the while boht the job I'm playing reckless with and my lying tongue when I talk with Professor. When I leave and hurry to the Silvers', I go with some money in my pocket but widoht my good feelings. Maybe I'm too scared that come evening Professor's going to ask me what personal business I mus' attend so early in the day. Maybe he'll go on and discharge me like he threatened one time and then I must take leave of the girls. When evening comes, Professor no say a word, but I feel a chilliness come off him and feel him watch me close, which worries my heart.

Next weekend I have a good amount of time for Brother Man's, but it's a bad weekend for winning and the money in my drawer dwindles down to nothing, so I have to make another trip to the bank. I get Zach for my teller this time, which never happened before, and a feeling half-bitter, half-glad fills me when I withdraw the last of my savings. Zach don't say a ting, because I'm a customer here, not a neighbor woman, and he's a man who knows some manners. That money was for Louisa schooling and Louisa clothes and toys. It has no use now that's any better than the one I put it to at Brother Man's. So I clear my conscience, just hose it down like a cement walk. And truth be told, part of me likes the emptiness in that account book, because that money for Lou often haunt me. What point to build a nest egg, when I've got no child to lavish it on? Still, I know someting's evil about thinking that way when there's a child somewhere in this world could use that money for her school fees.

With the fresh start this money gives me, I know I can call back my luck. Luck just took a rest is all. It's certain to be tonight my luck returns to stand by my side. But luck nah come tonight, unless that joker come to the side door and I'm standing at the front. Only advice I got for myself is "Concentrate, sister, concentrate," and if not tonight, then tomorrow you'll be getting back on di horse.

But now tomorrow is come, and nothing go better for me even though my mind's like a fist as it fixes on those numbers and my heart's certain I have them right. Still Joshie's ball bounces into the wrong box time after time, and I am borrowing very steady from Brother Man and scaring myself some. I try not to bring too many dollars with me each time I visit, but Brother Man don't want me stopping too soon, so he stands beside me, ready to make me a little loan, and my weak self can't resist what he offers. Each time I borrow from him, I put a scrap of paper marked with the amount in my drawer at home next to what cash is left, and I no bother pay him off. I just go in next time with a bit more cash, and I hope this day will be the day I conjure the right numbers so I can pay off all of Brother Man's loans at one time. Brother Man quits his flirting and his meanness both. He play the gentleman again, play the doctor who know all of what worries you and tries to soothe you some, but I don't trust him, and I wonder where in the world is Lucille, who's deep in debt to this man, and I don't see her anymore.

The days I spend at the Silvers' idle like a slow stream. I stay peaceful and mannerly there, but my heart is somewhere else and all my excitement bubbles within the earth neet Brother Man's house. Alcohol is costing me a sum, too, as Brother Man is not so cheap with his liquor with his old regulars as with his newcomers. I cyaan hold it against him that he runs a good business. I think of skipping the drink, but drink seems to go with the betting like horse and cart.

One evening, after coming home from the Silvers', I go into my drawer, and all I find there are scraps of white paper like one big sheet of stationery that's torn into bits, each one of them an IOU to Brother Man. My mind shapes a picture of Jill's letter from Ben Sands that she tore to pieces that odd moment when her mind seemed twisted. I wonder is my mind twisted now. I have no choice but go to Brother Man's with no more than what I have in my purse from Professor's last paycheck. I let the man give me a likkle more so I can put together a half-decent amount for my bets. Still, I know when to stop and don't plan to stay all day, like some of them. Just stay till I'm feeling myself. No point to keep up gambling beyond that. That would be throwing money down the drain, and I'm not that kind. All evening, Brother Man leaves me to my sport, but when I'm ready to go, he's by my side, close enough for only a whisper of air to run between us, and then his arm goes around my shoulder and he's breathing some words into my ear. "Come and see me a little later in the evening, cyan you, sugar dawta?"

I shake my head.

"What? Brother Man no treat you fine? No act generous and extend you plenty of credit?"

"I keep my gambling in one pocket, my personal life in the other."

"You keep everyting separate from everyting else," he says. "Got many more pockets than most. I notice that boht you, Indigo Rose. See how you blanch when the others take a photo or some likkle nonsense from oht they wallet same as if they pull a ratchet to cut you face."

"That's my business."

"You make all your personal life in the white man's world, don't give nuff respect to your own people."

"I don' waste my time boht who's my people and who's not."

"So fine of you," he says, and turns his mouth up like he's swallowed sour milk, walks off from me. But he can't let it go. He calls back to me across the room, for all the world to hear. "You seen Lucille around where you live?" Frank moves his eyes from the table to Brother Man, and Joshie takes his lip in his teeth. I shake my head, puzzled, and go on outside thinking the air outdoors figures to be less chilled than what's within.

I'm an angry woman as I make my way to the bus. I don't

like my pleasure complicated by that man. He looks too much at my figure and face, and into my eyes. I don't need him searching for a spot to enter my life.

I go there several days later, and Brother Man is too generous with his money, and charming as a prince, and him no say a word about wi get together for a drink. I forget what kind of care I need to use and take what money he offers, let Joshie turn that wheel all evening, until I am tired of betting, truly, though I'm just even for the night.

Late in the evening, I hear Brother Man laugh and say to Joshie, "Oh, too much coffee fill the bladder today." He strolls back to the tiny bat'room near to the Burma Shave clock. I hear him a-chuckle from in there and sing out, so all of us get to hear, "He's got the whole wo-orld, in his hands." I don't want my life mixed up with his, so the next day I do someting I never done before. I take a handful of jewelry belong once to my auntie and go to a likkle pawnshop down the street and loan it out to them for a bit of cash, thinking I'm going to start paying back what I owe the man, but my next trip there, my pocket is too full of dollars and my heart too full of the hunger, and I lay down all that money on Brother Man's table and go home late and tired and angry with myself and him both, at the same time as I'm restless to get back there and undo what damage I did tonight.

It's the first part of March. I pass a few quiet days at the Silvers'. The next time I go home to my flat, I walk in and someting in the room no feel right to me, but I can't say what. I look until I see an envelope that's taped in the center of my eating table. Seems it must be from the landlord, but I wonder at his a-use his key widoht my permission. That vex me, and frighten me. My mind turns to making a complaint before I even have the letter opened. When I open the envelope, there I see a typed letter that's not from any landlord, it's from

Brother Man himself and, oh, Jesus, my blood pressure drops so fast I mus' sit right down on the chair or pass out. Jesus Lord, what can that man want with me to make his way into my home and leave me these careful words?

I got to steady myself before the words can hold their place on the page. Then I see that Brother Man is telling me he is sorry, he is regretful, but my account with him is past due. Okay, okay, I can make good on that. I can catch it up, I'm sure of that. No big trouble there, I'll just find someting more to give to the pawnbroker. Me no need none of those tings anyway, they're just boht sentiment, boht tender feeling. I think of the hundreds of trinkets that lie in the Silvers' house, but no need to think that way. I got someting of my own I can give up, surely.

Brother Man's typing no end wid the words that say I'm past due. More is coming. He tells me maybe I will receive a visit from a couple good friends of his to collect what's owed him, and he would appreciate fi mi have the money, plus interest, set aside and available. He wants me to know that he can't be predicting just when these friend-dem might come by the house, as each one manages his own schedule, so I might want to be watching for them at any time of day or night. Oh, Lord, I feel how he loves to play with me, even in his letter. I'm just a field mouse. But the part that makes my heart stop is this last, where he tells me he's full of regret but has no choice but tell me I'm not welcome to come around to his establishment till my debt is paid, including his full interest. What a devil that man can be, playing with my heart so. I wish I had a drink to settle me, but I used up what likkle alcohol I had in my house. I could go across to Zach, but how can I tell him I lost my money. What will dat man tink of Indigo, all tangled up with samfai man, hugly man who play tricks on dem who foolish.

I try to busy myself through the day and keep my mind away from this new trouble, but that night after the sun begin its rest, I get a fantastic urge to get on the bus and ride to Brother Man's and see will he nah let me just bet what money I've got from my last paycheck. Someting inside raises a stern finger and warns me off of that, tells me don't even go near there now, don't cross Brother Man around his rules. I think of how Lucille stopped coming awhile, then en come back quiet and oversweet, half a zombie, watching Brother Man for his every nod and wink, and now it seems she's stopped coming altogether, and so many sly comments circulate around her name they get a person wondering what on earth happened to that big woman. I wrap up and go on out in the cold to the corner liquor store and get a bottle of rum and sip at it till I forget myself.

Sixteen

These next days are the hardest ones I've had for a long, long time. I'm at the Silvers', but all the while I have a deep, uneasy feeling about who is walking boht in my own house. The part that hurts me most is not the thought of Brother Man's henchmen come in while I'm there and break my bones; it's thinking about all Louisa's little pictures that sit there without me. What if somebody wanting to hurt me bad decides to tear them into pieces like the chits in my drawer? That picture makes me crazy, because those photos are all I have of my baby. I berate myself for leaving them there, open to harm, and want to get on the bus and go and gather them up, but I have no time in the day for that and don't need to answer Professor's questions, or Clair's, about where I go off to. So I suffer with the fear, and at the same time, Lord, if I'm not certain the only ting that would wash it from my mind is a visit to Brother Man's, the one place I don't dare go.

I wander into the library and pull out from the shelves the

photo album Jill put together. Though I never looked at it before except if one of the girl-dem shoob it under my nose, I go now and sit down on the sofa with the large leather book like I'm mother to these children, mistress to this house. There is Clair at the Lincoln Park Zoo next to the spindly baby giraffe, and me beside her, smiling, thinking some joking thought. I guess Jill's the one that snapped it, with that likkle zoom camera she loves that Mrs. Silver bought for her when she still knew someting about the girl's heart.

Next we are beside the birdhouse, where the strangest laughter comes from inside a hut of gray stones, each stone the size of a man's skull. Inside the first room are two African laughing terns, huge bird-dem, their beaks pointing to the ceiling, one bird's throat pressed to the other's, their long necks stretched like snakes and both laughing as odd as people likely to find themself one day in the asylum. We sidle through a curtain of bead ropes, and there's a nex' big laughing bird with a printed card undaneath that tells us this bird is "Kookaburra." The children and me see him grab a poor mouse who's trying to light-step across the floor. Mister Kookaburra holds the scrap of mouse by the tail and slaps it hard against a tree trunk. I don't know whether he want to kill it or crush its bones. Either way, Kookaburra's getting ready to make himself a meal. Poor mousie.

I close up the picture album and take a breath. *Bird got to eat,* I tell myself.

Just closing the book won't take me out of that birdhouse. I see Kookaburra lift his head and open wide his beak till the broken mouse tumbles down his throat. There's an ugly lump just sitting in his throat until he swallows once, and again, and then mouse in di belly.

"Oh, what a sight," I recall a-say to Jill. "Dat make me sick." Clair don't see it, I don't think. Her eyes are on a huge bird that look just like a songbird, but its face a white owl face, round and flat, as strange a combination as you could see. She points toward the Kookaburra and says, "I know a song about Kookaburra sitting in a tree. I thought it meant a bear, Indi."

All I can think of is Louisa's little song about Bunny Foo Foo bopping the field mice on the head. I start to hum it, and Clair surprises me by join in wid me. "You know that nonsense song, child?" I ask her.

"Sure. Little Bunny Foo Foo. Everyone knows it."

I shake my head and tell the girls, Let's go on oht the bird-house, I don't like this big, nasty cuckoo bird. Can't figure what he have to laugh at.

I put the photo book back on the shelf, because these memories do me no good. Memories never do, these days. I get up and stretch out some stiffness gripping my back and try to get on with my cleaning. All those ugly pictures from the birdcage turn my thoughts to places they don't want to go. There go Mr. Borotsky, a young man not much older than Jules, trying to get by in that monstrous place him sent to. I can't see how his heart's come clean after all that staining, but I believe it has, much of the way. And there's Professor in my thoughts, too, telling me alla the violence and misery many refugee come through, and some of them heal, and how he wants me to treat the children kinder or lose my job. Mr. Borotsky touches me in the way he worries about my roulette and notices the danger in the bullying looks Brother Man gives me when I bathe him in my ice water. Well, best I put that in the past voice, because alla that finish now. 'Cept Mr. Borotsky still ranking; I admire that old man.

I am upstairs, washing the extra bathroom behind the study, with four-foot as my company, when I hear the door push open downstairs, and wonder who is home so early. I think one of the girls mus' got sick at school and the teacher send her home. Or Julie, now she's a senior and afraid of no one—at least no one who's grown—mighta step out on her own and come home, after she fooled around till her heart's content.

I just keep on with my straightening—no need to run down and greet whoever—but Tennyson is on his feet and out of the study, and it surprises me to hear him standing at the top of the stairs, barking fierce as Toshie who three time his size. I head out and down the stairs with him racing in front of me, my heart beating faster than the Lord ever intended. When we get to the bottom of the stairs, he dashes to the white kitchen door, still with the sharp voice, so I push through it into the smell of the onions I fried up for my lunch, my mind on fire now with Brother Man and his goons. When I see Mrs. Silver standing beside my sink, reaching up to one of my cabinets, my heart slows, but my temper flares.

Tennyson never before met the girl dey mada, and he run half circles in front of her, biting lightly at the air like he want to nip at her legs but no cyan get around behind her to reach them.

"Mrs. Silver" is all I can say. How many months has it been since I've seen her in this house?

She rolls her lips in on each other, smoothing her lipstick, and makes a disgusted *"uch"* from her throat, and I recall how she nah like animal-dem and would only touch them if the girls pushed her to be nice to some dog or cat, and then she would touch the creature with the tips of her fingers. She is not so different from me in that. Me, I would pet whatever creature it was if I must, then go and scrub my hands and get the animal dirtiness off my skin, though this Tennyson is a clean dog and smarter than you woulda expect, so I come to where I put up with him.

"You surprised me, Mrs. Silver," I say. "You still carry a key to this house?" She is dressed as prim and tasteful as ever, in a navy-blue short wool skirt and a white silk blouse with a loose bow at the throat, though her face has a fallen-dough look it's taken on this past year and her skin is high colored and rough. Circled round in a ring of black makeup, her eyes are dull like stone, and her hair is dark at the root but bleached blonde at the tips. Frosted, she calls it, like someting the winter brought.

"I've got more than any of you think," she says in that draggy-tongue voice all her drugs give her, "and plenty more than your *Professor* knows."

I don't know just what she's talking about, but I long ago got used to that. "Professor and the girls are all out," I say. "Every one of them."

"That's all right. I just came for several things that belong to me." She marks her last few words like they are cork up with meaning.

"What here belongs to you?" I ask. "You take all your things, nuh?"

"I forgot two or three things," she says with another big air. "*My* things," she adds, like she and me in a fight over possession.

My mind lights on the girls she talks of wanting to take, and on Professor telling me she's hired a lawyer. "What tings?" I ask.

"Just some things of mine. Papers. I'll have to look for them, in the study."

"In Professor's study?" Alarm bells clang in my head.

"Yes," she says. "His study."

"Not if Professor's not here," I say. "You phone and talk to Professor when he come home." I feel like a big goose standing tall, flapping its wings to warn her away from that room.

"Indigo," she says in a sudden way, her voice sounding full of worry, "you had better be thinking about another job for yourself. When the girls come to live with me, you'll need some other work, won't you? To make ends meet?"

"Never mind about that," I say, brindling at her nonsense.

I follow her to the base of the stairs, the dog behind her at her heels, which remind me how Professor say this dog fashioned for herding, but I say him jus' a-hurry her out di house. While she climbs the stairs, she manages to kick out her foot to catch him in his little face.

"Aiii!" I give a scream. Right now, I wish he had a meaner spirit and the heft of a big shepherd dog. "I cyaan have you go in Professor study," I say, following her up the stairs. "I got to be in charge of this house while Professor is away."

She takes no notice of me and goes direct into Professor's room and pulls open the top drawer of his desk.

"I have a right to prove my case, Indigo. It's only fair. So I need the evidence I'm entitled to, of who's the unfit parent."

"That's not right, Mrs. Silver," I say. "A-go into someone's drawer like that, when they not home. You got to shut that up right away."

She laughs a nasty laugh. "I'll tell you about what's not right," she says. "I'll tell you about what that man you so admire's done to me, and then you'll know about what's not right. You'd be surprised, Indigo, to hear about your dear 'Professor.' "

"I don't need to hear that hugly talk," I say. "You close Professor drawer, Mrs. Silver. You get oht of Professor desk. That poison in your system mek you do tings that nah cyan be right. You cyaan even think of the children."

Now she glares at me. "Don't tell me about my children. And this desk is mine just as much as his. I bought this desk, for your information. I bought it at the Merchandise Mart, just like everything in this house. Everything in this house is mine."

"How you figure that, Mrs. Silver? That's crazy talk."

"The furniture and the pictures on the wall and the books and the children. We're not divorced yet, you know. Those kids are mine. They'll never be yours."

Now I am flabbergasted. "You think I want your children? I don't want any child not my own flesh, Mrs. Silver, and my own baby is lost to me, someting you already know. You get on out of that drawer, or I go on call the police." Now I believe I caught her attention. She knows the police know her, for all her problems with false prescriptions at the pharmacy.

She slams the drawer. "You're in trouble, Indi," she says. "And you've got no business talking about *my* faults. You should tend to your own business and don't worry about mine."

I don't know what she means by that but I don't care to listen.

"I could get you fired with what I know about you."

Is this someting real or just the bad talk Mrs. Silver so famous for? I twist my head, look at her crosswise, same as the likkle dog do when he want to ask you a question. "You don't have a lot of say-so with Professor these days," I tell her, bold as fire, but still I keep a-wonder what it is she tink she know to blacken me.

I hear the door open downstairs and don't know whether I'm glad or sorry someone's walked in on this. "Who is it?" I call down.

"Jill." Her voice floats up the stairs.

Oh, Jill, I think, wondering did she take notice of her mother's car out in the street. Jill's always the lucky one to be caught in her mother's ill wind.

"Come up here," Mrs. Silver calls down. "It's Mom." Her voice sounds so deadly to me just now I can't tell has she sweetened it up any for Jill.

I cannot see Jill but I feel her tighten. A few seconds pass, then I hear her moving up the stairs, slow as salve. She stops just below the top and looks across the landing to where we stand in the door of Professor's study.

"Hi," she says quietly, a stack of ten or a dozen books piled up to her chin.

Mrs. Silver turns her head to Jill but keeps her attention on me, too, as if she's got a gun to my head and no plan to let me slip away.

As her mother's eyes find her, Jill drops every one of the

books right on her own feet. They make a bangarang, but Jill makes no more than a squeak.

"What are you doing?" Mrs. Silver says to her, as if the child en make a choice to spill her books all over her feet.

The books scatter down three or four steps. Jill scampers after them, looking somewhat pitiful.

"So you finish looking for what you seek, Mrs. Silver? So now time come to go."

She looks at Jill, who's squatting, corralling her books, and says to her, "This isn't your business."

Jill has most of her book-dem cradled in her arms. She acts like she don't hear a ting, turns down the hallway, and goes into her room and out of sight. I hear her door shut softly.

Soon her mother follow after her and push open the door and say loud enough for Indigo hiez, "You think you can just walk away and shut your eyes and not see anything you don't want to see. You want to believe your father is a hero, but wait till you see what I'll show you, when I can get my hands on it. Then you'll know where you'll be a year from now."

I strain my ears to hear Jill answer her back. "I'm not interested in anything you have to show me." I picture her burying her face in her pillow and pressing her hands over her ears.

"I suppose you never heard the word *adultery*, but you may, soon."

"Who *wouldn't* commit adultery?" Jill yells, her voice suddenly loud and clear, and I can tell her fire's lit.

"That's fine for now," Mrs. Silver says. "You say what you please. And, by the way, I suppose you're not interested enough to ask what happened with my eye—who it was that helped me when you weren't there."

"No, I'm not interested," she says, her voice quiet again but fierce.

I feel a kind of thrill and in my head say, *You hold rock-steady, Jill. I always know you're the strong one.* Then I catch myself short, because haven't I tired of cheering for these girls who are no flesh and blood of mine? I slip by like a shadow and as I slide down the hall, I see Jill raise her head from the bed and look at her mada as if she want to say with her eyes, *What happened to you*? She stares at Mrs. Silver until her mother takes a step back inside the shelter of the door frame.

She pull in her breath, then let it out, then ready to start up again. "You'll be with me soon, all of you girls, and then you'll care about a few things." She adds, "Your friend Indigo, I'd think she'd be a bit more sobered by what happened in her life last year."

Lord, can this be? Is she talking about my child with that tone? I wonder again does she know someting of me and the problems that haunt me. I expect her to speak of last week, not last year, to jook me for my troubles with Brother Man. No way, though, can she know about that. Her world and mine never cross.

When Mrs. Silver go, I go back by Jill's room, and she is still on her bed, only now she's kneeling with her forehead buried in her pillow and her hip-dem up in di air like when she have misery from her period.

"She's not taking you girls," I say to Jill, and hope I tell no lie. "Her talk is no more than monkey chatter."

"She used to be okay, Indi. I remember. I remember when she was a good mother, a regular mother. Now all I feel for her is hate. I'm such a bitch now."

"Hush. No one going to blame you for that, Jill."

She shakes her head. "It's poison in me, in my heart. For my own mother."

"I know how that cyan feel."

I go on down to the living room and sit awhile, wondering why it is I bother to make such a show boht Professor's rights, even setting my body between Mrs. Silver and him door, when I ought to be seeing to my own life and not worrying over another's.

* * *

Three days later, I walk into town to do some errands for Professor, and take that dog along because he won't let up fussing at me. Heading back to the house, when we are near to the park with the old "climbing tree" all the children visit, I look ahead, and there's Clair racing back and forth, back and forth on the grass in front of that big tree like she is Charlie Chaplin in some kind of sketch. Her little skirt looks ready to catch a breeze and lift her into the air. Here it is, only forty degrees, with cold winds coming through fast as a line of buses, and Clair has on nothing but her pullover sweater and no jacket. I start to lift my hand and wave it, ready to call out her name and ask her what on earth she's doing chasing around like a person lost her mind, and half-naked as well, but just then her friend Franny comes out from behind the tree and Clair looks at Fran and holds her finger to her pursed lips and makes a sign to Fran like *"shhh"* and gives her a stern face, and that shooshes me, too.

Now I am close to the girls, and I stop behind some thorny bushes with shriveled red berries and watch to see what are these girls up to. The dog comes by my side and keeps quiet. Clair ducks behind the broad old tree with its low branches spread like a mada's arms, and Fran stands in front of the tree, looking this way and that as if she is a teif watching for her getaway car to come spinning around the bend. They cyaan see each other, but I see them both. Fran is restless, like someting growing inside her want to burst out, and she starts singing one of their camp songs that I hear by now more times than I care to remember. " 'There once was a man named Michael Finnegan, he had whiskers on his chinnegan. . . .' " Behind the tree, Clair begins doing the strangest ting I have ever seen. Right there in public, she unbutton her blue cotton-knit sweater and take it off so that she is standing in the cold, wearing absolutely nothing on top. Part of me gets set to race right out and cover her, and part of me is too shocked to move. " 'The wind blew 'em off, and they grew right in again,' " sings Fran.

She stops her singing. "Did you do it?" I hear her ask, her words punching the air in a loud whisper. I can't hear any answer from Clair, but Fran steps backward till she's leaning against the tree, then she reaches a hand behind her and around the tree, her eyes still scanning the street. She is opening and closing her eager hand, singing " 'Poor old Michael Finnegan. Begin again.' "

Clair's face now show so much excitement she look ready to launch herself to the moon widoht di rocket. She pass the sweater into Fran's waiting hand. Franny brings the sweater in front of her, and her eyes get wide from what she's got hold of, which tells her what Clair's nah wearing on her pale likkle body. Fran is jumping up and down. She gives up her post and rush around to Clair to force Clair's sweater into her hand and tell her, "Get it on. Hurry—you'll get caught." Clair starts giggling like she take leave of her senses. She squeals out, "Police," and circles her finger in the air like the spinning lights of a police siren and giggles and jumps some more and claps her hand over her mouth. Franny buttons up Clair's sweater, because Clair too busy jumping. When Clair's all dressed, Fran finally settles down and digs in her jacket pocket and pulls out someting she hands to Clair, and at that point I see enough and I go marching up there, the dog getting the girls' attention before me because all his quiet now turn to yapping and running circles round the children. The two girls are frozen side by side like Twin Pops, looking at me, their eyes all questions.

"Yes, I did see," I declare. "I saw all of it. The craziest ting I ever see in all my days."

"You won't *tell*, Indi," Clair pleads. "You won't tell Daddy. Please, please."

"What mek you so sure of that?" I say. "Tell me why would you girls do such a ting? And you *no* tell me a tale."

"We had a bet," Clair says, ready to spill it all out fast as quicksilver.

"Just fifty cents," Fran's thin voice says. "That's all I gave her. Two quarters."

"What would Professor tink of you two? You can give him a heart attack, Clair."

"Don't tell him, Indi. Please," Clair begs as if she will die from the thought of it. "Here." She reaches her hand into her jacket pocket. "You can have the money."

"Oh, put that money away, Clair, and come along home. Professor have nuff on him mind to worry boht widoht him know all you foolishness."

"Thank you, Indi, thank you," Clair says, and hangs on my shoulder, full of loving as if I just bought her a baby doll that coo and cry. "Here, Indi," she offers. "I'll take Tenny so you won't have to hold the leash."

I press my leash hand to my belly. "I en carry that leash all the way into town," I tell her, "so I can just as well carry it the rest of the way home." We all walk along together, me wondering what is in Clair's mind to do such a ting. Is she ready to have us all tink she have her mada's brain in her head? What comes into my own head then is a story the girls tell of their trip to Indiana last year and how their mother took too many of her pills and stumbled out the house in just her brassiere and baggies, and someone must have call the police, because the police they came by, their siren turning and flashing, and dragged her oht the yard, back eena the house. They asked the girls, *what's wrong with her, does she drink liquor,* and the girls boht die of shame. Just last night after that lagga head lawyer leave, those girls were talking about going to Indiana in the summertime. Jill was looking forward to visiting the frog pond by the house, and Julie was thinking about the beach and the suntanned lifeguards, and then this story boht their mada come up for telling one more time.

Seventeen

I step in like a stranger and squint my eyes over the space. I'm glad to see the dust lies unmarked, as if no hand has touched it. I have to stall awhile before I turn my eyes to where Louisa's pictures should be, on the shelf over the TV. When I see them undisturbed, I cannot stop my tears, so I sit and cry and all the while I curse myself for what I've done to bring us to this place. Me thinking I'm so smart and all the time as easy a prey as the rest. No different from Lucille, who lower herself direct into Brother Man's net. It's not my own wrecked life I'm hollering about now; it's the thought of some hugly man a-put his foul hand on my Louisa's pictures, which feels as if it would frighten her even now and take her from me one more time. I sit in my brown chair, Louisa's third-year picture in my hand, and can't move my mind from the thought of what kind of mother I am. What kind of mother could I ever have been to follow a whim to come to this America, which in the end is no different from any other place. Yet I leave my own child where harm could overtake her and tell myself I do it for her, for her future? What kind of mother could I be to mash up my life to where a stranger might walk eena my place and help themself to Louisa's pictures, to all I have left of her?

The saddest part is this: knowing what I know boht myself don't do a ting to make me be different from how I am. My want is more sharp than ever to find my peace at Brother Man's, and I swear if I had ten dollars, or even with my pocket flat empty, if I cyan noh that Frank open the door to me and Brother Man nod me in and offer me a lilly bit more rope to twist round my neck, I nah hesitate one second to climb on that bus. I understand now what Frank's big muscle-dem do for Brother Man, and I understand better someting wild in Frank's laugh when he joke boht what become of Lucille, but even that understanding wouldn't keep me from a-go back, fool that I am. I better say "sorry" to Jill, because now I know for certain who is the bigger fool.

Mama disapprove Papa's gambling, but she would nah turn her face from me for gambling now, because her face already turn. I know her heart become ice toward her Indigo. If she hear my voice, she just grunt some, never make a smile or crease the eye. What of Jill's poem now? *Some say in ice.* . . . Maybe that's the way, because how the heart can go cold.

I hold Louisa's picture close to my face and search in my baby's right eye for the tiny white spot in the brown that always looked to me like a grain of sand. I loved that little white spot like I loved every freckle and hair on my baby's head. No matter how close I look, I cannot find it. Not even a hawk's eye could find it in this hazy picture. I remember, too, the bald spot Louisa have on the back of her head, high up near the crown. It was a place no bigger than a pearl button, just a place where the skin was thick and no hair would grow. Louisa never knew about that spot. I never spoke of it to her, but noticed it whenever she laid her head on my chest or slept with her head buried in the feather pillow I got her at the Valley Goods store. I have no photograph of that spot, nothing

I can hold up to my eyes and try to burrow inside, hoping to see just one time more what I know was there. And at this moment I feel again that old feeling that says I no cyan bear to live out my life never laying my eyes on what Jah placed on Louisa's head to mark her as herself and no one else, or on that fleck of white sand He left in her eye. So that—that and Mama, because her heart surely harden against me the way I harden against those girls—is why I got to go back to Brother Man's or find another such forgetful place.

A knock comes at the door, and I open it to Zach. I am glad to interrupt my thoughts.

"How tings go wid you, Zach?" I watch his shy smile fill up and shine a little light over me.

"Oh, good. Good enough, sister," he says. He rubs his hand across his cheek, and I see he's not yet shaved. Never I see his face rough like this before.

"You hear from Cliff much lately?" I ask.

"Not so much. Him busy with his boy Jeffrey and trying to find a little work there in New York till he come home."

"Good he takes care of his son."

"Him a good father, Cliff," Zach says. "Him take that job serious. Well, I just come by to say hello to you, Indigo, since you gone all week on the job."

"All right, then," I say, glad he did come by and help me start to relax, wishing he might stay awhile but not thinking to open my mouth and say so.

As he's starting out the door, he scratches his head and turns back around toward me. "Someone give me a message for you, sister woman. I almost forgot."

"What message?"

"The man from across the road, the one with the hound dog, he come through my line at the bank, ask me do I live across from you. Then he say to tell you Brother Man send a message that he still tink about you, he not forget about you—meantime, don't want to see you."

I stretch my top lip into a snarl.

"That message mean something to you?"

I shake my head. "Cho! Not to me, mon."

"Seemed strange to me, Indigo—him thinking of you but no wish to see you—and odd to pass it to me on the job like that."

"Much about that man is strange." So there I give myself away.

The little bit of peace Zach brought is gone, and I drop my head and shake it.

"I'll leave you be, since you just come in the house," Zach says. "Maybe see you later in the day. You come by any time you want a cup of tea."

I am filled with all the thoughts of Louisa that Brother Man's sweet sport once shut outside my door. Now those thoughts come huff and puff like the big bad wolf, and I see how Brother Man made me grateful to him and to his quiet way of knowing how to keep me safe from too deep a pain. Bertha flutters in my mind, too, adding her piece to my misery. All I can see of Bertha's life is her sitting so heavy on the bed, shaking and crying, worrying over those pictures of her kids, her "heart and soul." I stay in my house and do nothing, not even my cleaning, and hear Zach come and go, come and go from his apartment, making so much noise I wonder does he want to fill my ears. Once I smell fish frying and soon he knocks on my door, but, though I long for distraction, I don't get up to answer and him too polite or humble to knock again. I'm afraid to go out and wander the streets because of who all could make themself at home in my place while I'm gone.

Adding to my trouble is Vincent. Though I try to keep the worry from my mind, I know that in two more weeks Vincent come to my door. I think of him like a messenger from Mama, as if Mama's been holding someting in her heart toward me ever since I left home, and since Louisa died, Mama's poor heart is set to burst, so now she no can bear hold it more and she send Vincent across the ocean to say her chastening words to me. This is what I am fearing all along, but I never tell it to myself until now. I feel how Mama's words may cut me, even coming from Vincent's gentle tongue.

I go back to the Silvers', and for once I don't mind being there, because I can lose myself in their lives and try and forget my own. This time I take Louisa's pictures with me, wrapped in a pillow slip, but the truth is I am too deep in my sorrow to worry much over what could happen to them. My baby feels so lost to me that paper pictures don't count for much. I am deep in sick-heartedness, and I curse Brother Man for holding back the medicine I need.

Wednesday evening, Professor comes to the door of my room, where I sit in the low light, crocheting. "Don't you want some more light?" he asks.

I shake my head, but he switches on a second lamp. "Indigo, have you seen Abraham Boronsky recently?"

"Borotsky?"

"Yes. Borotsky. He's the one. You know him. You told me that, didn't you?"

"Once in a while I see dat old man."

"I think he mentioned—last time I spoke with him—that he sees you from time to time. At some club you both frequent. Isn't that right?"

"Mr. Borotsky become a news reporter or some such ting, in his ripe age?"

"Maybe he's just worried about you, Indigo, isn't that possible? He's a good man, Indi, a courageous man. If you knew what he's been through . . ."

I feel a rush of the old, deep fear come into me. I think I might start to cry, right here in front of Professor. Don't know why that fear's got to come now, just because Professor talks of someone might want to save me some suffering and talks of a man full of courage, but it's the hopeful things that sometime twist my heart so hard I'm tight as a rag wrung out after washing. "Okay, Professor," I say, losing my spirit to fight him. "I know he's a good man. I've seen that for myself. Saw those numbers on his arm, too. Heard some of his stories, direct from the source."

All through my time at the Silvers', I narrow my mind upon one single ting. No more roulette wheel. No more Joshie. No more Brother Man. Mus' let it all go and stop yearning. Mus' cut it off 'fore it kill me and mus' figure how to pay Brother Man his money. If I carry on with it, surely they kill me one way or the other . . . kill me direct, with fist or ratchet, or kill me indirect when Frank and them do harm to what I have left of Louisa. All I need to carry in my mind is Vincent, my brother, who come one week Sunday. These my last days to ready myself, maybe fix some banana bread and tidy the house, and fix my mind to be strong enough for what my heart must soon encounter.

When I go back to my own yard Friday night, I make the bread and see it come out very, very nice, set it to wait in the freezer. I dust the house and tidy, sing songs, think nothing of Brother Man. The night is clear and pretty, with stars overhead, so I walk to the corner store, pick up milk and coffee. When I come back, I find a note slip under my door. The paper say, "Indigo, that man returned to the bank and asked me to tell you Brother Man do wish to see you now. Your friend Zach."

The words make my heart beat so fast it feels like a wild animal trapped inside my rib cage. *Jus' steady down*, I say, and set my batty down into my soft chair. *You got no more business with that man. Him nothing but badness and danger.* But I am a weak, weak woman, perhaps the weakest of them Jah put upon the earth, and I soon find myself in place at the bus stop feeling as if my own feet never carry me there. Cyaan even wait for morning like a woman with some self-respect.

The blue bus swing up to the curb as usual. With my eyes walking the ground in shame, I board the bus and let it carry me to the familiar stop, then I walk against a quickening wind to get to his door. This time I don't wear my plain clothes—because my mind never make preparation to go—but wear a little skirt and loose top and scarf wrapped around my head. I soft-step in the door and see some of them I know gathered around the tables with drink and laughter. None of them see me. The tables call me like a mada's open arms, but I lean my back to the door frame and stand, study the space in front of me. Brother Man is at his desk and soon raise his eye to me. "Indigo," he calls out with a sharp interest, directing all the other eyes my way till I want to dissolve in their light. I think, *Now that I stood all these eyes, can I go on over to the tables?* I've tucked a little money in my pocket just in case. But Brother Man strides over to me—his steps unnatural long, like a man raised up on stilts—and wraps my shoulder in his arm and turns me away from the tables and back toward the door I just come in. "Indigo," he says, "isn't it fine how people take trouble to deliver my messages."

"Um," I mumble. "You allow me back to the tables? That's why you call me here, don't it?" I am a nying'i-nying'i beggar.

"In time," he says, and laughs. "In time I do you that favor, but first you do me a likkle favor."

I shift my head, fearing his favors. "Sorry. Best me do no favor."

Wham! He's shoved my back to the wall so hard my head jumps back and hits a quips time after. "Jesus," I call out in a scream that's a whisper, and turn my head to the side as if he already smacked one cheek, and my eyes go out across the room to Joshie and Frank and them, but not a soul come to my rescue. He push me a second time against the wall, not so violent now but pinning me there with his hand on my shoulder so I know me cyaan move. My heart race like it may run right oht my body. "You want to think over that answer you give me, sister woman?" His voice is quiet now, for my hiez only. He drills me with his whisper.

I have no words to offer him back.

Brother Man digs in his pocket and pulls out a small, square envelope, such as a gift card come in. He puts it in my hand and I feel some padding inside, like plastic filled with air. "You a gwan take this where I tell you."

"I must go to work in the morning." I tell a lie.

"You go to work for your Professor after you do some work for you bredda. Anyway, this job set for tonight, midnight. It's a job best suited for the night hour. You well suited for the night hour, Indigo, don't it?" He shakes me again with his laugh.

All the starch is out of me. I think, *Just get it over with*. And don't be fool enough to answer his next call.

"Here is the address," he says. "It's a street corner not too far from where you live." He winks at me. "See, I attend to your convenience, Indigo, and don't put you out. It's just behind Redding Pharmacy. The drugstore. Good place for this. Seen? I bet you know where it is, right in your neighborhood. Someone wait for you there at twelve midnight. A boy. Bufu boy." He makes a girth like Joshie's with his arms. "No need to pass the time of day with him. Just wait for a boy gwan tell you it's too bad melon not in season. Then you hand him the envelope and be on your way."

I nod. "I go on and do your errand this one time."

"One time? Is that how you tink dis go, sister woman?" He places his hand neet my chin and lifts my head till I strain to breathe, then drops it, laughs like the Devil. I start to search out a safe pocket to hide his drugs, but while I look, he snatches the packet from my fingers. "Forget about it, Indigo," he snarls. "You tink I trust you now with someting of value? I just want to see the look on your face when you moon over that wheel you cyaan go near. Just want to see your pitiful face is all. Now, go on out of here and wait till you hear from me next."

I back away from him, move to the top of the steps.

"I keep my eye on you, Indigo," he says. "I keep my eye on you, and *your people*, and keep my ear to the ground." He finds another way to hurt me, talking about my people when he must know I lost the one most close and all that's left are across the sea. Surely he noh nothing of Vincent coming. He walks inside, lets the storm door slam. I see him bend over a woman I never see before and turn his charm to her. I hurry down the road, my breathing deep in relief, but I don't know whether I'm in Heaven now or Hell, because Brother Man cannot be done with me, not until I pay my debt, anyway, not until then.

Standing in the hall outside my door, smelling of fresh jasmine, he holds his small black hat in his hand respectfully, like he has come to see the preacher. He seems unready to enter my room, and I am not so ready to bid him in, but finally I do say, "Come in, then, Vincent." A tall, thin man now, when once he was a weedy boy, he seems a stranger to his long pants and overcoat and a stranger to my room. When he rubs his hand against his thin layer of beard, I wonder does it feel like Dada's face to him still and not his own. He cannot help but turn his eyes to each wall to learn the space about him before he turns to me. I see his eyes stop on the photo of Mama and Dada in their wedding finery and then, for twice the time, on the photos of Louisa that I set back on the shelf.

"Sit, Vincent," I tell him. "Go on, sit. Here, you take this chair." I pull out the straight-back chair that's beside my card table and drag over a second one for myself so we can sit across from each other. I smooth the white doily that decorates the table and sit, letting my chair stay back from the table.

"How are you, Sister?" Vincent asks me, his voice soft and careful as a gloved hand, as if we never played together in the dirt all those years and chased each other from one end of the field to the other, a-whoopin' and a-shoutin'. Now we are polite adult strangers far from those places we knew as children.

"How am I to be?" I ask him. "Getting by is all." I think how I don't even feel at home in this room we're in, because I don't know what hot-stepper planning to walk in and tear through my tings, and that thought jumps me right to the sick hunger for Brother Man's that doesn't go away, even knowing he's ready to rob and harass me, but I keep that whole pocketful of shaming tings my secret.

"All of us feeling pain this year, Sister," he says.

I do not noh what to say. Never did it occur to me that their pain would be like my own, they being all together and not guilty of any sin and not mother to Lou. "Not like mine," I say, but think that has a mean sound, and I look down, and for once my miserly spirit troubles me.

"We are all of us sorry for you, Indigo. Part of our pain is for your suffering."

This, too, surprises me, because I have carried them all in my mind so full of blaming. "Why do you come here to America, Vincent? You never had wandering in your blood like me, or like Papa." I wait but he doesn't fill the silence. "Mama send you to say someting to me?" Here is what I been fearing for all the days since Vincent's letter, though I could find no sign of it in his simple words.

"I have a wife now," he says, "and she is in need of deestant tings. Back home, you know, there are so few good jobs, and since Mister Gilbert do his work, everyone poorer than ever. I am looking to work here awhile, Indigo, just like you."

I come up on my elbows. "You have a wife, Vincie?" I shake my head. Nothing in this makes sense to me. Him come here to be like me?

He smiles. "Just last month. There was no time to write you and ask you to the nuptials. So I thought just to tell you myself, when I can sit across from you. She's here with me, in Chicago."

"Your wife here, in this city?"

"Yah, mon."

"Vincent, you marry. Kiss me neck! And Mama let you and she come here across the water to work, after what happen to Lou?"

He shakes his head, looking confused. "She tell me if I to come, I must come to Chicago and be near you. She believe two of her own over here more safe than one alone, and she worry more boht that than once she did. Mama send you someting," he says suddenly and with a boy's excitement, then he bends to pull out from his canvas bag a package wrapped in foil.

Though it is a gift, I open it with fear in my heart. It is twice wrapped in the foil that costs them dear, and takes me some time unwrapping. When the foil is removed and the sweet smell rises in the air, for a moment I cannot grasp that it is Mama's best coconut and almond cake.

"She worry that it spoil before I get here to you, because it so moist. I take pains to keep it cool."

Now I am crying, and when I try to stop and dry my eyes, the tears only come thicker until I am ashamed and shake my head in helplessness. "I am sorry. I never expect Mama send me a cake, not after all that happen."

Vincent is silent, and I look up from my tears to see that his face is gone blank. He doesn't understand me, and then the light in his eyes shows me that he does. "Louisa?" he asks, and says her name out loud for the first time. "Louisa taken from us? How could that be your fault? How could Mama hold you to account for that?"

"Where are Mama's letters?" I say. "For all these months, where are her words? Her comfort? Her message of prayer."

He shakes his head and hangs it. "I make no excuse for her, but can only tell you, Indigo, she has no words for what her heart holds. You leave the child *in her care* and the child die. What can she say to you? She is ashamed, so deep ashamed, and grieved."

I look up to his eyes to see does he mean it.

"All of us are one heart in tings like this, Sister," he says. "One heart that's deep wounded."

I sob and sob and must get up and go into the kitchen and cut Vincent some banana bread so I can compose myself. I cyan put no knife yet to Mama's cake, but preserve it whole. Poor Mama. I never write to her, never tell her no blame falls upon her. There she stands, suffering with shame and remorse and nah can move from that spot.

When Vincent readies himself to leave, he puts his arms around me, which he has never done in our lives. I smell the jasmine along his neck and understand him a grown man, who his new wife must desire.

"What's her name, Vincent? Your wife?"

"Teresa. She name Teresa. She a pretty-pretty gal and plump like tomato."

I smile.

"Mama say, 'Don't forget. Tell Indigo we love her so much.' Over and over, she tell me, 'Tell Indigo how we love her. Tell her how sorry we are.'" He lays his hand to his chest, where his heart is, to show me Mama's hand while she talk. Before he gets to the door, he pauses, and I see he has one ting more to tell me that worries him.

"What is it?" I ask him.

Still he cannot speak.

"Tell me, Vincent," I say. "I am your blood."

His eyes reach to me, they prepare to catch me. "Teresa, she wid child."

I should have expect this, by the hurry of their marrying, but the news wrenches my heart. I tink a moment of Cliff, who still is far away in New York, and slow my breath. "All right," I say. "Good news, then, for the family, nuh? Give she a kiss from me."

"Me and her look for a room to rent. I'll let you know when we have a phone and address. Then we make supper for you, Sister."

I nod. "One more ting, Vince," I say. "Anyting come of the investigation yet? You hear again from the police?"

"No. Nothing new. I don't know will they find the person, Indigo. You know how the police can be."

When that boy leaves me, I go into the bedroom and cry and cry and cannot stop for I don't know how many hours. I feel like each one of his words is a rose he hand me till he's given me a full bouquet. I don't mind the thorns. I want to bury my nose in the perfume and never lift it out. Even the news of the baby gives me joy as I let it eena my heart.

When my eyes are dry, I go sit at my dining room table and start to open the memory box that holds my Louisa father, start to hear its music, so sweet a song though I never learn the name. I think back to how I pull off that beautiful man clothes like a child unwrap a Christmas gift, how I feel alive in my body whenever he near. First time now, I ask myself what it woulda been like if Cliff's seed did make a child in me, give me a second child, maybe even a child who have a father. I don't make this thought into pain, just into wondering. I wonder, too, where is Steve Jones in this great big country? Does he have a wife and babies by now? Maybe he has a girl with Louisa's look, because Louisa had her father's mouth and curly lashes. I can only tink of that for one second and then I must put it away and breathe deep and slow, because if such a child were somewhere in this land, I would travel five thousand miles to find her, put my arms around her, hide my face in her hair to gather her perfume.

I let some time slip by. Then, after the sun go to rest, I pull out all my IOUs and Brother Man's little notes on what I owe and sit down at my dining table with a stub of pencil to try to figure my debt to him, but someting in his way of reckoning the interest tangles my thinking and I can't figure what I need to pay him to keep his cruel friend-dem from my door, so I gather my courage and take my fluttery heart to Zach's door, trusting he must know about figures from working at the bank.

I'm so grateful to see his face at the door, my full heart frightens me. "You recall that message you en bring me from Henry P?" I ask. "Message he carried from Brother Man?"

He nods. "Two of them. Both strange. Come, sit, Indigo."

He puts a silver kettle on the stove while I sit in his gold cloth chair, focus on steadying my breaths. He comes and sits across from me, hands on his bony knees, and I explain my predicament, try not to watch the worry build in his face. When his teakettle steams and whistles, he moves me to the kitchen, sits me down at his table, and shows me how Brother Man calculate the interest on my borrowings, so that soon I see I cyaan pay him off with the money I make, not if I live to a hundred. I strolled into that man's trap thinking my eyes were wide open but managing still to get myself caught tight as fur in nettles.

"I wish I could loan you something, Indigo," Zach says. "I'd do it in a minute if I had some to spare." He shakes his head, sorry. "After I pay my rent, I send what's left to Cliff to help with his son. The boy is slow and needs special schooling."

I think of Cliff's leather jacket, which must have cost a pretty penny and won't even keep him warm in the winter, but I am ashamed of myself for worrying boht how other people spend their money when I throw mine down Brother Man's plug hole. Professor would help me, I believe, and I think of asking him, but Lord, I hate to have him see me this way.

"I walked myself into it. Now got to crawl my way oht," I say.

Zach draws in his eyebrows in that serious-minded way that makes me want to call him "old man," but I hush myself for once, tired of my spleen.

"I wish you'd come to me sooner, Indigo, come to me like a friend, before you get in so deep. Wish you'd have come here before you even go to that Brother Man, a man who makes his sport of other people's sorrow."

I think of Borotsky, who seems smarter than most, who's lived a long string of years and lived through terrible trials. I wonder why does a man like that bring himself within reach of Brother Man's grip, but I have no answer to give myself.

"I know that man," Zach says.

"Hm?"

"The one calls himself Brother Man, as if he bredda to all."

"You know him?" I feel my heart's beating.

"Know enough to steer any friend of mine far from his door."

I can take no more of Zach's dark eyes, so I give a story why I must go to my own flat. Next morning, I'm back to the Silvers' with only my problems and no kind of solution. My heart is weary from alla my troubles but still holds a light that Vincent kindle.

When afternoon comes and Clair runs in from school and

sees that the day has got some hours of sunshine still left to it, she wheedles me into a-help with her hot chocolate stand, since Professor's birthday gift is on her mind once again. Soon she hauls outside her thermos of cocoa and the green-lettered cardboard sign she en hurry to write. Now I think she will leave me be while I start with dinner. But Lord, if that child don' keep a-run eena the house every ten minute to pester me for more hot chocolate. I don't know where she find her business out there on that quiet road, but okay, maybe she sell it all to the postman as him pass up and down the street, or maybe, eager as she is, she jus' follow behind the poor man and catch the neighbors as each come out to carry in the mail. Whatever her trick, she's in and out the house like lightning, too fast for me to stop her with "Who on earth you sell all this chocolate to?" I just make the cocoa and chuckle at the child, tink maybe her locate her trade earlier than most.

Professor has books to read in the evening, so they don't sit long at the table. When my dishes are washed, I go into the girls' rooms to put some folded laundry into their drawers and closets. Clair has a cupboard inside a walk-in-style closet that's big enough to sleep two Ja pickney. Set in the cupboard I find a blonde-haired doll with porcelain skin that looks like someone paid dear for it. It seems odd for Clair to have so pretty a doll tucked away. Seems most odd for her to get it—from Mrs. Silver, who else it cyan be?—and me not know, since Clair's not one to make a secret of any nice ting that come from Mrs. Silver, them so rare these days.

I find Clair in the library, sitting cross-legged on the floor, paging through the catalogues of costly store goods we get each day in the mail. "Hi, Indi. I want this horse and this Barbie." She points them out. "Do you like the Barbie?"

"That's what you plan to do with your chocolate stand money?"

"*No.* That's for Daddy. You know that. These are for me."

"Speaking of dolls, Clair, where you come by that doll in your closet? How come I never see her before today?"

"Um." Clair makes faces, bouncing her shoulders up and down like someting heetches her, saying no words. "The pony is fifteen dollars. Do you think that's a lot?"

"Well, what can you say to my question? Maybe then I give an answer to yours."

She turns her head away and picks at the carpet. "It's just from a lady I met."

"What you mean, a lady you met? That lady have a name, Clair?"

Clair shakes her head and looks at the space over my head. "Not really. I mean, she *has* a name. Everyone has a name, Indi. You know, there's a girl in my class named Terbal?"

"No one can name that. But serious now, a *stranger*? Is that what you mean?"

"You saw me bring it in when you were making more hot chocolate."

"Don't tell me what I saw."

She looks at me. "She didn't give me any candy." Her eyes go roaming again.

"A stranger give you a fancy doll, but since she give you no candy, that make it fine? Is that the story you tell me, Clair? Like maybe my brain shrivel from too long in the sun?"

She shrugs.

"What did this lady look like? What was her voice? She come to your stand? Is that why you sell so much chocolate in one afternoon?"

Clair's voice brightens. "She sounded like you, Indi, so I knew it was all right. She sounded just like you, and she was a lady and she didn't give me candy and I didn't go in her car. She bought hot chocolate, and she just seemed like somebody's mother or like one of your friends."

"So that's all you need to know, Clair? How do you know

she weren't planning to kidnap you, or cause you some other harm?"

"She gave me a doll, Indi, not candy. And she bought a whole pot of hot chocolate while we were talking. Three cups."

"Where's your head, Clair? How much more pain you tink Professor can stand? Now, tell me, what did this 'lady' look like? Tell me exactly what you see."

"Tall, Indi, and pretty. She had on a lot of feathery pink and green and blue dresses, and her skirts rustled and she smelled just like flowers. She was nice. She wasn't like a kidnapper would be."

"Oh, you know so many kidnappers, you know just how they be? What do you mean, she smelled like flowers? Like roses or someting?"

Clair tightens her mouth and shakes her head. "The little tiny white bells that come up in the garden pretty soon. There's a song about them."

Jah! I stretch my nostrils, because I know that smell. "What did that big woman say to you?"

"She just asked me if I could use another doll to go with whatever ones I had in the house. She said she figured I probably had some nice dolls in the house, but did I want another one. And I did." Clair lifts her eyes to me. "Oh, and she said she knew I liked dolls because my mother told her. See, Indi. She knew Mommy, so I knew it was okay."

"Lord, Clair, I thought you wiser than that. What else? Anything else she say?"

"She wanted to take me out for ice cream, but I was selling hot chocolate, and besides, it's cold still. She gave me the doll and bought three cups of hot chocolate just to be nice and because she was cold in those thin dresses, I think. Then she came back for more a while later. Nobody else did that."

I see some roads crossing and don't like what I see. Mrs. Silver tells me she knows some bad business about me. Lucille tells Clair she knows her mother. Must be Brother Man send

Lucille on an errand to learn boht me, and she smart enough to seek out Mrs. Silver. Lucille draw a different errand from the one Brother Man have in mind for me, but no less mischief in it.

"Clair, you frighten me," I say. "You must never take a gift—any gift—from a stranger again, no matter if it's candy or baby dolls or any other ting. You know how dangerous that cyan be? You know this world don't always be a safe place for children? You must know alla that by now, after what you see on the TV and in your own house. If this lady come around again, or anyone else you don't know comes around you and wants to ask you questions or give you tings, you must tell me straightaway, even if you must hurry home from someplace, even from school, because I need to know."

Clair nods. "Okay. Okay. Jill said Mommy was here last week."

"So what? She left with nothing."

"Did she bring anything?"

I shake my head. "Just herself." I stop myself from a-say more.

"Did she talk about the custody stuff?"

"A little. Just words, that's all it is."

Clair frowns and goes off, crestfallen, because what's good news to the rest of us is bad news to her, and I sit down on the sofa and start into a worrying that won't let up. How can I call the police, when I'd have to explain to them about Brother Man and my own bad ways? How can I do nothing, when Clair might be at risk? Only her little business operation stood between her and getting into that car, going who knows where with that crazy Lucille. That child's so hungry for love, she might go the next time. Though I warn her up one side and down the other, she can give herself some bobo excuse for why it's okay. My stomach starts to burn so bad I worry it's going to burn right through, give me a hole like that in the ozone layer Jill likes to worry over.

I think of going to search out Lucille. She stands out so, with her high build and her dress—she no falla fashin, she an original, for sure—that I noh I can track her, just by asking mongst the Jamaicans. But when I think of Lucille, all I see is her scared-rabbit eyes that flash her fear of that man. I know she fears him more than she ever fear me, so what use in try to twist that woman arm. I know what I must do, though the thought makes a scared rabbit of me, too.

After I clean up from dinner, I find Professor and ask can I go into Chicago while the girls attend school in the morning. I tell him it's personal business and tell him with my chin high and my voice flat so he is not going to ask what kind. He just tells me, "Yes, go, if you need to." It's not like Professor to ask a great many questions. I guess he feels he's better off ignorant, or he save all his wondering for his research.

Eighteen

In the morning, I put on a green dress instead of my maid's uniform or my bus driver clothes, because I nah wish to rile Brother Man more. I try not to think where I'm going. Plan to save my thinking for the bus journey, when it's too late to turn around, though my heart race. This time the bus arrive too fast for my pleasure, and it keep that brisk pace all the way; it weave like a dancer through the city streets. I climb down and into the neighborhood before I even fix my thoughts on what's to come. I set a good walking pace, despite the rough ice that comes when the slush freeze overnight in the spring. Best to act the part of Energizer bunny or bad Bunny Foo Foo and alla that, forget about the scared rabbit.

When I get to the red house, I steady my breath for one minute, then another, then say "Ready, steady, go" and move up, open the door, and find him looking directly into my eyes as if the door moving shock him awake like electricity. From the far side of the room, his eyes study me sharp and cold, but he makes no move in my direction. I have no courage to enter that room, where I been forbidden, so I *ah-hem* and then call out, launching my voice over all the people like a high-tossed ball. I let everyone hear me so I'm not alone with that man: "Let me speak wid you ohtside, mon, if you no mind." He frowns but raises a finger as he walks to his desk, so I know him soon come, more soon maybe than I can bear.

I let the door shut, almost ready to pray him turn me down and never come onto the stoop. I turn my back from the house to give myself a space that feels safe. My mind spins like Joshie's wheel, wants to spin away to another place where I cyan be safe, while my body fall down here on the wood. I talk to myself of Louisa, how I fail her, I neva protect her. I prod myself how I must stand up, must be tall, must be brave like a bear. *Indigo, you nah run from trouble, no matter how sharp him teeth. Him just a man. Truly.* Though she not my own flesh, I must stand up for this next child. Clair is not mine; however, this trouble that head her direction is mine, and that cyaan be right.

The minute I hear the door and know that Brother Man and I soon stand together, I say to myself, *Now you an actor, Indigo. You just pretend, play a part you see in a movie.* Him step out and show me his height, seem to flex fi me every muscle. I approach and bring my face so close to his I can smell his renk breath. I play my part right tru the danger that flows off him like wind. I want to be first to break the air with words. I jump on him. "What you thinking, mon, a-send Lucille after that child? How could you, mon? What kind of mischief in your mind?"

Him turn the head away like him pretend no one there talking in his face, then turn it back; lift his chin and beard, then lower dem, consent to speak to me. "Since when you worry your sweet self over what is in my mind, Indigo? You the proud-proud one cyaan worry boht no one but herself."

I hear it. I hear the hurt lion in him, and my fears tuck in a little. I speak more from my heart, less from my script now.

"You must never, never go up there and badda those children in they own yard. Hear what I say?"

"Last time I hear, it's a free country, sister. That's what they advertise."

"You nah free to go hassle that likkle girl. Even the law say that. You a hard ears man. . . ." I want to say his given name but don' even noh it.

He takes hold of his lower lip in his teeth, then spits it out and waits a second. "Which girl you speak about, now? Which one of them uptown girl-dem tell tales on Brother?"

My heart explodes. "Who else you send your she-devil to but Clair?"

"Why you think I mus' send someone to fill my shoes when I cyan go directly?" He smiles like him all in command now. "Unless, of course, I'm already occupy. Cyaan be a-go visit two pretty white girls at one time, no true?"

"Jah! Jesus! Who else you visit? Who else?"

"Sure have wild hair, that one. Maybe you help her with she grooming next time I have a date with her, dawta, so her no look so leggo beas'."

Jill, he's telling me he's been to see Jill. My fury is such, I think I may turn to fire.

"All of a sudden, you so interested in my life. Were never interested till now. Just interested in your roulette. Fall madly in love with that spinning wheel, with that foolish game. Interested in your white family, too, but that is where your loving ends."

"I'll get you your money, Brother Man. You nah worry boht that. I'll get your money, sooner than you tink."

"How you plan that, sister? You best sell the hot chocolate your own self, because I don't see that you make such big money from that professor in the suburbs. He'll spend his money on his girls, buy them pretty dollies and such, before he dig into his pocket for you."

"Forget about that."

"Oh, no, I forget it's the mada who buy the pretty dollies. Sorry, then. I forget my detective work. Still, Borotsky say Professor a big man at the university, but that don't mean he some fine, generous boss to di black nana, nuh."

"I wi get your money, Brother Man. You nah fret boht how. You leave that on my back."

He laughs and studies me. "I nah worry near so much as you tink, sister woman. And what mek you believe I even once trouble myself over that small piece of change you owe me?"

I frown. "You cut me off from di roulette wheel. Must matter someting to you."

He paces the boards, mek them creak. When he pass by me, he stop and say, "That money nothing but small potatoes to me, Indigo Rose. I just have a policy is all. And you no help persuade me to suspend my policy when you treat me widoht respect. Don't even wear a deestant article of clothing when you come here, except today when there's someting you want from me."

I get another sick feeling, seeing how I could have kept up my nice times had Brother Man not got it in his head to want me for a sweetie. Wonder did Lucille get herself stuck in this same pot of glue. I recall coming into Brother Man's time after time in my bus driver clothes, doing nothing to catch his eye. Again I brindle that a woman cyaan conduct her business in the world same as a man. Got to get caught in a sticky web of nonsense no matter what she do. But here I am, longing for gambling games again. I tell him, "You just keep your distance from those girls is all. Don't let me hear that you go again to visit them, and you nah send your people near them."

"Oh, now Indigo she in a position to threaten Brother Man. I like that!" He laughs an evil laugh. "Like I told you, sister, I do as I please."

My fear and anger rise again when he plays the Devil with me. "I kill you, mon," I say. "You hurt one of them, and I a-go kill you, simple as that. You understand me? You hear what I tell you?"

He laughs just to goad me. "Oh, now you the killer, Indigo. That's what it come to, I see. You who suffer so from one who kill your baby, now you come to be the killer."

"Kill the likes of you," I say. "You appear so smart a man, so wise, but look how you use what you learn. Only to evil purpose."

"The likes of me?" He flares up. "You something better than me, is that what I hear? Gambler. Debtor. Hard-hearted woman. What you have to make you so boasie?"

"This is no boht my pride," I say. "It is boht my girls." I see the sweat drip eena his eyes so he must wipe them with his sleeve.

"Your white girls," he says. "Your own girl long time neet the earth."

I wince. "You tink every second I take breath nah remind me of that. You dogheart man. No wonder that girlfriend leave you."

He slap my cheek so fast it is finish before I see it come.

My cheek on fire, I look at him and see him grab at his measly beard like he wants to pull it off, then he shouts, "Fuck that Lucille. Woman can't do a damn ting I tell her, no use to me at all—I ought to en send Frank up there with that doll," and he marches back eena the house, the screen door left to hammer shut behind.

When he goes, I am not moving, just standing thinking of him a-meet up with Jill. My body and heart shudder at that sight. Brother Man punches back tru di door. His eyes look ready to swallow me, and he is prepared, it seems, to tell me one more ting. But he says nothing, just stretch his eyes wider and wider. Then, fast as hawk dives to bird, he spreads his hand, thrusts it, and closes it around my neck, cutting my air. "Now, get this right, woman," he growls. "I do what I please, whenever I please to do it, so you no fuck with me, never. I kill you if it please me, and nah remember you long after, except for maybe the look on your face if I take time to do the ting myself. If you cyaan believe me, you go look up Lucille, see if you learn from her what I cyan do." He releases me, and I suck in air and try to slow my galloping heart.

I have no smart words for him, barely have words at all. "What do you want from me, to stop alla this? You want your coil or what?"

"You still a-think that bit of change mean someting to me? Neva mean shit, sister. But yeah, you go on and pay it just so you cyan get on out my life."

I am sitting in a seat halfway to the back of this bus, right hand gripping a silver pole, having no picture of how I walked myself here or got my batty set down in the seat. I must get Brother Man his money, but I can figure no fast way to do that, can only see to pay it back bit by bit with everyting I can save from what Professor give me, and that drip of cash don't seem enough to quiet me when I want to rip that Brother Man and his jancro spirit off of me and throw him out of my life. More than that, I got to worry boht those children.

I should be at the Silvers'—I'm due back there—but Lord, I'm not ready, so I get off the bus in downtown Evanston, just go and sit on a bench against the wall of the big transport station, no idea of what to do but let time steady me, and, Jesus, here come Louisa, her warm sudden eyes looking up at me, her nose wrinkling as she smile. All the little places on her I love ripple tru my mind. The white skin on her head where no hair would grow, the fleck of white in her dark eye, the soft brown tone of her hair just like Vincent's, and the feel of that hair—the texture and smell of it—when I twisted it into thin braids and prettied them with bits of ribbon. Lord, I got to scream out and shake my head to fling her out of there, since her picture inside my head tears me more than if a devil entered me. All of my heart is full with her, all of my mind crying to her no different than if she died yesterday. "Mama," I hear, "go on, pick me up, Mama," and I curl up on the bench and let the light of the station fade, "go on, spin me, Mama," let the sounds of people jostling and jiving fall away. I stop my fighting and sail off from this earth to where I can find her. I don't even stir myself when my body needs to use the toilet. None of that seems to matter, not even the fullness of my own bladder or the fact I'm late to my employment. There's nothing in this dreary world calls my name. I can let it all be. Maybe I'll make water where I lie and just lie in it like a baby. None of it matters. I'll just tink of Louisa and her baby skin and the smell of her when I checked to see was her diaper dry, checked to see was her hair combed proper, checked to see were her ears clean and fresh smelling, checked to see was she breathing easy at night—the joy of her in the next bed so wonderful it take my own breath away so I never stop checking her.

I lie on the bench like a body without a home. My eye scans the room as I try to bring myself back. In the corner is a phone booth with a directory dangling so heavy on a chain it could be a man been hanged. I think of the tilted phone booth by the Shell station, where me and Jill went after the driver kick us off the bus. Lord, what a day! The memory springs loose a laugh. I get up and go over and lift the five-pound Evanston book, set it on the narrow metal shelf beside the phone, turn to "Jones, Steven." Thirty listings under that one name just in this single book. How come my baby father have the same name as half the population? A Chicago book sits on the shelf. This one must have fifty of "Steven Jones" listed here. Sweet Jesus, the man is a tree hid in a forest. How could he a-stayed in the shadows like that, never step out and say, "Here I am, Indigo, here I am, India girl, come lay your head on my shoulder, cry some tears with me for what we brought to the sweet earth and lost"? I hear him call me "India" like he used to, him make me tink of someplace rich and strange. At times, he call me "Indigo Rose," no different from Brother Man. Did we mean so little to him, Louisa and me, that he never step out from his cover and call our names?

Who else do I know to look up? I go and look up my own name, just to see it in type and check they have me listed right. Then I look up "Borotsky, Abraham" and see there's just one of him. In all of Chicago, just one Borotsky. I start to get a sick thought boht what become of all the other ones once bearing his name, but my thoughts veer a different way and tell me like a sudden bright discovery that there's something nice, something real real nice, in how Mr. Borotsky's the only one. Must be lucky, too, because it beats the odds, being the ongle one when most of the names I see in this book are at least doubled if not times-fifty like Steven Jones. I dig in my pocket for change. Put in a dime and a quarter and press the numbers, listen to their pretty tones while I feel the memory of the old circle dials in my fingers, like on the phones back home. The machine asks for more change, and I feed it in, put my money on Borotsky, I tell myself. And then, just like something lucky, he answers right on the first ring. Might as well have been standing at that phone, waiting for me.

"Mr. Borotsky, Indigo Rosemartin calling."

"Indigo," he says, and his voice sounds light as skipping stones. "You're callink up an old man for a date?"

I laugh eena di phone, but while I laugh, my body starts to shake, and just like he's followed me into the station and slunk up behind, I feel Brother Man's hand so tight around my throat I can't breathe. Something in this old man's voice just lets the terror run free in me, like when a scared child catch sight of her mama and abandon herself to tears.

"When you call an old man, he is usually free. That is one of the pleasures of old age, to be available when called by a lovely young woman. Why don't you come downtown, my friend, meet me for coffee at the Basin Blues."

"Sorry, but I'm in Evanston, Mr. Borotsky, just come from Chicago, from Brother Man's." Oh, shit, what I been through with that man, what I been through. I don't see how I can endure this day.

"Oh. Is that so? Then I'll get on the bus, come and meet you at the Sweet Bar. That is, if you would like. Do you know where the Sweet Bar is inside the big hotel?"

"Yes, sir."

"A half an hour from now, Indigo. I'll meet you there at the restaurant. We'll talk. I'll buy you a nice piece of cake."

A nice piece of cake from Mr. Borotsky. I can breathe again. I call Professor's, and Jill answers. I tell her I'm held up some and ask can she keep a close eye on Clair until I come and can she go ahead and heat the oven for my roast chicken in half an hour. Then I walk to the nearby park to wait out the time. They have an old stone horse-and-general monument and circling it a patch of dirt feeds a few flowers, tulips and violets and some lilies of the valley. I pick all the sprigs of lily that are opened, which comes to just four. One voice in me says to pinch the delicate flowers off, one by one, and toss them in the soil, but I hold on to them. Don't need to act the part of Brother Man, whose heart so black.

Mr. Borotsky is beside the door when I approach the hotel.

"Indigo," he says, and reaches out both hands for mine.

I have the lilies in one hand, so I must offer them right away. "I know you like the fragrance."

"Oy," he says, surprised, and his face pales sharply. A tear bulges below one eye, frightening me. "Come. Come inside."

We sit in a booth, get menus from a young girl with Julie's dark-haired, bright-eyed look. He reaches up to touch the wetness around his eye. "I'm sorry, Indigo," he says. "The flowers startled me."

"Just four little sprigs of lily." I let him hear the puzzlement in my voice.

"Ach," he says, "but not to this old man." He draws in some air, and his eyes look wild, like a wolf someone's trying to muzzle, and suddenly his face looks too old to be alive still. "When I was in the camp, at the end of the war, the Russians came and opened the big iron gates, and those of us that remained wandered out into the valley. Some walked. Those past walking crawled on the ground. It was springtime, and the valley was so green, so beautiful. Who could believe such wicked, wicked acts—acts beyond speech, which is where your professor's research falters—were committed in that spot, in that cradle of nature's beauty, nature's generosity of spirit, all just a blink of an eye before that moment. It should have been a barren wasteland, to spawn such a sickness. It should have been the most hideous place on the earth, with every plant dead, or twisted by disease so ugly it would force your eyes shut. But it was green and abundant. Beyond belief, all beyond belief, yet it was so. We wandered out, the walking dead—how many of us left by then, I don't know—and the valley was blooming with flowers, with lilies. Lilies of the valley. *Can you see it, Indigo?* Thousands of them, like a carpet. I would have liked to lie down there, but I was afraid, afraid of the lash, of the bullet, afraid of the freedom, of life, of death, of the future, the past, afraid of . . . of everything . . . of the grass, of . . . everything, but I knelt down and lowered my head to the ground, which took what energy I had, and smelled those flowers, that grass, the earth, and tried to imagine that I was human still, and alive."

Mr. Borotsky scares me now, with his heart open so wide I want to run for bandages and tape. All I can do is nod. I think of Jill, speechless after my Louisa died, and give her a little pity. "Sorry," I say. "For all that you went through, Mr. Borotsky, Mr. Abraham."

"I know," he says. "I know, my dear. There is nothing to say.

So now you tell me why do you go up to Brother Man's on a weekday morning? You know by now he is a dangerous man, no? You know when I play against him, against 'the house,' I play against a man who is a hurt and angry spirit, who is not prepared to lose? You understand all that, do you not, that I pit my strength against his?"

"Just to discuss with him," I say, "to tell him he must give me a little breathing space to pay back my debt."

"But not to gamble any more of your hard-earned money?"

"No, sir. I try to be done with alla that."

"That's right, Indigo," he says. "Good. You put an end to that. Spend your money on nice things for yourself, or for those you love."

Here he goes, bringing in loved ones, but I don't bother to cut my eye at him.

Jill is outside, helping Professor by sweeping some light snow from the walk even as it falls. *Lord, do this winter never end? Not even come springtime?* I put on a thick sweater and a wool hat and go out and stand beside the front door. There's still a little light in the sky.

"Jill, let me talk with you a minute," I say.

"Here?"

"Why not here? Just stop your sweeping a minute."

She looks at me, surprised. "Okay," she says, her voice shy.

"I'm not here to trouble you," I say. "Just tell me about the man who come by and talk with you."

She shakes her head and shows me a baby's empty face. "A man?"

"I know about it. So you just tell me exactly what he told you."

"I don't know who you mean, Indi."

I hear in her voice that she's not fooling with me. "Didn't a Jamaican man—a tall man with a sorry-looking beard—come by somewhere and talk with you?" I think, *Maybe I'm wrong. Maybe Brother Man just empty words.*

Jill's face suddenly lights. "There was a man I talked to near school one day."

I take in a deep breath. "All right, then. Go on and tell me boht that man."

Now she looks like something pop eena her mouth that have a bad taste to it. "He told me he knows my mother, that she owed him some money because she'd borrowed from him and hadn't paid him back."

"Your mother? He say your mother owe him money?" *Don't nothing shame that man.*

"Something about Mommy telling him she needed the money for medicine and he loaned it to her out of pity."

I scowl at that. "Yeah, him so rich in pity. Don't you trust a word from that man mouth, Jill."

"But now he needs the money, because his wife's sick."

"Rhaatid!"

"So he wanted me to pay him back."

"Oh, Jesus," I say. "Jesus. Lies and games. Sanfi man, him. The man have no wife."

"Do you know him, Indi?"

I no cyan bring myself to speak it, but I nod. I can't see how I could heap more shame on myself if I set about to do just that. I nod some more. "Sorry I do."

"Does he really know Mommy?"

"What he tell you he going to do next? He say he come back for the money?"

"He said he would. He said *soon,* he'd be back soon."

"He poke his nose in and learn one or two tings about your mada, try to use them to his advantage." I think how Mrs. Silver must have learn one or two tings herself, try to use those to her own advantage, not so different from Brother. I think of the visit he promised me soon, the visit from his "friends."

"Why you nah tell someone about this, Jill? Tell me or tell Professor?"

Jill shrugs, drops her eyes to the ground.

"Your mother, right?" I ask. "All of that making you ashamed."

She nods.

"That's *her,*" I say, thinking this time it isn't even her, it's me, really—me, not Mrs. Silver—who's the shameful one. "That's her nonsense, not yours. It's nothing to do with you." The wind quickens, and I feel the cold and want to get into the house. "What were you going to do boht the money he demand?"

"Return Daddy's birthday present and give him the money. I thought that might be enough." Jill takes hold of the broom by its long handle and brushes a patch of new snow.

"I got to think about this, Jill, got to think about what to do. That man's angry with me is all. This have nothing to do with your mother. He not even know your mother, just sent out his spy woman to learn a little about her is all."

"All the gross stuff," Jill says, dispirited, "that's what people always know."

"I still cyaan figure how he learn boht the drugs, but that is his world, alla the renk tings."

I hear the phone ring faintly in the house. "I must think about that." As soon as I say that, I know my figuring won't take any time at all, because *I* am how he knows, because one day when I am angry at Professor and take too much of Brother Man's rum, I prattled on about Mrs. Silver and what Professor must put up with. So he don't need no scared-rabbit Lucille for that part.

Clair puts her head out through the door and looks at Jill. "Phone for you," she says.

"Me?"

"Yeah. It's Keith." She forces her words in a high whisper,

as if he is standing in the next room and she got to keep her words secret.

Jill lets go the broom, which falls to the walk, and rushes through the door. I am left there, again thinking I must find a way to pay back Brother Man, even if I have to borrow from Professor, because this crazy stuff too dangerous to continue. Clair pokes her head out as I stoop for the broom and stand it against the house. She walks out, no coat around her.

"Indi, is Keith Jill's boyfriend now?" she asks, her voice still in a hush.

"Starting to look that way," I say. "Go on in the house. It's too cold to be outside half-naked."

All of us are sleep in our beds the next morning when the phone calls me down to the library. Jewel says on the line, "Sorry to call you at your work, but I heard something I got to tell you about, Indigo."

"Um-hm," I say.

"You awake, girl?"

"Guess I am. Mostly."

"They found a woman half-dead in the street near where we live, most her clothes torn off her, attack by someone vicious as a pit bull. And Lord, it's scaring me half to death, girl. Too close to where we live, and too ugly and crazy a thing. I'm frightened to walk on the street, don't want to walk up to my own door all alone."

"The police—what they say?"

"They ain't talked to no one here that I know. They collected some evidence and drove off in the car. That's the last we hear from them."

"What they call her?" I ask. "The woman they find beat."

"Lucy, I heard one detective say."

I sit down on the floor. "Oh, Lord, so it's true." Where's he going to stop with his wickedness? "Don't worry, Jewel."

"Don't worry, girl? Why not? This happen right past our door. Might be you don't get the picture."

"This trouble don't bear your name. No need to fear for your safety."

"How you can say that, Indigo? You know something about this business?"

"Know more than I should. But now's the time for me to keep silent and don't make a bad mistake." Jewel surprises me, accepting what I say. Must be she's afraid something dangerous going to rub off on her if she learn too much.

I hang up the phone and go down to the kitchen to sit and, after some time pass, boil a cup of tea. It makes me sick how once I think him a great psychologist, so sensitive to how I feel about the family photos and trinkets that people pull out from their pockets and lace into their talk. Now I see how he's just storing up information like a gray squirrel, then want to use it for evil purpose. I catch myself feeling sorry for Lucille, though she do a bad ting by Clair, and who knows what other wickedness she is willing to do for that man, and that part I don't forgive. Lord, I must pay that bull bucka his money. Must pay him soon. Funny, I'm a-want Vincent to talk wid for comfort, though him my baby brother. But since he come to me the other evening, I see him in my mind all grown up, grown up into a good and deestant man.

The next few days I've got to wrestle my fear like it's a swamp alligator. Got to settle it down so I can think straight. It does me no good to waste my time picturing who's a-go to take hold of me from behind while I walk the street, who's a-go to pound down the door to my apartment while I sleep. I try to soothe myself like a mother calms a fretful baby, so I can think of what I must do next.

The last Saturday of April, I tame my pride and walk myself down to the Baptist church and in tru di heavy front doors opening to the sanctuary. I stand a minute and try to let the quiet feel of the place enter me, then wander the white corridors till I find a door that says "Father Davis" in gold letters on a smooth black nameplate. My right hand pulling at my lip, I breathe deep and rap on that preacher's door, half hoping to get back silence. Instead, I get a cordial "Come in," and I open the door to see Father Davis at his desk, looking strange to me with black reading glasses I never saw before. He grabs off the glasses, then laughs and shakes his head and says, "Now you know my vanity. Come in, Indigo. I'm happy to see you." He waits, then remembers he ought to stand up politely. He motions me to a wooden chair with a round seat and high, circling arms that make a place for me to rest my elbows. I am silent, looking around the place, taking it in, and finally he says, "How can I help you?" and I realize I have interrupted his work.

There's no more delaying what I come for. "I need a job."

"Have you *lost* a job?"

"No. I have a job, but I need someting more, someting part-time."

"Oh?"

He's wanting an explanation. I go ahead and say, "I lost my sense, got into someting I should have stayed oht of."

"Oh?"

"I have a debt to pay off."

"Acquired how?" he asks gently but as if it's his right to know.

My hard-ears self is going to balk right here and tell him some rude ting concerning what piece of this is his business and what piece is not, but I calm myself and remind myself whose faults are the bigger ones here and say, "Gambling. Nothing to be proud of."

"That character who calls himself Brother Man?"

I look at him, shocked, because somehow I still thought Brother Man's world secret.

"A lot of folks been taken in by him, especially the women. He likes to prey on women. Sorry to hear he dragged you down."

Again I am stunned.

"I heard his wife left him some years ago, ran off and broke his heart, left him a cruel man, though I make no excuse for him. But you, Indigo, trying to raise yourself up . . . now, that is something to be proud of."

"Jus' come a little late," I say. "People been kind to me this year. No need for me to cause them extra worry getting myself beat up or worse."

He nods. "Unfortunately, we have no cleaning work at all right now. That is already well taken care of by Manuel, my custodian. So I'm not certain we've got any work to offer, despite your need."

"Well, if that's how it is—"

"But possibly . . . no—"

"What?" Seems Pastor's teasing me.

"We might use some help in the kitchen Saturday and Sunday mornings. Do you cook?"

I nod.

"This job was Bertha's, and we've not filled it since we lost her. She was your friend, if I remember correctly."

"Yes. My neighbor. And friend."

"You would have to get here early Saturday morning and help with our breakfast for the poor. But you'll be working all through the week, so I doubt you'll manage an early job on the weekends as well. A person has to get her rest sometime, isn't that so?"

"I can manage, Pastor Davis."

"It's yours, then, if you want it. And it's appropriate for you to have it, since it was your friend's."

I leave thinking, *Okay, now I have eat my humble pie, so maybe tings go better for me in the future.* Still, I am nervous about Brother Man oht there meditating on what I owe him, ready alla the time to stretch his claws, him like a panther in a cage, pacing and ill tempered, restless for me to pay what's his, dreaming evil dreams boht me and the girls. I take to praying about it, just beg for him to be a little patient with me, keep his eye on some other field mouse and give me a few months at this new job to earn the money I need.

Nineteen

Clair and I sit side by side on the park bench, huddled against an early-May chill while we wait for Tennyson to do his business. A shiver goes through me, head to toe. "Ooh. Cold out tonight, Clair."

Clair pulls off her sweater and stretches it across my shoulders. "I'm not cold." The little garment resting on me, warming me, fills me with Louisa, and I lose all my words.

In time, the feeling eases. I turn to Clair. "Thank you. That feels warmer."

Tennyson finishes with what he needs to do. "Come," I call out to him. He trots to us and tucks his bottom to sit at my feet. "I never before see a dog so smart as this dog of yours," I tell Clair.

She smiles, proud because he is her own little dog, her birthday gift.

"No more strangers come visit with you since you and I have our talk, don't it?"

"No, Indi," she says. "Nobody."

When we go back to the house, I plan to read the paper, like I do each day now. I cyaan help scanning for stories of someone beat up, who might be another of Brother Man's unlucky souls. I give thanks that so far his long arm nah reach oht and grab me. "If someone does, you're going to tell me, right? We got that straight between us, no true?"

She nods, her face full of seriousness.

"Because you know what I tell you boht keeping safe, ya no see it? For your own sake and for Professor."

She nods.

"How much money you need for Professor's birthday pen now you finish with your hot chocolate stand?"

"Five more dollars. Maybe I can ask Mom."

"Maybe we do the chocolate again. One more day selling chocolate won't hurt. If you want to have another try after school tomorrow, go on."

Clair brightens, turns her body around to me. "I can?"

I nod. "Better do it now, before it come around to lemonade season. This time, I stan' oht there beside you."

Clair leans her head on my shoulder and closes her eyes.

When she lifts her head again, I see that inward look on her face. "What is it?" I ask. "You thinking about your mother?"

She shakes her head. "It feels tight in here," she says, and taps her fingers against her ribs so I can hear the thump of bone against bone.

"Tight like a sore muscle?"

She shakes her head.

"Is it your asthma?"

"Maybe," she says. "It's not cold enough, though."

"Feels cold to me," I say. "Get out your inhaler, in case you need it. And put this sweater back on."

She takes the sweater and rummages in her pockets for only a second. "I don't have one."

"Are you certain? You didn't look."

"I didn't bring one."

"Clair, you're always to carry one. I en hear Professor tell you that time and again."

"It's not that cold out," she says. "I don't need it when it's not cold."

I don't like the way Clair's voice is sounding, like she is measuring her words to keep from wasting breath on them. "We're going home," I say, and get up and take her hand. "You give me Tennyson's leash." We have only a block and a half to get to the house, where Clair has her inhaler, but her skin, which is usually pink as the inside of a seashell, has gone to gray and she has a scared look in her eyes. "How are you? All right?" I ask her.

She gives me a short nod.

I grip her hand and try to quicken our steps, but she stops me with the stiffness in her arm and with a shake of her head. The quicker walk has her breathing harder. I blame myself for that. "I'm going to carry you, Clair," I say, and push my purse strap way up onto my shoulder to free my hand.

"No," she says, and shakes her head. "Just walk slow with me."

"I better carry you. I'm strong as a horse." But I see I am frightening her with my worry, and that strains her breathing more, so I quiet myself and try to match my steps to hers, though my heart's going so fast it could have take me to the house and back ten times already and up the stairs to the bathroom cabinet where the inhaler's got to be.

It seems like forever, but finally we get inside the front door. I drop the leash and let the dog trot off trailing it. "You sit down in the living room and I'll get your medicine." I race up the stairs, and when I throw open the medicine cabinet door and see the little glass bottle with its peaked plastic top, relief floods my heart. I clutch it and run down to Clair and see the relief in her eyes, too, though she is too short of breath to speak. I sit down beside her on the sofa, praying she is well enough to work the ting herself, because I don't know how to do it. She puts it to her nose and draws in the medicine while I sit with my hand pressed against her back, thinking I can feel her lungs through her flesh. When I feel her breathing deepen and slow, all I know for a few seconds is the tripping of my own heart.

That night, when I go to my bed, I cry for myself, because somehow I am back to caring, which I never asked to be.

The weather is warm. There is no more ice in the ground. But in my heart, I still fight the change of season. I still pull my wrap around me, as if the icy winds were blowing even when the day is calm.

Next Saturday I am at the church by six a.m., cooking breakfast for the people who come in hungry off the street. I have only Manuel to help me, who no seem to know his way around a kitchen. "Who cooked with you last week?" I ask him. "Don't tell me you do this all yourself?"

"Pastor Davis," he says. "Since we lost Bertha, Pastor's my helper."

"Truly?" I say. "So he's the one I'm relieving."

"That man works hard."

"I thought him just a dry-land tourist when it come to hard work."

As I am serving scrambled eggs from the vat, I am unnerved to see Lucille come in the door, ashamed to meet my eye, still with a bandage around her head and bot' her eyes set in purply bruised skin. I tell myself, *Good you see this today, in case you get some crazy thought to take your little bit of wages and run on over to Brother Man's, try to cajole him into some new arrangement. Good you see what is real in this world.*

Lucille's got no choice but sidle past my eggs and bacon

strips. She comes along with her eyes on her tray and raises them just a bit to give me a weak smile and a whispered "How you been, Indigo." I let her pass and no trouble her with talking, though part of me wants to ask what happened, how did he catch up with her, and why so near to my house. That way, I can know what to fear and what to guard those children from.

Near to the end of the line, one more familiar face comes along. This time, it takes me a while to put a name with a face, but when I hear the voice, I know the name is Sanjay.

"Good day, Indigo," he says to me in his lovely English. "You should have taken the twenty dollars I offered that day. Remember? Then I could borrow it back from you now." He touches his tumpa arm to his forehead. "Not too many good days have come of late."

"Brother Man have a bad trap," I say. "Him know how to catch many rabbit." He laughs and passes.

When I leave the church and head to the store to buy food for my own pantry, I have only my red sweater tied around my shoulders. Winter is gone, and the birds in the small trees that line the streets chatter like granmadas.

When I arrive back home midday, I am weary. Since it is my day for rest, I lie down and sleep and wake midafternoon, unsettled. I don't mind hearing a knock late in the afternoon, because I can use some company, but I'm not ready for it to be Vincent, his brown cap in his hand, his face drained of color.

"Vincent," I say, "you surprise me. Come in. I get you some tea. Or you want food? I just come from the store earlier. Eggs? Or a piece of cheese and bread?"

"No, Indigo," he says. "No food. Just tea be nice." He sits in my chair before I ask him to sit, as if his body's too heavy for standing.

"What is it wid you, Vincent?" I ask when I hand him the

tea. "You look tired out." I don't tell him he is frightening me, that him worry me boht the baby.

"I have some news for you, Sister. Can't say if it bring you peace or bring you pain." It cyaan be boht Brother Man, thank goodness, cyaan be boht the girls. Vincent noh nothing boht those worlds. But still, there's the baby to frighten me.

I sit and examine his face, hope maybe to find my answer before I hear his words. My heart races. "Don't be timid, Vincie. Speak what you come to speak."

"It's about Louisa," he tells me, and make my heart pinch to a standstill, cut short my breath. "Mama send me some news."

"Okay, then," I say, pretending the waters are still, but the waves crash. "Go on and say what you got to. No more pain can come from that child now."

"They found the one who run her down, Indigo. They found the boy."

"Boy?" I say, all I know starting to slide.

"Yes, Sister, that's the part that troubles so. It was just a boy behind that wheel. Only thirteen years. Had a car that belonged to his poppi and was using it like a child's playting."

"What he name, this boy?"

"Earl somebody. Earl Potter, I think they say. All call him 'Earlie' where he live."

"How they find this oht?" I ask, trying to get myself back into the room with Vincent. "After near a year pass since Louisa death. And all this time, I hear nothing from the police and think them do nothing to track the killer down."

"This boy come eena into the police station one day, all on his own, not even a mada or bredda beside him. Tell the police he cyaan sleep at night, cyaan eat, him shaking and feeling misery all the time, seeing bad pictures in the mind. If he go to sleep, always dreaming of a big finger point his way, shake itself in his face."

"How do I take this eena mi heart, Vincent? What do I do with alla my hating?"

"I know," Vincent says. "It troubles me, too."

"Potter. That family live up on High Wind Road." When he is set to go, I ask Vincent, "How is your Teresa? How the baby?" I pat my belly.

"Good," he says. "Both good."

"When you bring that woman round to meet her new sister?"

He looks close at my face to see do I mean it and says, soft and careful, "The baby's showing now, Indigo."

"Naturally it is."

He smiles, "Soon. I bring her soon. She is ever so eager to meet you. She's lonely here away from home. Food taste funny to her, music sound wrong, clothes look ugly. Though the warming weather help her some."

"Soon the flowers bloom."

When Vincent goes, I try to do a little cooking, but my restlessness only sharpens and soon takes me across to Zach's door. He opens it before I finish my knock.

"Indigo, why you look surprise to see me when you just knock on my door?" He laughs. Not too many times have I hear him laugh. *Him have a pretty smile,* I say in my head.

"Come in, then." He steps back from the door to let me pass.

I see his tall brown hat laying on the table beside the armchair. "You're going oht. I come back another time."

"Come, come, friend. Me no a-go farther than to post a letter to Cliff. Him send you his regards, in the previous letter. Him have an affection for you, too."

I cyaan sit down, since I am feeling so fitful. I wander around his living room. "You make a nice place here, Zach."

"Thanks. I find a good home here."

I am by the open door that goes to his bedroom, my eyes

on the striped blanket tucked neet the mattress, along with the sheets. "Who teach you to make nice corners on your sheets?" I ask him. "Them neat as a woman's bed."

The laughing again lifts his voice. "This one you not believe, Indigo. Cliff, him the one."

"Truly?"

"Yes, truly. When I sleep over to his place when we bot boys in Jamaica, his mada, who is my Auntie Thea, she tell us to make up the bed proper before we go out and play in the yard, and Cliff know the way already and have to show me."

"I like a man who takes a likkle care with his tings." Mercy, if I am not feeling a wish to take Zach's hand in mine. Him a decent sort of friend to me of late, just like Jewel, and Bertha, too, before her life cut out from neet her so sudden. All of them stretch their heart to make room for me, even when they must abide the meanness that flourish inside me since Louisa die. I would like to take alla their hands in mine, just this once. I go ahead and do what's in my mind—walk up beside him and catch hold of his hand. "Someone raise you up a deestant man, Zach. More than most."

His eyes shine, but his shy tongue is still. I study his whole face with my eyes.

"You are surprising me, Indigo," he says.

"Surprising myself."

"You wanting a kiss, girl?" he asks me, quiet like he is but clear nuff for me to hear him.

I want to just nod my head and keep my silence, but I make myself say out loud so my own ears can hear it, "Go on, give a kiss, mon. Go on wid you."

"I don't mind," he says, and smiles, and we kiss and kiss again, his lips dry and soft, and let some time slide by and kiss a little more, and that is all we do, because Zach is a modest and respectful man and though I want to burrow alla the way eena his warm chest, I surprise myself by my timid feeling.

When it's time I feel I should go, I twist in his arm-dem, so he opens them and touches me only with his lovely eyes. "What, Indigo? You restless?"

"Time to go."

"If you determined. Glad you come. Glad you speak your mind."

I nod and turn away. "Glad for all of you," he says like he cyaan stop talking. He pats my shoulder all the way to the door as if he can't stand to let go of my body just yet. Lord, and I thought this one shy as a poor duppy man, but he a man, all right, just respectful.

When I get back to my apartment, I phone Jewel and ask her to come around and share supper with me, tell her I have more food in the pot than I need for one.

"How come I don't see you for such a long time?" Jewel asks me, sitting at my table, eating corn bread.

"Truth is, I got myself in trouble."

"What's that, girl? Women's trouble?"

"Ashamed to say."

"Go ahead. Lord knows, none of us perfect."

"Trouble with Brother Man's gambling games is what."

"Oh, Indi girl." Her voice is dressed in sorrow. She leans across the table. "I never should've introduced you. A lot of folk get carried away in that. I never should've dragged you over there."

"Quiet, Jewel," I say. "You never the one take me back there time and again, every chance I got. Truth is, I still am missing the place."

"You ain't going there no more, are you, girl?"

I shake my head. "He won't have me. Now I'm on his debtors list, and he intend to collect his money. But I'm all right. I'm working down at the church now. In time, that will get me money enough to pay that debt. I put out word through Henry P that Brother Man money come soon. I just hope he don't get impatient between now and then, like he did with Lucille."

"Lucille? Oh, no, child! That Lucy-girl, she ain't a piece of his work, is she? Lord, Indigo, you in danger. You let me help you. I got some money I can loan you. You pay Brother Man straightaway, get him off your back. Then you pay me as you're able. I shouldn't ever have taken you over to that evil place."

"It's two full months' pay for you. You got that much you want to trust to me, knowing how I am?"

"Oh, girl. You lose that much? I ain't got all that in my savings. So sorry, Indigo. You know I'd help you if I could."

"I think Brother Man be patient with me. Him like me better than Lucille." I eat a little of my stew and enjoy the strong yellow onion in with the meat and hope the words I say to ease Jewel's mind hold a crumb of truth, because I don't see Brother Man liking anyone on this earth less than he like me right now. "Vincent come by here earlier, and tell me someting."

"Vincent? Remind me now."

"My brother. Him come in April and get an apartment, him and the new wife. She just now expecting."

"Is that right?"

"He bring me some news about my Louisa. Mama no want to send it direct to me, so her send it tru Vincent, let Vincent come to me and deliver her message."

Jewel widens her eyes to take in what I want to tell.

"The police them find who kill Louisa. It was a young boy, from a family I know, a boy riding around in his daddy's car, just playing, fooling around like young folk do. Him take my baby's life undaneath his wheels."

"Oh, Lord, what a shame, girl, what a pity. Someone ought to keep more watch on the children."

I see her tighten up as she hears the other arrow her word-dem fling. "Hard to hate that boy," I say. "He been shaking and no can eat nor sleep since the accident. This all tearing his heart apart, they say."

"Just a pity, child. No one to blame. We best leave judgment to the Lord."

"A man I met at Brother Man's lose his arm in a foolish accident some young people cause tru a prank. Him hold no grudge toward them children."

"That's the best way," Jewel says.

Twenty

Time has come for Professor's birthday dinner. I am finishing up my cooking, laying pieces of almond on top of the green beans for a fancy touch, happy to be at the Silvers', where I feel farther from Brother Man's reach. I hear Clair playing a hopscotch game in the living room, jumping about and talking out loud to herself, full of her excitement about the gift she got Professor. I should tell her to take that kind of play outside, but the day is cool for May and the truth is I just as soon keep that child close where I can hear her.

Professor is pleased with my dinner of stewed chicken, green beans, and scalloped potato. Afterward, the girls want to go out into the living room and give Professor his gifts. The little dog sniffs at the boxes one by one so he can figure what's hiding in them.

"Open mine first," Clair says.

I can see Professor is impressed with the nice pen from Clair and then with the beautiful briefcase Jill got him, which

Clair makes him stroke with his palm to see how soft the leather is. Julie went to some trouble, too, and bought him a monogrammed bag for when he plays tennis and must carry his racket and balls and a bottle of water. When I see Professor smile over alla these tings, I think how Mrs. Silver hurt his feelings this same time last year, giving him nothing but a flimsy T-shirt that cause him shame. Some of that pain is past now, and I am glad for it.

At seven thirty, Professor is going on a date. The girls fuss over him like three hens clucking over their chick, just to get him dressed. When they finish, they each one look him over to give him their okay. He is going out with Miss Roberta. I have my feelings about that, but I don't say a word 'cept "Have a good time, Professor." Miss Roberta is such a skinny winjy ting, I cyaan see what good she do any man. But Professor got to make his own mind up. I don't see the girls cheering much for Miss Roberta, who don't seem to have much humor in her either. Even so, they fuss over Professor tonight, a-get him ready, because all of them love him. I do the same, because Professor been as good to me as any man.

The only one who's not right tonight is Jill. She smiles when Professor crows over the briefcase, but soon after, she sits by the wall and lets Julie and Clair do most of the tending of their fada.

"What's the matter with you, Jill?" I ask her after Professor kisses them all and goes off looking bright and sharp eye, like he's walking the high wire. "Professor loved that briefcase you gave him. Why don't you be happy as a lark?"

"I don't know," she says. "I'm just not in that good a mood tonight."

Later, Keith calls for Jill, and I shout to her upstairs to get on the library phone. When I go upstairs to fold the clothes I ironed, I hear her putting off that boy, who must be asking her on a date.

I go settle on my bed and wait. After I hear the phone set down, I call Jill to my room.

"How come you act so high up with that boy?" I ask her, quiet and no fuss. "I thought you and him getting along like doves."

Jill shrugs. "He's okay, but I have so much homework. I'll never get it all done if I go out."

"You would think you rewrite the Constitution or some such ting, Jilly, like all the world count on you to get it done just right."

She twists her mouth, like whenever my words burden her.

I get a hunch about this child's misery. "Your mother been after you boht someting?"

She looks at me, puzzled.

"She making you guilty all over again, so now you close the door on that polite boy and go back to dreaming over your summer boyfriend, Ven?"

She shrugs. "Not Ven," she whispers. "Ben." Then she giggles, which lets me know she nah feel too terrible.

"Sit beside me, Jill. I'm going to talk to you."

She gets a look like she's waiting for a blow.

"Just sit," I say and pat the bed. "This not going to hurt so bad. I'm not so hard-hearted these days as before."

"I know." She perches next to me.

"Look here, Jill." I start talking out of what my heart tells me. "Your mother is ill. It's sad, but it's the way it is. That's the first ting that's true. The second ting that's true is that you can help her very little, and you are always going to feel bad boht that. No one can take that weight off your back. It's part of the hand God give. Other people got other problems, like Professor always teach you." I wait awhile. "Don't let you mada stop you from your own life, Jill. There's no good in that, just two lives wasted instead of one. Do you understand what I'm saying?"

"But Ben writes me letters, and I think I like him better than Keith. I can't decide."

"Always easier to love the one who's far away. Ben is ready to be married to someone his own age. Didn't you tell me that one time?"

Jill nods, her head dropped down, and I wonder how much that girl can hear my meaning.

"So you go on and think about that. Think about where you best put your heart." Okay, I've said my piece, and now it's time to hold my tongue.

Later that night Jill goes out to meet that boy after all, and Julie goes off with her Scott. Clair complains how she's left all alone, but we spend a peaceful evening watching some TV till she falls asleep next to me on the sofa. I let her sleep awhile before I rouse her and send her off to her bed.

Professor comes in, his face a dark cloud, so I think maybe he nah have the good time he hope for with Miss Roberta.

"Where are the girls?" he asks me right away, and sits down behind his desk.

"Clair's in bed, where she belong, and the older girls are out."

"Both of them?" He is surprised.

"Yes. Both girls go out tonight."

"Jill's out again with that boy? Isn't she too young for that?"

"You think so, Professor?" I ask. "Jill is past sixteen now."

"Sixteen. Well, maybe it's just that I'm too old."

"You get the knack back in time. Maybe get you someone wid a kemps more fat on di bone."

He chuckles and stands up. "I'm getting a drink. You want a drink, Indi?"

"Tanks, no, Professor."

He goes into the dining room, where his two little bottle of liquor-dem stay.

I go into the kitchen to finish my cleaning. Then I shut the lights.

When I walk back through the living room to set out a few vases I washed, Professor is swirling ice cubes in a glass fill with liquor that ongle come halfway up the cubes, listening to some sad songs on his CD player, his head leaning back on the couch.

"Beautiful music," he says. "Listen to that, Indi. *Kindertotenlieder.*"

I shrug.

"Songs of the lost children."

"Okay, Professor," I say, my voice even, like a white sky. "Not my kind of music."

"Some of the best music ever written." His voice is gruff. "It wouldn't hurt you to listen."

"Songs of lost children? No thank you. I can do without that."

He tightens his mouth and nods, deep in his own world. "Yeah, Indi. Okay. Okay. Everyone in this household does what they want, anyway."

The next evening, Professor calls the girls around his desk. "You, too, Indi," he says. When we are gathered, he says to the girls, "I got a letter from your mother. It's good news, for once. She's going to drop her custody action. She says she's let her lawyer go."

Jill sighs, and her eyes tear up. She shuts them to keep us from seeing. "Good," she says. "Good. Good."

"Why is she?" Clair asks, her voice no more than a drip of water.

"Yeah, why?" Julie asks. "I bet she's planning some other way to torture us."

I make a face at Julie out of some old reflex that says, A child got to respect she mada.

Professor shakes his head. "It sounds like she's depressed. She doesn't feel up to fighting. She said you're all better off here, with me. She says she's not able to care for you."

"She could if she gets well," Clair says.

"I don't think so," Jill says gently. "I don't think she'll get that well."

"She used to be okay," Clair says. "I remember, sort of."

"It's better this way, Clair," I say. "You girls belong with Professor now. That's the way it's meant to be, from now on."

Clair follows me into the kitchen after Professor gets back to his writing. She hangs around, her mouth turning this way and that, her eyes reaching for the ceiling and the floor. She perches on one of the stools by the metal table that's against the wall. "Do you think she *ever* wanted us?" she asks.

"What you mean by *ever*?"

"Well. . . ." She has to give it consideration. "Like when we were born."

"Oh, Lord, Clair, yes, I think she did. Most mothers do. She's not so much different."

"Julie says she is."

"Julie's young. She don't see all there is, some of the time."

"Like what?"

"Your mother is troubled, that's all. She don't know what she wants. Don't know what could make her happy or make her right in the head. Every place you go—here, Jamaica, don't matter—some people not altogether right in the head. That's just the way, Clair, here, there, everywhere."

Clair screws up her mouth. "I thought if we went to live with her, she might feel like the other mothers. She would have her children, and then she'd feel better."

"Oh, Clair," I say, not knowing what to tell this child. "It ought to work that way, but it don't. She must feel right first, then be a mama to you."

"It worked that way with you, Indi," she says, and I think this takes all her courage. "You felt better when you had Louisa."

All I can say is "Yes, Clair, but that was different." And I know that's miles short of what she's needing. "Maybe another time I cyan try to explain that all to you. When we take a walk or someting, you and me, next nice day that come along." Then I think of a question I want to ask her, though I don't know what put it in my head. "Who took in that telegram that night, Clair? Who took in the telegram that tell what happen to my Lou?"

"Jilly did," she says, and stops, attends me, now widoht fear. "A man came to the door. It was raining. Jill went out to see what he wanted."

Jill know just how I care for my Louisa, how I always pet her little photo that I keep in my pocket or next to my bed. "Poor Jill," I say. And of course Professor the one call on the telephone to deliver that heartbroke message. Poor Jill. Poor Professor.

"And Jill went off to her long camping trip that next day?"

"Yeah."

Jill went away the next day with that message in her head: "Louisa dead. Killed by car. Funeral Monday." Oh, Lord. Words that do such cutting, words that take the breath of life from you.

"If something happened to me . . . ?" Clair asks, but she can't finish her question.

"Your mother's heart be broke."

The leaves seem like they sprung from the branches overnight. Birds wake up now before the sun, each one calling to the others. My time has come to go back to Brother Man and return him his first portion of money, with its teif's interest. When I finish serving breakfast at the church and get on that bus, I'm scared I won't do what I plan: hand over my money and walk out the door, turning my back on Joshie's silver wheel. I'm scared that money mean nothing to Brother Man, and him just laugh in my face and tell me, "What make you think you done with me now, sister, just because you give me this little bit of change?" I'm scared he's got a blackness in his heart for me that won't let up till I look like Lucille when they find her in the street.

When I see the house up the road, it looks quiet and shabby, set there barely breathing while spring grows up all around it. I push the door and see only six or seven people in there, then pick out the ones I know. My heart stirs, sharpens its beating, when my eyes land on Brother Man. I give a nod to Joshie and a glance around at the four or five men already thinking about their numbers this early in the day, then bring my eyes back to Brother Man and the slight, blonde-haired girl I never seen before who has her arm circled around his waist. Brother Man's eyes find me, and his face becomes a question. I lift my head and cross to him, nod, dig out the money that's in my pocket, and hand it to him. "This the first piece of what I owe."

He gives me a soft look and rubs his lips with his fingertips and says, "All right, Indigo. This fine gal be Suzie."

I nod and walk across to the door thinking, *That's it? That's it? He's going to let me walk on out?* I dare to think, *Maybe he nah bother me again,* and I'm grateful for that skin-and-bones girl and hope her heart never stray. My own heart feels light. I want to fly from here fast as a falcon, before the man have a chance to think and come chase after me.

When I get back to my own place, on the welcome mat in front of the door is a bouquet of flowers tied up in a silky green ribbon. *Lord, where did someone find these purple flowers?* I don't know what they call, but Professor's finished up blooming weeks ago. I go on in and set them in a cup of water, put my nose in them to check their perfume, then stand in the middle of my front room and stretch my limbs, glad for no more work today. Some sunshine lies across the furniture, giving everything a shine. A soft knock comes against the frame of the open door and I turn, and there is the one who must've brought the posies.

"How you doing, Zach?" I ask, and give him a smile.

"Indi girl," he says. "So nice to see you. I miss you all week long."

He comes beside me, and shy as both of us are, we are kissing right away, and before any time can pass, we are in the bed together and I'm not worrying myself over it like other times. He lies over me, his body like a canopy, placing no weight on me, just giving me shelter, casting his broad shadow over my body, using what nature gave him to make a bridge from his loins to mine. Lord, he brings me every good feeling.

"Where you find the sweet flower-dem?" I ask him.

He looks to me, puzzled, and shakes his head. Then he says, "Clifford's back in town. Maybe a little gift he give you." I laugh at my confusion, feel a second's nerves, since here I am in bed with Zach, with memories of Cliff and me called back. My eyes flee from his.

"I know," he says. "Cliff tell me about you and him. No trouble in that, sister woman. Just rest easy. Alla the pretty woman-dem get flowers from more than one man."

For a few minutes, the world feels nothing but good to me. I lie awhile in Zach's arms, watch the breeze fill my white curtains; then I must get up and set to tidying, because the room suddenly feels in need.

Twenty-one

I grew up beside the water but never been in a boat. Always I looked at them bobbing out on the water like bright beads, pretty and distant, and me never thinking to ride one. When I want to go far from home, I picture myself in an airplane, but never in a sailing boat. Now Julie says she's going to take us out in the sailboat that belongs with the house Professor rent for us.

"You'll drown yourself and your sisters," I say.

"I know how to sail," she says, her pride bruised. "From when I used to go to Camp Tamawok."

"Indians noh nothing boht sailing boats."

"You come, too," Clair says, and grabs my hand.

"I will not." I laugh like someone tickled my ribs with a feather. I shake my hand free from hers and run a few steps tru di sand.

The girls fill their arms with a portion of their gear and tromp barefoot across the burning beach, down to the water of Lake Michigan. First time I see this lake, stretching on like the sea, I wonder at its blackish color. My eye-dem find only a touch of blue or green in its heavy waves. It look to me like alla the dirt in the world wash down into it. After Louisa died, I wondered had all the world's tears found their way to this water and darkened it. But now I am accustomed to it and do not find it strange.

I slide on the thongs Jill bought me for the beach and pick up the orange life jacket and seat cushions and bags of Chee•tos that were too much for the girls to haul all at once down to the boat.

Julie uses all the muscle in her skinny arms to shoob that boat halfway out into the fishy-smelling water; then she steps through the bit of rough water that looks topped with whipped egg whites and climbs aboard. "You first," she says to Clair. Clair looks back at me, then wades out until the lake takes the likkle skirt of her bathing suit and floats it like a lily pad. I cyaan help but see Louisa in this child's young body. Julie gives her a hand and pulls her up. Jules points to Jill. "You push us off and jump in."

"I'm not going without Indi," Clair says, and jumps back out of the boat and struggles ashore.

"Oh, no, I'm not going, no, no, me no venture on dis boat," I say while she takes my hand and pulls me a few steps into the water. The rocking boat makes the cold water splash up onto the front of my shorts. "Oh! Jesus Lord!" I giggle as Clair pulls me up to my knees in the water, then waits behind me, pushing me to climb aboard. I see that she is frightened to go out with only her sisters. "All right, all right. I'm a-go now. Just keep that boat stand steady." I climb aboard, taking care not to rock it, until my feet are washed in the cool water that lines the bottom. Might as well kick off di shoes.

"You can keep all four of us afloat in this flimsy ting?" I ask Julie. "You know I cyaan swim for nothing. Don't spill me out in the deep water."

"Sure," Julie says, and nods as if there's no question of what she can do.

"You know how much I weigh?" I ask her. "I don't weigh like you girls."

"Don't worry." Julie hands me the life vest and helps me strap it on while Clair and Jill climb aboard. I am glad for the bright color. It give me some hope to think that if we tip over and all dump eena di sea, at least we'll be bouncing boht on the dull water like oranges. Someone might see us from a long way away.

Jill is the strongest of the girls. She pushes us off from the shore. I do as she ask and pull in the rope that trail behind us in the water, so now we float free. Jill leans over the side and paddles us across the waves to where the water smooths, then lays the paddle on the boat floor. Now it's Julie's turn. She lifts the sail and it flaps and suddenly catches the breeze and fills. We are bouncing across the water. "Oh, mercy! This nah what I expect," I say to the girls. "How can water feel hard like cement?" We race along like on an amusement park ride, and I giggle while the cold water sprays my legs. "Whoa, Julie knows how to run this ting, don't it?" I sit thigh against cold wet thigh with her and say, "You're good at this, Jules. They teach you this in camp?" For a minute I think how I could send Louisa to camp with the money I soon save, now that I'm mostly dug out of debt to Brother Man and still earning extra at the church. I wonder at all that child could experience, but no, I must return to knowing that never can be, and the remembering is sorrowful but calm, not terrible like it used to be. I turn to watching Jules, who is holding the tiller and also the sail. When she knows the wind is changing, she orders Clair and Jill to "come about," and they flatten against the deck and let the heavy beam below the sail pass right over their heads. I start to protest the danger but I cyan see these girls know how to do this right, so I choose to let them be. I ride at the rear end of the boat, beside Julie and the bar she calls the tiller.

"The tiller's connected to the rudder down below the boat," Julie explains to us. "When I move the tiller, the rudder moves underneath. That's what steers us—that plus the sail.

"We're coming about," she says to the girls, who hurry to make theyself flat as di rat-bat. We stay on a straight, easy course.

"Here, Indi." She pushes the tiller into my hand.

"No, Jules," I say, but I am holding the tiller bar. "Oh, no," I sing out. "I'm not the sailing type." Jules gives me the rope that lets the sail tighten or go limp. "Not bot of these," I say to her, ready to squeal.

"It's better that way," Julie says. "You work them together. Don't worry. I know how to teach you."

I keep hold of the tiller and the sail, too. Julie calls the sail a "sheet," and I keep my eye on it and watch to see that it stays smooth and unwrinkled, like a bedsheet passing neet my iron. At first my heart is in my mouth, but after a time I get easier with the jobs Julie give to both my hands and my head. I notice that Jill and Clair are dipping their hands overboard, running them in the water, making white bubbles like tiny strings of pearls, not even watching me anymore.

"Does Mommy know where we are?" Clair asks Jill, and I wonder where that thought come from. Did it float out across the water and into this child's head the way my thoughts of Louisa come to me? "She might be looking for us. She might want to see how my camp was last week."

"I told her you had fun," Jill says.

I feel sorry for Clair, how she still hangs on to thinking she is so much in her mada's heart. But then maybe Mrs. Silver does keep the girl in her heart in her own way, though her heart is more overrun by nonsense than most. "You can call her as soon as you get back," I tell Clair. "Where is Professor today?" I ask.

"He found a lady to ask for a date," says Clair.

"Well, good for him."

"I don't like her," Clair says.

"Do you know her?" I ask. "How you know she not your fairy godmother?"

Jill laughs. "She never met her. None of us did."

"I still don't like her," Clair says.

"You take this rudder back now, Julie," I tell her. "I had enough sailing for one day. No need to turn me into a sailing fool all in one afternoon."

Sitting back down on the white plastic seat, I think I may write Mama a letter and tell her one or two tings boht this day. I may brag a quips to Jewel, too, and Pastor Davis and Vincent. I hear Jewel telling me, "No, girl! Sailing a boat? You for real?" I hear her telling the others at one of her church parties, "You know what Indigo gone and done? That girl done sailed a boat!" Maybe I wi go along wid her next time and tell my own story. Maybe I wi get my own boat some day and learn how to sail it properly and take Zach out on the water, though first I wi have to talk away his fears.

I cyaan think of what Mama would say, cyaan even hear her voice. Too much time pass since we see each other last. I wonder would Mama get on an airplane and make a visit here if I send her the money. Or maybe I must go home and see her. Maybe I cyan get myself ready for that one of these days.

We are out in the middle of the lake, and now the wind has died down and the water is calm. It seems like we just bobbing, and I start to wonder are we to be stuck out here when the sun disappear behind the lake and the cold of night blow in. But Julie says we still move along just right, and I trust her as our captain.

"Come here, look," I say, because I spot someting floating right beside us in the water. I lean overboard wid care and tug at it, but its weight keeps me from hauling it up onto the boat.

Jill looks over, too, and says, "It's a rubber boot."

"A boat?" Clair asks.

"Boot," I say. "Just one rubber boot." Then I have to stop enjoying myself awhile to think about how did this boot come to be out in the middle of the water.

"Somebody drowned, Jules?" I ask, half whispering.

She shakes her head like she knows just what happened. "You always find stuff when you're out on a boat. People just throw it overboard."

"What sense in that?"

"To lighten their load so they can go faster, or just for fun. Or it's stuff they don't need."

"Some strange kind of fun," I say, still leery of finding some poor soul's boot in the middle of the lake. "Where's the other boot?" I ask. "And where's the person meant to be wearing it?" But no one answers me.

"It's like if I would decide to throw Jill's shoe over, and get her mad," Julie says.

"Didn't bring 'em," Jill says.

Jill takes the paddle and pushes the boot out from the boat, because it's lingering against our side, keeping us back. I imagine the lake like a huge bathtub. If you pull the plug and let the water drain out, you see all of what people have lost or thrown overboard, and you see all them folks unlucky nuff to drown.

"Get away from us," Clair shouts, and I have to laugh out loud at her hollering at an old rubber boot.

"All right, Clair," I say. "Don't get pesky. Boot have a right to be oht on the water same as us."

"Oh, Indi," she says. "Boots don't have feelings."

"Now, how you cyan noh dat?"

"Yeah," Jules says. "Have you ever been a boot?"

Clair can't help laughing at that degree of silliness. "It's still holding on to us," she says. "We can't get away."

"Call to it," I say. "Tell it, 'Look yu no bunks di boat.' "

Now Jill shocks me near to death, because she stands up

and pulls off her T-shirt and dives out of the boat into that water. I right away start screaming, "Jill, you come back in here right this minute. You'll drown. You know how deep that water is?"

She is standing up in the water, looking at us, paddling lightly with her hands. She shouts up at me, "It doesn't matter how deep it is, once it's over your head. Anyway, I can swim." She hoists up the boot, which is heavy with water, and turns and empties it, somehow keeping herself afloat widout use her arms. Then she sets the boot on top of the water, where it bobs away on the likkle wave-dem. She turns her back on the boat and swims a small ways out into the water, but it seems like a mile to me. *How did Jill get so bold?* I'm wondering, but maybe all of us change little by little.

"All right now, Jill," I yell out, trying to sound calm, but stern as a captain. "That's enough showing off for today." She comes on back and heaves herself up over the side and tumbles into the boat, so now I feel better and got to laugh at her nonsense, and the girls laugh along with me as we turn about and head back for the shore and think of checking on Professor, see how him fare with his lady friend.

Acknowledgments

I would like to extend thanks to my fine agent Alison J. Picard, who found a home for this book with Bantam Dell. There I was fortunate to work with three excellent editors Erica Orden, Margo Lipschultz, and Liz Scheier, all of whom brought intelligence, enthusiasm, and enjoyment to our work. Anne Winthrop Esposito contributed skilled and thoughtful copy-editing.

A number of friends—including some who are writers—read drafts of this book or offered other help. Ann Pearlman read and ably critiqued the manuscript, something she has done for me over many years, always bringing to bear her sensitivity to language and structure in fiction. Lois Kuznets Dowling read and re-read with her characteristic generosity and knowledge of literature. Judy Gray made available her fine editing skills, as she also did with my recent nonfiction work. Shaun Knibbs vetted my Jamaican speech, allowing me to breathe a little easier. Rose Diliscia Everett, Julia Davies, John Ware, Keith Taylor, and Judith Saltzman all offered help with particular aspects of this project. Finally, Deb Jackson was enormously supportive through her reading and response to an early draft of the book.

Many other friends and family members have been steadfast in their encouragement of my writing, through years of modest success and those of reward. To them, though unnamed, I extend my gratitude.

About the Author

Susan Beth Miller is a psychologist and the author of several nonfiction books on psychology. Her short fiction has won numerous awards, including two Avery Hopwood Prizes. She lives in Ann Arbor, Michigan.